HOW TO
EXPERIENCE DEATH
FOR BEGINNERS

JESSICA BRANTON

Charlie's Port Press / FRINGE

Charlie's Port Press / FRINGE Imprint
Atlanta
www.charliesport.org

Publisher's Note: This is a work of fiction. Names, characters, and incidents are a
product of the author's imagination. Actual Cartersville, GA, locales and institutions
are used strictly for atmospheric purposes. Any resemblance to actual people, living or
dead, or events in fictional or real locations is completely coincidental.

Cover Design © Jessica Jenkins

How To Experience Death For Beginners/ Jessica Branton
ISBN 978-0-06920353-7-5

CONTENTS

PROLOGUE

Some people say that your life flashes before your eyes when you die. What really happens is that you see all of the things you didn't do in your life. All of the words unspoken, the actions not taken, and finally the biggest and darkest regrets flash like lightning. How do I know this? Because when I was seven years old I saw my dad die, and I died with him.

I had been playing dolls in our bedroom with my twin sister, Christina, when suddenly I was hit with a fear so strong and terrible that I ripped off Barbie's head. A voice whispered, "Casey?" as I blacked out.

My mind was flung into the passenger's seat of my father's car. "Daddy?" I gasped, but he didn't hear me. I wondered where my body had gone and where Christina was. I watched my father's hands tighten on the steering wheel as the car slammed through the metal railing and into the river. Stop! I screamed in my head. He didn't die on impact. No, he continued to sit at the bottom of the river while watching death approach, and he was unable to do anything to stop it. Desperately, he flung himself against the windows of the car. The jammed door mocked him as he struggled. When the car hit the bottom of the river and filled up with water, that's when the memories came.

My father faded away and in his wake, I experienced his first kiss. I watched as he met my mom for the first time. She was so pretty as she smiled at him and shook his hand. He seemed so happy from merely meeting her. The rest of his happy memories flooded me: marriage, Christina and I being born, the last birthday we made our own cards for him.

Then other memories surfaced. A girl's tears rolled off her cheeks as I watched my father kiss another girl in front of her. His regret at not telling another girl he loved her flashed before me, and then a boy, his best friend, was being beaten up by a couple of bullies, but he didn't help. Finally, the biggest regret surfaced. Resentment filled me in horror as I watched him leave some woman's house before driving home to us. That was when the light left his eyes and he died.

When I finally came to, my mom was shaking me, and Christina peeked from behind her looking terrified. I burst into hysterical tears. "It's okay, baby. I'm here for you," my mom whispered in my hair, holding me close. But I knew it wasn't okay. What I had just seen was so real, like I was actually there.

I screamed repeatedly, "Daddy's dead!" Momma shushed me and laid me down to sleep. Christina looked at me, but remained silent. She crawled into the bed and wrapped her arms around me. Momma tucked us in and left. I whispered all the things I saw to her and I felt her arms stiffen. She placed her head against my hair until silent tears put me to sleep and Christina's soft snoring faded from my ears. Later, Mom came back in. I can still hear my mother whispering through tears, "How did you know?" I didn't know what to tell her.

I experienced death when I was seven years old. Ten years later, I found myself wondering if I would ever stop.

PART I
BREATHE

CHAPTER ONE

sluts, preps, and a golden boy

The screams of the alarm clock nagged me. School again, Monday through Friday. Days I would rather spend underneath covers. Why anyone would create something so evil is beyond me. The worst part was hearing everyone talk loudly in the halls. Between their vanity and hypocrisy, it was a wonder I could stomach the place. Not to mention the fact that every moment with someone else brought me closer to a potential death. Schoolwork wasn't great either, but I could find joy in that. Mostly, I hated the trash-talking jerks, the expectation to make conversation, and just the general cold atmosphere. School was a whole other playing field. And neither Christina nor I were winning.

The clock nagged again and again. I hauled myself out of bed and opened my closet doors. There technically wasn't a dress code if you were pretty enough to pass it, but mainly there were no hoodies, no hats, no glasses, and if your butt showed, only a select few got away with it. Not that I really wanted to wear booty shorts. I was plenty happy with my dark jeans and a midnight blue shirt.

I walked across the hall and banged on Christina's door. "Chris, it's time for school."

The door swung open and she looked at me with blue-green eyes. My eyes were a more silvery-blue, but really that was the only difference between the two of us. Our hair was long and black with the same silky texture. Our skin was a pale, creamy peach, and we each had a freckle above our right eyebrow. It was like looking into a mirror if I ignored the eyes and the expression. Right then, hers was in that shy smile she always had, and my face was undoubtedly blank.

"Come on, we're going to be late," I said.

She touched my shoulder. "You look pretty. Blue suits you." She whisked out the door. I put my hand where she touched my shoulder. *Maybe today will be a good day for her.*

—

I was still trying to shake off the shock of Christina's compliment in homeroom. She had developed Selective Mutism after Daddy died and I told her everything I had seen. According to the doctors and psychologist Mom made us see when we were younger, this was a coping mechanism for the trauma she underwent. She could talk and sometimes you could even catch her in a good mood where she'd talk for hours. Most days, however, she was as quiet as a mouse. She used to be so vocal when we were children. She'd always sing or tell stories, but it was hard to remember that happy girl. *I hope she's gained some confidence today,* I thought, walking through the school's hallways.

I entered math class shaking my head. I loved that class. It required enough brainpower to keep me from thinking about what I did to my sister when I talked to her all those years ago. I didn't feel like having my thoughts bombarded on why Christina would have talked and what could have changed.

As I walked to my seat, I glanced at Patricia who was examining her nails intensely. She was on a similar, if not slightly lower, rung of the popularity ladder as my best friend Danny was. Thankfully, this meant our interactions only coexisted when he dragged me to a big party or if she came over to say hello. Something about her always rubbed me the wrong way, but I could never figure it out. She looked up from her hand momentarily to give me a sickly-sweet grin, which didn't match her eyes.

I sank into my desk. The whispers around me grew. When teachers are late, students get loud. I sighed and stared intently at the book on my desk. *Ignore them and they won't be there,* I thought. I was sick of seeing the people around me, knowing that one day I might see them die. It was something I would prefer not to deal with.

"Class, calm down!" Mrs. Tawny said. She was a mousy, rather young woman for a teacher. Her brown hair was short and curly and she wore glasses too big for her tiny face. She continued when the class finally decided to obey. "We have a new student joining us," her high-pitched voice announced. "His name is Cameron."

Cameron walked through the door with his hands in his pockets, head down. He was so sun-kissed it looked like he erupted from its center. He looked like the picture-perfect California boy in his ripped cargo shorts, blue and white striped dress shirt, and thick leather bracelets. An edgy fashion contradiction that kind of bothered and intrigued me, but I couldn't figure out why.

"I expect everyone to be nice to him. He just moved from California." *Called it.* Mrs. Tawny mistook thirty gaping mouths as insults.

"Now why don't you go sit by . . ." She craned her neck and stood on her tippy toes. "Casey. Raise your hand, Casey." I initially sank into my desk but raised my hand like she asked. It's not like I could explain to her that I didn't want to sit beside yet another ticking time bomb. The "Golden Boy" smiled and sat beside me. Mrs. Tawny smiled too. "Today's lesson . . ." she continued, but I wasn't listening. I suspected no one else was either.

"Hey. I'm Cameron." He extended his arm.

"Casey." I tried to focus on the board, not wanting to get attached to him in any way. I could still feel his gaze and I shifted uncomfortably. *Please stop,* I whispered to myself, quickly growing wary of his staring. Not that he could know, but I didn't need to have another person that I could watch die one day and that had meant no more interactions. I turned to face him and raised my eyebrow.

Confusion colored his face as his arm retreated. He turned away from me and I breathed a sigh of relief that I wasn't caught in his gaze. Out of the corner of my eye, I watched as he rubbed his leather bracelet a few times before searching for something in his backpack. He came up empty-handed. "May I have a piece of paper?" he asked stiffly. I handed him a piece. When his hand touched mine, a shiver ran through my spine. His skin practically radiated heat. I quickly retracted my hand.

Even though I looked away, I felt his eyes on me. "Thanks," Cameron said.

The rest of math class was hell, consisting of me ignoring him, loud whispers, and a calculus problem I'd have to read about since I gathered nothing from the lesson. When the bell rang, I bolted from my seat.

—

I was calm by lunchtime, strolling into the cafeteria to get a slice of pizza. The Golden Boy didn't show up in my other three classes. I was extremely glad. I shook my head. At least it had looked like I would only deal with him once a day if he didn't show up after lunch.

I saw Danny at the far end of the cafeteria. Danny Mardox was everything I, and the rest of my friends, weren't: *popular.* And, despite his nerdiness, he was the most charming. He had dirty-blond hair, slightly tan skin with rosy cheeks, dark blue eyes, and a brain bigger than Texas. He'd been my rock since kindergarten, in a way no one else had. It all started with our love of pop rocks and me protecting him from bullies. Since then, not even his popularity or my tragedy could keep us apart. I sat beside him, my stomach growling.

"I'm telling you, he's coming!" Danny said, his hair hanging in his face like always.

Beatrix rolled her eyes. "Sure, sure. I've seen him. No offense, but we aren't his type." Everything about Beatrix was fiery and dramatic. She was clearly the co-star of our little group. She and Danny lived in a wealthy neighborhood, a place on the southern edge of town called The Waterford. She was the spitfire that always had something funny or shocking to say. "I mean, we're just too . . . too . . ." she trailed off, penciled eyebrows furrowing.

Tiffany's brown eyes filled with thoughtful energy. "I didn't think there was anything wrong with our group." Tiffany was the timid one. She always stood beside Christina, and she seemed to communicate with her in a way I couldn't. Christina nodded in agreement.

"What are you guys talking about?" I asked, chomping on my pizza.

"There is a new kid in school and Danny apparently made fast friends with him," Beatrix informed us. My heart stopped.

"You'll appreciate it," Danny said. "He's very . . . yummy." He raised his eyebrows in a suggestive way and gave me a wink.

I twisted my thumb back and forth in my hand, worried that I knew exactly whom they were referring to. Part of me had agreed with the "yummy" comment, though.

Beatrix was lost in thought, twisting the apple stem clockwise, a daily ritual for her. "Yes. He is very, very yummy."

"You're not talking about Cameron, right?" I said, wanting to disappear.

"Hey guys," announced a deep voice. "Sorry I'm so late. I had to stay after and talk to a teacher." The Golden Boy sat beside Danny and nodded at all of us, to my complete dismay.

"Guys, this is Cameron." Danny grinned from ear to ear. "Cameron, this is Beatrix."

She batted her eyelashes with a, "Hi." Her tone was incredibly flirty and I wanted to ask her to stop. I didn't want Cameron to intrude on our group of friends. I didn't want Beatrix getting him even more involved than he already was. "I hope we can get to know each other really well," she said. Beatrix stretched her arms forward on the table like a cat.

"Over there is Tiffany, and that's Christina, but they're really shy," Danny said. Christina gave a small wave and Tiffany gave a meek "hi," but continued eating. "And this is my best friend, Casey."

"Yeah, I've already had the pleasure of meeting Casey," Cameron admitted.

I gave him a small nod of acknowledgement, but not the satisfaction of speaking to him.

"I don't think Casey likes me very much."

Beatrix rolled her eyes. "Oh, pay no mind to *Casey*. Casey doesn't like talking to people she doesn't know."

"Why not?" he asked, trying to look into my eyes. I looked everywhere but his eyes. I didn't like how he singled me out among all of my friends.

Beatrix spared me a glance before saying, "Casey takes her friend group very seriously. You'll need a V.I.P. pass to get in. Or have known her before she was seven."

Danny sent Beatrix a warning glare, and I gave him a smile of appreciation. She closed her mouth quickly. Danny understood that I'd rather keep the past in the past. Beatrix, on the other hand, seemed determined to tell the world.

Cameron turned toward Beatrix. "What happened when she was seven?"

Beatrix seemed to glow and took a big breath. For a split second, her eyes darted to me, but I knew she wasn't going to stop. No matter what she said or how many times she said it, Beatrix was always defiant and knew it. "Well, it all started—"

"Beatrix!" I interrupted, annoyed beyond belief. "There is no need to tell him my story. It's too long and no one wants to hear it right now." Her face fell, but she didn't continue. All my friends assumed my father's death was what marked the melancholic change in my life. No one knew the real story. Not even Danny.

Cameron gave me a sympathetic look. "There are lots of stories like that."

I regarded the Golden Boy with minor interest. *Who is this boy who has smiles and a California tan? Why did he have to come to my school?* I caught myself admiring his blond hair.

"Hi, Cameron." I stiffened. Patricia's voice was like nails on a chalkboard. "Why don't you come sit over here with . . ." She was looking directly at me. " . . . People who are more like you."

I grimaced and focused on my half-eaten piece of pizza.

"Be gone, Satan! You have no power here!" Beatrix exclaimed, holding up two fingers in the position of a cross.

Danny rubbed his eye and forehead before turning to her with his best grin. "Now, now Patricia, be nice."

Patricia's own smile wavered. "You know your invitation is as open and free as his, Danny."

Cameron gave Patricia a thin smile. "Thanks, but I think these guys are more my style."

I had to cover my mouth to keep a giggle from slipping out. Patricia was not going to let up but it was fun to watch her squirm for a bit.

She huffed and flipped her bottle-blonde hair over her shoulder. She leaned in close to Cameron. "There isn't a time limit on my offer." With that, she flipped her hair again and walked away.

Danny let out such a huge sigh that my napkin fluttered. "I'm sorry about that, Cameron. She's a bit . . ." he searched for the right word.

"Of an attention whore?" Beatrix tried.

Danny rubbed the bridge of his nose. "Something like that."

"She doesn't seem all that bad," Cameron said. I exchanged an incredulous look with Beatrix. "But I can definitely see your point."

Danny's eyes narrowed. "She can actually be nice, but it's all about popularity and self-glorification. She's just . . . a tedious narcissist. Thankfully, you have us instead."

I rolled my eyes as Tiffany leaned close into Cameron. "It's nice to find a boy who hasn't fallen under her spell."

For a moment, I thought I saw my twin open her mouth, but if she did then she closed it just as quickly. I hunkered further down in my chair. *So much for her confidence level today.* Still, she was laughing at Tiffany's comment.

Perhaps the Golden Boy had more of an effect on my group than I thought he would.

—

"Hey, Casey! Wait up." I could hear the Golden Boy's warm accent in the distance. Wishing I could have just kept walking, I reluctantly slowed down in the jumble of the school parking lot. "Wow. You walk fast," he remarked, falling into an easy stride with me. I shrugged and looked at the ground. "You know . . . since I don't really know the town . . . I was wondering if you might show me around?"

I stopped at his words. *Why does he want to hang out with me?* I knitted my brows together and raised an eyebrow at him. "I'm sure there are other people who would jump at the chance to walk you around town, but I'm probably not the best pick."

"Well, what if I don't want one of them? What if I want *you* to show me around?" he said.

His bluntness shocked me. I was now even more apprehensive of this new boy. "Okay." I drew out the "ay" as I contemplated what to do. "You seem nice, but I'm really not looking for more friends right now." His frown caused me to pause. "Sorry."

"Okay, okay. I can see when my presence isn't appreciated. But can't you give me a try?" He put a hand on my shoulder and I froze. My stomach dropped to my feet like it does when I'm standing up for a big project. It was a bizarre feeling to have been touched by someone I

13

didn't know. I had spent so many years trying to distance myself that real contact felt nice. My hand reached for his, and I tried to move it off my shoulder. Our hands connected for a moment. "Pretty please?" His voice glided over me like honey.

I shrunk away once his hand was removed. Screwing up my mouth, I searched his face. Wide eyes, sloping smile, and dimples. This boy was definitely trouble, but I found myself saying, "I suppose," anyway.

"Great." He was like a glowing sun. Cameron didn't stop staring right into my eyes. "We can make plans tomorrow," he said, hopeful. Once his eyes broke away from mine, I found myself letting out a breath I didn't know I had held.

"Yeah, something like that." I turned and walked away.

"Goodbye, Casey," he called after me, giddiness in his voice. "By the way, call me Cam."

"Goodbye, *Cameron*," I called back. I swore I heard him chuckling. Rounding the corner, my brain raced to understand why he wanted me to hang out with him and how to convince him to go away.

The Golden Boy was proving to be a big mystery. The worst part was that I knew I shouldn't care but did. Looking both ways, I quickly crossed the street.

I felt myself getting more annoyed with each step. A sweet Georgia breeze flooded my senses but didn't calm me down. *Maybe I can just show him around and be done with it.* My best friend's grin fluttered through my mind. *Or maybe Danny will insist on his presence in our little group.*

I reached the bus stop and exhaled. Christina sat on the bench, her head cocked slightly. "Hey, Chris." I sat down as she waved at me. "Whatcha thinking about?" She shrugged in her usual answer. "Don't really feel like talking?"

Her face clouded slightly, and her eyes got a faraway look in them. I knew she felt really shy about her muteness. She swung her feet back and forth. "Not really." Her voice was so quiet I almost didn't hear it.

I gave her a half smile and we both stared at the ground in front of us. I reached over and gave her hand a small squeeze. She returned the squeeze with a bit more life in her eyes. Thoughts of Cameron dissipated as the bus pulled up. I got the same sinking feeling I always got when it was time to go to our wonderful home.

—

I opened my front door and the musty smell invaded my nostrils. Mom was passed out on the couch. A single note sat on the table beside her.

Dinner on the stove. Wake me up at 7 please. Have to work.

Well, at least she is going to work, I glowered. Christina walked over to our mom and touched her shoulder. She didn't move. "I doubt she's dead, Christina, so why don't we eat?"

The food on the stove consisted of poorly spiced hamburgers and plain potato chips. Wishing I could bury my head in a pillow and disappear into a blithe dreamland, I fixed us a plate. I could hardly stomach her bubbly silence. When Momma got a job, a job *I* helped her get, Christina seemed more vivacious. It bothered me that she rarely talked but would stretch her emotions to the max. I waited for the day she would crack.

"So, Christina?" I eased into what I knew would probably be a one-person conversation. "I never said thank you for the compliment this morning. So . . . thank you." A big smile stretched over her face. I shifted in my seat. "Did something bad happen today? I thought you were going to have a good day today." She bit her lips and focused intently on her hamburger. Methodically ripping at the bun, she rolled the tiny bits of dough into balls between her fingers. "I don't mean to pry but . . ." I didn't know how to finish that sentence. I stared down at my own burger. The silence was overflowing. My stomach momentarily protested. Closing my eyes briefly, I opened them once more and ate most of my chips and burger in a rush.

"I'm going to bed." Her face contorted with worry. "Don't look at me like that. I'm just tired." I cleared my plate and put it in the dishwasher. When I turned back around, I saw that she was only halfway done with her food. The plate was covered in circles of bread. "Don't forget to wake Momma." She gave me a quick nod but didn't say anything. I walked quickly to my room.

I fell onto my maroon bedding in a clump. Christina had to know how much she infuriated and worried me. Just how much I could take, I didn't know. The soft gold and maroon pillow blacked out the world and allowed me a silent wall against the wail I let out. With that off my chest, I flipped onto my backside and stared at the ceiling. A single crack crept from the far corner of the room to right over my bed. One day the ceiling was destined to creak slowly and fall right in.

My mind traveled to the Golden Boy. I didn't know if I wanted another friend, but he seemed persistent. But maybe we could be friends since he seemed nice enough. *Maybe even my boyfriend?* I laughed out loud at the thought of me having a boyfriend. Yeah, I was sure that a girl who could experience people dying was a real turn-on for a California boy. Besides, I barely knew the guy. Sleep called for me and made me sink. But it wasn't sleep that dragged me from my room. It was someone.

My mind took me outside. It was crisp and cool. Shock and worry clouded my thoughts. A girl was in front of me. She had dark brown hair and darker brown eyes. She walked calmly to her car. Darkness covered the world as the day turned to night. The pale girl didn't mind the darkness. Actually, she enjoyed the darkness. Yet so did the man who crept behind her. He was dressed head to toe in black.

There was no empathy in what he was about to do. After leaping forward and grabbing her from behind, he raised the knife and pressed it deep across her throat. She was down on her knees in stark terror, convulsing in front of the man who had just slashed her. In her mind, I saw that her last regret had been that she hadn't told her parents she loved them. The man in the ski mask seemed to stare right down at me, because I had become that poor girl in that moment.

I screamed as I was pulled back into my bedroom. My breath raced out of me with the thought of the man's haunting blue eyes, which would follow me for months. I had just witnessed a murder for the first time in my life.

the hamster that lived and other too close encounters

The brilliant blues of the eyes on the canvas still didn't match quite right. I stared at my portrait of the murderer I had seen in my "episode" two nights prior. It had taken me two days to get the courage to paint what I had wished was a nightmare. *Who is he?* I hadn't told a soul. My mind wandered to my wonderful best friend. *What would I say?* My cell phone buzzed.

"**Hey what's up? This is Cam.**" I stared at the bright screen in disbelief.

How did he get my number? Something deep down in me told me that it was probably Danny. I guess he didn't understand the whole small friend group aesthetic. "**Painting,**" I replied.

I looked up at the canvas. It was the best I could do to match the scene. I was just glad I didn't paint the death of that poor girl. I felt another buzz.

"**That's cool, what r u painting? Me? ;)**" I rolled my eyes. Cameron was cheeky, no doubt about that.

"**Nope. Not even close,**" I typed. What happened the other night hit me again. Squeezing my eyes tight, I attempted to erase the images from my mind. I covered the canvas and sank to the floor. *Why am I cursed with this "gift"? Why can't I just be normal?* A few minutes passed before Cameron texted me again.

"**Hey I'm sorry. I realize that was cocky . . .**" I smiled faintly. "**I guess when I'm nervous that happens. C I was wondering if u might wanna go somewhere tonight?**" I stared at the phone and wondered again about how to answer him. Another text buzzed my phone. "**Not as a date. Unless u want that. But seriously I just need to get out.**"

"**I'm sorry, Cameron, I would, but I can't. I don't feel good,**" I typed back. It was partly true at least. I read his text over again and felt my heart sink for him. "**Rain check?**" I sent the text before I changed my mind.

I got up slowly. Ignoring my covered canvas, I pulled out a new one and set it on the easel. I needed to get my mind off things. Absent-mindedly, I put black paint on my brush and fell into even strokes. The mechanical motions birthed a curvy foundation. I dipped the brush in a different color. Golden wings had spread within the central oval as the bristles kissed the canvas. I dipped the brush again. A smaller black circle filled the middle of the oval.

My strokes became more frantic. I felt the need to finish whatever it was. My hand, seemingly possessed, reached for a soft and sorrowful blue. With one final stroke, I was finished. I stepped back to examine my portrait. It was a brilliant golden eye with a single tear falling from it. *It can't be,* I thought, thinking of Cameron's eyes. Yet it was. The eye was too much like his to be anything but.

Why did I paint that? And why only his eye? I removed the canvas from the easel, suddenly eager to get away from all the paint.

—

"Well, what do you think?" Danny gushed over the phone. "I mean, Phoebe is really cute, but should I keep myself open for you know who?"

I was not enjoying the conversation. Danny wouldn't shut up about the one person in the universe I didn't feel like talking about. "Danny. I don't know. Who do you like better?"

"Uh knock, knock. I've only said I don't know for the past twenty minutes. Get your head in the game, girl!" he exclaimed. I contemplated going over to his house to smack him.

"I'm sorry. I'm just . . ." I sighed angrily. "Preoccupied."

"Am I being a bad friend? I'm so sorry. What's wrong? What happened?" His high-pitched whines seemed patronizing, but he was merely trying to help.

"I don't know . . . I just, I don't know."

"Oh come on, Casey. You know I'm always here for you," he said. I thought back to the killer and wished I could tell someone about it.

"Yeah. I know, Danny. I think I'm going to bed, but tomorrow we can talk, okay?"

His maudlin sigh washed through my ears. "Yeah . . . I suppose."

"And who knows; maybe we can go to the mall and scope out some cuties?" I asked, hoping it was a good apology.

He giggled. "Yeah, maybe, but we are talking about this, Casey. I mean it. Bye."

"Bye." I hung up the phone and stared at it a moment before putting it down. I fell back on the bed, slightly ashamed of myself. *His problems may not be big, but they are big to him.* Rolling onto my belly, I looked to the paintbrushes on my nightstand. My hand reached toward them and stopped.

I was sucked into a room, both organized and messy, but I didn't pay that aspect much attention. I softly gasped when a shimmering blade came into my view. It was from an X-Acto knife or a box cutter. Shaking fingers pressed the loose blade onto a left forearm enough to indent the flesh, but not enough to break skin. My mind was showing me Cameron. He lifted his right hand and repeated the morbid action all the way down to his wrist until a dark red bubble appeared at the blade's point. The silver razor clinked onto the hardwood floor. He made a tight fist, making the bubble grow, and then smeared the bubble into a bright red stroke.

Shakily, I reached for my phone . . . somewhere far away from the situation. A lullaby melody filled the air. Cameron looked down at the small cell phone in his lap that continued to ring. I could feel his hesitation in answering the call. Memories circled his mind, yet never really entered. His finger swirled the blood ever so slightly against the canvas of his forearm. I could feel a dark memory prodding: the memory of his mother? He focused in on the cell phone and picked it up. "Hello?"

I was snapped completely back into my bedroom. In my hand, the cell phone was clutched to my ear, allowing me to hear Cameron's ragged breath. I heard myself whisper, "Stop."

"Stop what?" he scoffed, frustrated.

"Cameron, it's me. Casey."

"Yeah . . . hey." His voice was heartbreaking. "Is there a specific reason you called, because . . . I'm kind of busy."

In the back of my mind, I saw Cameron with the blade right in front of him. He was still ready to do it. Ready to cut deeper. "Well, are you too busy to go out?"

A pause. "I thought you weren't feeling good."

"That was then." Lying to him wasn't going to work. "I was busy . . . I know it's a lame excuse, but I just *had* to paint. I'm sorry, but now I want to make it up to you. I need to get out too."

Another pause. This time it was longer. "Thank you for your honesty." *Don't pick up the blade,* I commanded him in my head. I watched Cameron close his eyes while the razor remained on the antique floor. "Where do you want to go?" His voice now sounded revived.

I exhaled, not noticing that I had been holding my breath. "You wanted me to show you around, right? Well, there's a cute diner downtown a few blocks from school on Main Street. I don't know if you've seen it. It's called Maximum's. I can be there in thirty minutes."

"I'll be there in forty," he said. In my mind, I saw him put the blade into a small envelope. The vision vanished when he was out of danger.

"Alright. I'll see you there," I promised, looking for something to change into.

"Yeah. See you there." I was about to hang up, but I could still hear him breathing. I had begun to ask if he forgot something when he said, "Thank you" and hung up.

"Thank you for not dying," I whispered into the silent air. Without a second thought, I pulled on my favorite blouse, ran a brush through my hair, and went to see my mom.

"Mother?" I unkindly nudged her.

"Hum?" she grunted, half-asleep.

"I'm going out. There are leftovers in the fridge. Please do not try and cook. We can't let this house go up in flames." I turned to leave only to find Christina, wide-eyed, looking me up and down. "Christina, did you hear what I just said?" Her blue eyes gazed at me without an answer. "Food is in the fridge. Don't let her use anything *but* the microwave, understand?" Only nodding graced me. "Whatever. I'll be back later."

Walking to Maximum's, I took in the first crisp air of the season. I've always loved fall weather and this was certainly no exception. Macabre thoughts about Cameron soon entered my mind. *Why? Why do you want to kill yourself?* An even scarier question then broke into my brain. *Did I cause it? Is this why he wanted to get out of the house?* Impossible. *Right?* A small part of me hoped that this dinner would help. My life was complicated *but if I could help him* . . . It seemed futile considering I didn't even want to be his friend.

I mulled over the vision. I had never had a vision that didn't end with death. Even the suicidal ones I saw, which thankfully weren't a lot, all ended poorly. *So, how did I see you?* Rubbing my hands together, I thought of the Golden Boy's wrist. *I want to help you.*

I focused on the concrete in front of me. *One crack, two, three, four* . . . . Before I knew it, Maximum's brilliant neon sign was in view. I entered and sat in a booth hidden in the shadows. Only I could see what was going on in the restaurant. The Golden Boy was nowhere. I waited.

A short, stocky waitress came to my booth. "Why, hello, deary. What can I get ya tonight?" Her voice was gruff from smoking too much, but comforting.

"Um, nothing yet . . . . I'm waiting on a friend," I said, slightly uncomfortable. She looked elderly, and considering the fact that they die rather quickly, it always scared me to interact with them.

"Nothing to drink?" she insisted.

"Not now, but if you leave a menu I promise to order when he gets here."

"Oh, it's a *he?*" She wiggled her eyebrows, leaving me mortified. "Well," she continued, patting my shoulder. "You just signal me when he gets here." With a well-intentioned smile, she glided away without realizing how terrible she made me feel.

I put my head in my hands. *She thinks that Cameron is my boyfriend and that we're going to make out. Well, she'll definitely be disappointed.* I shook the thought away just as Cameron came into view.

"Hey . . ." I said with as much enthusiasm as I could muster. He gave a small wave but didn't move. "You can sit down, you know." Cameron fell into the booth. His hair fell in his face, but he didn't do anything to move it. After a few seconds of awkward silence, I looked for the waitress. Another waiter apparently wanted our table, much to the old lady's dismay, and had started walking toward us. As Cameron continued to stare down at the table, I began to worry that this was a mistake. *How can I help him if I can't even help myself? What will going to a diner even do to help him?*

Concern colored my thoughts as the new waiter arrived. He stepped so close to the table that I feared he might go through it. His hair was black, medium, and had a slight wave that most girls would kill for. His clear skin was on the dark side of olive. Everything about him screamed "joker." But his eyes were the best part. They were a dark brown complete with green overtones. I had seen him before in school, but only now did I really notice him. His name was something like Adam or Aiken.

"Hola," he merrily greeted.

Cameron grunted in response and continued to stare at the table. His eyes squinted as if they were blinded by Maximum's bright lights.

"What do y'all want to drink?" The guy rocked a bit on his feet. He reminded me of a puppy.

Cameron looked at me inquiringly and I ordered for us. "Can we have two Coke floats please?"

"Be right back." He whisked away.

"Friend of yours?" He picked at his leather bracelet. There was a discolored area he was picking at. I briefly wondered if he had scars.

I leaned down a bit to try and look into his eyes. "You clearly don't know how small towns work. Here, everyone knows everyone. You don't have to be friends to be friendly, but you can't be rude or else that bit of information will spread to everyone."

"Weird." He cleared his throat. "Southerners are weird."

I leaned back and put my hand to my chest in a fake gasp. "I take great offense to that."

He looked at me. "I'm sorry but you are." I watched as his hand twisted the leather bracelet on his opposite wrist. If I tried hard enough, I could imagine the cuts they held underneath. "Still, maybe I can get used to it."

"So . . . what do you think of Maximum's?" I watched him comb the place, glancing again at the thick leather bracelets hugging his wrists.

"It's old-fashioned. Retro," he concluded, fondly eyeing the cakes and pies on the counter by the register.

The waiter returned with our floats and put them down with ease. We both jumped backwards. I hadn't realized it but I had moved closer to him. "I'll be right back to take your order."

Cameron's jaw was strong and clenched, his lips turned down slightly. He played with the leather bracelets on his wrist. "I like coming here, though. Every time I walk through the door, I'm sucked back into 1955." An awkward silence enveloped us again until Cameron's gaze found its way back to the table.

He removed the cherry from his float and took a sip. "You know, this just might have beaten the best float in California," he finally proclaimed.

"What?" I asked, my eyebrow rising slightly.

"There's this place on the beach called The Big Float. It has the best floats I've ever tasted—till today, at least."

"Oh . . ." I trailed off. I clenched my hands together and slowly rubbed my thumb up and down. "What's California like?"

His face lit up. "Beautiful. Bright. Sunny. Fun." His smile seemed as bright as the place he was describing. "Warm is another big one. Oh, and there's not as much rain as there is here. There's nothing but rich, ocean moisture. It's the best place to be." The smile on his face wavered.

"It sounds great. I mean, I've never been anywhere but this small town," I was embarrassed to say. "It honestly sounds like a wonderland."

He laughed. I was starting to like his laugh. It was deep and real. Not like he was trying too much. "I don't think I would go that far, but it's definitely better than wet Georgia."

"Hey, no need to bag on my state. It isn't the worst place ever. And it's been raining more this year than normal," I playfully warned him.

"Yeah. Sure," he said sarcastically. Stretching his arms back, he gave me a wink. "Georgia is pretty, actually. In its own way, I suppose."

"Oh, you just be quiet," I simpered as the waiter moseyed back to our table.

Getting his pad ready, he took our orders. "What will you fine people be having tonight?" Cameron's quietness grew again at the waiter's effervescent presence.

We only had one menu, and I was looking at it. "I'll have a Swamp Burger, no tomato please, cheese fries, and that's it." Once I finished, I handed the menu to Cameron. He glanced at it briefly before looking up at me, unsure, as if I was supposed to order for him since he was on my turf. "I suggest you try the Peach Burger with fries." His mouth gaped

26

open in horror, so I said, "Don't worry. Peaches aren't an actual part of the burger. It's really good." Finally trusting me, he nodded.

"Be right out," the waiter sang, leaving us to wallow in another silence. At least it was more comfortable than the ones before we ordered.

—

"Thank you for this," Cameron said as we reached my front door. The walk home had been just as pleasant as our meal. Not only pleasant, but also informative. The Golden Boy was growing on me.

"You're welcome. I actually had a lot of fun." I looked back at my shabby home. The rainspout was rusted. The once cheery, yellow paint was faded and peeling. The whole place appeared as if it were about to implode. Being with Cameron made me a little more self-conscious of it.

"I was . . ." he trailed off and looked down the road. "I've been in a bad place for a while, is all." *I know.* "Just, thank you. I guess I'll see you Monday?"

"Goodbye," I said. Again, we were closer than I anticipated. I took a step back. Now, we were about an arm's length away and I could breathe again.

"I had a lot of fun, too," he whispered. He rubbed his left arm with his right hand. "So, y'know, I was wondering—" The door opened. Shocked, I jumped back even farther from him.

"Chris," I said breathlessly, shaking my hair in my face. "You scared me half to death." Her blue eyes were wide. "What's wrong?"

Her mouth opened, and she had begun to speak when her eyes landed on Cameron. She shook her head sadly and started to walk down the hall. I rubbed the back of my head, embarrassed by my weird existence. "I'm sorry. I've got to go." I raced to her bedroom.

I moved down the hall to Christina's bedroom. She was crouched in front of her hamster's cage. "What is it?" I asked, kneeling beside her.

"My hamster," she managed to choke out. It didn't take long for me to figure out what she meant by that.

"Ohhh. I see. I'm sorry, Christina." One of the hamsters was on its side, breathing shallow, as if it were seconds from death. Her eyes were pleading, wanting me to help her. "I don't know what I can do . . . Let me go get a towel to wrap it in," I volunteered and fled down the hallway.

Cameron bumped into me. "Casey." He sounded embarrassed to be in my house without an invitation. "I'm sorry about barging in like this, but the door was open and then I just wanted to make sure everything was okay."

"Oh. Yeah." His chest was pressed against mine in the tight hallway. I felt his heartbeat sync up with mine as they both sped up. "I'm just worried about Christina."

"What happened?" He leaned back, allowing me to breathe. My mind was whirling but I shrugged off his lingering heat. "Sorry."

"Well, it's her hamster. I think it's going to die." I felt a tad dumb.

"Poor Christina." His empathy was genuine. "Where's her room?"

I was shocked at his kindness. "Um, right in here. I know it seems kind of stupid, but she loves her animals."

Cameron shook his head. "It's not stupid to be upset over something you love." He disappeared into her room.

How strange it was that just a few hours ago he was ready to harm himself, and now he was helping Christina. Questions about his stability warbled across my mind. Then, I couldn't help but chastise myself. *I don't know him.* I grabbed a towel out of the bathroom. *This is probably not going to do anything,* I predicted.

"Wow. You're quite the doctor," I heard Cameron say as I entered the room.

Curious, I glanced over their shoulders to see the same hamster that had been on its side, barely breathing. It was running on the hamster wheel. Christina stopped the wheel and pulled out the plump thing. Incredibly, it looked healthier than the other hamsters. She held it out to me as if to say, "See? All better."

Giving them an inquiring look, I asked, "What happened?"

Cameron shrugged and ran a hand through his golden hair. "Beats me. She was cuddling and whispering to it, and when she released it . . . it just started playing."

I couldn't fix my awe-stricken face. *That hamster was sick. No, it had been dying.* I dropped the towel and leaned into the doorframe. Christina, oblivious to my stupefaction, turned her attention back to her furry creatures.

Cameron's warm gaze caught mine. "Well, Christina, thank you for showing me your hamsters." She nodded enthusiastically but didn't acknowledge us any longer. He inclined his head to suggest leaving her room. I nodded and followed him out.

Walking through the hallway with him made me take in how sad our house really looked. Unkempt, walls flaked with dust, no pictures. I frowned at the sight. It was a happy relief when we were finally outside.

"I like your sister. She's very caring." He continued staring at me intently. "Your house is nice too. Quaint. I like that."

I gave a sarcastic laugh. "Quaint isn't really how I'd put it." I broke our staring contest by looking down.

He put his hand on my shoulder. "I like the house. And I liked tonight." He gave me a funny look but didn't say anything else. Long lashes framed his eyes. Sticking his hands in his pockets, he loped down the driveway. "See you soon, Casey Darling."

I slid through the door and into my house. My shoulder still felt warm from his touch. Looking out the window, I watched him continue toward wherever home was. I whispered to no one, "See you soon, Golden Boy."

CHAPTER THREE

two can keep a secret

Danny hugged me tightly as I got into his car. "Choking," I coughed as I squeezed him back.

"Sorry," he said, clearly not. "Okay, rules for today."

I groaned, a bit frustrated, but quickly simmered down at his look. He acted like a teacher lecturing me.

"One, you are going to tell me what was up yesterday." His navy eyes peered at me from the side. "Two, we shall find me a date. And three, I want all the details about you and Cam."

My heart froze. I didn't really want to talk about Cameron. Yesterday had been weird and the more I thought about it the more he worried me. I didn't know how to be friends with new people.

"Oh come on, Casey, you know me too well to think you can keep secrets from me."

I leaned my head against the seat and closed my eyes. "There isn't anything to say. He wants to be friends and I don't really want to be. But last night we hung out and it was fun. Besides, didn't you want dibs?" Turning to look at him, I put on my sunglasses.

Cascading sunlight streamed through the car.

His mouth formed a tiny knot. "True . . . but there's something about y'all. I don't want to deter you. As for your reluctance . . ." His eyes flitted toward me before focusing back on the road.

My stomach faltered. Danny knew everything about me, he *got* me, and he could probably feel my hesitation. I bit my lip and turned to face out the window.

Once again, I was hit with the question of why I didn't tell Danny about my problems. My whole *"experiencing death"* problems, I mean. Out of everyone I knew, he was the one I was most afraid to tell. I studied him in my peripheral vision. He appeared deep in thought and reached over to turn on the radio. He instantly perked up at the sound of Lady Gaga's voice. I realized that I didn't need to worry about telling him.

"Danny?" He kept tapping his hand and singing along with the radio. "Danny?" I tried a little bit louder.

"Yeah?" he asked while still singing along.

I hesitated. I couldn't burden him with this problem. It was too much for me and I knew it would be the same for him. "Um . . ." I scrambled to find something to say. "What were you gonna say about my reluctance?" I finally managed to sputter.

He flashed me a look and shook his head. "I love you, Casey, you know that, but I don't understand you." Danny moved his hair out of his face. "You're so afraid of new friendships and I don't get it. Tiffany joined our group and you didn't talk to her for the first two months." I could see him trying hard to focus on the road rather than me. "I remember the week after your dad. Scratch that, I remember the year after he died. I didn't know how to help then, and I don't know what to do now. But you can't keep yourself locked away forever." He finished in a whisper that made me shiver. The road to the mall suddenly became interesting. "Casey, I want you to be happy. And I think Cameron is good for you. I just have a feeling." A grin lit up his face. "And bi-best friends always have good feelings that *typically* come true," he joked.

I leered at my reflection in the window and turned back as we pulled into the mall. "Thank you, Danny. Now let's find you a date."

—

I scoured the mall for Danny's perfect match, drinking my Strawnana Smoothie. Out of every single boy and girl I had picked out (roughly 100, and that is only a *slight* exaggeration), Danny hadn't found any acceptable. "You have to *feel* these things, Casey. Dating isn't a game of chance. You can't always just go with what you get first."

"Okay. Over there, by the game store. Boy with the blue shirt, brown hair, and tall."

He craned his neck and looked at the guy I picked out. "Hmmm . . . I don't know. He looks like a jerk and he isn't my type. Can't you tell?"

I just looked at him. "Do you know how many times I've wanted to slap you today?"

Danny just shrugged. "Well, he wasn't the worst . . ."

"You're unbearable!" I pinched him.

"You know you love me," he declared.

"In your dreams." I stuck my tongue out at him and got the same response. As we continued to do this back and forth, people stared at us. I knew they were probably thinking we were some weird couple, but Danny and I were just in platonic love with each other.

"Hi, Danny." An eager voice met our moment. I turned to see Phoebe coming up to our table in the middle of the food court.

He became flustered. "H-hi, Phoebe," he stuttered dreamily.

"Whatcha up to?" she said with a bashful smile.

"I'll be right back, Danny." I had been hoping to give them some alone time. I walked over to the trashcan and threw away my smoothie. Looking back at our table, I saw Danny chirping away and Phoebe looking like she just won the lottery. I was amused.

Then I caught a flash of golden hair and skin. *Cameron,* I thought. I looked closer but didn't see him. I shrugged it off and started to walk back to the table when I saw it again. Except this time it wasn't just the hair and body I saw, but the place. Panic began to choke me. *It can't be him, can it?* My mind was yanked into another death scene. The killer was the first person I saw. His ski mask covered everything but his cold, snaky blue eyes. I tried to shout at him and distract him, but it didn't work. Then I saw Cameron. My world stopped.

Somewhere in the back of my mind, the part that still occupied the real world, I heard Danny call my name, but I ignored him. My feet carried me forward, but I couldn't stop myself. I was focusing on Cameron and the killer. Cameron's blond hair bobbed as he walked by a dumpster behind a department store. *"Cameron!"* I yelled at him, but he couldn't hear me.

I pushed through the crowd. My body wanted to escape outside. I wasn't sure where I was going, but I felt like I had to get there. It was just outside the mall. The killer drew out his knife behind the dumpster. Even with the mask on, I could tell he was sneering. Under his breath I heard him whisper something, but it was too low for me to understand. "Excuse you!" I heard someone say hotly as, in the real world, my body continued on a trek that I realized was leading toward the escalators.

Cameron turned around at that moment and two things happened at once. First, Cameron became surprised and tried to run. Second, I realized that it wasn't Cameron, but rather a Cameron look-alike with blue eyes, not brown. The killer stabbed him in the back just as I felt the smallest bit of relief that the boy wasn't Cameron.

The Cameron look-alike's happiest memories were ones about his first puppy, his first kiss, and the time he helped his little brother for a science fair project. My heart fell to the ground as I realized that he deserved my sadness just as much as Cameron. There were little to no bad memories, the biggest one being the time he fell and broke his arm. In fact, the boy's one regret in life was that he wouldn't see his brother grow up.

The killer sliced his neck with the blade and the vision disappeared. I looked at the fading sky through the vaulted, glass ceiling. My mind was loud with horrid thoughts. *Who is this man?* He enjoyed it. Somehow, I knew that. *Is he . . . is he a serial killer?* It was clearly the same man who killed the woman in Cartersville. However, the mall was thirty miles away. I usually only see deaths that are within blocks of me, or at least very short distances. *Why is he at the mall?* I found myself sobbing in the middle of the food court like a wretch. I was positively sick at the small bit of happiness I experienced when I realized the boy hadn't been Cameron.

"Casey!" Danny's voice was hysterical. "What on earth happened?"

Just then, flashes from security vehicles blinked through the mall windows and shoppers looked outside. The look on Danny's face made an inevitable decision for me. "Get me out of here. I have to tell you something."

—

"Oh my God! Why didn't you tell me this before?! Of all the things you don't tell your best friend?! This—*this* is not one of them!" he screeched in the car. I couldn't help but cower at his tantrum. Thank goodness I had insisted on driving. "How could you not tell me something like this?!"

"I don't know, Danny," I responded helplessly, glad I had to give the road my full attention. "I was afraid you would throw me in the crazy house."

His eyes looked like they might pop out of his head. Had the situation not been so terrible, I would have laughed. "I would never do that to you, Casey. You should have told me!" He complained like a five-year-old who couldn't have dessert before dinner. *His frustration is valid,* my mind whispered as I switched lanes on the highway.

"Danny, I couldn't be sure." I threw my hands up in exasperation, though I quickly brought them back down on the wheel. "I've been alone in this since I was seven. I wasn't exactly sure what anyone would say."

The sympathetic look on his face made me grimace. "You didn't have to be, though, Casey. You should have told me. All of us think you have epilepsy or some sort of fainting condition. Since first grade, you've been watching people die?!"

I couldn't hold it back anymore. Tears started to flow from my eyes. The once-pretty sunset in front of me swirled into a giant mess. I sniveled, "How do you say that to someone? How do you tell them what it's like to watch someone die? And to feel like you know them because of it." The world flew by as the car continued on its way. The road was starting to look like I had dragged a wet paintbrush across it.

"Shh, it's okay. I'm sorry." He reversed his energy, putting a hand on my arm. "At least now I understand why you're so quiet." He sat still for a moment, not knowing how to continue. "Is this also why you're so reluctant about Cameron?"

For a second the look-alike's death ripped through me. I hated Cameron for moving to Georgia, for being such a happy person who cut himself, for making *me* happy that someone had died. "That's why I'm reluctant toward everyone." I glanced at him. "But yeah. That's part of it."

He leaned back against the seat. "Is there anything else I need to know? Do you speak to aliens?"

That was the Danny I needed. "I'm still working on that one," I said as we pulled onto my street. Danny's laugh cut off quickly.

I looked at him and his eyes were glittering with sadness. "I wish you had told me. I could have been there for you."

I rubbed my eyes with balled up fists before putting them back on the steering wheel. "I never knew how to say it."

"Okay." I avoided his gaze. "I won't pressure you about your reluctance anymore but I need you to talk to me from now on, okay?"

I locked eyes with him. "Okay."

He reached over and gave me a hug that was hindered slightly by the steering wheel. In that moment, all the doubt about sharing my secret melted away. I gripped him tightly and thanked my lucky stars for this amazing best friend.

CHAPTER FOUR

death, drama, and other extreme sports

I slunk into my desk trying to draw little attention to myself. "Hello, Cameron . . ." I heard Patricia purr. I froze in the middle of reading my book.

"Hello," Cameron grumbled. I glanced up and my eyes met his. He gave me a show-stopping grin. My whole face lit up like the Fourth of July and I wondered if I was blushing. Surprisingly, the math class was already full, so he couldn't sit where he had sat before. "Mind if I sit here?" he asked Patricia with forced happiness.

I was practically blinded by her beaming smile. "Of course."

"Morning, class." Mrs. Tawny seemed a bit frantic for a Monday morning. Her hair was disheveled, and she looked like she might fall apart at any moment. "I'm sorry I'm late, but today has been very hectic." She dumped an armload of stuff on her desk. "Many of you have heard about this weekend, and for those of you who haven't, I'm sure your peers won't hesitate in telling." She stretched on her tiptoes again and let out a short breath. "Last night, someone your age was killed at the mall. He was from Cartersville." I ducked down. Mrs. Tawny looked old and haggard for someone young and jumpy. "Although he did not *go* to this school we should all keep him in our thoughts and prayers. This is a very tragic event, and one that should not be taken lightly."

The whole class sat in complete silence. People died all the time, even some young adults, but never in our town and never in our age group. Peggy, Patricia's best friend, popped her gum and asked, "Who was it?" Everyone turned to look at her and she took the looks in as if we were paparazzi.

I gritted my teeth as Mrs. Tawny addressed her. "His name was Sam." I looked down. *Sam,* I thought miserably. More than anything, I wish I hadn't heard his name. Before, I could've seen the boy as just another human, but now I saw him as a real person. One with hopes and dreams. One who wanted to see his little brother grow up.

At that moment, Cameron decided to turn and face me. His face portrayed nothing at first. He had texted me again during the night, but I couldn't bring myself to respond. We searched each other's faces, but I personally couldn't find anything.

"Class, I want you to be careful," Mrs. Tawny sweetly requested. "I know that seems juvenile, but I don't want to hear about anything like this happening to any of you. There was another incident recently, as you might know. I'm not saying they were related, but . . . just be more alert when you're going about your business. Alright?" I was struck by how much Mrs. Tawny actually cared.

"How did they die?" barked a voice from the back.

"Zombies," another voice said.

"That's disgusting," Patricia sneered.

Mrs. Tawny held her hands up to the opening floodgates. "I don't think we should focus on the details of the situation. We should just be aware that we have lost a *young* person in the community and try to be as careful as possible. Why don't we turn to calculus?" The class collectively moaned, and the lecture began.

—

"Isn't it just unbelievable!?" Beatrix asked as she leaned against the locker beside mine. She flicked her hair behind her shoulder. With crossed arms, she had told me everything she knew about the murder that had occurred. My polite "hmms," and "wows," didn't seem to placate her.

"It's crazy," I said. I stuffed the last textbook in my bag and hoisted it onto my shoulders. The weight made me hunch over slightly as I shut the locker door.

Her face drooped momentarily. "Are you okay, Casey?" She raised her own book bag a bit higher. "Cause, I am now realizing that was a bit much?"

I gave her a half smile. "Maybe, but I know how you are."

She lit up and slung an arm around my shoulder. "I am glad you are always here for my performances." I rolled my eyes. A few feet ahead of us, the Golden Boy caught my eyes and waved. I waved back. "Do you wanna hang out tomorrow?"

I looked at my good friend of several years. Exuberance shone through her eyes. Everything, from her hair to her bright yellow toenails, shone brighter than I could.

Just as I was about to answer, Cameron walked up to us. "Hey," he said, his voice as soft as the gold in his eyes.

"Hello," I repeated awkwardly. He was blocking our path. I tried to smile and act normal, but his eyes seemed to waver between being his and being Sam's blue ones.

"What are you guys up to?" He rotated his leather cuff around. I watched him watching me. It made my heart flutter uncomfortably.

"Casey and I were just talking about Sam and potentially hanging out!" she said as she gave him a big smile.

"Sam is?"

"Hello, the guy that was murdered? Didn't one of your teachers tell you?"

"Oh, right. Mrs. Tawny mentioned it. I can't believe it. It's awful," Cameron said.

"Isn't it though? I mean one second he's fine then—"

"Beatrix." I pinched the bridge of my nose. "Not again, please."

She gave me a guilty half smile. "Sorry. I'll tell you about it later, Cam." She started to walk away from us backwards. "Oh, and Casey, please let me know about hanging out, okay?" With a quick wave, she was out the door.

Cameron and I stood in front of the lockers without saying anything for a few minutes. Pursing my lips, and groaning under the weight of my bag, I looked back at him. His eyes locked with mine and with a nod of his head we left the school together.

Walking beside him, I couldn't stop staring at him. The heat radiating from him was kind of comforting. Every few seconds, our arms would brush against each other causing me to jump a bit each time. Soon we reached a bench in the park a few blocks from the school. I liked that he had chosen this place because it was one of my favorite thinking spots. When I sat down, he sat strangely far away from me. His eyes darted nervously.

"Um, so, I texted you last night." His voice fluctuated ever so slightly. "Did something happen or?"

I moved my hands back and forth over my jeans. "Yeah, I mean no. I'm sorry, I was hanging with Danny and then I just sort of went to bed."

"Oh, okay." He took a deep breath. "Good. Cause I was afraid you were mad and I didn't really get why but I wanted to find out why. Cause, if you are mad, and if it's for something like me coming into your house, then I just want you to know—"

"No." I cut him off with a firm look. "I am sorry for not texting you back but it doesn't mean anything." I shifted in excruciating discomfort. "Is that all?"

He scooted closer to me. "Well, I want to know why you don't like me." My body skipped a beat. His hand ran through his golden hair.

"I don't *not* like you," I said.

"Okay, but that, why do you feel that way? Can we not be friends? I mean, your other friends seem to like me." The beautiful scenery seemed to dissolve until there was just the Golden Boy with a shy smile and a piercing stare.

I took a deep breath and closed my eyes. Today was too stressful. First the news about Sam, then a Chem test, then lunch, and now this. He was looking at me like I could help him, could fix him. As if I didn't have any other problems. His hand touched my shoulder again. It was lighter than the touch from the other day. "It's complicated."

He narrowed his eyes. "Too complicated for friendship?" His hand left my shoulder and I watched as he hooked one of his fingers underneath his bracelet. "Please. Be honest with me." I lifted my head and found a rude awakening. The colors, which had just been at a dizzying boost, were dull and drab around Patricia, who had approached us.

"Cameron." Her shrill voice was even worse on my nerves today. "How are you?" She glanced at me before turning fully towards

42

Cameron. Now staring at her back, I felt all the energy drain out of me.

Without a second thought, I grabbed my books and started on my way home. "Casey, wait." I turned to see the Golden Boy running behind me, leaving Patricia in the dust. His hair flopped in his face, causing my heart to make a similar motion. "Where are you going?"

"Home. I'm tired." I continued walking.

"Casey." His intensity made me pause. "I want to finish our conversation."

"And I want to go home," I said, but didn't move. I squinted up at him, the sun hurting my eyes. Sunlight tumbled through his golden hair and lit it on fire.

"I'm new here. You said at Maximum's that in a small town every-one knows everyone else, but right now I know no one . . . I have no one." My heart somersaulted. When I looked at his eyes, I found them staring at the ground. His mouth was a thin line and his hands were in his pockets. I stared at the leather bracelets. "I know people don't really ask to be friends like we did when we were kids, but I'm trying to ask you because I like you."

I like you my brain repeated. Now it was my turn to stare at the ground. I remembered my conversation with Danny. Spreading one of my hands out I watched as the shadow grew on the ground. "Patricia could be your friend. Or Danny. Or someone else."

"I don't really want to hang with Patricia. She reminds me too much of some people back in Cali. Also, if I'm friends with Danny then I'd end up being around you anyway."

"You're gonna have to put up with my quirks." We locked eyes for a few minutes of silence. Then his face lit up.

"Quirks I can do." He reached out his hand. "Friends?" My mouth curled up involuntarily as I gripped his hand.

"Friends," I said.

"Great!" He bounced slightly and we both began walking towards my home. "So, do you want to hang out tomorrow, *Darling*," he said, stretching the first vowel in my last name.

His confidence and happiness were more intense than the sun. It was hard to say no to. "I can't do tomorrow. Maybe next weekend?" I struggled to gain an intelligent thought. "Is there any way I can come over to your house?"

Something dark clouded his face for a split second before the smile was back. "We can definitely hang out next weekend instead, but I'm not sure about you coming over. But your mom won't care, right?"

"No . . ." I said, thinking of how terrible it would be if he met my mom. I crossed my arms as he stopped walking beside me. I looked back but didn't stop.

"I'll see you in class tomorrow," he said.

As he walked away, I opened my phone to text Beatrix and told her we were good to hang out tomorrow. Chewing on my lip, my finger hovered over the send button. I finally clicked it and made my way home.

CHAPTER FIVE

not every rain cloud makes a rainbow

The world outside was invaded by gray thunderclouds and thousands of raindrops pounding the pavement. Memories of Beatrix and I dancing in the rain had entered my mind. I smiled momentarily at the storm before realizing that I was with Cameron instead of her. It would have been a perfect day for us. We had spent a day together over the week, and I had apologized for being short with her, but things still felt stilted. I just needed more Beatrix time before things would be right between us.

"Is it really raining again?" Cameron glared out the window. Looking at my phone, I decided I would text Beatrix when he left. I was nervous that he was sitting in my room for the first time. It was weird to think of him as my new friend.

"Well, it *is* Georgia," I replied from the chair opposite him. Having a boy in my bedroom was weird, especially considering how little I knew him, but he seemed nonchalant to the fact. At least we weren't too close since I stayed in my chair.

He turned to face me with a bright-as-the-sun smile. "Yeah. California weather isn't so moody. At least there I could go outside EVERY day."

"Sheesh, I swear Georgia isn't that bad. Besides, we *can* go outside," I said, trying to mimic his smile.

"Sure. If we want to get soaked."

Looking hard at the Golden Boy, I suddenly had a good idea. "Come on." I stood up.

"Come where?" His whole body tensed up on my bed. Maybe it was the five cups of coffee I drank earlier, but I wanted to dance in the rain like I did with Beatrix when we were little. I wanted to convince the Golden Boy that there was some charm to Georgia's rainy days.

I grabbed his sleeve carefully to avoid touching his leather bracelet and bolted from my room. We were out the door and under the skinny slant of the roof when he stopped me. "What are you doing?"

"Come on, scaredy cat," I taunted him, but he didn't budge. "In case you're wondering, this is what *friends* do."

"Then I'd rather not be friends," he joked.

I ran into the rain and looked up. Water pelted my face. The chilly drops fell into every pore. It felt as if all negativity was being washed away. I closed my eyes as if I were becoming renewed. After a few minutes, I looked over at Cameron, who was staring at me intently. "What?" I asked, nervous about my behavior. Sure, I loved the rain, but maybe I shouldn't have shown him such a strange and personal side of me.

"Nothing. It's just . . . you look so . . . I mean, you're so . . ." he stuttered. The rain came down harder. He stayed on the porch.

"So what?" I was curious now. My clothes clung to me in awkward places, but I honestly didn't care. Rain always made me feel clean.

He finally entered the rain. Water fell on his hair and immediately darkened it. His eyes were like two bright smoldering embers. He was no more than two feet from me. Water hung from my eyelashes. "So how do you like it?" I had to talk over the increasing rain.

"It feels good," Cameron acknowledged. He wiped mascara from my cheek, smiling down at me.

"Thank you." I pretended not to notice how his shirt clung to his body. A small heat trail tingled where he had touched my cheek. "Now close your eyes." He complied. "Lift your head back." His eyes opened questioningly. Laughing, I pushed his eyelids closed. "Trust me, it feels good." He reluctantly faced the sky without looking. "Let the water wash you clean." He did. And I shook away the continuing guilty feeling that I had not only been short with Beatrix but I missed her. My head also toward the sky, I felt my entire body relax. I loved the feeling of having water wash every part of me away.

Then I saw a flash of something. A flash of something I didn't want to see. A gasp ripped through me. I lost all connection to the world around me until only the sensation of Cameron's hands kept me from losing myself.

"Casey?"

I couldn't answer. I was too far into another experience with someone who was about to die. My mind traveled into the park across town. Dellinger Park, surrounded by woods. It was normally filled with people, but the impending rain had kept it empty. I froze as I saw the next victim in town. "Beatrix?" I whispered when I realized what had been happening.

I saw Beatrix jogging down the wooded path. My rain was just about to reach her as the purple clouds moved her way. She looked up at the sky at the first few sprinkles. The heavier drops felt wonderful combined with her sweat. The tiny iPod headphones blasted her eardrums. I heard the song she was hearing in the back of my head. It was a favorite of hers.

"Beatrix!" I screamed, but it was no use. Beatrix slowed down to a stop and let the rain wash her face. She opened her mouth and wet her tongue before turning around on the trail back toward her neighborhood. She ran right past the killer but didn't see him. She was running with her eyes closed, enjoying the fresh rain. He stepped out behind her and began to follow her. I screamed again, "BEATRIX!"

Music continued to play in her ear and my head as the killer advanced. She looked behind her for a second and saw the man in black. She instinctively ran faster. *You're overreacting,* she thought.

No you aren't. I was maddened. The man sped up. She glanced back a second time and understood this was no joke. He was really trying to catch her.

He caught up quickly and grabbed her arm. Beatrix screamed like a banshee and clawed at his face. The man released his grip and Beatrix ran away from him, screaming as loud as she could. "Help! SOMEONE HELP ME!" her voice begged to the empty park. I tried to snap myself out of it to help her, but there was no use. The killer tackled her again. She fell. His knees fell on either side of her as he put his hand over her mouth.

His knife lifted above her head. "Please . . ." she mustered. Loud lyrics continued to pummel her ears. She screamed before the knife slashed her neck. I saw her biggest regret so quickly. The thought that she would never be famous flashed through her brain as the knife kept on and on, slashing and stabbing. The killer had almost taken her head clean off.

I found myself screaming in Cameron's arms as the visions faded away. "Casey, Casey, it's okay. I mean—are you okay?" I snapped out of

48

my trance and sat up, slowly looking around.

"What happened?" I asked, my voice shaking. The world around me was pale and dreary. It was as if all the color had been washed out.

"Well, I don't know. I mean, I heard you cry out and I opened my eyes, but yours were wide open and blank. Then I called your name, but you fainted. Your eyes looked like you were looking at something, but nothing was there . . ." His eyes tried to search mine, but I looked away.

Normally I can snap myself out of it, or someone else can, I thought worriedly. "Sorry."

"Sorry?" He chuckled ever so slightly. "Sorry for what? I don't even know what just happened." I instantly realized he was cradling me. "Are you okay?" His eyes caught me like a deer in headlights.

His face scrunched together. "What else happened?" I whispered lightly. He was so close to me that the rain was barely hitting me.

"You were yelling about Beatrix." He moved a piece of wet hair out of my eyes.

I gasped, "Beatrix!" and pushed away from him. "Oh no." *How on earth could I have forgotten that?* Anger propelled me forward. I grabbed my cell and called Beatrix, moving to the porch to keep the phone dry. I obviously got her voicemail and panicked. Cameron followed me, lost. I frantically dialed Beatrix's mother. Her honey voice answered on the first ring. "Hello?" A clap of thunder made me jump.

"Mrs. Tay, I can't reach Beatrix and I think something bad happened," I said, aware that Cameron was watching my every move. The stupid rain wouldn't stop pelting me, even on the porch. I suddenly hated the rain.

"Oh. Well, Casey, she just went out for a jog, but I'm sure she's on her way back, because it just started raining. I'll tell her to call ya when she gets back."

"No. Please, Mrs. Tay. Listen to me." My voice was shaking. Cameron put his hand on my shoulder. I shook him off. He gave me a questioning look, but didn't try again.

There was a pause. "Well, what do you mean, you think something bad happened?" Mrs. Tay said.

"I can't explain it right now, but I think she's in trouble. You have to go find her!" I found myself shouting at her mother, who paused for what seemed to be five minutes.

Mrs. Tay took a deep breath. "Well, okay, I'll go wait for her outside."

"No. She's in the park. Go to the park." I brought my hand up to my face and scraped my palm against my cheek. I knew my behavior was erratic and problematic but I had to make her understand.

I heard rustling and figured Mrs. Tay grabbed her raincoat to go search for Beatrix. It would take her a few minutes to reach the entrance of the Waterford, which was directly across from Dellinger, where Beatrix ran almost every day. "Casey, is this a joke? You're scaring me."

"Just go to the park! I had a dream that she was hurt in the park!" I turned away from Cameron and cradled the phone against my ear and shoulder. I fidgeted with my hands. "Please keep me on the phone."

"Alright . . . I'm going toward the park . . ." I could almost see Mrs. Tay wincing at the rain, concerned about my call but turned off by its strangeness. "I'm getting in the car now so it will still be a few minutes. I'm just gonna leave you on speaker in the cup holder for now."

I closed my eyes. They were close to the entrance but I knew that between Beatrix's usual route and the entranceway to the Waterford, it would be a few minutes. I dropped my phone to my side. I turned back around and looked at Cameron. Seeing the worry on my face, he grabbed my hand. I tried to pull away again, but he held firm and wouldn't let it go. His mouth was slightly open like he couldn't force himself to close it. "What is happening? Did she hang up?"

"No, she's driving. It'll take a few minutes, though."

"Casey." His eyes pierced mine. "Are you okay?"

I shook my head. From the speaker in my phone I heard Mrs. Tay's voice. "Casey? Are you there? I'm in the park now and I am parked."

"I–I'm here." I hated how rough my voice sounded.

"I guess I'll just keep going until I see her." Her breathing picked up as I presumed she started jogging. "I really don't understand why you're so—Oh, oh my God." I closed my eyes tightly, as I knew exactly what she was seeing. I pictured Beatrix, lifeless on the trail, covered in blood, her throat slit wide open, and her mother rushing to her side. Red hair, redder blood. "Beatrix?" Mrs. Tay whispered again. "NO! BEATRIX! Oh my God!" A clattering sound cut off her phone.

I closed my eyes and fell to the floor, my phone still clutched to my ear. The images left me. They resided just outside my mind. "Casey?" Cameron asked. I felt him lower next to me. The porch boards creaked with our every move. "Casey, what is going on?" I scooted away. I couldn't touch him. We just kept staring at each other. Eventually, I turned away from him and focused on a small puddle at the edge of the porch. "Casey?" he asked a bit more forcefully. I knew he needed answers, but my lips wouldn't move. I couldn't speak, my body birthing convulsions. We were just tangled in a disturbing reality.

"I've got to go." I turned from him and stood. Raindrops camouflaged my tears as I braved the water again, which had now turned into a bona fide storm. Floorboards creaked as Cameron followed me. I looked up into the dark clouds. The sun had come out in a little corner behind us where clouds parted, far away. There was no rainbow.

Cameron grabbed me and pulled me toward him. It hurt as his fingers dug into my arms, but I didn't care. "Casey, what just happened back there? You fainted. Then you called Beatrix's mother and told her something bad happened." I focused on his hand. The rain bounced along his knuckles. "Why won't you answer me?"

"It's nothing!" I yanked my arm from his hand. *Stop touching me,* I wanted to screech at him. *Don't you understand I don't need you to touch me right now?*

"Nothing?!" He raised both eyebrows and shook his head gently. "Casey, stop. You can trust me."

"We're friends, right?" He nodded vigorously. "Then as my friend, I am asking you to go away right now."

The wind rippled through the air and a thunderbolt knocked the ground like an earthquake. Cameron gawked at me. "What happened to Beatrix, Casey?" His voice was a low thrum. "She's my friend too, now. I may be new, but I deserve to know," he insisted, putting his hand on my shoulder yet again.

"She was murdered a few minutes ago." I shook off his hand and ran all the way across town toward the park without looking back.

—

It probably took me twenty minutes to get to Dellinger's entrance. Sirens had plagued my ears all the way. Twilight was approaching when I arrived at the pandemonium of flashing lights. I never realized this town even owned ten police cars. My knees almost gave way when I saw paramedics pushing a gurney from the wooded area. The air had a distinct feel of death. *Why aren't they moving fast? Is she gone? Don't they need to declare a crime scene? Is this real? Where are they going?* My mind was a whirlwind of fear. I shook my head at the questions and the answers I knew.

After a few minutes, they put the gurney into an ambulance and it left silently. In a cluster of officers, Mrs. Tay stood numb as the ambulance rolled away. One of the officers was talking to her. "Did you get even a glimpse of the man?"

"No. No one was there. I went to check on her and she was . . ." Mrs. Tay could not continue.

Another officer chimed in. "What made you run into the woods to check on her?"

"C–Casey!" Mrs. Tay screamed and pointed as she discovered my presence. Everyone looked at me. "*She* called me and told me she thought something happened to B–Be–Bea . . ." She rushed to shake me. Her grip was violent and harsh, which was completely unlike the normal Mrs. Tay. "How did you know?! HOW DID YOU KNOW SHE WAS ATTACKED IN THE PARK?!" Her hands were cutting off my circulation as she gripped my arms in a desperate vise.

In sheer terror, I turned to the officers for help. They began studying me and exchanging suspicious looks with each other. One in particular emerged who had more authority than the others. He seemed about forty and had one of those stupid blond handlebar mustaches. His hair, in contrast, was the dullest shade of brown, and was cropped. On top of that, he looked tired and his breath smelled like coffee. "I'm Officer Golding. Casey, was it?"

I felt unfriendly to his suspicious tone as other officers pulled Mrs. Tay off of me. "Yes, sir."

He put his hand down slowly, resting it on his handcuffs. "I need to ask you a few questions, okay?"

No, it's not okay, I thought, but was ready to comply.

—

Everyone had moved into the Tay household within minutes. Some authorities were oddly using dishtowels to dry off. With all of them talking to each other in various uniforms, it wasn't difficult to decipher the chaos that was police, firefighters, and paramedics. I was sitting on the brown leather couch in the living room, wondering when my interrogation would begin. I watched Officer Golding speak with two detectives in the hallway for what seemed to be an eternity. The two had just arrived in suits and were clearly about to take over. I assumed they wanted to talk to Beatrix's parents first, but I knew they would be coming for me soon enough. They talked to Officer Golding and then moved into another room. I became more nervous as Officer Golding approached me with his notebook. "Okay. So how close were you to Beatrix?"

"She was one of my best friends," I replied, looking at a coffee table picture of Beatrix with her parents on a camping trip. I heard Mrs. Tay sobbing in the dining room nearby. The detectives were probably speaking with her and Mr. Tay, who had been working but rushed home to the incident. I was excruciatingly uncomfortable and writhing in pain. My goose bumps felt like microscopic razors all over me.

"Mm hmm," Officer Golding mumbled, jotting something down. *Why isn't everyone going to the hospital? Does this mean she is really gone? Can no one save her?* Despite what I had seen, surely Beatrix, dramatic, amazing Beatrix, was alive. I had kept staring at the picture on the table. I felt horrible for her parents, but Golding kept the momentum. "About how many years was she one of your best friends?"

Was? My stomach reacted to the past tense. "For a while now."

"Have you had any recent fights with her?" He peered down at me as I looked away from the Tay family camping picture.

"Um . . . no," I shot at him, insulted. "Why?"

"We just have to ask these questions to understand what happened, alright? And where were you during this incident?" he asked.

"What are you implying?" I felt my skin flush in anger and I started to play with my index finger to keep my hands from shaking.

Officer Golding looked me dead in the eyes. "Just answer my question." His voice was authoritative, but I didn't feel like listening to him.

"I think I deserve an answer first. Because I can assure you that I didn't kill her." My voice rose sharply.

"I am not accusing you of killing her. We have to ask these questions to establish—"

I cut him off. "You listen to me, Officer Golding. I would never harm Be—" I swallowed hard and looked at the rain pelting the windows. "She was one of my best friends. I'm telling you." I closed my eyes at the past tense. "Look, I have someone who can vouch for where I was all afternoon, okay? I promise you that I didn't kill her."

His milky brown eyes finally filled with compassion. "Okay, I understand." He wrote down more notes. "Can you tell me where you were this afternoon and who you were with?"

"I was with a boy named Cameron. We were at my house." My cheeks blushed as the officer memorialized that fact in ink.

"Does Cameron have a last name?"

"I'm sure he does." I tried like hell to refrain from snapping, but I wasn't doing a very good job. The officers shared skeptical glances.

"Okay, we need to find this boy, Cameron, and speak with him. Was he also a friend of Beatrix?" Golding stared at me, waiting for an answer.

"Define friends." The officers shook their heads and gave me incredulous looks. Sighing, I squeezed my index finger and finally realized they were merely doing their jobs. "I'm sorry. I'm just upset, okay?"

"That's alright, we understand." It was obvious that Golding was used to intense situations and kept on going. "Does your friend Cameron also know the victim?"

I cringed at the reference. "Yes. He knows Beatrix. I mean, he *knew* her. We all go—went—to school together."

"I see. Well, here's the situation. Mrs. Tay informed us that you called her and told her that her daughter was in trouble in the woods. Mrs. Tay then ran into the park across the street to find her daughter dead on the trail. Now, how is it that you knew your friend was in trouble?" The officers all stared at me . . . waiting.

I didn't know what to say. I had never been more frightened in my entire life. All eyes were on me and all clocks were ticking. "I don't know. I really don't know." My lie was all that came out.

Officer Golding wrote one more thing in his notepad and closed it. He motioned for another officer to come over. He whispered something in his ear and the man left towards the dining room. I shivered on the couch, wishing I were anywhere but there. They decided to have the police escort me to my own house. I would then wait for the "suits" to follow. It was strange protocol to say the least.

CHAPTER SIX

my dreams aren't normal and neither am i

I sat in the back of a police car, very glad the lights weren't flashing or the sirens blaring. Apart from the circumstances, it was the most peaceful ride I'd ever taken. My eyes were closed and everything disappeared around me. Tears flowed silently from me. The car began slowing down once we got to my neighborhood, so I opened my eyes back to the world. The officers rolled up to the curb in front of my house. The light in Christina's window was on. I didn't feel like talking to her. The idea of telling her about another loved one dying was heartbreaking. I then wondered if Cameron was still there.

"Is this it?" asked the officer driving.

"Yes." I remained in the back, not sure what I was supposed to do.

He turned to look at me through the cage that separated them from criminals. "Why don't you go inside, get dry, get warm, and the detectives will be over to talk to you when your mother gets home."

How refreshing that my mother has been called. I let him open the door. Then I turned away without saying goodbye and walked up to the house. I saw Christina's curtain open slightly. There was no telling what she thought, seeing the police car out front and me walking up to the house soaking wet. I opened the front door and closed it quickly. Christina was already peering out of her room at me. I ignored her and looked out the front window at the officers who remained in their car with the lights off. *Are they just going to stay there? What am I supposed to do? I don't want to talk to the detectives.* A shiny black car drove up and parked behind the marked vehicle. *Speak of the devil.*

"Don't ask," I told Christina, who was wide-eyed. "Oh wait. I forgot. You don't really talk," I snapped maliciously.

Christina was offended and looked as if she were scared of me. "You know I try my best, Casey," she said quietly.

This made me feel more horrible than I already did, but I hated her for the silent act. I hit the wall with both fists. "Beatrix is dead." Tears fell quickly from her eyes. She pulled me in close, shaking. More tears streaked down our faces as we embraced each other.

The commotion of police officers moved in rapidly. I could hear my mother getting out of her car and confronting them. "What the hell is this?"

I heard one of them reply, "Something very serious has happened, and we need to ask you and your daughter some questions."

Taking a deep breath, I walked around the corner and took in the scene. My mother was hugging herself, damp, in front of the two detectives. A man, who looked a bit older than my mother, stood next to a woman who was about my mother's age. The man was tall, long, and overall lanky. I half wondered if he'd collapse like rubber. In comparison, the woman was fierce-looking with bright orange hair and a blocky frame. Probably hearing me come in, my mother turned to face me.

"Casey! Do you know what this is about?" I gave her a slight nod and slid further into the living room.

"Ma'am, I'm Detective Tal Davis and this is my partner Detective Mary Alden and we would like to ask your daughter a few questions if that's okay?" the man said.

My mother's head bobbled between the two of us before she finally stepped out of the way and gestured to the open living room. The two detectives walked over to me and shook my hand one after another. Detective Tal had a light touch while Detective Mary gripped my hand with more authority. Together, we all sat awkwardly around the coffee table. I stared at my hands as they rubbed against each other.

Tal cleared his throat and said, "I'm sure you know why we're here, Casey."

It was a shock hearing my name in his voice, but I figured he had probably been briefed by his colleagues. I narrowed my focus further on my hands. Spotting a speck of dirt under my nail, I attempted to clean it.

Mary cleared her throat and leaned closer to me. Even with my attention on my hands I could see a blurry version of her face in my peripheral. Her eyes were kind. "Casey, may we talk to you about Beatrix?"

"Beatrix?" At my mother's voice, I finally looked up. Her brows were knitted together as she stared at me, which caused annoyance to flare up in me. For once I wanted her to know what was happening without me telling her.

"Yes, Beatrix Tay. She was murdered a few hours ago."

My mother's hand flew to her mouth and I thought I saw her eyes watering. I didn't realize how much she had liked Beatrix. She had barely come around once we hit high school because we had assumed my mother didn't like her. "My God," she said behind her hand. "Casey, did you . . ."

My own eyes watered momentarily but I shook it away. "Yeah, I knew," I said, looking back down at my hands.

There was a moment of silence before Tal began to speak. "I can only imagine how hard this must be for you, but we need to ask you some question's if you don't mind?"

"Okay," I said in a voice that was barely a whisper.

"How did you know about Beatrix's murder?" Despite Mary's gentle voice I couldn't help but hate her for asking that question.

I didn't answer. There was no correct way to answer. Only the truth would keep them from accusing me of being in cahoots with the killer. The only thing I knew for sure was that this conversation would suck. My mom interjected quickly. "I don't understand what relevance that has. What about *us*? Will *we* be safe? I mean, Beatrix was a close friend with Casey. What if we get att—"

Tal's raised hands silenced her. "There is no need to panic, Mrs. . . . Darling, correct?" My mother answered with a nod. Mary shook her fiery hair, which seemed to contrast with her kind eyes and yet I had seen a hint of anger in them. "A teenage girl is dead, and your daughter—" her piercing eyes landed on me "—knew exactly where she was and what had happened. Unfortunately for your daughter, that is very suspect. We want answers, and trust me, we'll get them."

My cheeks heated in a wave of embarrassment and hatred. My mother's annoyed sigh echoed through the room. "As I said, my daughter was a great friend of Beatrix, and she is in shock right now. Don't you have empathy?" I sent a silent thanks to whatever being existing outside of Earth that made my mother rational and sober.

Tal gave me a once-over. Standing up, I decided to pace the living room and pray that the shabby décor might possibly eat me. The two detectives exchanged looks that I imagined said: "Another time?" "No, now." "Perhaps this isn't the place." "Maybe it should be."

"I'm not sure my daughter is up to questions right now."

"Mrs. Darling, there is no way we can leave this house without asking a few questions. The one Mary raised being a very important one." He turned his attention to me. "All I need you to do is tell me what you were doing during this afternoon, your relationship to Beatrix, and how you know what you know."

He said it so calmly that I had to stifle a chuckle. That's all he needed to know? *Might as well ask me what the last digit of Pi is.* Everything but that last answer was simple. "I already told the police at Beatrix's house where I was and you know we're friends."

There was a pause and Mary narrowed her eyes at me. "And how did you know about her murder?"

"I told the police—"

"And now we're asking you, Casey. I would suggest you answer."

I rubbed my hands over my face. "Like I said, I was expecting a call from her and when I didn't get one I panicked."

Tal opened up a notebook from his pocket and wrote something down. "And do you normally panic when someone doesn't call right away?"

"If you were with another friend why were you so fixated on her phone call?" Mary crossed her legs as she looked up at me.

My decision to stand suddenly seemed like a bad decision so I turned away from them and paced a bit more. "No, I don't normally panic, but I mean I guess it was warranted, right? And, Detective Mary, I was expecting the call like I said, so when I didn't hear my phone go off I decided to pay attention to it a bit more."

"Uh huh, I see," Tal said as he scribbled some more.

Mary leaned forward on the couch and put her head in her hand. "Mrs. Tay said you sounded quite panicked."

I stopped in my tracks and through my hands up in the air. "I didn't kill her, okay!" I looked between them and couldn't figure out their faces. "Please, she was one of my *best friends.*" I leaned up against the wall. My breathing was heavier than I expected. The two detectives exchanged another look with each other, but this one was indecipherable.

Tal stood up. "You seem very stressed." Those eyes bored into mine and I realized there might be more to his frail lankiness. "We'll come back another day . . . Soon. Perhaps when the search warrant comes in." My mom looked mortified at that. "Before I go, Casey, are you sure you don't have any more comments about Beatrix's death?"

I froze, unsure of what he knew. I fibbed again. "No. There isn't anything to comment about. I was just worried about her. We were sup-posed to talk to each other after she went running in the park. It started to rain, and she hadn't called me. I got worried, so I called her mom. I thought I was overreacting. But I guess I *wasn't* overreacting, was I? Because there is a serial killer on the loose, you know. Isn't there? This is the *third* death, isn't it?" My spasmodic fit of words sounded like rambling to me.

The suits quietly condemned my body language, waiting for me to say something else, digesting my thin story. "We can't really comment on the nature of the kills around Bartow County." Mary took a deep breath and leaned forward. I saw a flicker of kindness in her eyes. "We are *sorry* for your loss. I hope you'll help us with this particular case." They moved towards the front door, temporarily satisfied, but I knew I would see them again.

Soon after the detectives left, my head still reeling from the talk with them, I made my way to the cemetery across town. My car shuddered on the wet ground. Once there, I headed to the gates. Moisture clung to the bars and graced my skin as I leaned my head against them. They were wrought iron and cold. I stared across the abyss of tombstones. It seemed kind of pointless to actually go in now that I had reached my destination. Squinting hard, I saw my father's marker. I bit my lip to keep yet another tear from falling. *What is a bit more water going to do to me?* I wondered to myself as I observed my still wet clothes.

"Casey?" a too familiar, timid voice asked. "Is that you?"

I can't believe it. Without turning, I addressed Cameron. "Yes." He walked up in the same blue shirt and jeans he wore earlier, wet like mine, so he probably hadn't been home. "What do you want?"

"Well, for starters . . . world peace, a happy life, good health . . ." I rolled my eyes at his sarcasm. "A group of friends would be nice."

I sighed softly. "That's some pretty big jumps. Why are you here anyway?" Gripping the bars tightly, I lay back so my body was almost parallel to the ground. I glanced up to find his golden eyes inviting me in, but I shut them out by counting the bars that had begun to loom above me.

"Oh? Is this not public property?" Unlike his usual cheery demeanor, his words were clipped.

I looked up with surprise.

"For your information," he continued, "I like coming to cemeteries, too. And after what you did earlier, I needed time to think before I went home."

My cheeks burned as I pulled myself up. I turned away from the bars so that I was finally facing him. He was looking down so I couldn't see his eyes, but his body was shaking slightly. "Cameron?"

"I sat on your front porch for a long time because you ran off like an idiot after telling me Beatrix was just murdered. So, then what? Let's see . . . Oh right. I waited there for about an hour until the rain cleared." I withered under his empty gaze. He ran a hand roughly through his hair. "Christina came out. Probably wanting to know why I was sitting on your porch like a dumbass, but she never asked, which was polite of her." He gave me an acerbic smile and my bitterness grew. "Even if she had, I was too busy being creeped out. That hit close to home . . . you telling me Beatrix was just murdered. But then, you wouldn't know that." I gripped the bars tighter, unsure what to say because I didn't know what he meant. "How do you expect me to feel?" He remained silent for a moment, seemingly fighting an internal war. "Anyway, I got tired of waiting for you to come back, so I came up here to chill out because . . . like I said, I like it here."

Is he joking? No way he frequents my cemetery. But I didn't say anything. His words were scattering against me like the rain from earlier. I pulled against the gate so that I was closer to a normal standing position.

"I saw you over here and decided that you might want some comfort. I didn't mean to intrude." He finished snidely, his hand grinded against his leather cuffs.

I had no idea what he meant about murder hitting close to home. This entire situation was agonizing and absurd. "I am genuinely sorry about earlier. I should have explained but . . ." I trailed off, uncertain what to say.

He gripped the bars close to me and mimicked my earlier pose.

"Y'know I think you're interesting and you're pretty, in a mysterious way. You seem smart . . . but I'm ninety-eight percent sure you're crazy. Certifiable."

I was nervously flattered. Looking at him, I realized he was just as crazy as I was. I could tell there was something more to him and his story, but I couldn't place my finger on it. I crossed my legs and leaned back against the gates. "You're right about the crazy part."

He laughed. The first genuine laugh I had heard since before the detectives had come over. The sun was gone and the streetlights had flickered to life. Fresh tears welled in my eyes, and I started crying again. My eyes were burning. I was so tired. "Hey. Hey, don't cry." He stepped away from the bars so that he was right in front of me. I dropped my head towards the ground to keep him from seeing. Crouching slightly, he peered up at me despite my attempts to hide. "I'm here for you."

"I appreciate that, but it's not that simple." He blinked. "You want more than that, I think." He bit his lip as he stood up and I followed him with my eyes. Scratching the back of his head with his hand he looked away.

"I don't have to. I'm trying not to and, I know you have friends, but it seems like you could use another one." My heart did a flip at his kind words. Taking a deep breath, I leaned forward and wrapped my arms around him.

I shouldn't have been surprised by his warmth after all our time together, but it was engulfing. The initial contact had obviously shocked him since it took a minute before he returned the hug. It was nice. I hadn't realized how starved for contact I was. "Thank you, Cameron. I don't know why you want to be my friend and I don't really know how I feel about that. I don't know how to feel about a lot of things. My friend is dead. I don't want to push you away. This is just so messed up."

"Then don't," he suggested. "It's pretty simple. Don't push me away." His voice was soft in my hair. "Now, please tell me what happened to Beatrix, and how you knew?"

Shivers ran through me as I pushed him away. My phone buzzed. It was Christina wondering when I'd be home. It was already nine thirty. "It's kind of late. So, later?"

His eyes glanced over my face before he finally nodded. I squeezed his shoulder once before going to my car.

—

I collapsed on my bed like a pile of bricks. The interrogation had sucked all the energy out of me. Going to the cemetery apparently didn't help either. "Casey," my mother commanded. I groaned inwardly. "Phone."

Rolling off the bed, I stretched like a cat and walked to my mom, who was holding my phone. *My mom used to be so pretty.* I looked at the bags under her eyes and the stringy light brown hair. I grabbed the phone I left downstairs. "Hello?"

"Casey?" Cameron's voice made my heart shudder, but I had to put on airs of normalcy in front of my mom.

"Hi, Cameron." My head pounded in defiance of conversation. Swallowing the pain, I continued, "So, did you get home alright?" I went back into my room for privacy.

There was a long pause. "Yes," he said quietly, "but I still have so many questions. I know you said later and maybe this is too soon, but what happened? Why did I find *cops* at my house?"

Tears turned the room into a kaleidoscope. I closed my eyes to keep them from escaping. "She d-died. Didn't the detectives ask you questions?"

"You were right?" I could practically see the bewildered look on his face. "God, I'm so sorry, Casey . . . I—my God."

A bitter choking-slash-chuckling sound escaped me.

"And what detectives? There was just a group of officers that were here. When they began asking questions my Gran told them to get the hell off her property and called her lawyer."

Wish I could've done that, I thought ruefully. "You didn't tell them anything? They didn't ask you any questions?"

"I said that you were a liar and I didn't even know you." The smile in his voice did little to comfort me. His personality was a cross between a hurricane and low tide; then again, I was right up there with him. "I'm just kidding. I said . . . uh . . . we were just hanging out at your house. Then they asked how you knew about what happened."

I cringed. "What did you say?"

His reassuring response finally let me breathe. "Don't worry. I figured you wouldn't want them to know that. *I* don't even freakin' know what in the hell about that, but it probably has something to do with you *fainting.*" His pelting words paused, attempting to get me to answer. "Anyways . . . I said you were expecting a call from her and got worried when she never responded. I figured you would say something like that, so I thought I would . . . you know."

Despite me being absolutely mortified, his voice was calming. "Wow. Thank you, Cameron." I grabbed one of my pillows and hugged it tightly, plagued by the memories of the day.

"So, um, I know it is pretty soon afterwards, but do you know anything about the funeral yet?" That one hit me hard in the gut.

"No." I imagined seeing everyone at the funeral—all the tears and condolences.

"Oh . . . um . . . do you think that when you know, you could maybe tell me? And also give me a ride?"

It seemed harmless enough. His nervous voice made my mouth quirk up to one side. "Yes, of course."

"Thanks. I really appreciate it." There was a long breath. "And if you need someone to talk to . . . well, obviously you have Danny and all of them, but I'm here for you as well."

"Thank you," I whispered. It was terribly kind of him after everything. "I'll talk to you soon."

"Goodbye, Casey. Be safe." The phone clicked off.

—

I was twirled into a circular dreamscape. I opened my eyes slowly to find myself waltzing in Cameron's arms. After a final dip, I smiled and closed my eyes. That was when I felt the world almost drop under me. Afraid, I opened my eyes and found that Cameron wasn't the one holding me. A faceless man with shadows in his hair and snake-blue eyes leaned into me. Screaming, I pushed away, and the man disappeared.

"Cameron?" I screamed into the darkness. Spinning around quickly, I saw Beatrix. "Beatrix?" I whispered. She smiled brightly. "Beatrix." She took a step forward and fire encircled her. Beatrix screamed loudly. "Beatrix, I'm coming!"

As soon as I got to Beatrix, she burst into flames like a glorious phoenix and vanished. "No!" I screamed. The world around me dissolved into dark nothingness.

"Don't worry," the blue-eyed killer said. His distorted voice wrapped around me and threatened death. A blinding light shot through the air. His flesh bent back into a grotesque mass of muscles with blood flowing freely from it. "You'll be joining her soon." His evil cackle evaporated as if he were smoke.

The smoke enveloped me. It clouded my mouth, making me choke. Soon it was gone and I was drowning in water. My dad was in our old car in front of me, beating against the glass, trying to get out. I wanted to call to him and help him, but I couldn't move. His eyes caught mine and he started screaming but I couldn't hear him. Finally able to move, I swam closer to him. "Why aren't you doing anything?" his voice screamed through the windshield. The scream cracked the windshield and the water rushed forward with me in it.

Suddenly it was dry and I dropped to the ground, disoriented. "Casey?" I heard Cameron whisper. Looking up, I found him far in front of me. He reached his hand out and I ran to him. But when I tried to grab his hand, mine fell through his. Cameron's smile was sad and sweet as our eyes met.

"Cameron." I begged him to stay. "Cameron."

"I'm sorry," he murmured. With that, he faded away like a ghost. Christina's bright face flashed before me. I ran from that place. I ran as far as I could but couldn't escape.

I gasped when I woke up from my dream. My room was pitch black with only the glow of my small red alarm clock. It cast shadowy figures and remembrances of my dream onto the walls.

Christina sat beside me. "Oh, you scared me." Her arms wrapped around mine. "You miss her too. Don't you?" I whispered into the dead night. I felt her nod. "You miss *him* too." Christina's body tensed.

"I don't know how I feel, Casey. That's why it's so hard for me to talk. Because . . . because I don't even know what I'm thinking half the time." I looked at my twin's droopy eyes. She picked at her nails. They were incredibly close to her skin.

I turned on the light and looked around my room. It was void of the things you would typically find in a teenager's room. There were a few choice pictures of my best friends, but none of my family. Not a single poster graced my walls and there were only books to show the places I had been. I closed my eyes as I digested what our lives had become. An empty room. A heavy presence. Things too dark to be considered "life."

Christina tapped me on the shoulder, shaking me from my stupor. "What?"

"Cameron messaged me. We're taking him to the funeral?" She pulled out her tiny cell phone. On it held a single message from him. *"Thanks 4 letting me ride with u guys 2 the funeral. Hopefully soon I'll get a car & we won't have 2 worry about that. Talk 2 u soon."* I looked at the miniscule screen. It still seemed relatively happy. He seemed, to me, an enigma.

"I kind of like him. He seems nice," she said. I shrugged as she gave me a quick kiss on the cheek.

"I'm sorry about yelling at you earlier, Chris."

She gave me a tilted smile. "I know you didn't mean it." Getting up, she turned out the light, leaving me with darkness. I stared at the ceiling till morning came.

CHAPTER SEVEN

goodbye

The funeral happened a week later. By the time we finally got to the graveside service, I was irritated and just plain exhausted. Mom was nagging me. Mrs. Tay kept glancing at me like I had all the answers. Cameron refused to leave my side, which didn't bother me, and the minister recited the "Beatrix will be happy in Heaven" speech. I clutched Beatrix's favorite flower, which was the iris. Just the feel of it reminded me of all the times I had passed them to her for a job well done in one of her plays. Cameron focused his eyes on me as the coffin sank slowly into the ground. I eased up to the grave. The casket was black and depressing, the complete opposite of its now unfortunate owner. I softened at all the pictures and flowers being thrown onto the casket and finally watched my iris float down six feet to join them.

The sun seemed to make the world cheerful. Turning, I gave Cameron a small wave. He just nodded and let me go. I walked over to where Danny, Tiffany, and Christina stood. Danny broke away from their conversation and pulled me into a huge hug. He could do so much without even saying a word. Tiffany sniffled behind us. I saw tears dripping from her eyes as I left Danny's arms. She clutched Christina. "Hey," I said softly, as not to startle her. Her head bobbed softly. Beatrix had been like her older sister. It was no wonder she was falling apart.

"So . . ." Danny attempted to give me a grand smile. "How about this weather, huh? Nice day out," he said while he looked at the ground.

I let out a half-giggle, half-sob thing. "Sure is . . ."

"Oh, please don't cry. If you do it, I *know* I will." We all gave a small chuckle. Not because it was really funny. But between all the tears and death, we honestly needed his humor. It felt like a breath of fresh air.

Tiffany pulled Christina into a tight hug and we quickly joined. It was the sweetest, silliest, saddest, and cheesiest group hug ever. The sobs erupting from Tiffany seemed to fuel the entire group's emotions. We all pulled away after a few moments. "Wow, we look rough," Tiffany remarked, her voice quivering.

I examined the funeral. Many people from school were there, along with their families. It was pretty packed. I looked over toward my dad's tombstone and found someone standing there. Whoever it was had blond hair and seemed interested in the ceremony. I took a small step toward him, ignoring my friends for a second. "Casey?" Danny asked, but I was too far away.

The man seemed familiar. I couldn't really distinguish his features because of how far away he was, but I couldn't stop looking at him. The man took a step forward and I finally understood what I was seeing. His eyes were bright blue and snake-like. It was Beatrix's killer. *Maybe?*

Fury and confusion took over. I started to push through the crowd. The man disappeared from sight. I walked faster. I couldn't let him get away. "Casey?" someone was calling.

I ran up to the grave and looked around the area but came up with no killer. "Where did you go?" I whispered.

"Behind you," Cameron said, making me jump.

"Cameron, good God, you scared me," I exclaimed, touching my heart as it sped up. His eyes regarded me with concern.

"Sorry. I saw you walk off and I was afraid that someone had done something or that you had lost it . . ." He trailed off.

"Oh, no. I'm fine . . ." I looked at my father's tombstone. "I thought I saw something."

"What did you think you saw?" he asked.

I shook my head. "Nothing. It's not important."

His frown deepened. Walking past me, he examined the tombstone. He crouched beside it. "So . . . whose tombstone is this?"

"My dad's." I turned back toward the funeral. The crowd was dwindling.

"I'm sorry." I shrugged. "Casey? I wanted to say that I'm sorry about your loss, but I hope it gets better. I'll leave you guys alone to say goodbye. I can walk." He gave me a brief but tight hug and then started home.

I watched as the distance between us shrunk him. I looked back for where the mystery man might have gone. I knew in that moment, only one thing would satisfy me. Beatrix would be avenged, because tomorrow the hunt would begin. I headed back toward the gravesite. Evil thoughts prodded my head.

The grave was cold and everything opposite of Beatrix herself. I found it incredibly unnerving. My friends stood over the six-foot abyss. "Cameron didn't wanna come?" Danny bumped hips with me.

I shrugged and massaged my fingers. "He said he wanted to let us say our goodbyes."

"He's nice," Tiffany said. Christina nodded in agreement.

"Well, hopefully," Danny said dragging out the word hope, "he'll stick around." He winked at me, which caused me to blush and scrunch up my face.

"What? Alls I know is Beatrix is smiling down on you right now, because she sooooo wanted some of that." Leave it to Danny.

"Okay. I get it. He's nice."

"And adorable."

As my friends poked fun at me, my cheeks continued to burn. To get my mind off of their comments, I turned toward the crowd, which had dissipated. The twilight illuminated a few stragglers. It was time for our own little memorial. Tiffany was sitting beside the tombstone, curled up close, and Christina's fingertips barely brushed the granite marker's surface. The pain in the air was palpable.

"Are we ready to do this?" Danny's nervousness rolled off of him.

We simultaneously produced memorabilia that was near and dear to our beloved friend. My token was a small, stuffed pink dog that I slipped out of my purse. It was bright and joyful. She had actually won it off one of the carnies when we went to the fair. It had only been knocking down pins, but she was so proud that I gladly took it. She had split her cheek muscles from grinning so much that day.

"Okay, no crying." Danny took over. His own cheeks were covered with tearstains, but no one remarked on that. "Beatrix would want us happy. Tiffany, I think you should start."

She looked startled but agreed, standing at the side of the tombstone. The rest of us sat around the rectangular hole, careful to not fall in. I ended up at the other end, meaning I would get to say something about her last. "I brought a picture," Tiffany's meek voice whispered through tears. She turned it around and I immediately recognized it. In it, Beatrix's head was thrown back, loud and proud, while Tiffany was bending in half. She was laughing so hard. "Y'all know how shy I am, but with her . . . I don't know. I just felt so free. I loved her. She's my sister . . . well, *was*, I guess. She was my sister." Christina rubbed her arm. The graveyard crept into darkness and the trees seemed to sway in slow motion. She continued with an unsteady breath. "I remember one time she convinced me to go up to this huge group of guys and start flirting with them. Then out of nowhere she called them 'jerks' and walked away. I was just stunned. I didn't know what to do. When I asked later, she just said, 'I heard them making fun of you one day, and just now they were making fun of Danny.'" We all smiled fondly. "She was our protector." Quietly, she dropped the picture onto the casket.

"Okay," Danny said, dabbing at his eyes. "Stop making me cry!" he yelled, half teasing, half serious. "Christina?"

She pulled out a beautiful flower, obviously fake, but bright red with gold tips. Most importantly, it was a giant iris, Beatrix's favorite. She gently dropped the flower down and sobbed. "Y'all know—y'all know I can't talk as easily as I used to. Beatrix never cared. She embraced me. I'm so lucky, or I guess, I was so lucky to know her." Tiffany wrapped her arms around her and cried too.

I exchanged a solemn look with ever-prepared Danny, who pulled out tissues. "Here," he said and passed them to the girls. "Beatrix was really one of the best people I ever knew." He produced a colorful Mardi Gras mask. "Do y'all remember what she did to get this?" My two friends looked up, but were still wrapped in grief. My heart lurched, but I nodded to please Danny. He cleared his throat and continued. "There was this really small carnival one year for Mardi Gras. And of course, it was the only one we've ever had." He gave us a meek smile. "Anyway . . . there was this cute, cute guy and he had these masks. Of course, he was also a jerk." Danny's eyes narrowed. "He had been selling them to everyone, so I went up to him and asked for one."

My mouth curled up on one side. I remembered this day very clearly. I closed my eyes at the story's ending. A pounding pushed against my temples and my eyes clenched tighter. I opened my eyes and returned my attention to Danny.

"When I asked, he said, 'Sorry, I don't sell to fags,' and just turned back around." He gave a tiny smile, as did the two other girls. "I was willing to leave it, but Beatrix wasn't gonna have it. She walked over politely and asked for a mask. He gave her one and turned his back on her. Then she hit him in the head with the mask and jumped on his back, taking this dude down." We all chuckled slightly. "It wasn't long before he was running away and left his masks with us. Beatrix picked out this gorgeous thing and gave it to me." He smiled fondly. "Thank you, B . . ." Danny said, dropping the mask onto her new home.

"I brought this," I whispered, holding up the stuffed pink dog. My throat threatened to collapse on itself, but I quickly cleared it. "Life after my dad was . . . hard to say the least. Christina and I became reclusive, but we had three great friends to help us." All of us shared a smile. "Although we were complete opposites, I always appreciated what she did for me. Beatrix was the first one to drag us anywhere, and the annual Bartow County Fair was the first major event she managed to get us to. Beatrix certainly loved her fairs. While we were there, she, of course, couldn't resist playing the overpriced games. She kept insisting she was going to win me this dog while you three rode some rickety rides." My voice got louder as I continued. "Finally, she did. 'Its name shall be Sal and she shall be there to help you no matter what.' And that's what I kept Sal for. This little dog steadied me when I went through one of my vis—episodes." I quickly covered up "visions" with the epilepsy episodes my friends thought I was somewhat prone to. "Though this little dog has helped me a lot, I think it needs to go with Beatrix now. I've had a good life with Sal; now Beatrix can have a good afterlife with her."

Tiffany scoffed through a sob. "Afterlife." She shook her head bitterly.

"Don't be such an atheist, Tiffany," Danny said, giving her a half frown.

"Don't be such a Christian, Danny," she snapped back. We all looked at her. "Sorry, guys, it's just . . . She's dead. Her throat was slashed by some horrible monster and now she is in a better place?"

My mind floated to the various visions I had about people. I wasn't exactly Christian in the traditional sense, but I believed in an afterlife. A good place, a bad place, and possibly something in between. Yet throughout all my visions, I never got to experience the beautiful afterwards. Just the painful end.

"God, the stabbing," Danny said, placing his head in his hands and successfully rubber-banding me back to the tombstone.

Christina's eyes widened with horror.

"She was probably in so much pain when it—when that monster jumped her in the park. Where did he even come from?" Tiffany continued.

Good question, I thought, looking at my quiet friend.

"Isn't he supposed to be . . . somewhere in the woods, hiding?" Danny asked.

"I don't know," I whispered to both of their inquiries.

"He deserves to die. He deserves whatever comes after death. Whether it's pain or nothingness, *he* is the one who should be rotting in a grave. Not our protector."

"Tiffany," I finally admonished, but a part of me agreed.

"Come on, Casey. You know you're wondering too. How it must have felt? What she must have been feeling? Who that abomination was who killed her? Where she is now?"

If only you knew that I knew the answers to two of those questions, Tiffany.

"Heaven, Tiffany." Danny directed her attention back to him. Christina's wide gaze glimmered with the hope of his words. "That's where she is in my mind. She deserves that." Christina and I nodded enthusiastically. "Atheist or not, we both know that she deserves Heaven. As for the killer, I'm a Christian, but right now . . ." He trailed off venomously. A plan began to form in my mind, and I realized that the killer not only deserved to die, but deserved to die by someone . . . like me.

Tiffany began to sob once more. "I'm sorry. It's just—she was our best friend. She was our armor, and you're right, Danny; I may not believe it, but she deserves Heaven. I just think that we deserve *her*."

Tears dampened my cheeks and I pulled Tiffany into a hug. Danny and Christina joined us, so that we were once again in an almost cheesy embrace. Yet we sat like that at the precipice of the afterlife. Lost friends. Hugging in a graveyard.

CHAPTER EIGHT

bloody research

Rumors had swelled that a full-fledged serial killer was on the loose. I could still feel the disconcerting last memories of one of our science teachers, Mr. Patrick. He was murdered on the trail, also while jogging, in Dellinger Park. Once more our town was blasted by the mystery killer's reality check. Everyone had a theory, a motive, a suspect. All of them were wrong. One autumn Friday in my glorious high school, the students piled into the smelly gym like sardines during last period. I didn't have to know what the assembly was about to dread it. The last time our school had an assembly, a policeman dressed up as a dog said, "Drugs are ruff." This was no doubt more excruciating. I rolled my eyes as Danny and Christina scooted closer. I had been distant toward everyone since Beatrix's funeral, with Cameron in the peripheral the whole time. It's hard being the new person in any group, but having a death thrown into the mix was worse.

Whatever it took, I would make sure her death was avenged. After all, I was the only person still alive who had seen the killer's eyes.

Tiffany clutched Christina's arm and Cameron sat in front of me. He turned around to give me a grand smile that I gladly returned.

"Students . . ." Principal Benton's voice boomed. His chin and neck bloated, reminding me of the nickname we had given him: Bullfrog. "I would like all of you to be polite as we welcome detectives Mary Alden and Tal Davis from the Cartersville Police Department." I froze.

I shifted uneasily on the crappy bleachers. Cameron glanced back at me, but I just shook my head at him. My heart panicked as Detective Tal began his spiel. "Kids. I'm sure you're quite aware of the recent murders around this area." Danny glanced at me nervously, but there wasn't anything I could do to calm him. Detective Tal continued, "Now, law enforcement is doing everything possible to ensure safety in the community, but we are here to ask several very important things of each of you."

"Bartow Slasher! Bartow Slasher!" some genius shouted from the back.

Mary Alden's firm voice took over with a slight echo. "Detective Tal and I have some tips on how all of you can remain safe." The students rustled in their seats, submitting themselves to the inevitable. Only a few idiots in the back were talking. "First of all, we are issuing an eight o'clock curfew."

The crowd erupted into a massive thunder of resistance, directed at Bullfrog Benton himself. Pretty foul language pounced toward the podium. Well, pretty foul for a school assembly. One guy dared to yell out, "Curfew my ass! I don't need to be told when to go to bed! I'm a freaking senior, for Christ's sake." I shook my head as anonymous curses continued to pop from the crowd in its own bullfrog chorus.

"Silence!" Principle Benton demanded. His face was fire engine red and he looked like he would give us all forty paddles if it were still allowed in the public school system. "I will not stand for disgraceful behavior."

"Then sit down, croaktard," I heard someone yell. I looked back to see the biggest and most stupid jock, Ryan Arnold, huffing on his feet. His cronies chimed in, "Bullfrog! Bullfrog!"

"Ryan Arnold! Detention!" Benton screamed. Ryan shot a bird in defiance, which went undetected as he fell onto the bleachers with the rest of the muscle clan. Cameron turned around and gave me a look that asked, *is this normal?* I nodded with disdain and turned my attention back to the authoritative trio. My hands rubbed together.

Mary Alden pressed on, unmoved. "We realize this decision is unsavory. However, I implore you to understand the gravity of the situation. You also must not panic. The curfew is to secure order and prevent further incidents." The resistance slowly subsided. "I would think this student body would respect the necessity of a curfew, considering it has just lost two of its very own."

The whole crowd became silent upon being reminded of Beatrix and Mr. Patrick. "Also, we want to suggest that everyone stay in pairs. No one should be out walking alone, especially after dusk."

A flurry of whoops and whistles happily concurred. "Party at Arnold's!"

Really? Ryan Arnold's father was the Chief of the Cartersville Police Department. The sheer stupidity of my high school was going to force me into a mental institution. Principal Benton regained composure. "This is a serious time in our town's history. We haven't had anything this significant happen since the blizzard." Strangely, this resonated. It was probably because everyone remembered the horrible blizzard a decade ago and the trouble it caused, which was actually not worth all the school we missed in its chaos. "This is really serious, folks. A serial killer is in the area. We have lost one of our students and one of our teachers. This is no time for jokes. This is no time for disobedience. And this is certainly no time for disrespect." In the background, I heard the slightest sound of snickering. I dropped my head into my hands. *Can y'all please be serious?*

When I turned around, I found Patricia and Ryan snickering over their phones. Part of me wondered what they were laughing about while the other part felt pure annoyance. Sure, it was a stupid assembly, but the subject matter was anything but. Patricia caught my stare and offered a coy smile. I turned around quickly and waited for the assembly to be over as the concerned voices at the podium turned into Charlie Brown jumble. It took another thirty minutes of patronizing advice, calming down the crowd, and utter torture before it was *finally* over.

Most of the kids were breaking off into their respective cliques, planning devious soirees. In conjunction with such an occasion, there were discussions about how to obtain mind-altering substances and various forms of entertainment on their ways home. Fun screams and tire screeches filled the parking lot as mischief was conjured by Cartersville's youth. I ran to my car and backed out of my space before my friends could catch up to me, because I had a plan. It was difficult to avoid the many almost-car-wrecks from careless teenagers entering Church Street. All I could do was pray in the sanctuary of the beat up Escort I shared with my mom and sister. So that was what I did. All the way home.

—

The killer couldn't be allowed to live. For some reason, I felt that it was up to me to find him. It was a surprisingly sunny day considering the forecast noted a major storm approaching. I dropped off the car at home, slipped on "suitable" hunting attire, and hopped on my bike. October was in full swing and it was as if the world had been painted brilliant reds and oranges with pokes of golden rays. I missed my neglected paint set, but there was too little time to paint the beauty in the world. A rough wind ripped around me, and the trees swayed to the music they created. For one blissful moment, I closed my eyes and just remembered calm and happiness. It felt foreign but was still comforting. Reaching into my pocket, I pulled out a small pendant Beatrix had given me. "This is for you, Beatrix." With that, I hopped off my bike and entered the brick building.

The library was as lively as a tomb. The bald librarian barely looked up as I made my way past him to the computers. It seemed as if only the elderly were librarians, which made me wonder what they did before. Within minutes, I was logged on and searching Google. "Killings in Cartersville, Bartow County, Georgia," I muttered, typing the words into the search bar. A website called *Bartow Crime Stoppers* looked promising. I clicked it and an article about the recent killings bore yesterday's date. *Perfect.*

> The Eyes of a Killer
>
> By: Joy Freeman
>
> A serial killer known only as the "Bartow Slasher" has riveted Cartersville. The culprit has the whole town cowering in fear.

I couldn't help but roll my eyes at the comment but continued reading.

> It appears that the killer is searching for a variety of people

to attack. Detective Mary Alden stated, "We have leads on possible witnesses and places he could be, but we can't resolve these killings yet." Victims include Victoria Pendrake; Beatrix Tay; Don Patrick; Sam Riesling.

"This person is sick," Officer Golding stated. "All we know is that no one needs to go into the woods alone, the park alone, anywhere at night alone, and generally . . . we are urging everyone to travel in pairs and report anything suspicious." More on potential DNA testing as soon as information becomes available.

One witness has not been reported to the media. Det. Alden stated, "We are respecting her privacy, but she is considered a person of interest at this point. We have no further comment on her identity."

Rage colored my vision at Mary's remarks, and I scrolled away from that section to the end. I knew exactly what "witness" they were talking about and didn't appreciate it. *No matter,* I thought. *Now I know where to start.*

The police are now searching the woods around Dellinger Park, where two attacks occurred, for forensic evidence. The other crime scenes have been evaluated. It is quite possible that the perpetrator is a resident of Cartersville and living and working among our citizens.

"Whatcha reading?" I whirled around to find Cameron looking over my shoulder.

"Nothing," I snapped quickly. "I mean, just something for a project . . ."

His eyebrow raised in curiosity. "About the woods?"

My cheeks felt like flames. "What? Do I not seem like a nature lover?"

Cameron's golden eyes narrowed. "Not really." His tone was the low note of a cello.

I crossed my arms and raised an eyebrow. "Still enjoying this Georgia weather?" I asked through the awkward silence.

He laughed hard. "It's certainly a stretch from California. But I like the rain more now, after . . . you know." My cheeks grew hotter. "With the sunshine going away maybe you would want to—"

"I'm busy." I squirmed in my black, military-type attire, dark green bandana covering my braids.

"Are you supposed to be some vigilante now?" There was his signature smirk.

I twirled my chair and turned off the computer screen. "That. Is none of your affair."

"Bartow Slasher," Cameron scoffed. "What a joke. I guess 'lunatic' is too cliché? Why do they give these losers stupid names?"

"No clue," I said. "But he'll be a dead loser soon enough, and I don't care what people call him then."

"Whoa, Miss Hot Stuff. Psychic detective on the hunt." His cocked eyebrow took me back to when he saw me witness Beatrix's death.

"It's not what you think."

"How do you know what I think?"

I gathered my belongings and readied to leave. "How did you know I was here?"

"Actually, I just picked up my brand new Beetle and thought the library might be a nice place to stop . . . since I happened to see Casey Darling parking her bike out front." He rattled his keys.

I rolled my eyes with a laugh. "Congratulations on the new wheels."

"My grandmother's awesome like that. You want to go for a ride?" Out of the corner of my eye I saw him fidget with his leather bracelet.

"I have my bike. Sorry. Maybe some other time." He seemed, for the first time ever, like a scrawny, cold bird. Defeated. "Okay?" I asked, taking care not to make him fly away. My hand rested against his skin and his heat chilled me to the bone. Then out of nowhere, I saw his skin melting in a blanket of flames, part of my soul dying with him.

I pushed back against the chair. Visions blanketed me in an unmoving ice storm. All I could see was Cameron dying a thousand different deaths. I wondered if I would ever be able to see anything else again. Then it was Beatrix. Her head almost completely detached. My dad's lifeless body floating in water, and then Christina pale and unmoving, something I was sure to see eventually. They weren't even real visions, but they were real to me. Or very, very close to being that. "I'm sorry I—I have to go."

The confusion plastered on his face was thick. "Why are you leaving?" It struck me that maybe I should stay with him, but I couldn't imagine his death again. "Aren't we friends? Do you want to talk to me? I am here for you if you need me."

"Later . . . later, we can talk. Please, I just need air." I leapt out of my chair.

Surprisingly, no pleas followed after that, nor did any footsteps. I was grateful, but also a bit afraid of leaving him so suddenly. I walked out the glass doors, and into the blue skies, which stretched to infinity. I hopped on my bike and began pedaling. My pace quickened. It wouldn't be long until I found the woods and I could start my search for clues.

it always happens in the rain

I ended up on the gravel trail in Dellinger Park where Beatrix was murdered. I wasn't looking for the exact spot or anything. I just wanted to be near her. She had always given the best advice when it came to things like boys and new people. I had never needed it. *Of course, when it's too late, I need your spunky advice,* I thought ruefully. I combed the area thoroughly to no avail. I finally sank into the ground, burying my face in my hands to keep someone from potentially seeing my pain. There was still the occasional jogger or walker and I was sure I looked like a lunatic myself. *What am I doing here? How is this helping?* I looked at the ground in front of me and watched as a worm squirmed around. *Maybe I should keep myself away from people . . .* my mind proposed softly in a spot too far to reach. *Why do I have to keep running away from people?* Then I thought of Danny. Christina. Momma. *Can I give up everyone I know and love? Wall myself off like my sister? Shut myself out? It's not fair.* I placed my balled up hands over my eyes.

Allowing myself to wallow in pity, I didn't realize an hour had already passed. My mind kicked into overdrive when I became cognizant of just how alone I was in the last place Beatrix Tay was alive. The sun still shone in several bright spots, but the inevitable forecast was moving closer in dark purple. No major creepers were to be seen, but something didn't feel right. Someone was watching me.

Squinting through the trees, I got up unsteadily, and it was like my air was cut off. Uncomfortable warmth poisoned my wrist. Looking down, I saw nothing was different, yet it itched like crazy. The second I began to scratch at it, images of waves beating against a boulder like a wet pendulum flickered in my head. The murky water was some version of gray, blue, green and even some yellow mixed together. Off to the side was a boy I knew all too well, blood flowing freely from his wrist. Bending over, he let the water wash out his blood into the greenish stream. Cameron was in the park by the lake. I frantically moved through the trees for sight of the pond. *Why is he doing this again? Why out here?*

Exiting the patch of trees, I saw him at the boulder. His eyes were hidden behind his eyelids. I tiptoed in fear until I was ten feet away. "Cameron?"

He wiped the tired frown off his face and opened his eyes to me. He pushed off the boulder and hid his razor behind his back. On the ground, his leather bracelet was turned upside down. "Casey?" My eyes moved to his red and runny wrist. I reached my hand out toward him as if he was a wild animal. Cameron was stoic, effortlessly hiding the razor behind his back. Drops of blood had spotted his jeans. "What are you doing here?"

"What are *you* doing here?" I pressed firmly.

"Reflecting."

"That's not what it looks like to me."

Leaning down, he awkwardly picked up his bracelet with his right hand. He walked away from me and toward another part of the gravel trail. "Sometimes things aren't what they seem."

I followed him. "Cameron . . . what did you do to yourself?"

"Nothing. Leave me alone."

"Oh, so now you want *me* to leave *you* alone?" I stopped him and forced him to let me see his wound. "Why did you do this?" I took off my bandana and wrapped it around his wrist.

He walked away from me, pressing the bandana to stop his own bleeding, his Doc Martins crunching the gravel below his feet. "Oh good God, what is it with you, Darling?" His eyes flashed angrily as he turned on me. "It's what I like to do. Why do you care so much?"

I followed him closely, but I didn't talk for a long time. "We're friends . . . I thought." He clasped the leather bracelet over his bandanaed wrist to keep it secure. "Was it something I did?"

"Don't flatter yourself." His eyes were glued to the leather.

The first thunder rumbled in the distance. "Cameron." He stopped but didn't turn around. "You knew I'd be here. Did you want me to see?"

Another long pause was broken up by rolling thunder. I walked in front of him so that I could see his face. Finally, he looked into my eyes with a blank expression. Fear knotted my insides as I searched his features for an answer. "It's not that simple."

"Nothing about this is simple. But are you telling me that after you saw what I was reading about the park that you came here. For me to find you? *Slitting your wrist.*"

He stepped off the trail and walked over to a tree. Leaning against it he examined his bracelet and the wound. Blood had begun to discolor the bandana. "Yes, I saw what you were reading. And, yes, I thought maybe going to the woods would be fun and lead me to you, but then . . ." He bit his lip and I took a step toward him. "Then it became too much. I needed to just . . ."

My heart sped uneasily through me. I wanted to touch him, but something stopped me. This was obviously a bigger problem than I understood. There was no telling what might hurt him, set him off, or even help him. I twisted my hands together. "Cameron—"

His cold eyes ripped through me. "Besides, I thought a friend would be nicer about all this." He shuddered. Pushing off the tree he turned back towards the lake. "So, did you catch the killer?" He changed the subject, continuing his travel away from me. His calm cadence bothered me.

"Cameron, I want to talk about this." Those words, so similar to what he had asked of me, rang through the quiet air.

"You probably don't want to know my story," he said.

I stared at the boy I'd met two months ago. The boy who was nothing like me. So full of life one moment but careless the next. The new boy who had become a wonderful addition to my friend group. An addition I thought would never happen. Images from my earlier vision warned me to be cautious, but I ignored it. "I want to know everything." *Definitely a glutton for punishment.* He flipped the razor through his fingers, playing with it. I wondered if he did that when he was deep in thought. "Will you please tell me your story? I won't laugh. I won't hate you. I won't run away."

"Promise?"

"Cross my heart."

He took a giant gulp of air and started down the trail. "I never intended to move from California." I joined him when the raindrops arrived. "Even with everything that happened between me and my dad, I would have never left my mom; I would have stayed behind." We shuffled toward a gazebo.

"I guess my dad had always been a psychopath, but my mom

didn't notice until after she married him. On top of that, he was a drug-gie. All he did was drugs. All he cared about was drugs. And if either my mom or I got in his way about it, he was relentless. Maybe it was the only thing that made him feel." We reached the gazebo and watched the downpour develop. He sat down before he continued. His arm lightly brushed against mine. "He would hit us, cuss at us, but thankfully not too much more. One day, though, he pushed me over the edge . . . and I cut myself. Deep. It almost killed me." He showed me the scar. I sat down next to him and finally understood the thick bracelets.

The beginning of his story bounced around my brain as I played with my hands. Cameron was someone I never would have pegged as a cutter, despite what I saw in the first vision with him. I never could have imagined the real story behind the Golden Boy. How it could have been worse than mine? And yet he was still so happy a lot of the time. Or maybe that was just what he wanted people to think. I analyzed the time we had spent together and it seemed different in retrospect; he was just as broken as me. *All he wanted was a friend,* I thought. I turned my face toward him and found him staring back. At that moment, my heart sped up and I realized that I did actually care about him and that maybe my crush was real. I didn't want him to die or hurt himself. I laid a hand gently on his. He jumped but then grabbed on to it.

"My mom found me that night. When she saw the blood, she freaked. Took me to the hospital. Told me that she never wanted to see that again and if I ever did it again I was in big trouble. She started crying but promised, 'We'll get away from him.' I believed her, of course, so I stopped cutting." He looked at me with pain in his eyes. "She was sticking to her promise, too. Saving every penny she could possibly find and keep-ing it hidden." He took a ragged breath. "We were almost out of there. One day, though, my dad found the money." His hands tightened over mine.

I squeezed his hand back wishing there was something more I could say or do. He bent toward me and looked me in the eyes. My heart stuttered. *Itching with cravings,* I thought, glancing at our hands. He needed someone. And maybe I did too. He let out a slow breath before continuing.

"I came home from school to find him yelling at my mom after he was on a bender. When I saw him hitting her, I froze. He saw me staring at him, and when my mom realized what was going on, she turned to me. Her lips were puffed out and swollen and she had this look of terror. She tried to tell me to run, but just as she was going to . . ." I could feel his muscles tense in my hand. Cameron started to tremble, and I rubbed my fingers across his smooth skin, wanting to comfort him, but unsure if I was helping. "He stabbed her with a knife. I screamed. He just looked at me with glazed-over and dead eyes. The lack of empathy still shocks me. And then, he said the craziest thing. 'Help me put her to bed.' I couldn't breathe. I felt like my world was torn to pieces. And the world kept spinning and spinning. I wanted nothing more than for it to just stop spinning."

My brows furrowed together. I couldn't believe the Golden Boy's story. It was so horrible. I didn't know what to do, what to say. I felt like I was thrown onto a roller coaster I didn't even know I was going to be on and strapped in, riding over tall hills and jerky turns. His eyes were so sad. It made me wish I had been friendlier in the beginning. It looked like he had gone behind a cloud. *Am I supposed to say something? Am I supposed to do something?* There was only rain and soft thunder for a moment. "What then?" I whispered.

A cruel laugh escaped from his lips. "The cops came. A neighbor heard all the commotion and dialed 911. While he was dragged away, he kept screaming that he would kill me. I was thirteen. I was freaked out.

I went to live with my grandmother. We stayed there till it was time for his trial. For years I'd been fighting that bastard and his heroin and his cocaine and his liquor." He shook his head. "It took my mother's death to get him locked away forever." He choked away tears.

"So, he's in prison?"

"He'll rot where he is. I wish he could have been executed right in front of me."

Ignoring my bubble, I put my arms around Cameron. The rain pelted our faces, coming into the open gazebo. *It all happens in the rain.* "My grandmother moved me out here, so I could start over. You're the only one who has made it seem possible that I could start my life over."

"Why me? You don't even know me."

"Because you have just as many secrets. And one day, you'll tell them to me. I mean I know we just met but . . ." I looked away from his piercing eyes, not wanting to open a can of worms just yet. "Like the day Beatrix was killed." He lifted my chin back up to him. "I haven't pressured you to explain what happened."

"I'm not ready yet."

"I know."

"I want to know more about you first."

"Okay, let's see. I used to be a wild card; tried drugs myself. Lashed out at the world. Wild parties in the City of Angels." There was a short pause as I imagined the shady side of the Golden Boy. "I've never had a real girlfriend, either." He said it like he knew I'd never had a boyfriend, but our reasons weren't even in the same ballpark. "Where there's dating and Coke floats and gentleman crap. If I wanted a girl, I would just date one and move on. I didn't really care about them and I know that's wrong." He chuckled at his own observation. "Anyway, I don't want to do that anymore. I want to be better." His eyes cut to me.

"I moved here to better myself and climb out of my hole." He wiped the tears and rain from his face. "You've been too quiet. What are you thinking?"

What am *I thinking?* I questioned. "If you want to climb out of your hole, why are you hurting yourself?" I finally asked the obvious.

"I figured you would wonder that. Who wouldn't?" My eyes pleaded for an answer. "I don't cut *deep* anymore."

"That's a cop-out."

"Have you ever been in such pain that you have to escape? I think of my mother . . . how I didn't—couldn't help her, and I get this over-whelming sense of guilt that hurts more than you can imagine. I cut to alleviate that emotional pain and turn it into something tangible. It puts me in control." He made a tight fist and then opened it slowly.

"Will you stop?"

"I'll stop in my own time." We sat in a long silence. Yet again, I watched him fidget with the leather bracelets. The rain wasn't letting up. I was freezing and didn't know how much longer I could sit out there, even under shelter. "Come on. I don't want to talk about this anymore. You're cold."

"We can wait to see if it stops."

"We're in Georgia."

"It might."

"Yeah, right. Come on. Let's bite the bullet."

I surveyed the imminent yuckiness as I debated my options. I did not want to run on a trail that my friend was murdered on, in the rain, to get into Cameron's brand new car. However, he grabbed my arm and started running before I could protest. Our hearts racing in the frigid rain, his midnight blue Beetle stood as a beacon of potential warmth when it was finally in sight by the lake. He opened my door and I carefully got in, taking as much care as possible to not dirty the interior. The car smelled of crisp leather and him. I sank into the luxurious fabric and felt as if I were in an embrace. Rhythmic sounds of tires against the pavement and windshield wipers against glass created a somber ambiance that was eerily romantic all the way to my house. Part of me was nervous about the sad boy beside me. I couldn't understand why he did what he did or what he gained from it. But as I looked at him out of the corner of my eye I found myself more intrigued than worried. Maybe he could explain everything. Thank God my mother wasn't home, because I was inviting the Golden Boy inside.

CHAPTER TEN

walls are meant to be torn down

One hour later, I was still wringing water out of my hair, but it was in the comfort of my warm pajamas, our comfy couch, and Cameron shifting uneasily underneath the covers, presumably from the effect of his near-nakedness. "Okay, I'm just going to say this." He pushed himself up on the couch and towards me, careful not to make the covers fall off. "I think I like you. I think I could want to be with you. I don't know if you feel the same," he rubbed his bracelet, "I sort of hope you do, and I just wanted to let you know." His eyes caught mine in a dagger of intensity. "But more than that, I want to *know* you."

I flinched slightly, unsure of what to say or how to say it. This honesty, this rawness, scraped against my walls. I still didn't feel ready to tell him about me. What he said, and what he had done, plagued me in a way I couldn't shake. Part of me wanted to tell him that I did, in fact, like him. The other part was almost impenetrably walled off. "I know that and I understand, but I'm not sure I'm ready to talk to you. To tell you everything. And . . . I'm still so confused by you."

Cameron put his hands back under the covers and looked out the window. "Can you tell me something? Anything?"

"We're friends," I whispered. "That's what you asked of me and that's what we are." His eyes shot toward me, but he didn't say anything. "I—I'm . . . still just learning about you. For most of my life I've kept myself relatively walled off. Beatrix wasn't wrong about my reluctance to gain new friends." A sigh escaped him and I found his eyes moving rapidly beneath closed eyelids. "I appreciate your honesty and your friendship. That's something I don't want to lose. But we've only known each other for a little while, and while I think I may like you too that way, I just don't know . . ." I wanted to say that I was sorry. That I wished things could be different. The only thing that kept me from saying anything was my cowardice. After so many years of only interacting with my friend group, I found myself unable to open up to someone new . . . and important.

His eyes opened once more, and he focused on me. "I guess . . . I guess I understand that. I don't want to lose you as a friend, so I'll stop prying."

"Thank you," I said intently.

"You're welcome," he replied, formally. "What about the clothes?"

I shivered at the thought of his blood-covered t-shirt. "Probably not much longer." A corner of his blanket had shifted toward me when he moved, and I had begun to play with it. "I wish I could have let you borrow something to wear, but my dad's clothes are in storage."

"Casey. I'm home." My mom strutted into the room, shaking out her jacket. She smelled of cigarettes and cheap perfume and was in complete disarray. "Oh . . ." Her eyes combed over our attire and how close we were sitting. I rocked backward. "Cameron, right?" she asked cordially.

"Yes, ma'am," he rumbled shyly. The gray cover didn't seem to be able to hide his humiliation.

"You rode with us to the funeral." My mom's eyes were cold and calculating. I didn't like how she was assessing the two of us. *I'm not doing anything wrong.*

Cameron nodded. "Uh-huh."

An awkward silence thudded into existence. Then Cameron and I spoke at the same time:

"I should really go home."

"Wanna stay for dinner?"

I raised an eyebrow at his contorted face. "He doesn't have to leave, right, Momma?"

Lips pursed, she said, "Of course not."

My blood boiled, but taking in a calming breath, I turned back to Cameron expectantly. "No, thank you. My grandmother will be worried." He picked himself off the couch, suddenly not caring that his clothes were still tumbling in hot air. His boxers hung low on his lean but muscular body. His golden skin glowed and had a slight sheen. Despite the fact that I had seen him shirtless when I gave him the cover, I couldn't take my eyes off of him. My mother's eyes seemed to both narrow and grow bigger at the same time. He folded the blanket in a perfect square.

"Um, his clothes are in the dryer . . . can you get them?" The look she gave me would have made the Devil cower. Without another word she went to retrieve them. "I'm so sorry. But you know you had to get out of those clothes. They were soaking wet and you needed to get warm or else you might get hypothermia or something, and there are just no boy clothes here, but I should have—"

"Casey," he said abashedly. "It's okay, I just need to leave." At that moment, I don't think I've ever seen him look so pitiful. I reached over and pulled him into a hug. He was warm and after an awkward second of him just standing there, his arms surrounded me.

"Excuse me," my mother said, clearing her throat loudly. I once again became aware of just how little clothing he had on.

"Thank you." He whispered in a voice that was almost too low to hear.

"Here are your clothes." Momma dropped them on the couch, turned on her heel, and went to the kitchen, probably thinking a beer might help. I twisted back to him.

He uttered a shameful, yet easy laugh. "I have a feeling your mom doesn't like me anymore." I rolled my eyes, not really caring. He picked up his pants and shirt and put them on; they had a few stains from the blood and water, but they were small enough that it wouldn't render them useless. Without meaning to, I watched as he stretched his lean muscles by putting on both items. Cameron caught my stare and gave me a small wink. I spun around, mortified. "I'm decent now," he teased softly.

Facing him, I realized how true it was. He wasn't frowning or embarrassed or even depressed like he looked seconds ago. His mood swings were utterly astonishing. Maybe it was the wrong way to process them, but I was intrigued. He practically basked in joy. "You seem happier now," I caustically noted. My mind flashed a picture of him with red wrists again, but I quickly shook it away.

"I appreciate everything you've done for me." He self-consciously put his hands in his pockets, but the bulgy bandana prevented him from shoving his left hand too deeply.

"Of course," I replied quietly. "Just don't . . ." My voice trailed off, unsure of the correct way to phrase my worry.

He nodded, understanding. "I'll see you Monday, right?

I mean . . . that's something friends do, right?" A playful smile tugged at his mouth. "See each other?"

"They do." A corner of my lips lifted. "Sounds like a plan."

Once I gave him his keys, he left. I watched him through the window. My heart puttered after his fading car. I felt awful for what he had gone through and my earlier reluctance to befriend him. The rain ran down the glass and made me shake. It didn't cleanse me. It didn't wash away my problems. *Why does this happen? Why does he have to like me? Why do I have to be this way?*

My mother entered the living room surprisingly beer-free. "So. Seems like you and Cameron are really close." I made no response. "Why were all of his clothes off?!"

I looked at her in horror. "They were soaked. So, I *dried* them. You might have noticed that I am wearing pajamas, not underwear."

"So, I noticed." I was taken aback by her response. "We need to talk, young lady." Everything about her was off. Her posture was mature. Her tone was angry. Her arms were crossed. It was like she had finally become my mom. Her green eyes flashed. "Sit." It was not a suggestion.

I sat down in the chair in front of the couch. Everything about her ticked me off. I crossed my arms, confounded that she was becoming so righteous. "Talk." My response was also not a suggestion.

"Don't you take that tone with me. I am the mother here, not you. Now why was he over here tonight?"

I glared at her. "I got a ride because it started raining. Do you have a problem with that?"

"What were y'all doing?"

I gaped at her. "We were talking. Is that a problem for you? Because if it is, I suggest you lighten up. People talk. It's why English was invented in the Dark Ages."

She sighed and stood up. "I don't like you hanging out with that boy. He worries me. At the funeral, he was so quiet. He in general is so . . ." She was struggling with the words. I found her accusing tone highly offensive. "So may I ask if you did anything with him?"

"Mom! I'm still a virgin. And even if I wasn't, I don't believe that is any of your concern." My hands curled into half fists.

In response, she put her hands on her hips. "It is too my concern. I am your mother whether you want me to be or not. And I will not, will not tolerate what you just said to me. Until you turn eighteen, or I drop dead, I am your mother. Like it or not. Do not think you have any right to keep anything from me. That boy is trouble and I forbid you to see him."

My heart froze over in abject anger. Since when was she the one in charge? What made her think she could control my life? Forbid me from seeing him. That was *not* going to happen. "He's my *friend*, Mother. We *are* gonna hang out and you can't stop us."

She got in my face. "Yes I can."

I burst out of my seat and pointed a finger in her face. "How *dare* you!" It was bad enough that I had been inconsiderate to Cameron, but for her to force me to ignore someone? She had no right. "You don't know *anything* about what goes on between me and Cameron."

Her mouth was wide open and she was fumbling to keep up. "I don't know if you've forgotten . . . but I am your mother. What is wrong with you?"

I laughed darkly. "You're my mother? Oh please. Where have you been for the past ten years? Who puts our meals on the table? How are you able to pay the bills again? Who got your lazy butt a job?"

"Casey . . ." She was searching for words in the air but came up with nothing.

"Dammit, Momma! *I've* been the mom all these years!" I couldn't control myself. All those years of saying nothing. All I could do was scream at her. I couldn't take being so quiet anymore. I just couldn't take it. I stood up straighter and watched as she wavered beneath my gaze.

Her face was as red as a cherry tomato. "Don't—don't . . ." she tried to say.

"Don't what, Momma? Don't speak the truth?" My words were nothing but shouts. I no longer cared. "God, you are so incredibly clueless." I felt my tone fall down a few degrees. "That's why Daddy was able to cheat on you." I let that register for a moment. "That's right. Daddy Darling was having sex with someone other than you. Someone *better* than you. Thanks for proving my point." I turned away quickly but walked slowly to my room.

I didn't get far before I saw Christina's blue-green eyes widen. The look on her face angered me even more. "What? What is it? Is this situation too much to handle? Are you unable to talk?" I glared at my twin. "I thought so. You're no better than her and I'm sick of all this crap." Christina's eyes filled with tears as she fled down the hall.

That was exactly what I wanted to do. Run away from everything. Run far away, forever. If not forever, at least for a few hours. I slammed my bedroom door. Having no need for anything in the room, I opened my window. Another storm was brewing, one inside of me. Tides were turning and there was no going back. I knew I needed to go back and apologize but didn't have the energy or the heart. The graveyard would be perfect in the pouring rain. It should be a permanent condition, washing away the sins and sorrows of the deceased. It was too cold.

I closed my eyes, imagining the rows of the dead. I had memorized where my dad rested long ago. His grave was bare and boring. Even the writing on it seemed stupid. "Loving father, husband, and son." Yeah right, in whose world? I sighed and pictured the tombstone. "I don't know if I should hate you or love you, Daddy." I rested my head against my window frame.

My wrist started throbbing. I looked down and saw a small trickle of blood. My heart froze, and all of a sudden I was in a small bathroom, looking at Cameron in the mirror. No, it was *me*. I was Cameron. He looked down at the razor blade and pressed down deeper. This time it was the other wrist. Burgundy drops trickled down his tan arm.

This will end tonight, I thought furiously. I shook myself out of him, put on my shoes, grabbed my coat, and climbed outside. *For once I'm glad this house is one story.* The rain flooded me as I focused on the task of getting to his house. I didn't even know where he lived, but my feet carried me to him. Cherokee Street. I recognized the blue house in the blur inside my head. No memories had come to me, which meant he was still alive. But I knew it wouldn't be for much longer if I couldn't find him. Instead of worrying, I ran faster. *It's all your fault,* my brain roared at me. *You should have helped him. You should have been a better friend. If he dies it will be your fault.*

Suddenly, I was in front of a house. It was his house. It had to be. Pale blue with gingerbread trim. Two stories. The only light on was upstairs, which I assumed was where Cameron was suffering. I sprinted to the door and pounded on it. "Cameron!" I screamed. "Cameron, let me in. Please." I heard some shuffling upstairs and then a door opening and closing.

The door opened and my heart jumped to my throat. "Casey?" He was confused. I looked at his wrist and saw a bloody rag tied haphaz- ardly around what must be the cut. "What are you doing here?"

I pushed him back through the door and dragged him into the living room. A small part of me noted that the room was expensive looking, and not only had style, but a cozy feeling. "Where is your grandmother?" I asked, looking him in the eyes.

"At work. Why? Why are you here, Casey? I thought you didn't want to talk to me anymore tonight." He threw the words at me like bullets. Even though I had said a lot earlier, I had a few shots of my own.

"Yeah, well, I didn't want you to kill yourself either. And just because I don't want to tell you my whole life story today doesn't mean we aren't friends. My God, Cameron, we just talked about all of this." His eyes widened with questions, but I ignored them. "Where is your first aid kit?"

He looked like he was about to argue, but I suppose the look I gave him shut him up, because he just said, "Under the sink in the kitchen."

"Okay." I gave him a quick once-over and sighed. "Sit down," I said, using the same tone I did when I tried to calm Christina down after a pet died. I grabbed the first aid kit and a wet washcloth and went back to find him lying on the couch. His eyes were closed. My hand skirted the length of his injured arm. "Again, Cameron? I *just* asked you not to. You *just* did this a few hours ago."

Cameron grabbed my hand with a wry smile. "You know, for someone who's afraid to be close to me, you sure are touching me a lot."

My face heated up. "Can you please be serious?" Without another minute of hesitation, I took the wrist with the rag on it and untied it. Seeing the cut, I gasped. The line was red and angry looking. As the air hit the wound it began to bleed again. "Why do you keep doing this?" I whispered.

"Takes away the guilt."

I sighed. I wanted to pursue the question, but I knew this wasn't the time. "Nothing you've done or haven't done warrants this. Sit up please," I commanded, looking through the first aid kit. After a few seconds of rumbling around in the box, I found Neosporin and some bandages, along with a whole lot of other things I was sure I would never know what to do with. I pressed the washcloth against his cut softly and gently cleaned away the bit of dirt.

"How did you know I was cutting myself? This time . . . and earlier?" he asked after a few minutes of silence. I didn't look up immediately, but his eyes were drilling into me. He must know something was wrong with me.

Internally, my heart raced, but I just said, "I didn't. I was coming to apologize."

I finally met his steady gaze. An eyebrow had cocked up slightly and his mouth was a thin line. He stared at me intently. "If that's true, then why were you screaming and pounding on the door?"

Uh-oh, my brain whispered. "It was cold and wet."

"Why didn't you drive?"

"Not enough gas."

"Why didn't you just call me then?"

"That would have been too impersonal."

"Why do you care? I thought we fixed it. Like you said, we were fine."

My answer broke off in my mouth. *I can't tell him the truth, can I?* "I thought we were fine but clearly not," I said, gesturing to his bleeding arms. "Besides . . . I do care," I whispered softly. I screwed off the top of the Neosporin and started to squeeze the gel out. He stared at the top of my head for a long time, but I caught his look.

"Imagine that," he said quietly. I focused on the cut and was happy to see that not only was the cut cleaner, but the blood had stopped flowing. "You never really answered how you knew I was cutting myself or why you are soaking wet again."

"You didn't ask why I was soaking wet." I let out a loud breath. "I can't tell you how I knew." I finished putting the bandage on his cut and looked into his golden eyes.

"Why not?" he asked. "Don't you trust me? After everything I told you?" His hand grabbed mine.

"You promised you wouldn't pry." I shuddered as his touch seemed to spread to every vein in my body. His heat warmed my freezing veins. He must have thought my shudder was from my wet clothes, because he suddenly leapt up and said, "Let me get you something dry to put on. It's your turn now."

"Wait . . ." I tried to say, but it was too late. While he was gone, I decided to look around the living room. A few pictures of the Golden Boy as a tiny little boy sat on a shelf above the television. Every camera had caught him laughing or smiling so big, I was surprised it fit into the picture. His golden hair and eyes glowed and I could see just what a happy child he was. It made me wonder when it all went wrong. I picked up another picture of an older woman, who I figured was his mom.

The woman had worry lines all over her face, but she didn't look that old or sad. Her face was half turned to the camera and half turned toward the little boy in the picture, as if she knew she had to look at the camera, but she didn't want to miss a second of him. Her hair was a darker color than Cameron's and her eyes were browner, but the resemblance wasn't doubtable. From the way Cameron looked at the woman in the picture you could tell how much he loved her.

"Here you go," Cameron said, walking back into the room. "These might be a bit big, but you kind of have the same build as my grand-mother . . ." He trailed off as he saw the picture I was holding. "What are you doing with that?"

I thought he was going to snatch it out of my hands, but he came closer instead. "That's my mom."

"She is really pretty," I said.

"Thank you. I miss her a lot." His hands reached around me to touch the photograph. "I think she would have liked you." I gave a small nod, intensely aware of his arms around me. "I know I do."

I leaned into him. "I thought you only *thought* you liked me."

His chuckle rumbled against my back. "Fair enough." We stood there for a moment. "I'm sorry about prying. You're right, I did promise I wouldn't."

"I'm sorry about earlier," I mumbled. I turned around and blushed at our closeness. "But, I'm glad I'm here now."

"Put on these clothes and then we can talk if you want." I nodded and waited for him to leave. "What?" His eyebrows rose.

"A little privacy, please?" I said. His cheeks were flushed, and he stammered something about getting water, fleeing into the kitchen. Still laughing, I put on a warm California City sweatshirt and gray sweatpants. I smiled at the warm and relaxing clothing. "It's safe," I announced, sitting on the couch.

He came in with two glasses filled with cold water. "I see you made yourself right at home. This is good." I tried not to smile as he sat down beside me. He handed me a glass, which I eagerly drank from. "Thirsty much?" the Golden Boy asked. I just rolled my eyes and punched him on the arm. "I'm not going to pry, but I want you to know I'm still dying of curiosity."

Protests bubbled to the surface of my lips. "If I tell you, you'll probably think I'm crazy or you won't want to be my friend anymore."

"Casey, I like you too much for that to ever happen. And I already think you're completely crazy. I won't push it, but what about a story for a story." He adjusted pillows and reclined for whatever he was going to hear. My heart was sick of being quiet and was ready to throw up all of my thoughts. "Let's hear it, Darling."

"You wouldn't understand." I was searching for any reason not to tell him right then.

"That's a cop-out," he parroted from earlier. "Gran's a nurse. She won't be back until tomorrow morning. You have the floor."

Looking into his eyes, I couldn't hold back any longer. "It all started when I was seven years old . . ." I told him everything. How my dad died and how I experienced it. About how after the funeral I realized I would have to be the head of the family. I told him about how I forced my mom and sister to move so we could actually afford food and a house. I told him about my mom drinking and doing drugs. I told him how frustrating it was to live with someone who's mostly mute. I told him everything up to the more recent events. Like my mom *finally* getting a job. And me getting a scholarship to KSU but being too afraid to do anything about it, because I didn't want to abandon my family. And then . . . I got to the fight with my mom just before I almost beat down his door. And, of course, how I saw and felt him cutting in the bathroom.

The entire time, he just listened. Cameron really listened. He didn't nod or patronize me. He just digested everything. I didn't know if it was a good or bad thing. When I got to the part about feeling him cut himself, he stopped me by saying, "How close was I to dying?"

I let out a shallow breath. The thought of him dying was absolutely terrifying. "The thing is, you weren't all that close. I mean, I didn't get any memories or any regrets. I just felt your feelings. And when I see someone die, I always see their memories and regrets."

"Like I said, I don't cut deep." He stroked his bandaged wrist. "Maybe your power has developed more now that you've gotten older. Or, maybe I was close to cutting deep." He almost relished the idea of being close.

"Maybe," I said, but not really agreeing. I turned to Cameron and looked him right in the eyes. "You know, I didn't forget my question either, Cameron."

He looked sincerely confused. "What do you mean?"

"Why did you cut yourself tonight? It can't be about guilt over your mother every time, can it? Does it really hurt that much? I mean, you already cut yourself earlier today." I felt the danger creep into my tone.

Cameron's gaze left mine and he muttered something unintelligible. I grabbed both sides of his face between my hands, feeling a sharp tingle pass through our skin, and forced him to look at me. "Why did you do that to yourself?"

"Doesn't matter, Casey. If pain plagues me, I have to escape it somehow." His beautiful eyes rolled over my features. "It's really complicated, because it is a bit about my mom. It almost always is, but this time I was . . . I was also sacred of losing you, okay," he whispered softly. A long sigh escaped me. "I know it probably seems silly to you. I don't expect you to understand. But this helps me feel better." He took a deep breath of air. "I'm glad we're friends but I do actually like you and I wanted you to be the girl I was my new self with."

I let out a trembling breath. "You're right. I don't understand." I watched as he shuddered. "But I'm trying, and you have to promise me you won't do this. I'll be here for you. You have friends and you can't do this to them." He looked down. "Cameron, you have to *promise* me that, no matter what happens, you will not cut yourself again." I felt my heart plunge to the ground at the thought of him cutting himself.

"I can't deal with it sometimes— Sometimes, even a seemingly small thing bothers me and—"

I moved a hand from his face and put my index finger on his lips. "Cameron, *promise* me. You can never, *ever*, do that to yourself again. No matter what happens between us. Whether we date or don't date or be friends or don't be friends." I felt tears spring to my eyes. "Because your life is more than just you and me, and it's more important than any guilt you could have . . . Don't throw your life away for *any* reason. Least of all, me. I won't stand for it."

He was silent for a few minutes. "Okay," he mumbled faintly. "I promise." His hand wiped a stray piece of hair behind my ear. "I won't do it anymore." I released him as a calm washed over me. "I also promise that it wasn't just about you, so . . . don't, y'know, feel bad." He fidgeted with his bracelet. "Can you promise me that we're going to try and be real friends?"

The light bounced off his tragic eyes. This problem wasn't fixed, and maybe it wouldn't ever be, but I wanted to be there for him. I said, "I promise that I will be there for you, but only if you try to stop doing this." Satisfied enough, we both settled into the couch next to each other, not talking, not needing to.

CHAPTER ELEVEN

actually happy

I guess I must have fallen asleep, because I woke up to the smell of pancakes. I smiled against the back of the couch. Turning around I sleepily opened my eyes to find Cameron splayed out on the floor beside me. Realizing what it meant that he was still beside me, I panicked. *His grandmother must be home and it is now Saturday morning.* Careful not to step on him, I forced myself to walk into the kitchen. Behind me, he let out an endearing and soft snore.

A small older woman stood in the kitchen with her back turned to me. She had bronze hair streaked with silver strands. Her posture was strong and her hands moved decidedly as she made the delicious food I smelled. I didn't know if I should talk or wait until she said something, but I didn't get much of a chance to figure it out. "Why, hello there," she said when she turned around. Her voice was soft but strong and slightly coarse. Now that I could see all of her, I realized how much she looked like Cameron. They had the same eyes, but hers were infinitely wiser.

"Hi," I replied, cautiously.

"You must be Casey?" She peered at me behind small glasses.

"Yes, ma'am." I was nodding like a bobble head. I walked closer to her so that she could turn her attention back to the food, but I could also see her face.

"Cameron's told me a lot about you. It's nice to finally meet Miss Mysterious." She smiled as she pulled a pancake off the griddle. "He seems a lot happier since he's met you."

"I'm sorry," I blurted out, not knowing what else to say. She looked at me questioningly. "I mean, about falling asleep, you know, in your clothes. It had been raining. We didn't do anything of course," I continued quickly, wondering just how beet red my face was inevitably turning. "I mean, I was just tired after I got here . . . I guess, and we were just talking and—"

"Whoa, now calm down." She chuckled softly. "I have nothing against you spending the night. I might have wanted a little warning so I could fix the house up a bit better, but you're fine, child. You're just fine." She turned her attention back to the pancakes. "Ever since Tina died . . . well, let's just say Cameron hasn't been himself. I was hoping Georgia would change that. Turns out that a girl by the name of Casey might have." I looked down. "Will you grab a plate, please? They're in the left top cabinet." Now I knew where Cameron's bluntness came from.

I reached up and grabbed a plate. They were white and simple. The vast difference between it and my life was astonishing. "I don't know if I'm helping him all that much," I admitted softly, remembering last night.

She turned around to inspect me. "He isn't the most stable right now. I don't think he'll be very stable for a while, if I'm perfectly honest." I handed her the plate and kept going as she put pancakes on it. "You are tough, aren't you? You seem kind and I appreciate you standing your ground with him. He needs a friend."

"He's so fragile. What if I do something wrong?" I shifted uneasily in the bright kitchen. Warm sunlight bounced off the yellow walls. In the daylight I felt like an intruder.

"'What ifs' don't matter. Sometimes all you can do is just give it a try."

"Yes, ma'am," I said trying to feign confidence I knew I didn't have. "I will do all I can to be there for him. Thank you . . ." I trailed off, not knowing what to call her or think of her.

"Just call me Anne. Now go wake that boy of mine and tell him breakfast is ready. I'll put it on the dining room table." Anne grabbed the plate of pancakes and went presumably to the dining room.

I walked back into the living room. Cameron's back was to me with a blanket thrown over half of his body. Golden hair turned the color of honey in the sunlight streaming from the window. It was amazing how comfortable he looked considering he was sleeping on a hardwood floor. I got on my hands and knees in front of him and shook him softly on the shoulder. "Cameron," I whispered, "breakfast is ready."

He turned toward me and opened one sleepy eye. "Hmmmmmmmmmm . . . Mmmmorning, Casey. You didn't have to make me breakfast," he mumbled sleepily.

I chuckled softly. "I didn't, sleepyhead." He stretched up from his position and gave me a lazy smile. The leather cuffs on his wrists slid down, exposing his new bandage. My heart started beating a mile a minute. His eyelids slid down yet again.

"Are you two going to eat breakfast or what?" Anne yelled at us from in the dining room.

Cameron's eyes flew open. "She's home?" I nodded, again with the bobble head thing. "Did you talk to her?" I kept nodding like an idiot, not really understanding why he was flipping out so much. "And . . . ?" he inquired.

"And we're fine. She didn't freak out." His eyes closed in relief and he smiled. "Are you ready to eat?" He jumped up in a whir. Leaning down he offered his hand and pulled me up.

"I suppose I am." His gold eyes rested on our still clasped hands. We both let go at the same time. "Let's go."

I went back to the kitchen after freshening up in the bathroom. "It's about time, you two," Anne teased. "I thought food was supposed to send teenagers running to the source." I laughed at her remark. "Sit, sit. This food can't go to waste." I put two pancakes on a plate and stood back awkwardly as they fixed their plates. "Morning, sleepy boy," Anne said, smiling at Cameron.

"Morning," he grunted, stacking six pancakes on his plate and drowning them in syrup. "I'm hungry."

"Hungry? It looks like you're serving a plate for someone half-starved!" Anne exclaimed, giving him a kiss on the forehead.

I couldn't help but become uneasy as I watched the happiness all around me. Together, we walked to the dining room and sat down. Cameron immediately dug in. I swallowed the pancakes hard. I felt like a burglar. Like someone intruding on their lives. On *his* life.

The cute dining room walls were a calming green and the table was small. Lace curtains allowed rays of brilliant sunlight to fill the air. "So," Anne interrogated, sitting at the head of the table. "How did you two sleep?"

Despite the politeness of her blunt question, my heart started pounding like I was in trouble. "Fine," Cameron said with a smile. "Casey was awesome company." Anne's smile met his own and I could tell that they knew when each other was lying. There was an honest love between them that I really liked.

My own countenance was at a loss at what to show. Here I was with this incredibly intriguing boy and his wonderful grandmother and I could barely eat the delicious meal. I felt like they were going to start interrogating me together at any moment.

Anne's crystal-blue eyes washed over me. "Are you okay, hon?" I nodded mechanically and ate a bite of the pancake. It was perfectly sweet and moist.

Cameron's eyes also looked at me suspiciously. "Casey, please, she isn't going to convict us or anything for you spending the night."

I sighed to myself. "I'm glad to be here, I—I just feel like I'm interrupting." Suddenly the pancakes weren't all that delicious.

"Nonsense, young lady." Anne smiled brightly at me. I could see the resemblance between her and Cameron even more when she smiled like that. "Any friend of Cameron's is welcome in my house. Besides, we could use another girl's touch around here." She finished with a wink.

I laughed a bit and popped another bite into my mouth.

"Thanks for embarrassing me further. You might as well tell her I'm a slob," Cameron shot playfully.

"Well, she probably already knows that," Anne said, cutting her second pancake. I hadn't even realized we were almost done; I personally had been eating on autopilot and found myself full.

"Thanks." Cameron's smile caught my eye, and I physically couldn't put another morsel in my belly. "Hey, we'll be right back, Gran. The pancakes were perfect, as usual. Because you're perfect, as usual." She responded with a happy shake of the head, which led me to believe it was a common phrase between the two. He then led me out of the room.

"Thank you very much, Anne. I enjoyed breakfast. Um, I guess I'll be right back?" I said, having no idea where Cameron was leading me.

The porch looked neat and classical in the daylight. The air was damp, coating my throat and making me feel refreshed. I appreciated the dew on the ground. I had never realized how pretty those drops could be on grass. Cameron leaned against the rail, sitting on the porch swing. I took a spot a little less than an arm's length away, my heart racing. Last night should have made this easy. We were friends after all. But if anything, me opening up to him like that increased my vulnerability tenfold.

"Thank you," he said, shifting closer. I could feel the heat radiating from him. *Oh God.* He grabbed his leather bracelet and twisted it tightly against his wrist. "For last night, I mean." I avoided his eyes the best I could. "May I kiss you, Casey Darling?"

The air around me seemed to constrict and I froze. "What?" My voice sounded strangely detached, breathy, curious, shy.

His eyes met mine earnestly. "May I kiss you?"

"Cameron," I scolded half-joking. Confusion vibrated through me. However, looking into his golden eyes I found a feeling rich and deep that I couldn't name. I dropped my eyes back to the floor. "We're supposed to be friends."

"And we are and we can be but . . ." He licked his lips. "I've been dying to kiss you all night. Just a kiss, no strings attached?"

It was a stupid suggestion. A kiss with no string attached. He must have known the potential problems and implications a simple kiss could have. And yet, staring at his lips, I found myself in want of him. "Yes." It was barely a word at this point. "You may kiss me."

Gently, he crossed the short distance between us and his lips covered my bottom one as if it were the first kiss of my life (and it was). My eyes stayed open until bliss enveloped me. I closed them as pleasure overtook me. My first kiss was softer than I imagined it would be. But it was real. Soft pressure and heat. It was as if I were floating high above my body, attached only by the tingling sensation of my bottom lip. All I wanted to do was giggle but instead I kept quiet.

"See?" His breathing was heavy. "No strings whatsoever." We were still inches from each other and I felt my own heart beating harder than expected. Then, out of nowhere, I got an image of the killer's blue eyes. I don't know why, but I pulled away quickly.

"What?" His eyebrows did that confused one-higher-than-the-other look. "What did you see?" he asked gently.

"Nothing." I shrugged it off. "I just got a glimpse of Beatrix, the others, the killer's eyes. They haunt me."

His face dropped like a bomb. "I'm sorry."

"It's okay. Happens every once in a while. Little flashes." Cameron picked at his leather cuff. "Beatrix and blood. A blurry mess." I took a shuddering breath and forced a tiny smile. "It just comes and goes at odd times. Sorry."

"Maybe this was too much?" His beautiful eyes soothed me and the world faded away. He gave me a gentle squeeze before putting distance between us.

"No. It was nice." We smiled at each other and agreed to go inside without saying anything else.

After finding Ann clearing the table, Cameron said, "I'm going to take Casey home, okay, Gran?"

She saw my face and softened. "Just be back before dark tonight. They got that curfew instated now."

"Thanks, Gran." He pecked her on the cheek. I grabbed my coat and pajamas that had been washed and folded. We put on our shoes and entered the warming sunshine. Anne's clothes were comfortable in the crisp morning.

"I won't tell anybody your secret. You know that, right?"

I nodded gently, increasingly aware of the space between us.

"You aren't mad about what I did on the porch, are you?"

"It was the gentlemanly thing to do. Nicely done," I answered. "But no strings attached, right?" We locked eyes with each other. I was glad that I had allowed him over my wall, but the way he was looking at me set my heart ablaze. I blushed and looked down, unsure what to think of his intensity.

"I'm glad . . . and right. No strings attached." He chewed once on his bottom lip and his eyes flickered to my lips. I looked out the window before we caught gazes again. "None at all . . ." he whispered. We drove toward my house in silence, his hand touching mine in between shifting gears.

Before I knew it, my house was in sight. Images of me cussing out my mom and yelling at Christina flashed through my mind. I sighed. *It is not going to be fun to walk in the house.* Cameron looked over at me cautiously. "What?" I asked, tucking a stray piece of hair behind my ear.

A sweet smile flashed through his features. "What do you mean?" He drummed on the steering wheel.

"You seem so shy all of a sudden?" I responded.

He laughed and my stomach flipped. "I'm not. I mean, why would I be, because, y'know, we just had a nice night and that was really it and, well . . ." He ran a hand through his hair. "Would you want to go to the dance together?" At my wide eyes he scrambled to add an "as friends" to the end of that sentence. "Friends go together all the time, right? So, we can go together . . . as friends."

I found myself smiling at the boy I had met two months ago, and really liking him. Somewhere deep inside of me, panic swirled. I was reminded that it might be too soon and "no strings attached" might not have been an honest statement. "I think that would be fun." His face lit up. "But right now, I unfortunately have to go inside."

His hand squeezed mine and I melted. Part of me groaned at my gushy feeling and the other part realized that I might be creating some strings of my own.

"So today . . . or any other day . . . you won't *do* anything? To your-self, I mean." I asked, catching him off guard.

"No. Because I promised my *friend* I would never do that again."

"If you need me, you know I'm here for you, right?" I gave him an investigative head tilt.

"Yes, I know and I appreciate it." His smile grew. He looked at his cuff and tapped it once before looking back at me. "I'll see you later." I sucked in a breath and pushed myself out of the car. He situated him-self to drive and gave me a small wave. We went our separate ways. He home, and I to my doom.

CHAPTER TWELVE

close encounters of the serial kind

The front door creaked as I peered into my living room. As far as I could see, my mom and Christina weren't around. I walked in slowly and turned around to shut the door as quietly as I could. Peering down the hallway I saw that Christina's door was closed but that was it. I went to the kitchen to get a bit of water.

After grabbing the pitcher of water from our fridge I turned around and found Christina staring at me. I jumped a little which caused a bit of the water to dribble down the side. "You scared me, Chris."

She didn't say anything but crossed her arms. I sighed and put down the pitcher. I turned away from her and grabbed a glass for my water. "Are you getting breakfast?" Turning back around I found her glaring eyes. I rolled my neck around in a circle and examined my sister. She seemed relatively awake, but considering it was close to eleven that didn't surprise me. "So . . . how'd you sleep?" She rolled her eyes and walked over to the cabinet beside me to get a bowl out of the cabinet. I fidgeted with my hands as she aggressively shook cereal into her bowl. "That bad?" I tried to play it off as a joke.

She slammed the box on the counter and glared at me. "Oh, I'm sorry, I thought you wanted to adopt my 'mute' state."

I flinched at her words and brought my attention to the floor. "I'm really sorry, Christina. I didn't mean it, but Mom just pissed me off—"

"Yeah, well, she was kinda upset too, Casey. She spent a lot of her night crying. Where did you even go?"

I pinched the area where my fingernail met my thumb. "It doesn't matter." I turned my attention back to her. She was completely stoic. "What does matter is that I am sorry for what I said to you. That wasn't fair or right, and I am truly, incredibly sorry. Is there a way I can make it up to you?"

She quirked her mouth up to one side and looked down at her bowl. With a large sigh, she grabbed the milk that was sitting on the counter between us. "Not really." I watched her pour the milk into the bowl. "I just get to be mad at you for a bit, okay?"

I grabbed the milk as it slid over to me. "Okay." With a parting smile, she left the room and I ate at the dining table alone.

—

Later, and being as quiet as I could, I changed into more hunting clothes, grabbed my jacket, and prepared to leave my house with the knife I had kept hidden in my nightstand. As I left my room, my eyes lingered on Christina's door. She hadn't said anything to me since breakfast and I half wondered if I should tell her I might not be home for dinner since it was already five o'clock. Deciding that her version of being mad at me meant ignoring me, I walked down the hallway.

My thoughts drifted into unrestricted territory: Beatrix. My free hand traveled to my jacket pocket, which held the old, blue pendant Beatrix gave me. It was time for the killer to be finished. I gnawed at my cheek inside my mouth. *Think, think.* My sanity was teetering. It had felt primal, making me stronger. There was part of me that enjoyed being a complicated vigilante. I thought back to the newspaper article. There had to be something in Dellinger Park. Why did the cops think he was staying in the woods?

When I walked outside, I found Danny's car sitting in my driveway. I peered through the windshield to find Danny's mouth in a frown. I rubbed the back of my head and gave him my best smile. He rolled down the window as I walked over. "Hey Danny. What's new?"

"Are you out of your mind?" Warmth flooded my cheeks. He raised a hand to keep me from protesting. "Get in, we're going to Maximum's."

Inside his Accord, the silence was stifling. He didn't say anything and his radio blared pitifully between us. I shifted around, constricted by the seatbelt. I was painfully aware of my outfit and its purpose. When we finally got to Maximum's, we both went in without a word.

After sitting down, he finally decided to talk to me. "Are you *mad*?" Danny asked. His eyes were ginormous. "What on earth were you planning on doing?"

I squirmed. "Nothing." I looked down at the table.

He sighed. "Casey, I'm worried about you. I know about your earlier escapade through the woods." I opened my mouth unsure of what to say. "Cameron and Christina messaged me. We're worried for you."

I looked at the menu, unable to focus on any of the words.

"Hola." The waiter with the greenish brown eyes who had once waited on Cameron and I was smiling at our table. It was driving me crazy that I didn't know his name. *Adam or Aiken.* I looked for a nametag but found none. "What can I get y'all to drink?" he asked, and I finally remembered him from my Spanish class. *Alex! That's his name.*

"Coke?" Danny asked me. I nodded. "Two."

"Be right back."

I brought Danny back to the conversation, wanting to avoid a fight. "Hunting," I said, disheartened. "I was gonna go hunting."

Danny blinked at me from across the table, knowing what I meant. "Do you even have a plan, Casey? You can't just run through woods looking for a psychopath. They have FBI people for stuff like this. My mom said they're already here in Cartersville. You don't know what you're doing."

"Well, neither do the police apparently, since they haven't caught him yet."

"They might not ever catch him for all we know. Some serial killers prey for decades, you know. Nobody ever caught Jack the Ripper or Zodiac."

"I have to do *something.*"

"I want him found just as much as you do, but this is not the way to do it."

"But I just can't sit idle. Maybe I can find a clue. Maybe I'll see his eyes again and point him out. I've seen his eyes. They haunt me. I can't get them out of my head."

He slammed his hands down onto the table. I jumped and looked at him with wide eyes. "Dang it, Casey. I'm sorry, but this is not the way to help. You have a 4.0 grade point average and got accepted to Kennesaw. You have scholarships lined up. Since when is Sherlocking a serial killer a plan of yours?"

"Since our friend was murdered." I thought back to the newspaper article at the library as Danny digested my answer. "I can find him and point him out." I squeezed my hands into fists.

"This is crazy. You're crazy."

"I HAVE to find him, Danny—"

Alex returned with our drinks, very curious about my yelling whispers. "And what will you fine people be having this afternoon?"

"The Cluckin' Burger." I smiled as if nothing was wrong.

"And you, sir?"

"I'll have the same," Danny said with a flirting lilt.

"Be right out." Alex gave him a cheesy wink before strutting away.

I wanted to puke instead of eat, but my body needed food. My intensity returned. "If I find him—"

"Exactly, *if* you find him you'll do what?" He grabbed my hands. "You are seventeen, Casey." I wrenched my hands from his and put them in my lap. I focused my eyes on my flattened hands. "This is not the thing to do and if you really want to find him, why not start by looking downtown. It's possible that he's in *here.*"

I looked around. For a late Saturday afternoon, it was more crowded than usual. Patrons filled the booths with laughter and the bar with quiet conversations. A pair of girls giggled in the booth in front of us. I tore my eyes away from them and focused on the wrapped silverware in front of me.

"Just stay out of the woods."

I realized how stupid I was being. It wasn't like the killer would jump out and say, "I'm here." I felt like the world's stupidest girl.

"You're right," I whispered. I looked back up at him to find him slurping his Coke loudly.

"Good," he said. "I'm glad you're coming to your senses." He spun the Coke glass around a few times. His eyes seemed far away. "Don't do stupid things anymore. Okay?"

"Okay."

"I've been worried sick about you, Casey. All of us have. I've texted you ten times today and called you twice with no answer." That made me feel so guilty. "Cameron and I discussed your hunting habits today, you know. I thought about telling your mother."

I scowled at him. "Okay, I've already agreed to stay out of the woods." I slouched down further in the seat. "I've only done it once anyway."

Danny began rubbing his forehead. "But you were obviously gonna do it again." He pointed at my attire. "You haven't talked to me since the funeral. I'm afraid you're gonna hurt yourself or mess up your life or be freaking killed." He looked furious, but I knew he was just concerned. "Why have you been ignoring everybody?"

"I'm sorry. I've just been . . . introspective."

"Just talk to your best friend, okay?" He held up his hand in a pinky promise gesture. I couldn't help but smile. I clasped his pinky between mine. "Like, what happened with you yesterday? Christina said you got in a huge fight with your mom and that you were rude to her?"

I clasped his pinky tighter together as shame ran through me. "Cameron *and* Christina texted you?" He nodded. "Yeah, last night was not great." I released his pinky and sat back against the booth.

"Then why aren't you talking to me about it?"

I looked at my best friend. His normal infectious happiness seemed dull. After everything that happened with Beatrix, I could only imagine how much of a toll it had taken on him. We had been like the three musketeers when we were younger. "I'm sorry, Danny. I've felt awful about last night and then things happened with Cameron and . . ." I looked him directly in the eyes. "I don't even know how you're doing."

He gave me a half chuckle. "Casey, life sucks right now. It's senior year, there's a killer on the loose, and well, you know. But," he leaned forward, "what helps is knowing I have great friends like you." I smiled at him. "So what exactly happened with Christina and Cameron?"

I told him about my fight with my mom and misdirected anger with Christina and then, after a bit of prodding from him, I talked about sleeping over at Cameron's. "Honestly, it was nice but weird, but also in a good way."

"Right, right." Danny sat back and stared off into the distance. "I really think he might be good for you, Casey."

I blushed as Alex came over and set our food on the table. "Do y'all need anything else?"

"Nope!" we said at the same time, which made us both giggle a bit. Alex left with a grin splashed across his face.

"Seriously, you should consider locking him down now or I might just have to make a move on him."

I rolled my eyes as I picked the onions off my burger. "I'm sure I'll manage if you take him away from me."

"Your loss," he said, crunching on a French fry. I threw the straw wrapper at him.

"Now, can we start talking about your life? We haven't talked about you or your love life in a while. I don't even know the latest parties."

He put his hand on his heart. "Well, I simply have to tell you everything then." Just as I was about to eat a French fry, he yanked it from my hand and plopped it in his mouth. "But first, no more hunting or whatever it is you were planning to do tonight, okay?"

"Okay." I smiled at him and stole a fry off his plate. "But no more stealing my food."

Danny's laughter filled the room and we continued to talk and eat for hours. It was nice to talk about the ins and outs of normalcy with my best friend. For the first time in a long time, I hadn't felt like I was missing the person right in front of me.

—

I leaned against Maximum's cool wall, basking in the sign's comforting glow. The moon was rising in the sky, but I couldn't see it. It was a new moon. Streetlights had invaded the town, and I felt like the whole world would go dark around them. Thanks to Danny, my head felt clearer than it had in weeks. I really should have been better to my bestie. The night's blanket of darkness made me regret saying no to his ride, but he was gone. *Christina will be here any minute,* I thought to myself, looking at the time on my phone. I desperately needed to talk to her. We hadn't been on the best terms since I yelled at her and though I had attempted to apologize earlier it didn't work. I rubbed my eyes and tried not to think about the four people who died. There was a time and a place for that and me waiting for Christina alone at night was not it. I wrapped my arms tight around my body as a cold gust of wind blew.

Suddenly, I was blown by the same wind to a different place. My mind was taking me on another twisted journey. The light of Maximum's glowing sign reached the back of the restaurant, but it wasn't nearly as strong as it was out front. It threw perfect shadows, easy pockets of darkness for someone trying to hide. I gasped as I saw Alex's black hair and brown-green eyes. The killer leapt out from behind the garbage can and—

I shook myself out of the vision quickly. *Move around the side!* Still disoriented but gaining my senses, I ran. The night colors blended together, but I knew what was waiting for me. It felt like I was in slow motion as I rounded the corner. I saw the killer, right in front of me, fighting Alex. My heart did a happy leap that Alex was still alive and fighting. Vision became reality. I was grounded. There was a nasty scratch on Alex's cheek, but he was relatively unscathed. His exhaustion was evident, and the killer seemed to know this and was about to finish Alex's young life. My grounded body ran forward into their grunts and violence.

The killer's back was large. He was oblivious to the fact that I was behind him. Alex's eyes met mine and widened in bewilderment. His body was fighting back on the ground, almost defeated. I pulled the knife out of my boot. Alex's eyes grew even larger. I closed my eyes, took a deep breath, and tackled the killer. A loud *oof* sound escaped him as my body collided with his. The collision caused my grip to loosen, and the knife flew out of my hand and into the wall. "Crap," I said, latching onto the killer.

His body was hard through the black outfit he wore. He stood up, supporting my newly added weight, but stumbled drunkenly. I clawed at his mask, trying to tear it off. He realized what I was doing and rammed me against the brick wall. I groaned and released him. It took a lot of strength not to scream as the bricks scratched and tore my skin as I slid down them. The killer turned to face me.

His snake-like eyes seemed to glow in the dark. In that moment, I saw every killing he had done. He took a step toward me, but Alex tackled him. The two of them flew through the alley, landing a good ten feet away. Alex managed to get up before the killer. I scrambled for my knife and then positioned myself beside Alex.

The killer scurried to his feet, his mask slightly askew, allowing me a peek at his tanned skin. I had almost got the mask off earlier. He let out a demonic growl and took off down the street. We never saw his face.

"Come back here. You coward!" Alex called after him. My eyes bugging out of my head, I clamped my hand down on his mouth.

"Are you insane? Let him go!" I said, begging into his intense eyes.

"He can't get away! I can't let him escape after that." He started toward the killer. I gripped his arm and fought with might to keep him behind the restaurant with me. The scratch on his cheek was bleeding heavily.

"Yes, yes you can. Please!" I held my ground and implored him to listen. He looked at me, and I caught the same peppy expression he had with his customers. Suddenly the alley was too creepy and small for the both of us. "You need to call the police, but—"

"Was that the killer? Like . . . THE killer?" he interrupted. He raked his hands through his hair before throwing them up in the air. Then, like a little kid, he rocked gently forward on his feet, his eyes bright. "Holy crap!" His large, warm hands wrapped around my shoulders. We gave each other a huge hug. "Are you okay?"

Affected by his happiness to be alive, I laughed breathlessly. "I'm not the one who was just attacked. But sure, I'm fine." We let go of our embrace. I looked up and saw security cameras, panicking.

He gave me a charming smile. "Good. I wouldn't want anything to happen to you. You were amazing, man." He got out his phone.

"Alex, wait."

"You remember my name. From—"

"Do those cameras work?" I was freaking out about the cameras. Detective Mary's eyes scraped the surface of my mind.

"Oh, right. That's awesome! We got him on tape! Oh my God, it's going viral, man!" He started dialing the phone.

"Wait." I grabbed his wrist tighter than any sane person would.

"What?" He backed away, giving us both more breathing room.

"We have to call the police."

Everything about tonight spun around me.

I didn't know what I was going to do. "I know, just let me think for a minute."

"Alright, sure." He stretched out the vowels in "sure" slowly. "Why don't you want to call the police?"

"No, I do, I mean I know we have to—no, *you* have to call the police, I know, but . . ."

"So let's call." I paused to really look at this boy. He had just fought with a serial killer and *won*; you could practically see the adrenaline pumping through his veins.

"Remember Beatrix Tay?"

"Uh, vaguely . . . yeah."

"Well, the cops interviewed me after she died. She was one of my best friends." My throat began to clog, but the panic allowed me to fight through the sadness. "It's a really long story, but before she was murdered she was jogging and didn't answer her phone and I got worried and I called her mom and told her to go check on her, and she was . . . dead. The cops thought it was suspicious. And here I am again . . . and the killer just attacked you."

"Whoa." His eyes were electric. "That's intense."

"Yeah."

"But you didn't do it. You came to rescue—"

"But I was *HERE*. At another *scene*." I was in a frenzy trying to convince this boy how perilous the situation really was. "Don't you see? I'm not exactly *un*suspicious."

"Whoa." It seemed like he agreed with me, but as he gave me a once-over, I wondered if he thought I actually might *be* suspicious.

"Alex . . . you saw me eat here tonight. I heard you screaming from the front of the restaurant. I came around back. That is all. I promise I didn't—"

"Alright, calm down." He ran in place as he paused momentarily. "I guess—I don't know; I guess I can hide the tapes."

I was shocked that he suggested such a thing but impressed nonetheless.

"That's illegal and wrong and . . ." *Helpful,* my brain generated, as I grew more horrified.

"Casey?" I nodded and tried to breathe. "I thought I was a *goner.*" He laughed and screamed at the sky. "I almost *died* just now!" Sparkles shone through his eyes. Despite the situation, his mouth fixated into a wide grin. "Crap . . . we let him get away. They'll never be able to find him now; he's long gone, whoever the hell he is."

"I know." Anger at the thought of him still on the loose painfully ripped at me. However, the run in with him convinced me of my own inability to do much against him. "I don't know what to do. Just call them. I'll have to deal with it." I gave up. "Oh . . . and can . . ." I grimaced. "Can I have the tapes?"

He looked at me long and hard before nodding. "Did you get a good look at him?"

My brows furrowed together but I obligingly answered him. "He has blue eyes and he's big." *Horrible, snake-like pale blue eyes.*

"Six four?"

"Sure. Something like that." I was wondering where he was going with this.

"His knife. It was a buck knife. This guy's killing people with a buck knife." *Who cares what kind of knife it is,* I thought with a raised eyebrow.

"I don't know what a buck knife is. A knife's a knife."

"Well, I do. I can just tell the cops he attacked me . . . I fought back and he ran away. I'll describe the knife," he suggested quietly. "They'll be thrilled about the new evidence."

"And if there's new evidence then they might not care about the tapes?" I said finally catching on.

"Exactly. You can't even see the images on there anyway; it's blurry and dark. You can't even tell which employee is taking out the trash or havin' a smoke. The guy was in a ski mask and in black." He put both hands on my shoulders. "If I just tell them everything we saw, it will be enough."

"How do the tapes work?" I asked.

"Ancient VHS. There's a pile. Every twelve hours you take one out and put another one in. They won't notice if I give you the one in now. I'll just put in a new one and not record, so it'll be like somebody forgot to press the button."

"Wow." I couldn't figure out why he would do such a thing for someone he didn't even know. "You would do that for me?"

"You saved my life."

"I appreciate it," I said, putting my hand on his. We both released each other, and I took a step back. I let out a big breath and shook my hands. "I promise I'll do everything I can to keep you from getting in trouble."

His mouth fell a bit, but it was back to its earlier grin in seconds. Again, he gave me a soul-searching look. "Thanks. I trust you. And I'm going to tell them you didn't do it. Unless, you have a crazy, giant doppelganger." I finally returned his smile.

"Just don't tell them anything about me." I hugged him with all my might and he returned the gesture. As he called the cops, I texted Christina, "**Never mind. On my way.**" Alex quickly got me the tape and I was out of there in a flash, running all the way home.

I slumped against my doorway. *Now I just need a long, hot shower.* Today had been too long and too stressful. I opened the door and found my two least favorite detectives waiting in the living room with my mother. Christina was nowhere to be found, which was probably a good thing.

"Hi, Casey," my mother said cautiously. She was groomed and put together. Her eyes quickly assessed me. "The detectives just want to ask you some more questions." Judging from the way she gawked at my appearance, she probably agreed that it wasn't going to look good in front of the detectives.

Mary's red hair framed her stern face. "It's late. We will try to be as brief as possible, but we need some information," she said with narrowing eyes.

Destroying the urge to roll my eyes, I sat beside my mom. She smelled just as good as she had before she left for her job. It was still a shock to see her so clean and free of beer fug. The detectives looked at my condition and tried to communicate between each other without talking. Mary decided to jump right in. "Detective Tal and I think you may be a good kid and we don't want to fight with you. But unfortunately, we can no longer ignore the connection between you and the incident with Beatrix. It's time for us to explore all of our avenues." Mary leaned back and connected her hands in her lap.

"We need to know what you know about that murder. We know you know more than you're telling us." Tal leaned forward. *If only you knew what just happened with the killer. I've seen him face to face now.*

My mom rubbed her temples. Fidgeting with my hands, I did my best to avoid their gazes. "I told you. I don't know anything. The thing with Beatrix was pure coincidence." Christina's head peeped around the corner of the shabby wall. I gave her a small smile. She waved but rose her eyebrows in a questioning expression. Her head tilted at my appearance, seemingly eager to know why I texted her not to come. I also tilted my head as to why she didn't inform me the detectives were at our house.

Mary's head snapped towards Christina, who quickly disappeared. Mary looked at me with a raised eyebrow. "This is serious, young lady. These connections are intense. The implications, serious."

"Well, it's the truth. Believe me or not." I stood up, fully intending to leave.

"Sit down." Her voice was steel in the middle of winter. Regretting standing, I sat back down. "Now, Casey . . ."

"Mary?" Detective Tal intervened. "I'd like to talk to Casey, alone."

Sending Tal a small glare, Mary obliged. Tal rubbed his head tiredly. "I'm sorry about that. She is very stressed about the case. We both are."

"May I ask exactly what is going on? When are you gonna catch this guy?" my mom asked, sinking into the couch more relaxed.

Tal heaved a sigh. "I don't know. He doesn't seem to have a purpose. There are no motives for hurting any of the victims." He stretched. His navy-blue suit seemed out of place in our living room. "It's like nothing we've ever seen before. The GBI and FBI are now offering some help. We just don't have the resources . . ." I resisted shaking my head at *poor* small town Cartersville.

"I'm so sorry. This is awful," she said earnestly, resting her hand on his arm. I shot my eyes to my mother. Her posture was very open, and if I wasn't mistaken, flirtatious. I almost gagged.

"It's alright, ma'am." He smiled back at her. "Would you mind getting me some water?"

"Of course," Mom said, nearly knocking the table over by getting up. While Tal watched her leave, I rolled my eyes. Without my mom, the room seemed too quiet and very awkward. Ironically enough, a clock ticked in the background, as if to prove that even in the real world, a ticking clock is the sign of awkwardness.

Detective Tal cleared his throat. I may have liked him better than Mary, but I still didn't want him as close as he was to me. "Casey...I know you don't know me. But you *can* trust us and we need to trust you. You are an important lead for us. I know it's a big responsibility and you're young, but we need you to cooperate. Has someone threatened you? Are you scared to tell us the truth?" I rubbed my lips together so hard it was almost painful. "Everything you say will be completely confidential."

I looked at him and tried to see if he was being honest. There were giant bags under his eyes, wrinkles cascading across his forehead. Looking at him then, I realized I couldn't help but believe him. The tapes in my purse seemed to glow hot beside me. "To be honest . . ." I had gripped my bag so tightly my nails had begun to dig into my palm. I couldn't tell him. At that moment my mom came in. We both leaned back, and I quivered as the tension in the room diminished. I did my best to cover the bag with my body.

"Here is your water, Detective Tal," she said, handing him a cold glass of water.

"Thank you, but it's just Tal, ma'am."

I groaned at their chemistry.

"As I was saying, *Detective* Tal," I continued, butting into their gush-fest. "To be honest, it probably wasn't anything more than the fact that I had plans with her. Maybe friend's intuition; I don't know, I got worried. But I promise I have no idea *who* the killer is. Or *where* he is. And I can assure you, *Detective* Tal, that it isn't *me*."

He stared at me for a few minutes before sighing. Throwing his hands up in the air, he gave me a disgruntled reply. "I know you're not the killer, Casey. But I'm not so sure you don't know *who* he is. Or *where* he is." Taking a big gulp of water, he put the glass down and turned his attention back to my mom.

Mary Alden stepped back into the room, having run in from the porch. "Tal, we have to go. *Now*."

"I apologize for the inconvenience, ma'am. Thank you for allowing us into your home." Detective Tal stood up. I knew exactly why they had to go. My stomach dropped to the floor as I thought about the tape sitting in my backpack.

"It wasn't an inconvenience at all. And please, call me Lynne." My mom, *Lynne*, offered Tal her hand like an old-fashioned debutante. "I hope you can figure everything out. Everybody's on edge around here. You certainly seem capable of it." I ran from the room, refusing to subject myself to any more of their flirting. I grabbed fresh clothes and made my way to the bathroom, not giving a crap what they talked about. I had just turned on the water when I heard the front door close.

"Casey." My mother's voice was calm and clear. "Come back here, please." I turned off the water and did what she asked. After all, I hadn't seen her since our fight. I found myself face to face with a woman who looked like my mother but couldn't possibly be. Her hair hung in soft curls. Simple, yet thoughtful makeup framed her features. Washed clothes lined her gorgeous figure. And finally, she smelled like flowers. No beer, just flowers. It was one of the single most shocking moments of my life. She self-consciously tugged at her fixed hair.

Her eyes grazed my completely black ensemble. I'm just glad she couldn't see the knife in my boot. "Can I talk to you?"

"I suppose."

"What you said last night? It really hurt me, Casey." I flinched. "I deserved it, though. I have been a horrible mother to you and Christina." Her voice cracked and her eyes watered. I had to force myself from dropping my mouth like a fish. "All these years I've been so depressed about your father. I mean, not just his death . . . I knew he was cheating. But for so long I denied it. I can hardly remember those years, let alone the ten I've spent wallowing in myself."

"Momma . . ." I struggled with words. Everything seemed to have changed now. I found my voice and my mother found her brain.

She cut me off. "No. Don't console me. I am proud of you and your sister. So much has happened, and I wasn't there, but you two girls are both beautiful and accomplished. Even if Christina barely talks . . ." Her tone was new, and it was clear that she had no idea how to continue. "Just . . . thank you for snapping me out of this. I really needed it. I went to an AA meeting tonight. Do you know what that is?"

My eyes widened in response. "Yeah. I know what it is. I'm glad you went."

"Me too." I could tell how difficult this was for her to admit and *do*. "I'm gonna get better. You aren't alone anymore." She walked up to me, tentatively. "I love you." Her hug was brief but lightened me in a way I didn't know was possible.

"I love you too, Momma." I meant it more in that moment than I did when I was seven. I used to say that every day when I was little. It felt good to say it and mean it again. She smiled softly and walked toward the door.

"Oh, and Casey . . . I like Cameron. Just . . . no more boxers and pajamas, please." With that, she was gone.

Reaching the bathroom's safety, I peeled off my shirt for a warm shower. The water sent wonderful shivers down my spine. I couldn't keep myself from groaning when I stepped out of the warmth and into the much colder house. It's amazing how much a good shower can help.

I settled myself deep within my maroon blankets. Within minutes of snuggling under the covers, I had fallen blithely asleep.

dancing like a fool

Crisp autumn weeks continued uneasily through Cartersville. After the killer's last murder attempt, which was Alex, he had grown surprisingly silent. Our town was weary to say the least, waiting every day to get news of another victim. But the rest of October was devoid of our serial killer. Cameron and I became closer friends. Danny continued to tease me about our "friendship" while everyone else playfully ignored him. Even Christina had begun talking to him.

November was a gust of sharp worry. The killer had been dormant for over a month, making everyone wonder when he would surface and who would be his next victim. Although our town floated through November without a killing, the cops didn't let up.

Finally, December appeared, shaking the trees into their shocking state of bareness. Freezing air morphed our student's skanky clothes into much more covered outfits. Kids flustered over the Winter Dance, which Cameron had invited me to, but the adults remained agitated shadows. Prom had been cancelled. The annual fair had been cancelled. Cartersville was no fun at all and Christmas was leaning precariously.

I refrained from biting my glossed lip for the thousandth time as we reached the gym lobby. My heart rate picked up and I wondered what I was doing. Everything about me was new: the makeup, the shimmery dress, and my confidence. I pulled at the blue fabric, wondering if it was too much. Obviously, everyone dresses up for dances, but since we were going as a group I wondered if I looked more ready for a date.

Cameron had agreed to pick me up and when we arrived at the dance our group was nowhere to be found. He was so close I could smell his cologne, something with a lilting, sweet but spicy scent. He really looked amazing in his dress shirt and maroon tie (which complemented a lot of his features).

As we stood in line, a group of friends in front of us complained about how late we were being let out this year.

"I can't believe they kept us here for so long," said a girl with bright blonde hair.

"Yah, like, Christmas is only a few days away. My family barely has any time for a vacation," a dark-haired girl said.

The line moved forward as they left and we moved up so that we were standing in front of the ticket booth, which was really just a fold out table covered with light blue paper.

"Tickets?" the gaudy girl at the table asked without making eye contact. She looked absolutely miserable for handling this administration, but that changed when she eventually looked up. "Oh, hi, Cameron." Her smile exploded on to her face and she batted her eyes multiple times. "You can't possibly be alone." She put her head in her hand and leaned forward.

I fidgeted nervously. It wasn't a date, but looking at her staring at him with those eyes sent flames of jealousy down my back. I turned my attention to the decorations.

Cameron shoved his hands in his pockets and rocked backwards. "Nope! I've got a whole group waiting inside, at least I think they're inside." He smiled at me.

My jealousy dissipated, and I felt stupid for even feeling that way in the first place.

"I'll take two tickets please," he said politely, putting the money on the table before I could protest.

"Sure," Debbie said. It felt good to have him beside me as we walked through the entry to look for our friends. Balloons, crepe paper, snowflakes and punch. It was a picturesque winter dance scene out of a high school storybook. Pathetic and hilarious.

"Sorry about that. Debbie's in my lit class. She won't leave me alone," Cameron whispered into my ear as we headed toward friends.

I looked at him inquiringly just as Danny walked up. "Hey, guys," he said, bouncing up and down. Phoebe had her hand intertwined with my incredibly adorable best friend. His tux was all white with a giant rainbow bowtie, and topping her black dress was a cute rainbow necklace that really completed their picture. "We've been waiting for y'all forever. It's boring at the moment. The music is very blah." Danny was gesturing like crazy. Phoebe seemed at a loss and I gave her a knowing chuckle.

"Weirdo." "Gay." Derogatory whispers blew through the air behind us as we met Danny and Phoebe. Popular or not, some people couldn't seem to leave Danny's sexuality alone. My friends seemed unmoved, but I started to worry that the night might come unhinged. Once we reached the table, I couldn't care less. Christina's head was thrown back in laughter, her hair was up in an elegant bun, and her red dress shook with holiday flair. Tiffany had her hair curled and was wearing a beautiful, yellow, flowing dress.

"Having fun?" I gleamed. Both of them nodded enthusiastically. Danny started up a new ramble with Phoebe and Cameron. "You look gorgeous, Tiffany," I said.

She blushed graciously. "Thanks, Casey. I love that dress you're wearing." I sent my thanks in return. "I love it in here. It's almost magical. So happy midterms are over!"

Christina's head bobbed happily in agreement. "It is, isn't it?" Confidence exuded from my quiet twin.

"It is very pretty . . ." I mumbled to appease her. I reached out and squeezed her arm lightly. Glancing around at all the mingling, I realized that even though the decorations sucked, the night didn't.

Out of nowhere Lady Gaga's "Just Dance" pumped through the speakers. "Oh. My. God!" Danny exclaimed, shaking ecstatically. We all laughed at his obsession.

"Hey, Danny, let's dance," Cameron suggested brightly. My heart glowed. "If you don't mind?" He addressed Phoebe who shook her head with a laugh.

"Sure. But, Cameron? You can't keep him," Phoebe warned.

"Awww . . . well, one should be plenty." Danny pulled Cameron to the floor. "Come on, pretty boy. *Just dance!*" The whole crowd was shocked as two boys (the new hot one and the popular gay one) took over the floor.

I don't know where they learned to dance, but it was quite possibly the funniest thing I had ever seen. Danny shook his butt and jumped around, while Cameron tried to maintain some dignity and cool factor by swaying. He eventually just started to act like Danny. They both failed miserably at being normal. When the song ended, the whole crowd (who had given them the center, probably more for their own protection than for the two boys' happiness) burst into an awkward applause. Christina, Tiffany, and I went berserk and started for the boys. The bromance didn't last, unfortunately. Because though most people at our school loved Danny and his funny ways, and happily cheered him and the new kid on, they weren't the only people there. Ryan and Patricia's gang roamed the forest of the crowd and they, for some reason, despised Danny and what he stood for. A real blowup had only been a matter of time.

"Nice dance, faggots!" I heard a voice call out above all the cheer. I froze, my heart beating hard against my chest. As flawless as a movie scene, the entire crowd turned in silence. Pushing through the sea of students gathered around, a dressed-up Ryan and Patricia smiled at Danny, and then at Cameron. "I mean, really . . . and Cameron. I never knew, dude. I'll have to watch out for you now." Cameron's whole body seemed to pulse with rage. Danny, on the other hand, put himself in between the two of them.

"Ryan, you know there is no need for that. I thought we were cool." Danny crossed his arms and raised an eyebrow.

The DJ's speakers pumped bass again, preventing chaperones from detecting the budding altercation. Finally able to move again, I quickly found my way to both Danny and Cameron. I draped my arm protectively around Danny's shoulders and held Cameron's arm. "Let's go," I said softly, hoping they would agree. Slowly both of them nodded. We turned our back to the jock.

"Oh, I see how it is." Ryan's voice sounded like nails on a chalkboard, just like Patricia's always did. "Y'all's little 'girlfriend' comes in and suddenly we all have to go." Ryan's warm breath brushed against my neck. I released both of the boys and spun around to see his eyes, way too close to us. In that moment, I realized how icy blue they were. He put his hand on my shoulder and squeezed. "You don't have to protect them. I was just teasing." My blood cells stuck in their position at his touch.

Cameron's hand flashed through my peripheral vision, and before I knew it, I was separated from the jock. "Don't you *ever* touch her again." Cameron's voice was deadly.

Ryan, who had been pushed back a good two feet, just snickered. "Who do you think you are? I can touch whoever the hell I want." He looked me up and down. "Not sure if I want to, but I could." Fear coursed through my veins. *Oh no. This is not going to be good.*

Clutching Cameron's arm, I felt his muscles tighten in consummate fury. He took a step forward, but Danny ferociously jumped in Ryan's face. "Don't lay a finger on her."

"Oh whatever, queer. Patricia could take your gay ass." Patricia momentarily shrunk under his words. However, she quickly shrugged and glared at me. Now it was my turn to take an angry step forward. Ryan held up his hands in mock fear. "Oh no! Is it the Bartow Slasher? What will I do?" He took a step closer to me and suddenly the space between us was unnervingly miniscule. His eyes flashed, making me shudder. Cameron shoved him from the side.

"Back off, Arnold."

"What? You're standing up for the Slasher?" He smirked. "I mean the detectives were saying you might have an accomplice," he said with a look back to me. "Learning a whole lot about who you are, Cam, and I gotta say it's pretty sad."

Cameron stood up a bit straighter. The whole crowd was eerily still and quiet with music blasting through the gym. In the corner of my eye, I saw Ryan's buddies shift toward us. Christina and Tiffany weren't in my field of vision, but I imagined they weren't reacting well.

"Look, I've heard it from my dad. We know that she's probably the Slasher, so let me be a hero and detain her." He looked me up and down. "I'm sure I know how to make her talk."

Danny walked over to Cameron and crossed his arms. "Are we taking this outside, Arnold?" Cameron's golden eyes were mere slits, and in the dim light, he looked serious and almost evil.

Ryan shook his head and laughed. I could see a few teachers glance our way, but no one did anything. Still, Ryan frowned as he examined the crowd. "Gladly," he said. The two boys walked slowly out the double doors with a sizeable audience in tow. We had reached the chilly night before administrators and teachers even noticed anything bad was about to happen. One or two looked over before we made it outside, but they probably assumed a cluster of people had just exited early. If the situation wasn't so dangerous, I would have laughed at their obliviousness. Christina's hand slipped into mine and I looked up to see a horrified expression on her face. Tiffany was a few inches to her right. Her face mirrored Christina's.

Out of nowhere Danny leapt on top of John, a friend of Ryan's, and proceeded to hit him. Ryan took a fast swing, but Cameron luckily ducked it and jabbed Ryan in the stomach. Everyone moved into the action, closing the once-big circle. A huge "Oof!" sounded to my left. I saw Danny and two other boys fighting furiously. Danny was in a headlock by John, and a boy named Fred gladly pummeled his stomach.

Anger coursed through my veins, red hot and ready for a challenge. I started toward Danny when Phoebe appeared in front of me. She shook her head, not letting me pass. "What?" I said.

She grabbed my arm tightly. I could practically feel the bruise forming. "You'll only make it worse on him . . . on *both* of them. Maybe not today, but later." I saw her point. Ryan was definitely not one to step down. Plus, this had been a long time coming. Still, I had begun playing with my hands nervously.

Cameron and Danny managed to flip John over their heads and into Fred. John's eyes widened in surprise, and Phoebe and I clamped hands with satisfaction and worry. I broke away from her just in time to see Ryan's fist connect with Cameron's nose in a not-so-satisfying crack. My whole body twitched, seeing him in pain. Cameron shouted and reached for his nose. At that very instant, Ryan's other fist collided with Cameron's eye.

Cameron definitely looked worse than Ryan, who, so far, only had a cut underneath his eye. Ryan smiled triumphantly as he got in yet another blow to Cameron's lips. Unable to control myself, I ran in their direction. Patricia stepped right in front of me. "I'm so sorry about Ryan. He's a real athlete. People should think twice before trying to mess with him," she said, sardonically.

I didn't dignify her comment with a response. Cameron finally gave Ryan a swift uppercut. "Whatever," I said.

"No, honestly. Men can be such pigs." She twirled around in a way that left her beside me, not in front. "Poor Cameron. Maybe I can nurse him back to health . . ." she wistfully suggested. Cameron landed another hard punch to Ryan's side, sending him down. "And don't worry. Maybe Danny will be put out of his misery. He's been clinging to the top rung of the ladder for too long now. I don't think Mommy Mardox can get him out of this one."

"What is your *problem*, Patricia? Danny has been nothing but nice to you and you're really gonna try and drag him down right now?"

Something flashed in her eyes, but she quickly shook her blonde hair off her shoulders and put her hands on her hips. "Oh please. Danny *never* cared about me, so why should I care about him? It's all politics, sweetie, and truth be told he's failing miserably. Soon he'll be another has-been like your dead friend B—"

My fist collided with her jaw—quite nicely, I might add—before I even registered what I had done. She backed away in horror with her hand clutching her face. Her friends began coddling her as I turned my attention back to the fight. Alex, who had appeared out of nowhere, had Fred sitting down, looking worse for wear. Alex's brown-green eyes glimmered as they caught mine, but quickly turned back to his prisoner. He certainly became one of us that night. Phoebe was pulling Danny off of John.

"Damn!" I heard Ryan bellow. My attention shifted to where Cameron held Ryan on the ground. His hand was wrapped around Ryan's collar and he gave him one final punch causing Ryan's head to collide with the concrete.

Cameron stood up straight glaring down at him. "Don't you dare bother us again," Cameron demanded, panting. Ryan woozily stood up. Holding his head in his hand, he took a wobbling step forward.

My group gathered together as he spit out blood. Patricia rushed to Ryan and began babying him but he shrugged her off. "You'll regret this. You all will." His gaze locked on Danny and he pointed at him. "I don't care how much pull your family has or how many people you know. You're a *freak*. You're *nothing*." Cameron leapt after him but I managed to pull him back.

With that, their group left us to our own devices. I looked at my best friend. He was staring at his own hands periodically opening and closing them. For having been in a fight he looked surprisingly okay. His bowtie had been ripped and his lip was cut, but I couldn't find any other major injuries.

Alex was patting Cameron on the back, who was eyeing me carefully, but I couldn't focus on him in that moment. "Danny," I asked walking over to him. After a moment, he looked up at me with tears in his eyes. "Are you okay?"

"Yeah, yeah, I'm fine." He hiccupped as a tear rolled down his cheek.

"Oh, Danny." I wrapped him in a hug. Our original group closed in and comforted him as he sobbed. After a minute or so he gently excused himself from our cluster. Phoebe, who had stood awkwardly off to the side, gave him a quick hug. "Are you going to be okay?" I asked him.

He nodded and gave me a broken smile. "Yeah! You know me. Besides, I wanted to hang out with Phoebe a bit more tonight."

"You did amazingly, Danny," she said with a smile. Her hand rubbed circles around his back. "I mean, you had two guys at once." She shook her head. "That was insane. And, sure, Alex helped but I'm sure you could have done it by yourself." She kissed Danny's reddening cheeks. "I mean, look. You only have one cut."

"Thanks," he said softly before turning to Cameron. "Now *you* were awesome. You took every punch like a man. And, I mean, wow. You beat the hell out of him. Thank you. I needed to stand up to them for once in my life . . ." He brushed his hair back into place.

"What are friends for?" Cameron said giving him a fist bump.

Cameron rubbed the back of his neck but winced at the movement. "Hey, are you okay?" I asked him.

He stretched slightly and nodded. In a sharp movement, I watched as he twisted his nose to the left. I heard a sickening crunch. He moaned as I cringed. "Yeah. Now I am." Blood poured out of his nose and I could almost see his black eye forming.

Alex put out his hand to Cameron, who shook it and gave him a pat on the back. "Thanks, Greene. You're alright."

"No problem."

Christina was examining the three boys with reproach. *Just because you have a visceral response to violence doesn't mean you can look in disdain at your friends,* I thought bitterly and resisted scowling at her. "Um, wow, Cameron. You need . . . medical attention," Tiffany said glancing around his face.

Out of the three of them, Cameron looked the worst. Before he could protest, I spoke. "Well, I'm glad that's over with." I clasped my hands together and turned to Danny. "Do you promise you'll be okay with Phoebe? Cause I'm here to talk about what happened?"

"Seriously, I don't wanna mess up this party. We can talk another time." He gave me a pointed look and snuck back into the dance with Phoebe.

"Thanks, Alex."

He gave me a smile. "Y'all want to go to Maximum's?" Tiffany and Christina nodded. He looked at me expectantly.

"Let me try and fix him up and then we'll probably come." The girls both gave us one final look before they headed to their cars. Finally, I faced Cameron who was wincing as he continued to touch his nose. I knocked his hand away. "You look awful."

He exhaled. "I'm not even in pain." At that moment, a big rush of blood escaped his nose and hit the ground.

I shook my head. "There is no need for overt masculinity."

"No," he said, dragging the word out. "I'm not being overly masculine, because I *am* fine."

"Come on," I commanded. Looking left to right, I commenced sneaking back into the high school. "You're hurt."

He tried to justify his defiance. "No, I'm bleeding. There is a difference."

"Please." I kept dragging him down the corridor. The nurse's station was not far. His hand was rough and warm in mine. We made another right and reached the nurse's office on the left. Luckily, it was empty and unlocked. We turned the lights on.

Cameron hopped onto the patient's bed like a little kid. He swung his legs and watched as I searched for gauze and such. "Really, Casey?"

"*Really*," I countered, pulling out the rubbing alcohol. I turned back to him and flinched, truly realizing the damage. His eye was growing red and purple, his lip was split and bleeding, his nose had bright blood flowing from it, and his shirt was ripped, showing a small cut. He demurred. "Stop. You should be glad there's someone to help." I poured a small amount of alcohol on a pus-yellow rag. Gently, I wiped clean the blood. "Did you realign your nose?"

He laughed softly. "Yeah, I did." I nodded and examined it. It looked fine, but I wasn't a doctor. I pulled away and ripped open some Band-Aids. After cleaning the cut on his neck, I put a small one on it. "If only it was Scooby-Doo," he said, laughter in his eyes. I rolled *my* eyes and looked back at him. Taking care not to hurt him, I positioned his head so that I could see his black eye close up. It was pretty big and looked bad, but really all I could do was put ice on it. Realizing that there was no ice in the office, and that the cafeteria was closed, I stepped back to examine him once more. It looked like I hadn't done anything. I sighed and wiped my hands against each other. "Thanks for being my nurse. It doesn't even hurt anymore," he said, touching his cut lip.

I focused on his eye. "I thought you were 'just bleeding.'"

He made a small chuckle sound. "Yeah, you're right." He swung his legs again. Seemingly absentmindedly, he began rotating his leather bracelet. "You're pretty good at this whole nursing thing."

I shrugged. "I bandaged up my sister and I whenever we got hurt. Plus she's brought home so many wounded animals that I found it was better to be prepared." Looking around the room, I found a bandage for the cut under his shirt. Content that I had done all I could do, I leaned my back against the bed so that we were beside each other but examining the room. Taking a deep breath, I leaned my head back, so I was facing the ceiling.

Cameron's head turned toward me with a pensive look. "What do you think of everything that happened?"

I closed my eyes. "I think it was stupid, but inevitable?" Opening my eyes, I threw my head forward and pushed off the bed. I spun around. "I can't believe Ryan, and then Patricia. It's all so stupid." I ran my hands down my front.

"Fair enough." He tapped on the plastic frame. "Sorry we had to leave so early." I scrunched up my lips and shrugged. "Hey," he pushed himself off the bed and walked over to me, "what's wrong?"

"It was just a sucky way to end the evening and so early too. I didn't even do anything." *I didn't get to dance or eat crappy food or . . .* I looked up at him. "I'm just glad y'all are okay."

He grabbed my hand and squeezed. My heart unwillingly leapt forward. "I'll help make up for this evening one day. Maybe we can even dance sometime?" He held up our hands but winced.

I couldn't help but laugh at his cute notion. "I'd like that but for now I think you need to rest." I wrapped a cautious arm around his waist, and we walked out of the school and into the night.

CHAPTER FOURTEEN

painless

I woke up with a smile on my lips. It was astonishing, that after all that had happened, happiness was the most prominent emotion. Stretching my back, I looked at my phone to see Danny's response to all of my texts after the dance. According to my phone, he really was feeling better. Still, I decided to get up and go check on him.

I quickly changed into some real clothes and literally ran into Christina. "Woah, sorry, Chris."

She smiled at me and rubbed her sleepy eyes. "No problem." She yawned. "I wasn't exactly paying attention."

"How was Maximum's last night? Sorry we didn't stop by."

"No problem. It was fun though. Alex is awesome." She yawned again and shook her head. "Is Danny and Cameron okay?"

"Cameron is fine but I'm actually going to Danny right now. Do you want to come with?"

She shook her head. "Nah, but thanks. Tell him I hope he's okay."

I gave her a wave as she walked toward the kitchen and I walked out the door.

The crisp December air reprimanded me for lack of a big winter coat, but I refused to go back inside to get one. My bike was rusting on its side and I wondered how much longer it would last. *Hopefully till I get to Danny's,* I thought as I kicked off and down the road. Strong winds pushed me around as I wondered about him. Sure, he had seemed fine yesterday, but it was obviously a big problem. I just hoped we would have a good talk. In my pocket, my phone buzzed.

As I turned on to the road leading to the Waterford, a cold breeze nudged me to a different place. I blinked several times to try and focus on the road, but it was no use. My body tumbled off of the bike and into the grass as I realized who I was looking at—Danny.

His screams filled my ears as I watched him run from the killer. The masked killer was hot on his heels, but Danny was doing his best. Danny looked back and almost tripped as he scrambled to gain speed.

Wrenching myself away, I picked up my bike and raced to the woods. The rough handle bars pinched at my now raw palms. Thanking God that I was already close to Dellinger, I tried to force myself back into Danny but it wasn't working. It was almost as if I was blocking the vision somehow. By the time I reached the entrance, the vision of Danny had reentered my mind.

Off in the deep part of the woods I watched as Danny hid behind a tree. He was breathing hard but kept his hand over his mouth. I pedaled faster than I thought possible, considering I was mostly blind. I shook off the vision and, realizing I was going the right way, allowed it to rein me back in. "Danny!" I screamed. *What will I do if he dies? If I see him die?*

My luck had finally run out as my bike hit a rock and sent me spiraling to the ground. Pain from my already injured palms momentarily blacked out my vision of the world. A heavy surge of rage fueled me back on my feet. In my mind, I watched as the killer walked in front of

Danny. As they had what must have been the deadliest staring contest, the killer twirled the knife in his hand. "Run!" I screamed, unsure if he could hear me.

Killing my best friend would be too much. I would never survive it. Trees flew past me in a blur. Everything seemed to come to a pinpoint, then fade into the blur. My brain couldn't process anything other than where I had seen the killer. Rocks and roots threatened my every step, but I couldn't stop moving forward. All the trees blended into a sea of green and brown, keeping me from knowing where Danny was. I listened to every sound over the beating of my heart. My nostrils flared as if I could smell him.

"Someone help me!" Danny's voice ran through me like a train as I tripped over a root.

"Danny!" I screamed back. My feet picked back up in his direction. "Danny, where are you?"

Though I thought I had gotten close to him I found that his voice was far away. "Someone, please!" He screamed again. In my vision I couldn't see the killer anymore but that didn't mean Danny was safe. He turned around in a circle and I saw a large cut in his shoulder. I ran faster.

"Danny!" My voice echoed back at me, but I don't think he could hear me. I bounced off of a tree with coarse bark scraping against my sweater.

Somewhere deeper into the woods and to my left, I heard Danny continue to scream for help, but it sounded wordless. Taking an abrupt turn, I ran in his direction regardless. My breath was coming in short gasps, and I couldn't feel my frozen hands anymore. I stopped and screamed at the woods. "You asshole!" No response. I whispered to the ground. "Danny . . . where are you, Danny?"

Behind me, a branch snapped. I swiveled, just in time to see a black mass that charged at me—and shoved a knife right through my heart.

—

Dying wasn't painless, but it wasn't filled with pain either. I watched as my mother wrapped Christina and me in a blanket. I saw my dad's hand resting on her back. I saw Christina smiling as she opened her hand. In it rested a beautiful locket she got me for Christmas. I heard Danny's laugh as he danced with Cameron. I saw Beatrix bragging to all of us that she got the lead in the school play. Danny, Beatrix, Christina, Tiffany and I all hugging. I felt Cameron's soft kiss. All of my fondest memories lifted me into a world I wanted to inhabit.

Then a weight, as heavy as lead, rested on my shoulders. It was my parents shouting. I saw my dad dying again, then Beatrix. I examined myself, so alone and without anyone. Even with my friends right beside me. The reluctance with Cameron. That one time Danny and I cussed each other out. Fights with my sister. It was all there. My mind reeled, and suddenly fear struck my core as I realized I was about to see my biggest regret. Now I understood the fear of death everyone else had. It was then I gathered that I could never do what I always wanted. My biggest regret: deciding to shut everyone out that fateful night when I was seven.

I screamed, but I had no voice. I resisted, but I had no will. Something dark blanketed me. My darkest memory was coming. If I had a body, I would have braced myself. Death's grip had me finished . . .

—

"Breathe, dammit," I heard a breathy voice say. My mind fast-forwarded into motion. Three fast gasps erupted through me, and suddenly I could see again. Christina's blue eyes filled my vision.

"Christina?" My voice was healthy and normal. I shot upward and nearly knocked into her.

"Be careful, Casey," Christina warned. I blinked once at her voice. My hand clutched my chest. It had healed, but as I looked down I found that a scar remained.

"I died," I said. "I died!" Clenching my eyes closed, bracing myself, I opened them and looked down. Blood covered my shirt. Instantly, I looked back at Christina. Something in her had changed. She seemed to glow with life, but her eyes had dimmed. "What's going on?"

"Are you okay?" Christina asked, avoiding my question.

I was dumbstruck. Her voice was a razor of reality, but I still couldn't focus on that right away. "Danny!" I gasped and tried to run.

Christina stopped me. "Danny's not here. We have to go!" There was a small jingle from Christina's pocket. Whipping out her phone, she brought it up to her ear. "Oh, thank goodness it's you! Yes, I've got her." Listening intently to the person on the phone, she turned to me and mouthed, "Are you okay?" Her face was shockingly calm.

"Um . . . yes?" I felt fine. Well, at least my body did. I scanned the woods, looking for the killer. I knew I had died by his hand. I wanted him dead.

"Yes, I heard from Danny a bit ago. It was brief but he's okay." I felt every atom of my body collapse with relief. I must have looked like I was going to actually collapse because Christina rushed over to support me with her arm. "Where are you?" Christina proceeded to drag me toward God knows where.

"Where are we going? What's going on? How am I alive?!" My voice wavered in pitch. *I don't like this. I was just dead. My whole life had flashed behind my eyes. All of my memories were a slideshow. It was just like every other death I've experienced.*

A fierce expression marked Christina's features as she put a finger in front of her mouth in a shushing motion. "I'll explain later," she mouthed once more, noting the depth of my panic. "Where do you want to meet? Cameron? Cameron? What do you mean hold on? Who?" *Cameron,* my panicked mind questioned as Christina listened to whatever he was saying. "Where are you now?" Christina's eyes got extremely big and she forced us into a sprint. "Cameron?!"

I could see our sad Escort parked at the entrance of the park. Ending the phone call, she looked at me and I saw a thousand emotions flicker across her face. "Cameron is in trouble. We're supposed to meet him outside the county. The detectives found the tape you hid." Briefly I remembered my stupid plan with Alex to hide it and I almost vomited in fear. "He called to see if I found you . . . he was close to the bridge . . . where Daddy died . . ." My heart has never dropped that fast. "The phone cut off. We need to go *NOW.*"

CHAPTER FIFTEEN

breathe

"I don't understand!" I yelled at her, throwing myself into our Escort, which was parked by the pond. *What are you talking about, Christina? What just happened? What is going on with Cameron? What is going on with* you? *AND WHY WAS DANNY IN THE WOODS? I'm going to kill him myself!* That last thought settled uneasily near the spot where I had been stabbed. I didn't voice any of those questions as Christina forced the car into reverse, digging up earth with the tires. "How am I alive?"

"Okay, I know you just died, but let's start from the beginning." It normally stunned me when she talked but this time was different. It was still relatively breathy, something I was told was common with her disorder, but there was a strength unlike anything I had ever heard. I looked at her in wonder.

Her hands gripped the steering wheel firmly. Her eyes never left the road during her spiel. "About five minutes after you left, the detectives arrived. I tried texting you but when I didn't get a response they announced they had a search warrant. I don't know what possessed you to hide the security tape but they found it in minutes. Momma was furious and went with them to the police station. Something about watching the tape on their equipment and *arresting you.* Even though I knew you were going to Danny's I couldn't get him on the phone so I headed to Waterford. When he finally called me to tell me that he had been chased and that he thought he had heard your voice I almost crashed the car. I went immediately to Dellinger and searched for you. It didn't really take long but I kept texting Danny and then Cameron for help. We're all terrified! You might get arrested and Danny was almost killed!"

I leaned back against the seat unable to process what she was saying. They found the tape, the tape I hid, and now I was going to go to jail. That was a felony charge. My scholarship seemed to flutter out of my fingertips. I put my head between my legs and tried to focus my breathing. Christina almost ran off the road as she shook me. I snapped up and gripped her thigh. "What happened with Cameron?"

Christina drew in a jittery breath. "He was heading to Dad's bridge, and out of nowhere I heard him yell 'Holy crap,' and there was this sound of a car hitting him and . . . the phone cut off." My eyes pierced her soul. Her eyes pierced mine back before she flicked them back to the road. "Before he was cut off, he said a guy wearing a ski mask was right up on him and kept hitting his bumper."

Oh my God, the killer's after Cameron! That's when I saw it. Another episode gripped me and wouldn't let go. I felt fear rip through Cameron's mind as his car made its way to the southernmost bridge in Cartersville, which crosses the Etowah River. *No, no, no,* I repeated over and over again. He wasn't going to die like my father.

Why am I just getting this vision? I wondered if my death was causing me to play catch up with everything that was happening. "Christina, drive faster!" I tried to pull myself out of the episode while remaining inside Cameron's head. I gripped the dashboard in front of me. One second it was Cameron, the next Christina. "Chris, we have to reach him! Cameron, wait for me!" I urged both of them, feeling Cameron's terror and Christina's determination. I briefly wondered why I had been able to focus when it was Danny.

My vision flickered back to Cameron. His car hit the cement guard-rail and flipped right over it, falling into the river with the same jarring impact as my father ten years ago. His head hit the wheel, reopening wounds from the dance. After the impact, the car teetered and began to sink. He looked around, panic rising with the water, first at his feet, then his shins, then his knees. *NO!* I was beside Christina again, who spotted broken glass. "There's the wreck!"

I leapt from our car when she pulled over and grabbed a tire iron from the trunk. "Meet me at the riverbank!" I took off running to the railing and leapt into the freezing, unknown depths of the current below. The frozen water locked me into place, and the tire iron dragged me down quickly. Cameron looked up through the car's windshield. The water rushed into every crevice as he took in a final breath. I could see his pleading and fearful eyes as he struggled to keep consciousness, his body unable to fight for lack of oxygen. Adrenaline coursing through me at his death, I used all of the strength I had to slam the tire iron into the windshield over and over until it cracked and caved. I grabbed a lifeless Cameron and swam us towards the river's surface.

That was when the memories started. I saw his first day at school, him meeting Danny, our first and only kiss, and his mom saying she had saved up a lot of money. *No!* I kicked harder and harder until I burst out of the water with a heaving gasp. I saw a moment with his mother in perfect clarity when she leaned over as he cut out Christmas sugar cookies. *Not the regrets,* I implored, verging on hysteria. *I can't lose you too, Cameron.*

I reached the riverbank and dragged him into the weeds. I furiously pumped his chest to no avail. The regrets burst through him. "No, no, no," I pleaded, not knowing what else to do.

A regret flashed where his mother found him cutting. He regretted not avenging his mother. I felt all of his pain flooding me and I knew his biggest regret was coming. Then, like a meteor, it hit me. Cameron watching his mother being killed by his own father. His biggest regret tore through me in terror. *"Help me put her to bed,"* his dad said, as a rush of darkness stole Cameron away from me.

I clutched him and sobbed. I lost him. I would never get him back. I would never see his smile again, look at his caramel eyes, and hear his laugh. Cameron was dead. I looked at his wet face and cursed every higher being I could think of. "I've only just met you."

"Casey?" Christina whispered. "Move."

"No." I hugged him tighter and resumed CPR.

"Move, Casey, let me see him!" Her voice was strong and clear, despite her lack of using it.

I couldn't stop staring at his lifeless body but her gentle hands made mine release him.

"Trust me," she said. She knelt beside him and put her hand on his heart. Leaning down close to his face, she conjured a miracle. "Breathe . . ." she demanded softly. A small breath escaped her and fell into his lungs.

"Christina?" I murmured. "What are you doing?" Cameron's chest began to rise. I moved in closer and saw his eyes flutter open. He choked, gurgling out brown water from the river. I felt another hysterical release of laughter escape me. I leaned in close. "Cameron!" He kept choking and vomiting. I pulled him into a hug that was too tight, but I didn't care.

Christina fell onto her back, looking up at the sky. Cameron eventually regained his senses and breathed with ease. We looked at Christina, *us* now speechless. She took a few deep breaths and closed her eyes, the color returning to her pale face. Intertwined and shivering, we studied my sister, who had claimed the role of leader. Sirens wailed in the distance. She regained her calm and turned to us with another order. "We have to get out of here."

PART II
MORTEM MOBO

the not so great escape

Cameron was on his feet before I could speak. "Christina's right, Casey. I know you have questions . . ." Cameron eyed both of us, steadying his breath. "I do too . . . but right now, we need to get somewhere else." My surprisingly confident sister and recently risen-from-the-dead friend were standing next to a bridge where a car crash just occurred. I had died just minutes ago but was miraculously alive with no wounds. And to top that off . . . my best friend was sort of missing in action and the cops were after me. Sounds about right.

"Okay, let's go." At once, we climbed the bank and clambered into our car, Cameron behind me, Christina beside me. My brain shot into motion. I gripped the wheel, took a deep breath, and made a very illegal U-turn. "We have to try and get Danny." The air in the car was stuffy and filled with unasked questions. Protests began to interrupt but I raised a hand. "I need to see him. I know you've heard from him, Chris, but . . ." the rest of my words were choked off. I gripped the steering wheel tighter.

Out of the corner of my eye I saw Christina nod once. "Last I heard he was on his way home. But if his mom is there then we're screwed.

She probably called the air force."

I groaned at her truth. Danny's mom was a force to be reckoned with and I was powerless against it. "He's hurt." The car swerved as my hysteria rose.

"Casey! Maybe I should drive." I barely heard Cameron's plea as I sped toward Danny's house.

"No, no, I got it." I let out a deep breath. "His back was cut by the killer."

"Then the cops probably are there. Casey, we can't go there," Christina said.

"We have to," I said through gritted teeth.

"It's gonna be really difficult," she pressed.

"Then get him on the freaking phone!" I screamed.

Cameron's hand landed heavily on my shoulder. "We need you to get to Waterford without killing us so please calm down." I glanced in my rearview mirror so that I could see him.

"I'll call him again." Christina frantically fiddled with her phone.

"Okay, so . . . Let me get this straight." Cameron spun his bracelet. "You went to save Danny in the park because he was being attacked. You didn't save him, but you did find him, right? How did you get to Christina and why didn't you guys go to his house?"

My gut flipped over as I glanced at my sister. She shook her head ever so slightly. "Christina found me, but we never found Danny. I have no idea if he's okay, so that's what we're going to find out."

We rode in silence until we had reached Danny's posh neighborhood. I stroked the steering wheel as I turned down the streets. "Christina, thank you for saving me," Cameron said.

"She saved me, too—"

"You're welcome!" Christina interrupted me quickly. At my

raised eyebrows and Cameron's confusion, she replied, "I mean, we're both saving her from jail, right?" I looked down at my dark t-shirt. The brown water and mud had washed away any evidence of my blood. It didn't take a genius to figure out that Christina wanted her saving my life to be a secret. The question was, *why?*

"Yes. Thank you," I played along, feeling guilty at keeping a secret from Cameron, but if it meant pleasing my seemingly cursed twin, I guess there was justification, at least until she told me why.

"Oh dear," Christina murmured. Danny's house had four ominously perched patrol cars on his curb, guarding Chief Arnold's SUV. "Casey, the chief of freaking police is here."

"I freaking know, Christina." I gritted my teeth and continued driving past his house. "I'm not doing anything till I see him and know he's okay."

"Obviously he's okay, Casey," Cameron said, putting his hand on my shoulder. "There are cops at his house."

I shook my head. "That doesn't mean something worse didn't happen."

Christina's phone dinged. "He's okay! His mom had his phone."

"Thank you, Lord," I whispered, turning the car around in a cul-de-sac.

Christina kept texting and the phone kept dinging. "He will meet us near the pool house."

"Yes. Thank you," I kept repeating while heading to the neighborhood pool house. The three of us ducked down for five minutes as cars passed by. I was finally able to exhale in relief when I saw him reach the parking lot. Sure enough, Danny presented a dashing smile when he dove into the backseat. "Danny!" I exclaimed, jumping against my seat belt so that I could turn around to see him better. *You have to unlock it, smart one.* I untangled myself and awkwardly squeezed him from the front seat. "You're really okay!" He winced from where my hug had affected his dance wounds. It seemed like the wound from the killer was barely a scratch.

"Yep!" he squeaked, releasing himself from my vise. "Are *you?* Why aren't you answering your phone? Why are y'all wet?!" His navy eyes tried to compute.

"I'm perfectly fine," I said.

"My car's at the bottom of the river. A man in a ski mask flipped it over a bridge," Cameron offered. "I died and Christina saved my life."

Danny shook dramatically with speechlessness.

Christina cleared her throat.

"What?" I asked at her tension.

"The detectives. And cops," Christina sputtered. My face shifted, and I observed Danny, who was now shaking even more. "We have to get out of Cartersville. The cops are after Casey."

"Why . . . what . . . WHAT DO YOU MEAN THEY'RE AFTER HER?"

Cameron nodded in agreement. "Look, we gotta go, man. We'll explain later. Glad you're okay."

"ARE YOU KIDDING ME?!" Danny scoffed. "There is no way in *hell* y'all are going anywhere without me. I had to freaking climb out of my second story bedroom—realize I said *second story*—pass by the cops who had moved on to questioning my hysterical mother, and make sure she didn't see me, because since I got in a fight last night and just told her I was attacked by a serial killer, I was lucky to go to the *bathroom* alone, let alone my bedroom! Was that you calling me in the woods? *I'VE BEEN FREAKING OUT, CASEY!"*

"Yes, but I couldn't find you," I explained.

"That's how I got away! Did you see the killer—"

"No!" Christina interrupted again.

I gave my sister an impatient glance. "The cops are looking for me, probably to *crucify* me." His brows knitted in confusion. "I kinda, sorta, hid some evidence a few months ago." He fell back against the seat.

"O-M-G." He hit the back of my seat. "What the actual hell, Casey?"

I flinched at his words even though they were valid. "I don't know what to do but I know I'm in a *lot* of trouble." He got the message loud and clear. "Anyway, you got away and Christina picked me up." I looked at my sister for approval. "And yes, the killer also flipped Cameron over a bridge just now and Christina saved his life. So, there's that."

"Okay, whatever. Everybody's alive, let's just go. *NOW.*"

I rubbed my hands together. Briefly, I noted that my palms were free of their earlier injuries. "Danny, you should stay here to report what's happened. Aren't they taking you to the hospital?"

"I can't go back there now! Mom's gonna freak when she hears all this! Beatrix! Alex! Cameron! *Me!* Why is he after us?"

"*We don't know!*" Cameron, Christina, and I said in unison.

Danny was beside himself. "Why did you hide evidence, Casey? *What* evidence?" I couldn't answer. "Just go. We have to get you out of here and then . . . I don't know. Cameron and I will come back and tell everybody what happened. I don't need a hospital." Danny ignored my guilty eyes and produced his shiny Amex card. "But *you're* gonna need a place to stay?"

For a moment, everything felt okay. That was, until more police sirens swelled in the distance. We clasped our seatbelts quickly. "You do know how much I love you. Right, Danny?"

"You save me, I save you." He winked as we bolted out of the Waterford, passing several police cars, including one that I swear belonged to Tal and Mary. I didn't breathe until we got on the highway.

hostile hotel

"I'm going to need to see some ID," the clerk said. It was a dump, far from any hospital or nursing home for my added comfort. I couldn't say I blamed her annoyed tone. Here were four teenagers, only one with an ID claiming he was twenty-one. She was probably suspecting we would be doing more than sleeping, since there were two boys and two girls. On top of *that*, Cameron had a black eye, a piece of tape on his nose from the dance fight, and was still bleeding from the crash. Yet we both had on brand new clothes purchased from Target in a haze. We were a ragtag, *charming* bunch.

"Of course you can. You know, I get that *all* the time and it just baffles me. I mean, I must look twenty-one. Why do people mistake me for seventeen?" Danny rambled on nervously. For someone as smart as Danny, you would think he would know when to be quiet. I gave him a death glare to help.

The girl squinted her eyes. "Uh-huh. And why do you really want the room?"

"Oh. Um . . . well, you know, it's not like it's for something *illegal* or anything—" he huffed.

With a "whatever," the girl handed Danny's shaking hand the room key. It was just our luck that she didn't seem to care too much about her job. Or maybe it was because of Danny's Amex card. Needless to say, we entered the elevator in the clear. "I think I did okay," Danny boasted as we shook our heads at him.

For a second, I imagined we were completely normal teenagers. Our only worries: Danny getting his fake license taken, not escaping the cops, and the psychotic killer out to get us. Our biggest event: Having an unsupervised blast with two supernatural twins.

"Thank you, Danny." I kissed my best friend on the cheek.

"Are you kidding? Of course! My parents always say 'for emergencies only,' and . . . well, this definitely applies. Plus, they're not on the account, so they won't know where we are." His lighthearted voice fell flat with his words. We all knew that this emergency was deadly.

We walked to our room, punched in the key card, and opened the door. Inside was a large bedroom with two beds. A couch sat in the living area that I assumed folded into a bed as well. There was a coffee maker on a long table, complete with cheap accompaniments. I headed immediately toward it. Tonight definitely constituted coffee.

We headed for the bedroom and, with a bit of effort, all managed to squeeze onto one of the beds after throwing Target bags of new clothes, snacks, and whatnot by the wall. Cameron sat crisscross in front of me, Christina outstretched by my side, and Danny sprawled at the very edge, his lanky body hanging off the sides. There was a long moment of silence as we relished being safe and hidden. The past three hours had concluded, and we hadn't even debriefed. "So . . ." I began. "What exactly happened with you, Danny?" *Might as well start with the easiest thing first.*

In a dither, yet brave-faced, he began his speech. "The killer, who I will now call 'K' because Bartow Slasher is too good of a name for him and to keep from taking too long, obviously found me while I was walking by the woods."

"Why would you do that? Don't you remember the police telling us not to go into the woods?" Christina scolded.

He exhaled for a few moments. "Look, I know it was incredibly stupid of me. And I yelled at *Casey* for being in the woods alone. But after the dance . . ." He looked down for a minute before he continued. "I wanted to talk to Beatrix about the fight and what Ryan had said." I opened my mouth but stopped when I saw him shaking his head. "I know I shouldn't care about what Ryan said, but I still wanted to share with her the beautiful night we all had and how much I wish she had been there. I wanted to visit where she died instead of her grave, because that was the last place she was alive. The last place she could have been able to hear the story." He shrugged sadly.

"Danny, you can't do that in this kind of situation," Christiana retaliated. "You could have been killed."

"I just wanted to talk to her again." I looked at my best friend and his puppy-dog eyes.

"I can't believe you did that," I said in a low voice. "But I do understand. I get a freebie to yell at you for doing something stupid next time." I was trying to get him to smile. When he finally did, it was a sad one.

Christina immediately continued with worry in her eyes and voice. "This is no time to joke, Casey! I care more about the safety—"

"I was perfectly safe! Well, until K showed up . . ." Danny interrupted.

After glowering at Danny, she continued. "I just want you safe, Danny."

"I'm safe. If you'd let me finish my story, I could describe *how* that came to be." He received no argument.

Thank you, I thought, relieved to be back on track.

"As I was *saying*, K apparently saw me standing by where she was killed and I guess started stalking me, but of course I don't really hear him. Then, for some reason, I feel the need to look backwards and there was K. So I freak out and take off running as fast as I can and, *of course,* it's in the freaking opposite direction of where my house is and everyone else. I can run fast, y'all! Did you know that? I should go out for track."

"Danny!" I gave him a look to try and refocus him.

"Sorry. Anyway, I'm flailing my arms and screaming for help." The memory resurfaced. "I see his black outfit in the corner of my eye and so I decide to feint a right, nearly missing his knife." My breathing sped. I could see Danny, so panicked, so afraid, it was all I could manage to keep still on the bed. "Of course, just when I thought I was safe I rounded a tree and found myself face to face with him. That's when he slashed me." He rotated around and pulled down his shirt to show off where he had been hit. There was a thick bandage there, which I assumed was from his mom. "But then, miracle of all miracles, I hear you answering my call. You came to save me 'cause you're *psychic*! This is so incredibly far out." He looked at me for confirmation and finally I managed to nod. "I wanted to try and find you but I was so afraid of where K was that I turned tail and ran to my house. I'm sorry I left you behind." He smiled sheepishly at me.

"No, that was smart." I reminded myself to breathe.

"All I know is I called 911 while I was running, then Christina because you weren't answering, then Mom, then she freaked, then police came, then you guys came. Oh, and now I find out you and Alex Greene hid security tapes. And here we are."

Again the room was silent. My mind raced as I tried and failed not to dwell on the past few hours. *Danny was safe because of me.* Not even in a cocky way did I think that. The killer had heard my screams and for some reason abandoned his chase. *Had he recognized my voice? What does he want from us?* My thoughts swirled around the mysterious man in black.

Danny reached over and patted my leg. "I'm glad Christina found you before K did. That would have been so horrible." He cringed with that final sentence. Trying to do it slyly, I studied my sister. *What does she want me to say?* He cocked his head and looked at me. "Speaking of . . . what happened with you and K?"

For a second, the ghost of a blade entered my body, but not wanting to raise worry, I shrugged it off. "Well after . . . I mean once . . . I tried to . . ." I trailed off as both of the boys gave me questioning looks. I tugged at the hem of my new shirt, conscious of the matching new scar beneath.

"I found her!" Christina piped up. "She was petrified." I narrowed my eyes at my twin. This lying game was twisted and dangerous.

"Well, I didn't know detectives were looking for Casey. My mom ended up calling the FBI, GBI, SWAT team. We're lucky she doesn't have the president's number. I was finally allowed some breathing room after Chief Arnold talked to me. I told them everything I knew. Including the part where I heard your voice. I'm sorry, but I didn't want you to die, Darling. I was *freaking* out. Mom wouldn't let me go back. My dad had to physically restrain me. And she took my phone. I had to steal it back."

"I'm glad you're safe." Christina and Cameron nodded in agreement.

"Stupid detectives. I don't know how we escaped through the neighborhood without being stopped," Danny said, looking at all of us with a small smirk before returning to a grim expression. "But honestly, this cut is nothing. I was so afraid, and my mother was a blustering tempest . . ." He convulsed. I poked him with my toe, since it was closest to him, to show my support.

"Don't worry, Danny. I don't blame you. None of us do." I smiled. He responded with a smile of his own and it seemed as if a weight lifted off his shoulders. At that moment, the coffee pot stopped gurgling. "Anyone want some?"

"Yes, coffee." Cameron popped up right behind me. We fixed two cups then were back on the bed. I leaned my head against the wall.

"What about you, Christina?" Cameron asked her. Her eyes widened. "I mean, what's with this magical power nobody knew about? And you're also talking a lot more than usual."

A slight blush colored her as she bit her lip. "It didn't just appear recently. I've had it as far back as I can remember." This was news to me. My powers took forever to develop, or so I thought. She squirmed beneath our stares. I reached out and put my hand on her shoulder. "One time, when I was five, I touched a dead squirrel—don't look at me like I'm crazy . . ." She froze with her lips pressed tightly tighter.

Danny cleared his throat and tried to put his best smile out for her. "Go- Go on, Christina."

"Never mind." She turned her attention to the wall.

I put my hand on her shoulder. "We want to know, Chris."

Danny's head bobbed erratically. "We really do. I'm sorry it's just a bit weird." Cameron nodded his own head.

Twisting her hair through her fingers, she continued. "I touched the squirrel and it rolled over, looked at me, and took off. I didn't really *understand* it till I was ten or so and I've been trying to figure it out ever since. Unlike Casey, I can use my power when I want. It seems like you can't control when your episodes happen or who you're around, but I can. Ever since Daddy died, since Casey talked to me about what happened, I felt broken," her voice tightened on that word, "it's been so hard to talk to any and every one." Her hands began roughly combing through her hair. "But right now, I know I have to step up and talk more so," she gulped, "I'm trying."

"Why didn't you tell me, Christina?" I whispered, flabbergasted. *How bad is it for her?* I wondered.

"You didn't tell *me*, Casey." She twisted a large strand of hair through her fingers. "Anyway, those were the years I learned how to control my power. I saved Cameron's life! That, in itself, is a miracle," she continued with relish. "Besides, I knew there was something . . . misguided . . . that you were dealing with as well." I laid my head on her shoulder. It felt like I finally understood her. "I didn't want you upset with me for having a power. I could tell whatever going on was plaguing you and that you hated it."

I shook my head hard, but everyone else had moved on. "This is fascinating, and we are *going* to talk about this, but we should figure out what the hecking heck we're gonna do about the police," Danny said.

I pinched the bridge of my nose and closed my eyes. He was right. When I opened my eyes, they were all staring at me. "What?"

Christina sighed and rubbed her temples. "You should have seen the detectives at our house— No, you should have been there. They are one hundred percent going to arrest you." I found myself trembling at her words.

What are we going to do? My head fell into my hands. Thoughts were slamming against my temples. A warm hand lightly touched my knee. "I know it sounds crazy, but we need to go to the police station," Cameron said.

Looking into his honest eyes, I knew he was right. "What if they arrest me?"

Danny said, "We'll be there to help. I think Christina may be the only one of us not in trouble though."

Cameron pointed at himself while tilting his head. "What did I do?"

"You left the scene of an accident." When no one responded, Danny continued with, "That is actually really serious."

Cameron's face dropped, and he pulled his hand away from my knee. "Dang it, you're right."

"So, we're all equally screwed?" I asked.

"Except for me," Christina said.

"Yeah, except for you," Danny said. We all stared at each other.

"So, tomorrow I'm gonna throw my life away? No graduation, no college, just a jail bird?" No one met my eyes. "I— we, we can't afford bail, guys."

Cameron leaned forward and locked eyes with me. "You will not be alone in this . . . but we need to do it. Besides, if I get arrested then we could be jail pals." He laughed halfheartedly and twisted his leather cuff.

I stared at the rotating leather. "We'll tell them that you aren't the killer at least. Maybe between my testimony and other evidence, they'll be lenient." Danny shrugged at his own words. "Speaking of which, what exactly do we know about K?"

"Yeah, any ideas on who the killer could be?" Cameron wondered, looking at me. The other two followed suit.

"How am I supposed to know?" Cameron patted my leg in comfort and Danny did the same to my foot. "I can't figure this out alone. I mean, sure, I see visions of him, but it's in a blur and he wears a mask. I'm also being bombarded with a million memories from a soon-to-be-dead person, but I can always see his eyes. Other than that, I only see a vague silhouette."

"Ugh, why do we have to have such an *annoying* K?" Danny said. He threw his arms out in front of him and plopped his head into the bedding. Barely understanding his muffled voice, he continued. "I freaking ran from the guy and can't tell you anything. What about you and Alex?"

"Alex?"

"Yes." Danny popped his head back up at my ridiculous question. "You and Alex, like, fought him off. Then you stole the tape where K can actually be seen."

I squirmed. "You can't really see anything according to Alex. The footage is apparently terrible, but who knows, maybe it would have helped the detectives." I sighed and slammed the back of my head against the wall. "I do know that his eyes are a vivid blue." I sighed in relief to have it out in the open. "The only one who even has a similar eye color is Ryan." Cameron and Danny exchanged a glance. "I mean, his dad *is* the police chief. He has access to weapons. He's very cocky and mean. The killer is kinda big like Ryan. But it's not him, guys. That would be crazy."

"Oh. My. God. It is *totally* Ryan," Danny said.

"He sure is a big enough asshole to kill someone and not even care," Cameron admitted. "And he's going after me and Danny? After last night?"

"Ryan is totally K!" Danny said.

Christina narrowed her eyes and propped up her hand in a what-do-you-mean gesture. "Is this a joke? We have no real basis. Besides, how exactly does this help Casey?"

"Maybe if we tell them about the dance."

Christina shook her head. "Y'all didn't see the detectives. They're very determined." She eyed me carefully. "I think our best bet is to tell them you're psychic."

My mouth dropped open. "You want me to tell them 'I see dead people?'"

"Don't give me that look—"

I cut her off. "I'll give you whatever look I want, because you're insane. We live in Cartersville. *Cartersville, Georgia*," I said, enunciating the syllables. "Some of us still can't believe that the North won the Civil War and think a black president was as normal as an alien! I'd be tried as a witch and burned at the stake." Christina replied by rolling her eyes.

"That's a tad much, Casey. Not everybody thinks Obama was Satan down here," Danny stated matter-of-factly. "However, I do agree with what you're getting at." He turned to Christina. "There is no way they would even consider believing her. You can certainly try," he brought his arms up in a shrug, "but we should be considering worst case scenario."

I blew a stray piece of hair out of my face. Cameron thumped the bed twice. "Tomorrow is going to suuuuck." He pressed a finger against his temple.

"No duh, dude! They thought she was suspicious before," Danny guffawed. "They probably think she's K!" Danny froze and gave me a sheepish smile when he saw my wide eyes. "But we're gonna try and fix that. Plus, the tape shows you beating up K."

"I just hope Alex isn't in a lot of trouble," I said.

"I wouldn't worry. His dad works with the District Attorney. Mrs. Greene plays tennis with my mom every Tuesday. It will all work out." Danny's jocular social existence was all encompassing. Small town politics work wonders when you have connections, and Danny seemed to have them all.

"I definitely hope so," I said. After rubbing my face with both hands, I observed our small group. "Let's go first thing in the morning."

"Fine. But we're gonna do everything we can to keep you from actually being arrested," Christina said as she grabbed my hand. "And we'll all help you find the killer. You don't have to be alone anymore." My smile wobbled at her growing one.

Danny and Cameron placed their hands on top of ours. "No one will be alone," Danny said with fortitude. "But I'm getting in the shower now." He dramatically popped up and rushed into the bathroom. I got off the bed as well.

"That's fine. The three of us can decide sleeping arrangements and then we'll shower after you." It was hard to resist my best friend's effervescent attitude, even at weird times.

"Perfect!" He opened the door and squeezed me into a hug before disappearing again into the bathroom.

I turned to my sister and Cameron. "I don't care where I sleep." Cameron's back popped as he stretched out on the bed. Christina got off and stood beside me. "Or about the shower."

"Then you should shower next," Christina directed at Cameron. "Casey and I take longer showers." Something felt off with her words. She shuffled her feet and gave me a deliberate look. "And unless y'all object, I figured Casey and I will take the fold-out couch and you and Danny could crash in here." Cameron simply shrugged and closed his eyes, already looking comfy on the bed. "Awesome. Well . . . Casey and I are gonna fix our bed."

"What's going on?" I whispered as we entered the living area. It took us a few minutes to unfold the bed. Eventually, I tried to break my twin's silence. "I'm so confused right now, Christina."

"I know, I know." She searched for the right words. "Look, I don't want them knowing I saved you." I raised an eyebrow. "I can't really explain why right now, but I want you to promise me that you won't tell them you actually died."

I chewed on my bottom lip and watched as she grabbed some extra blankets. Furrowing my brow, I considered the situation. I wanted what was best for her, but there were a lot of questions that required answers. "I need a bit more than that, Chris. They know you can heal people now, so why the secrets?"

She gave an apologetic smile. "You don't need to know . . . yet. I don't want *them* to know. You and I need to talk about it alone but we can't do it here. Please, just promise me." Her eyes met mine as we finished draping a comforter over the bed.

"Fine, I promise," I huffed. Her face of joy did little to ease my worries about the situation. *What in the world did she have to tell?*

—

Christina was the last one to shower and by the time she had begun I could already hear Danny snoring. I stared at my palm and ran my thumb over it gently. *What all can you do, Chris.* I looked up and found Cameron leaning against the doorway between his room and our make-shift bedroom. His legs were crossed, and his hair lay matted against his forehead. Feeling a bit embarrassed by the towel on my head, I leaned my head to the side and let it fall to the floor with a thud.

"Are you sure about going to the police tomorrow?" he whispered, pushing off the door and coming closer to me. I patted the bed and he sat beside me. "I mean . . ." he let out a low breath, "that's intense."

I picked up the towel and began twisting and untwisting it. "Yeah, but I mean, I gotta. I can't just run away forever." I screwed up my face. "There isn't much of a choice." I peered at him. Since he was sitting so close to me I could feel his body heat through our clothes. "What about you? You, you know, died today."

A shudder rippled through us and caused our skin to connect. "Yeah I don't know how I feel about that." He began scratching at his bracelet. "I mean, I am glad I'm alive but . . ." the scratching became more intense, "I can kind of remember that feeling. The weight of the water on my chest." My own breathing felt shallower. "I think a part of me wanted to, wanted to . . ." His droopy eyes searched mine.

The hand playing with his bracelet was shaking slightly. I put my own hand on his. "I was so afraid that you were dead forever. That I'd lost you." He looked to our hands and then back up to my face. Hand still shaking, he reached up and lightly touched my cheek. I let out a soft breath.

"Don't think about that." We were inches apart now. I looked at him through my lashes. Before anything else happened, Christina opened the bathroom door. Cameron slowly leaned away and gave me a half smile. "Night, Darling."

"Night, Cameron." I raised a hand in goodbye.

CHAPTER THREE

cars just aren't safe anymore

"Thank you for breakfast, man," Cameron said, rubbing sleep out of his eyes.

"No problem. Emergency. Remember?" Danny put up his credit card and signed the bill.

The sun streaming in from the windows was killing me. After settling into our beds, it had taken forever to fall sleep. All I could think of was the killer, and even more than that, talking to the police. Christina bounced beside me, earning a sideways glance from yours truly. I still needed to speak with her.

"You okay there?" Cameron's warm eyes met mine. "Well . . . as okay as you can be, that is."

I gave him my equivalent of a happy grimace. "Not bad, for the situation. What about you?"

"What can I say? This beats explaining to my grandmother how my car is at the bottom of the river and I ran away from home."

"At least you told her you're alive." I stretched and took a good look around the restaurant. They had decked their halls with a decent sized Christmas tree and a couple of fake pieces of holly. We still had a few days till the actual holiday. I was terrified that I'd be spending it in jail. I couldn't believe Christmas hadn't been paused after everything that had happened. It was more of a ho-ho-homicide than a jolly Santa laugh.

Danny groaned. "You think *your* situation is bad? Don't even get me started, pretty boy. My mom is friends with Chief Arnold's wife, and holy crap, that lady almost had a cow when she realized who I was friends with." Perched in a corner of the restaurant, I couldn't help but look around at his non-whispered voice. Returning my attention to our table, I poked my eggs with my fork. They were pretty good, but my stomach seemed keen on rejecting even the idea of food.

Danny pushed his back against the booth. "Okay, I know we're nervous and we gotta go talk to the police, but I really have to talk to you guys about your powers. Hello!"

Cameron offered a small nod of agreement. "Sorry, but it *is* kinda cool and you both haven't said enough about it."

I shushed them as our waiter refilled our water. "What do you want to know?" I asked.

"Anything? Everything? I mean, you told me a bit when we first discussed it but now Christina as powers too?"

I fiddled with my hands. "It's a curse," I said at the same time that Christina said, "It's a gift." We eyed each other.

"I have to watch everyone I love die. On top of that, I see people I don't even know die."

"Sounds like something you could use to help people," Christina said crossing her arms and leaning back. "Besides, we're two halves of the same coin and my powers are fantastic. Yours can't only be a 'curse.'" Her use of air quotes around the word curse made me narrow my eyes.

Danny placed his hands a little too hard on the table and looked rapidly between the two of us. "Um so," Danny bounced up and down, "How does it happen? What's it like? Why is it hard to stop it? Is it painful? Do you know what's going on in the real world during a vision? Have you met anyone else who has it? Why—"

"Danny!" Christina and I cried simultaneously. I inhaled deeply, as if I was the one who had talked for almost a solid thirty seconds without breathing. I'm not sure how it was possible, but Danny single-handedly asked the deepest and hardest questions and managed to direct them toward both of us. Cameron leaned back in his chair, a delighted smirk on his face.

Shaking my head, I answered Danny's questions in the same way he gave them to me. "Not sure, horrible and tiring, how should I know, sometimes, again sometimes, and no, not yet." When I finally stopped to take a breath I found my answers had even surprised me.

Danny looked thoughtful, but then nodded in satisfaction. "Christina?"

Christina's shoulders trembled as she readied herself. "It's all about contact and speaking. When I touched that first animal I was five. How? Well, genetics?" she questioned with a laugh. "It's not like I've really asked anyone before. As for the rest of the questions . . . they don't quite apply to me. Although I will say that it is anything *but* painful. Actually, it's amazing, like giving a part of my s—" She paused and looked at us cautiously. "It feels great."

I scoffed at her. "What if it hurts you physically, Christina? You have no ideas of the implications."

She raised an eyebrow at me haughtily. "What do *you* know, Casey? Our powers are probably connected by genetics and since *I've* never had an issue—"

"Okay, well, I watch people die. So maybe you're just being naive about your power."

Running her hands through her hair roughly, she leaned forward. "That definitely sounds awful, but maybe you can find a way to save them. It doesn't have to be bad. Actually, if I were you—"

"If you were me?" I cut her off and jabbed my fork in her direction. "If you were me, you'd feel bad and you'd be scared as hell to get close to someone, because what if they started to die? You'd see it all—"

"Stop complaining. It could be much worse." Christina matched my tone perfectly. "At least you don't have to worry about your power not working. Some animals never come back from their hits—"

"I know that hurts you, but you cannot possibly compare that to—"

"Yes I can! You have no idea how hard it can be to—"

"Guys!" Danny stopped our screaming match. The few restaurant patrons focused their eyes on us. "This is not what I meant by sharing information about your powers." He turned to my sister. "Christina, your power is really cool, like, *really cool*, but you can't seriously compare it to Casey's." She sat back in a huff and crossed her arms. "And Casey, we're here for you but try not to yell at Christina. She just doesn't understand. None of us do." He gestured to our group.

I rapped my fingernails against the booth and eyed Cameron from my peripheral vision. He was resting his chin in his hand. It surprised me that he hadn't said anything. "Okay, any other questions?" I asked.

Danny raised an eyebrow at Cameron who shook his head. "What? No questions, none?" Danny asked, furrowing his brows at Cameron's lack of curiosity.

"Nope. I just want to make sure everything about the powers situation is as okay as it can be . . . for powers." He bit into a muffin.

I sent him a sly half-smile after taking a gulp of coffee. "Okay. Any other questions can be voiced later." I leaned forward. "Is there anything else about K?"

"OH." Danny's eyes lit up as he copied my movement. "Any more ideas about him? Besides the fact that Ryan is totally K. It is a he, right? Cause K didn't feel very feminine." His eyes lit up at the use of the nickname he had christened the killer. "I mean, yeah, last night we established the blue eyes, but . . ." He shrugged.

I knew what he was thinking: *But there has to be something else.* "We are still teenagers, guys. Like you said, it's not quite up to us to find out who the killer is." Of course, that gave me three wide, disbelieving, disagreeing sets of eyes. "Okay . . . that's hypocritical of me and wrong. Obviously, this isn't going to go away any time soon." *Ha. I wish.* "I *am* currently suspect number one."

"Stop saying that, miss Debbie Downer." Christina exhaled angrily. "For all you know, they could go nuts and believe you without a single doubt. You said the tape shows you saving Alex from the killer."

"Yeah! And go punch Ryan in the face, just like we did, and lock him up forever. Score!" Danny was way too into the Ryan possibility, even though it was certainly plausible. But I chose not to point out the flaws in that theory.

"So, I'll go in, talk about what I know, *possibly* tell them how, but at least convince them I'm innocent. What should I tell them about leaving after Cameron's accident?" I wondered aloud.

"Considering the fact that my car is at the bottom of the river, they might believe an, 'oh we weren't sure what to do' situation, but it isn't probable," Cameron said shrugging. He leaned back and clasped his hands behind his head. "They're definitely throwing me in jail too." He shook his head.

Danny had another plan. "If I were you, I would *not* tell them K ran Cameron off the road. It's another situation you're connected to. Why throw in another one, right? Say . . . y'all didn't know what to do. You were following Cameron because y'all were trying to get out of town fast, right, and he lost control. Then, because he lost control, y'all started following Cameron who was afraid of dealing with his grandmother, *because he just totaled a brand new Beetle*, and wanted to get away with you. And that's that. You say all that until they actually believe you're psychic." Danny looked up at the ceiling and rhythmically tapped his hands against the table. "Nevermind. It's pretty important that K is trying to kill us all. You're right though, Cameron. I think you'll probably have to deal with leaving the scene of an accident no matter what. And, wait. Do we really know that it was K who ran you off the road?"

"He was wearing a ski mask."

"Okay, it was K." Danny noted Cameron's deadpan remark and looked at me. "Are you sure this psycho isn't Ryan for real? He's messing with us. Or messing with people connected to *you*."

Rubbing my thumb's knuckle, I gave his idea a thought. "It would certainly be nice if it was. Because then the world could be rid of two awful people." I shook my head. "There's just no way to know. Anyway, I'm not going to tell them anything about Christina's power, no matter what. The purpose of this whole thing is to get them off our backs. Not give reason to look closer. We don't want them locking us *both* up." Christina agreed with a nod.

"Okay. We have a plan." Danny was almost done with his forensic architecture. At my distress, he added, "Sorry, Casey. I just fear that we won't really be able to help you no matter what they believe. But it's the only way to explain why you have been involved."

I sighed, and spun around the saltshaker in front of me. "You're right, Danny. I wish you could." The restaurant was predominately empty, meaning it wouldn't be much longer till it was time to head home. "Let's go."

—

Screams ravaged my ears. "Casey?" The concerned voice didn't belong to anyone in that moment. Only when I felt my hand hit the car window did I realize that I still had a body. That didn't matter at that moment.

The smell of burning rubber, putrid and hot, scorched my nostrils. Screeching, twisting metal flew through the air. Massive piles of cars were scattered around like the broken glass that littered the road. To my left, a little girl lay there with a broken arm and glass protruding from her chest. I was ripped into her subconscious.

"*Mommy, I want the big one.*" The blond girl's pale skin shivered around a tiny puppy. "*Bowzer wants a piece of cake, too!*"

Her mother laughed. "*I'm sure he does, honey,*" she replied, slicing a big piece for her. "*But he'll get a special piece later.*" The little girl nodded enthusiastically as her mother loomed closer. Suddenly, I was the little girl, and her mom was smiling over me. She looked down at the cake. On top was a giant 10. Her birthday had happened a few days ago. As we devoured the cake, I used the strength I had finally gained to pull out of her.

Out, I was shocked to find that I was back at the wreckage, but not with my friends. My heart started beating faster. It was bad. Plenty of deaths. An old man dragged me into his death.

"*But, Georgia, you can't leave yet,*" he whispered to her corpse. The room held the musty, clean smell of a nursing home. The old man's soul pulsed and I felt drawn into him, but I stopped myself before I was totally sucked under. *"I didn't say goodbye."* His biggest regret concluded his death.

I gasped. There were too many people. So many fumes. Too much death. They clouded around me, vapors jamming the space around me. Death choked me and surrounded me; it was all I could do to remember *I* was alive.

"Lily, I said no!" A cute teenage boy laughed as his girlfriend danced out of his reach.

Where on earth did that guy come from? the truck driver thought just as he slammed into the bus with a sickening crunch.

One more route, the bus driver thought, loading on the last kid. *"Come on, class,"* she heard the teacher say as they piled on her bus.

Suddenly, I heard a bloodcurdling scream. It was from me, but I couldn't disconnect from the wreck. Death pounded on my skull, and somewhere in the back of my mind I felt my body flailing. I was trapped. *I'll witness all of this,* I thought, the panic allowing another death to drag me under.

"Good boy!" a skinny, freckled kid exclaimed, hugging his golden retriever.

Then he was crying:

"Mommy, look?" His arm dangled uselessly at his side.

No! I exclaimed, wrenching myself from the boy's bad memory. Playing tug of war with the ends of all these people demolished my body. I vaguely wondered what was happening back in the car.

Abruptly, five different memories of the crash bombarded me.

"HOLD ON, KIDS!" The bus driver screamed as she swerved, quick but not quick enough, to avoid the semi. *God, please help us—*

"No!" The semi driver instantly panicked as he watched the bus plunge into a ditch. *"What have I done—"*

"*Not much longer, dammit,*" the man, Dennis, said into the phone. "*Traffic tends to take a bit.*"

"*Well not that long,*" a woman replied from the other end.

"*Look, Jan, work was terrible; can we—holy crap!*" Dennis said as the semi impacted him head on.

"*Help! Please!*" two girls cried, clutching each other. I was forced into the brown-haired one's head. *Please, God, if you are out there, please protect me and Holly—*

Each version showered me with pain. They all kept coming, every death with all its memories. People laughing, crying, screaming, hugging, living, and finally dying. I couldn't feel my body; I couldn't scream. Finally, and blissfully, I fainted.

—

"Christina, please stop already! You cannot save everyone and we *have* to get your sister out of here." Danny's hysterical voice washed over me.

"I . . . I can save one more. I just—I just need time. That guy . . . just caused a crash. More can survive," Christina replied, far away and anxious. At that moment, I wanted nothing more than to comfort her, but my body wasn't allowing for any leeway in my movement. I also realized how wrong she was. All of those people were dead. Their memories no longer bombarded me; it was through fate alone that we had even managed to escape it.

"Christina, there's no use! We have to help Casey!" Cameron's voice was a sunray in the dark. I twisted towards him. "I'm right here, Darling," he said as he grabbed my hand. "Christina, come on!"

Slowly, I popped open an eyelid, which I immediately regretted. Through the back windshield, I could see plenty of the wreckage behind us. Beside me, Cameron was half in and half out of the car. The whole interstate was cluttered with burning pieces of twisted metal and black smoke. Using as much strength as I had, I managed to pull myself into a sitting position. Bracing myself, I looked out the windshield.

Christina's small frame bounced from place to place as she frantically attempted to heal people. Danny had begun to drag her hysterical figure toward the car, leaving the burning and trashed wreck behind them. Her shirt was covered in so much dirt and blood that I could barely tell it was white before. It looked like her body was convulsing.

Once in the car, Christina's sobs dissolved into quiet sniffles. Danny's hand gripped the steering wheel, but we didn't move. "Christina?" I muttered, leaning toward her. My head throbbed painfully at the small amount of movement. Memories of the awful event threatened to control me.

"Mhm-hmm," she affirmed, staring back at the scene.

"Are you gonna be okay?"

At my soft voice, she finally turned toward me. Her eyes were red and tear-filled, but at seeing my pale and shaking face, her lips curled up slightly. "Yeah. Are you?"

"Yes," I replied. Danny put my miraculously unharmed car in drive and rolled through the median. He was able to creep right onto the highway, as the wreck had blocked all moving traffic. The open road was ours. No one said anything for a very long while. I realized the phone had been yanked out of the aux cord. The silence was deadening while Danny hit the radio button. A news update blasted through the speakers at an extremely high volume. Danny quickly scrambled to turn it down.

"For those of you who just tuned in, there has been a massive pileup on I-75 Northbound involving a tractor trailer and multiple vehicles, including a school bus." All of us let out barely audible gasps. "The cause is unclear, but fatalities are imminent. Details on injuries will be reported, so stay tuned. Those traveling northbound should expect delays up to four hours. Anyone with information about the wreck should report them immediately. Now about the weather . . ."

Christina's sniffles grew again.

"Should we . . . tell?" Cameron asked, unable to finish.

After a moment I sat up straight. "Yes. Look at Christina's clothes." They were covered in blood and smoke and oil and dirt. Then a thought struck me. "What exactly did we see?"

Christina was thoughtful. "I saw . . . the cars start flipping . . . but the semi-truck was first."

"I saw that too." Danny's exuberant personality was nowhere to be found. "Something happened to it, and then all of the cars started braking. We barely survived, y'all. I had to slam on the brakes, because that car in front of the semi swerved so close to me, I had to dodge it. That's what took us into the median. Its brakes lit up, but it just kept going. Asshole! It was almost like he was *trying* to hit us. Did anyone see that?" There was a collective affirmation.

My head pounded with the previous memories. "Did you see what the person looked like?" I managed to croak out.

Danny cocked his head to the side but kept his eyes firmly fixed on the road. "Um, I was a bit more focused on the driving, so I didn't get a good glimpse." I watched as his eyes narrowed through the rearview mirror. "Why?"

"Well . . . I just think . . ." All eyes found mine. It was worse than being under a microscope in a busy science lab. My mouth dried up, but I knew it was better to voice my thought than keep it to myself. I pinched my finger and stared at the floorboard. Cameron had scooted closer to me as much as he could with the seatbelt. "That . . . could that have been the killer?" I watched their eyes grow fearfully.

"Oh. My. God." Danny gripped the wheel and breathed in and out in a calming rhythm.

"Casey. Are you sure?" Cameron examined my eyes.

"No . . . . Of course not, but it's all a bit convenient isn't it? A crash happened just as we are heading home and, Danny, you said it seemed like he was coming straight for us, right?" He nodded but didn't say anything. No one did for a few minutes.

"Why was he here?! Why did he cause that wreck?!" Christina's eyes grew wider by the second.

"Oh. My. God," was all Danny could say over and over and over.

"Why did he do that? How could he do that? Does he know where we are??" Christina's shrill voice pierced my ears.

"I don't know!" I cupped my hands over my ears. "It might not have even been him, but I'll tell the cops about it."

"I hope they can help. Or else we might end up in some serious trouble." I knew my twin was right. "Either that, or all of us are going to end up like Beatrix."

I didn't argue with her anymore. Christina reached for my hand and held it the entire way to Cartersville.

CHAPTER FOUR

yay ... interrogation time

The building was tiny and brightly (too brightly in my opinion) lit. The woman behind the counter seemed to think I was wasting valuable living space after hearing why us teenagers were there. Even though everything felt new, I found plenty of scuff marks on the door and floor.

After a few uncomfortable seconds, detectives Tal and Mary burst through the lobby door and gestured for me to go through it. I half expected them to handcuff me, but they remained stoically by the door. My friends whispered encouragements as I glided to the detectives, who took me into their custody. Mary had her usual stern look, but even Tal looked displeased. Tal pointed to Danny, Christina, and Cameron. He firmly addressed the receptionist, who was actually just another uniformed cop. "Don't let these three go *anywhere*." I meekly waved goodbye as two officers entered the lobby to oblige Detective Tal. My friends shifted in their seats as Mary closed the door behind me.

We passed through the buzz of officers talking on phones, writing, and looking at walls of maps and pictures, trying to find Cartersville's notorious serial killer. It looked like they had called in extra manpower, because the few cubicles weren't enough to accommodate everyone. Some of them eyed me as I walked by but kept about their business. Detective Tal led us down a hallway and stopped at the last room on the right. He gestured for me to go inside after opening the door.

A black gentleman in a sharp suit sat at a long conference table, looking out of place; everything about him appeared important and strong. Brown and sharp, his eyes followed me as I entered. Two white gentlemen in suits sat on either side of him, wearing FBI badges. I was so focused on the three captivating men, I didn't even notice my own mother until she turned around and stared at me. My heart sank.

"Please don't turn me over to the FBI. I'm so sorry about everything," I said, looking left to right at the two detectives beside me. "I didn't do anything, I swear, and I know everyone says that but—"

The black gentleman raised his hand with a slight chuckle, and I slammed my mouth shut. He pointed to a chair at the head of the table and addressed me in a deep voice. "You must be Casey. Why don't you sit down?" Doing as I was told, I focused on my mother. Her mouth was set in a petulant frown, which told me she had been there for a long time. When her eyes met mine, I could tell that she was dying to tell me something, but in the presence of the three men at the table, she kept her mouth shut. Tal and Mary sat down next to her.

"Okay," was all I could muster before complying.

How do I get out of this nightmare? My mother and two detectives with wary eyes sat directly across from three FBI agents, and I had just been offered a seat at the head of their table. *I am so screwed.*

Detective Tal spoke up first. "Casey, this is Agent Harling." The black man smiled and nodded his salutation. "These are agents Smith and Mulligan." The two men on either side of Harling remained stoic and watchful. "The FBI has come to aid us in the investigation and they want to sit in on this interview."

Suddenly, it seemed as if the world had sharpened, taking both my heartbeat and my breath away from me. "The FBI is really involved with this?" It was a tad hard to not gulp loudly. Mary narrowed her eyes.

Agent Harling gave another chuckle and took out a notepad from the many files before him. "Anything involving a serial killer typically attracts the FBI. No need to worry, though. We're only here for the bad guys." He gave me a wink. I instantly relaxed in the chair.

"So . . . this is just an interview?" I couldn't believe I was only to be questioned by these guys. I was more or less expecting an immediate arrest.

Mary shook her head. "It *could* have been an interview, but you've made that impossible, Casey." She shifted through some papers in front of us. "You were at two scenes of a crime before yesterday. Then, you hid evidence from one of those crimes and ran away from a third one." She shuffled the papers back together. My cheeks felt unnaturally hot. Mary leaned forward and clasped her hands in front of her. "Now, you're a minor, which is why your mom is here, but everything you've done leads to jail time." She opened her hands at me. "So, we're going to need you to cooperate."

It felt like my throat was clogged and I desperately tried to force air down it. Harling gave me the once-over and offered his opinion. "She doesn't look that capable of murder . . ." I breathed a sigh of relief. "But when you've been in the field as long as I have, you know that looks can be deceiving." *So much for that,* I groaned inwardly. My mother's leg bounced up and down rapidly as she looked around the table. After a minute, she buried her head in her hands.

"Tal and I have been very lenient with you, but that's ending. You hid evidence and then ran out of town. Do you have any idea how guilty you look? How absurd you've been?" Mary said.

I squirmed in my seat. "I haven't done anything wrong." I tried to hold out from answering questions as long as I could.

"Young lady, that is the biggest lie you've told," Mary said.

My mother sort of jumped out of her chair and wagged her finger at me. "You have done so much that's wrong! How do you know so much about what is going on? Why did you run away? Where did you go? I haven't slept all night!"

"I didn't really get much sleep last night either, Mother."

My mom ripped at her hair. "Casey, *what is wrong with you*?! Please just tell us what you know already!"

"Alright, Mrs. Darling. Let's calm down," Agent Harling said lowering his hand in front of him. Tal and Mary looked down at the table with similar scowls. *Interesting. They do not like him.* "Now, it is obvious we have questions for Casey. But it is also obvious that she wants to tell us something. Or else she wouldn't have come of her own volition. I think we should calmly figure this out."

Tal and Mary looked at each other and shared a secret conversation. I could almost feel sympathy for them, as they had had their case stolen by the FBI. The other FBI agents didn't flinch at any of this. I actually wondered if their eyelids had blinking capability. Mary leaned back in her chair and finally spoke up. "Maybe she'll listen to you, Harling." She turned her head away from me.

Closing my eyes, I focused on what I needed to tell them. "Okay . . . I came here to tell you everything you want to know. I know it looks very bad that I knew about Beatrix's murder, and that I showed up in the alley behind Maximum's when Alex was attacked, and hiding the security tape, and that I ran away last night with a group of friends." I finished vomiting the words and gazed at the detectives.

Tal shook his head. His arms were crossed. "It doesn't just look bad, Casey, it *is* bad. I don't think you understand how bad."

"I *know* it's bad."

Mary glanced back at Tal as I tried to keep my composure.

"Then why do it? Why put your life in jeopardy?" His brow furrowed as he finished his question.

Putting my head in my hands I pushed into the table. "It's complicated . . . Where do I start?"

Agent Harling cleared his throat. When I looked at him, I found him staring intently back. He stretched his palms upward. "Let's start with the lesser of two evils. Why did you run away with your friends?" Agent Harling's voice was a calm drop of water in this turmoil. Suddenly, talking became easier.

"I was scared."

"Of what?" he asked.

"That there is a serial killer in Cartersville who is attacking people I know, people I don't know, and . . . the police think I have something to do with it."

"*Do* you have something to do with it?" he asked matter-of-factly. I brushed my thumb over my knuckles.

"No. I don't. But I have . . . *information* about it," I admitted as Mary and Tal shifted in the squeaky chairs.

"And what is that information?" Harling began writing.

"Um. Well . . . I knew about Beatrix right before . . . or *as* she was being killed, because I saw it in a . . . um . . ." I looked at the cops in the room as their eyes bored into me. Unable to concentrate, I quickly closed my eyes and took a deep breath. "In a vision."

Mary scoffed and was about to interject, but Harling stopped her. "Just let her finish." I was liking this man more and more every second.

"But she's being ridiculous!" Mary said rising from her chair. "Visions, I mean." Harling shot her a look.

"I want to hear what she has to say." Mary's eyes locked on me and for a moment she said nothing. She slowly sunk back into her chair and crossed her arms. "Go on, Casey."

"A vision is the best way I can describe it." You could almost hear everyone's judging thoughts. I gulped down the excess of spit in my mouth as I revealed my darkest secret to them. "I have many of them. I have seen almost every murder that has been done and attempted by this psycho, who has apparently made Cartersville his prime hunting ground." Agent Harling nodded and leaned back in his chair, wanting to hear more. I refused to look at the detectives as my confidence grew. "They're horrible and vivid and I've had them all my life. When I was seven, I witnessed my father's death on a bridge while I was still at home. I knew that he was dead. And he was. Dead."

My mother had tears streaming out of her eyes and reached out to me. "Why didn't you ever talk to me about this after that day?"

"Because it's not exactly the best conversation in the universe, Mom." I felt bad about her tears, but I didn't quite know how to console her in this situation.

"But you should have told me more! I remember!" My mom was on the verge of hysteria.

Agent Harling reined us back in. "Mrs. Darling. If you can't control yourself, I'm going to ask you to leave. Do you understand?" My mom sat back and hid behind a wad of tissues. Harling calmly focused on me again. "So, you've had them all your life? These visions?"

"Yes."

Harling continued pulling it out of me. "Describe them."

"They're all different. I just . . . feel what the people are feeling. See their lives flash in my head. Their regrets. Their joys. It happens in a blur."

Harling looked at his fellow agents. He wrote something down on his pad, which I couldn't see. He showed it to them. They both nodded.

I spoke up again in fear that I was losing him. "I promise all of you. I had nothing to do with any of these murders. Beatrix was one of my best friends. I had a vision of her dying and knew something bad was happening to her." Tears clawed at my eyes and throat, but I pushed them away. "I ran all the way to her house in the rain. I was horrified. But she was already dead. I knew that, and I still ran to her in hope." Tal and Mary kept shaking their heads, but I continued to appeal to Harling. "I also knew that Alex was being attacked, because I had another vision. So, I ran to Maximum's back alley and he actually needed my help. I *saw* the killer in my visions and I *saw* him that night when I helped Alex. But I am not the killer and I do not know who is."

Harling looked at both men on either side of him. They gathered a few files and notepads and then left the room. My mother sat, wide-eyed, shaking. It felt so good to be released from my secret, even if they might not believe me. My fate was at a distance, currently, because the police knew. Detectives Tal and Mary were speechless.

Harling deftly kept the information flowing. I was amazed at his lack of any visible emotion. "What does he look like?"

"He wears a black ski mask and dresses in black. He has a large build, muscular, tall. But the most important thing is . . . his eyes. He has piercing blue eyes that seem to cut right through you. I don't know what his hair looks like or if he has tattoos. I don't really know anything else about him, other than he enjoys this, because of his eyes."

"Listen, kid," Tal said walking closer to me. He put one hand down on the table and used the other one to point at me. "You're in a lot of trouble and spinning tales isn't going to help you."

Mary's eyes seemed, surprisingly, filled with sympathy. "If you're honest, maybe we can help you, but this vision thing is ludicrous. If this is all true, you would have no reason to hide that tape."

"But I was afraid y'all would act like this!" I had shrunk in my chair from Tal's sudden closeness but now I pushed myself closer against the table. "I'm telling the truth, I swear!"

"I believe her." My mother looked at me with tears still clouding her eyes. "I know she is telling the truth, because I was there when she told me about her father's death! I promise! I remember."

Agent Harling's response could not have been more soothing. "It might seem ridiculous, but that doesn't mean it isn't true." Relief happily bombarded me.

"Please, I didn't kill those people. I know all of these things because of my visions." I tried one last time to appeal to Tal and Mary, but they weren't looking at me. Tal backed away and went to lean on the wall behind Mary.

"It just seems too unrealistic and then you hid the tape—" Tal began but I cut him off.

"But I've already explained why I did that. Because I was *scared*. I am *still* scared." I thought about everything I hadn't said and tried to keep it together. "There is a serial killer walking around town. You act like I am the only one who could possibly be the killer. But I'm not. You can see that clearly on the tape, right? And, I know this is also going to look bad, but my friend got into a car accident yesterday, as I'm sure he will tell you, and we didn't know what to do, so we got out of Cartersville. Christina was with me, so she went with us. I told my friend,

Danny, we were leaving, and he wanted to come with us. I was tired of being in trouble for things I didn't do. I was confused." I didn't know what else to say to convince them to ease up. Tal and Mary just looked at me in complete disbelief.

Harling kept pressing, but I didn't mind at that point. "So, is there any way you might be able to prove what you're saying is true?" He stopped and held his earpiece as if someone was communicating to him from somewhere else, but none of us could hear the information. He wrote something else down on his pad and then looked back up at me.

I said, "You mean, like, take a lie detector test?"

Harling seemed amused. "Well, yes. Polygraphs are helpful. But I wonder if there might be another way. Can you give us a description of everyone who has been killed by this man in black?"

Tal argued, "How is that going to prove she didn't do it herself or doesn't know who did? It's been all over the news."

"Maybe there are victims we haven't found," Harling stated flatly.

Mary Alden's eyes narrowed. "Well I think she needs to take the polygraph. It might get the real truth out of her."

I closed my eyes tightly before turning to Harling and his questions. "Yes. I can give you a description of everyone the killer has killed or tried to kill. I can also give you a description of everyone who was killed an hour ago in the accident on I-75." Agent Harling froze. For a brief moment, I saw his composure drop. "I can tell you what they were thinking, what they regretted, and what they loved most about their lives. And I have never met a single one of them."

Agent Harling looked deep into my eyes and I thought I saw a hint of sympathy in his. He then wrote something down on his notepad and stood up. "Excuse me for a moment." He left the room. I stewed in the presence of Tal and Mary, who couldn't believe me, and my own mother, who almost appeared dizzy from the twenty-four-hour whirlwind she had just endured. We all sat there in silence for a while until Mary spoke up.

"Casey," she said in an almost whisper. "You may be in a lot of trouble, but lying isn't going to help."

I squashed my hands together. "I don't know how else to tell you that this is the truth."

Tal added, "I used to think you might be a good kid . . . but you're turning into a real piece of work, Casey Darling." My cheeks burned in defiance.

Agent Harling came back inside and sat down. "Okay, Smith and Mulligan have been talking to your friends out there. Apparently, there were fatalities on I-75 that all of you witnessed?" He addressed Tal and Alden. "It wasn't this jurisdiction. Emerson. By Lake Allatoona." The detectives wrote that down.

My mother interjected dramatically, "Oh my God! Were y'all hurt?"

"Do I look hurt?" I asked her.

Harling took control again. "Well, apparently your sister, Christina, tried to help some of the victims, but you decided to leave? Because it was no use?"

Detective Mary laughed. "What?"

I tried to nip this line of questioning in the bud. "I know what you're thinking. Yes. There was an accident. Danny was driving us back to Cartersville so that I could come and talk to *you*." Panic was flooding beneath me, but I continued on. "A few cars hit each other on the highway. Danny missed them and ran into the median. We saw the pileup. Well, they saw it more than I did. Around that time, I had fainted . . . from all the visions of all of the deaths. Christina got out to see if anyone needed help. It was no use and paramedics were showing up. We knew we had to get *here*, so we got back on the interstate and drove to a *police station*. We obviously weren't running away from anything and we had nothing to do with the accident. Our car wasn't even hit."

Detective Mary glanced at Tal and then back at me. "It seems a little convenient that you were indisposed. What have you gotten yourself in to? What all are you connected to?"

Tal passed a quick glare to Harling who leaned back in his chair, surveying the dismay of both detectives. "It *is* very interesting. Doesn't mean it isn't true." He studied my broken mother and then finally came back to me. "Tell you what. I want to hear more about these visions. I'd like to hear more about these people you've seen 'die.' Agent Mulligan is arranging for you to take a polygraph. That is, if, Mrs. Darling, you consent."

"I consent. She can do it. If she wants to do it." Even though my mother was finally on my side, I didn't know what to say.

"Yes. I want to."

Harling wrote something else down and said, "We have someone here who can administer one. He's been on site as needed and will be ready to go in a bit."

My mom happily said, "Bring it." Despite it sounding funny, I felt a twinge of embarrassment.

Harling didn't laugh but seemed glad things were moving along. "Sounds good. But while he is setting up, I'd like to talk to Casey alone."

"Is she going to be arrested?" my mom asked.

Harling shook his head. "For now, I want charges against Casey dismissed." As the detectives protested, Harling raised his hands. "After I talk to her and see the results of the polygraph that may change, but for now I believe her. She's young and made a mistake, albeit a really big one, but she is clearly not committing these murders and clairvoyance is not a crime." I smiled at Tal and Mary's sour faces. "Just don't hide any more evidence, or you *will* be arrested." I nodded profusely.

The detectives stood up and walked out of the room without looking back at me. My mom got up as well and looked at me. "Just don't lie, Casey. You have some explaining to do later, but right now . . . you'd better tell this man the damn truth. Do you hear me?"

"Yes, Mother. I 'hear' you."

—

The polygraph was excruciating, but not as bad as having to go over every brutal detail of the killer's activity when I spoke privately with Harling. Although he made it easy to trust him, it was difficult to recall everything. Plus, it was intimate details that I hadn't even gotten to go over with Danny and the rest of my friends that knew. Yet, I still agreed for him to record our conversation before the test. I told him about the woman at the mall . . . the Cameron look-alike . . . Beatrix . . . Danny in the woods . . . Cameron and the bridge . . . the car crash . . . all of it.

Afterwards, he thanked me. I asked him if I would be able to talk to him instead of Tal and Mary. He said it would depend on the results of the polygraph and if he could convince them to do that. Apparently, the investigation was merely using the FBI for support at that point. However, if the cases were not solved soon, the Bureau would then take over whether the CPD liked it or not. Apparently, that sometimes happened. I told him that would be nice.

He then took me to another room. A pudgy man with horn-rimmed glasses indifferently greeted me and told me to sit in a chair. The man explained the rules and circumstances of the test and how important it was for me to relax. Surprisingly, I was able to do so despite being hooked up to seemingly hundreds of wires, which could determine my entire future. What followed was an hour of me responding "yes" or "no" to a series of pretty tough questions pertaining to my life, my friends, the killer, the victims, and the killer's MO. All while three FBI agents watched impressively behind glass.

CHAPTER FIVE

parental troubles served with some healthy family problems

"Casey!" Danny exclaimed as I came back into the lobby. "Are you okay?"

The events were still unfolding, but I attempted to smile for his benefit. "Yeah, I'm fine."

I found a sad and worried Christina. "What's going on? Momma said they gave you a lie detector test?"

"I passed." Danny and Christina squealed at the results. I shushed them as best I could. "That means they dropped the charges but I'm not sure if Tal and Mary believe me. Regardless, it's no longer up to them."

Danny felt personally vindicated, even though it was about me. "Ha! Suck it, suckers!"

I continued explaining, "There's this FBI agent, Harling, who listened to me and convinced them I was telling the truth. They didn't want to hear it, but I asked for the polygraph and he totally believed me. Harling asked if he could be my contact through their 'investigation' and if I have any new information or whatever, I'm supposed to call him. So I don't have to talk to them much anymore."

Danny was pleased. "SWEET. See? I knew everything would work out. Now you're an FBI psychic. That so rocks. They're gonna make a television show about you."

"Okay, listen. I don't want anyone to know about all this. People think I'm weird enough." Danny and Christina lost their luster. "Not even Tiffany." Christina began to protest. "Until I'm ready. Have you told her you can bring things back to life?" She obviously hadn't thought about that and looked to Danny for help. "Are you going to tell Phoebe?"

"No. You're right. Got it. No problem."

Our mother re-entered the lobby with Mary, who directed her to the reception window. "If you would just step over to the glass, Mrs. Darling, she will get you the paperwork so we can get out of your hair."

As they tackled paperwork with the receptionist, I finally noticed that our group was missing a person. "Where's Cameron? And your mom?" I whispered hurriedly.

Danny huffed. "Well, they put him in jail—"

"Jail!?"

"Yes, but his grandmother is on her way to bail him out. Apparently, you really can't leave the scene of an accident without going to jail and stuff."

"Oh my God, are you kidding me?"

Christina cut in. "But he'll get out. Anne was actually really nice about it. She's kind of awesome strange. In a good way. But Momma's pissed, Casey. She was already here today when we got here—"

"I know all that. I could care less about our mom right now. This is none of her business." I remained silent for a few minutes. "Anyway, Danny, where is your—"

"Danny? Danny!"

"Speak of the devil," Danny lamented just as the outside door flew open. Danny's mom was a flurry of bling. She was judgmental, conceited, and protective, which basically meant she was the quintessential example of the dignified class in small towns.

"Thank God you're alright! Are they charging you with anything?"

"No, Mom, I'm fine." Danny tried to calm her down as she smothered him with her body. When she finally released him, she looked at me. "Casey."

"Hi, Mrs. Mardox." I tried to sound as poised and polite as I could.

"Do you have *any* idea what your actions have done to Danny's and my reputation? You are a disgrace."

I tried to open my mouth, but Danny intervened for me. "Mother, you're being a bit irrational."

"IRRATIONAL!" she shrieked. "Do you know how many people have come up to me, worried about your future? 'Oh your poor son,' they say. 'I knew that Casey girl would get him in trouble one day.' 'She's always been an outcast.'" Mrs. Mardox kept spitting out insults. "But this is awful. Some people are saying you're an accomplice, Danny! An *accomplice!* To a serial killer! All because of that little witch. Don't even get me started on my—"

"Whoa, Rachel," my mom said, coming between Mrs. Mardox and me, who in her fit of anger had decided to stick her finger in my face. "There's no need for worry. Your reputation is well intact, as is your son's. *We* both know the town wouldn't dare cast you out. And as for my daughter, I'll be dealing with her."

"You'd better be dealing with her, Lynne. I will not—"

"I gotcha, Rachel!" my mom hollered. "Go fill out your paperwork and go home."

In a stew, Rachel Mardox headed to the counter, muttering about our low standards. Danny gave me a sympathetic look, but remained by his mother's insane side as she flung open her Gucci purse and slammed her pen on the counter.

"Come on, girls, let's go." Christina and I followed our mother out with our tails between our legs.

—

It actually felt good to be home—that is, for a moment. "Where on earth do you think you're going, young lady?" my mom blurted as I started toward my room.

"My bedroom?" I said calmly. "Problem?"

"Yes there is a *huge* problem." The panic she had at the police station had melted off somewhere in the car ride home. "Yesterday, I wake up to find two detectives—"

"Whom you've seen before."

"Your sister but not you. And they tell me that you hid evidence!"

I cut her off as she glanced at Christina. "Hey, I'm just as shocked as you are about everything! I didn't know the detectives were there until later that night."

"But they had a search warrant, Casey! I felt so violated."

"I know I messed up big time about the tape."

"Then, after everything I've found out, I learned that you skipped town! You spent the night at a hotel? With *boys!* Danny's mom was hysterical—"

"So? She's dramatic. And Danny's my *bisexual* best friend who I've known for years, so it's not really 'boys' plural."

"Stop interrupting me!!" she finally snapped. "My God, Casey."

Christina shrunk into the couch. "I am trying to get on to you, which is my—*my* job and you are ignoring me. It is incredibly disrespectful."

I felt my eyes widen. "Don't you 'my God' *me*, Mother. Since when did *you* decide to become a parent? Christina and I were doing fine on our own."

"Shut your mouth." Her voice dropped to a deadly whisper. "You have no idea what I've been through—"

"What about *us*, Mom? Have you ever wondered, even for a second, why you have a nearly mute daughter and one that *clearly* hates your guts?" I stared at my mother. She could be so pretty if she wasn't so horrid. "*You* know *nothing* about us. You can't expect me to just step down from being a parental figure after ten years like everything's normal."

She was quiet. "There is something you don't know about our family."

I tried to catch her eye, but she wouldn't meet mine. "Whatever it is . . . maybe I don't wanna know."

"YOU DON'T UNDERSTAND!" My mother's wail was more frightened than angry. "Please. Sit down." Looking at each other, Christina and I shared a feeling of horror. We had never seen our mother so desperate (which was saying something). She left the room.

I looked at my twin and sat down. The last thing I wanted to do was have a serious conversation about *anything*, but something morose kept me glued to the cushion. Two things struck me as Momma reentered the room. First, she was truly terrified. Second, she was clutching a giant book that I hadn't seen before. It was battered, the pages a little mustard-colored, but the dark blue leather was holding up well. I yearned for an explanation. She opened the book. "I've known you two would have powers. I'm not sure what I was expecting, but this was not it."

"What do you mean 'you know'?"

"I know Christina can save animals. I've never said anything about it until now, but I've seen her do it."

Christina was mortified. "Did you know about Casey?"

"Yes. Not really. I didn't understand it. I knew I would eventually." We didn't know what to say. "I know, because . . . your father had a power too. A gift."

Christina vocalized what both of us were thinking. "Wh—what?"

"What is that book?" I couldn't keep myself from crawling forward to get a closer look.

"His family called it *Mortem Mobo*."

"What on earth? Is that Latin?" I asked, freaking out a little.

"Yes," she replied. "It means death plague or disease. According to your father, far back into his ancestry, their family was cursed. By witches." I felt like I couldn't breathe. "I'm not sure why or how. But it's meant to hurt . . . or drive the person insane."

"H—how?"

"Well, I think you know how, Casey. How you . . . *know*? About a person's death or something?"

"But what about my power, Momma?" Christina touched the pages of the book. "I *save* people."

"I know. I don't have all the answers, sweetie."

"But how—" I stood up.

"Wait! What does this book have to do with it?" Christina asked.

"I'm not sure, hon. It's a history book of the curse. From what I've found, no two are the same. Your father's doesn't sound like either of yours." She looked both of us over. "I know that's a lot to process, but the book is yours to keep."

"Why did you keep it from us?" I pressed on.

"What does it matter? She's giving it to us now."

I wanted nothing to do with that book. It gave me a bad feeling. It annoyed me that Christina was so drawn to it.

"Feel free to browse it whenever you want or need to. It might help. My side of the family doesn't have any curse, but you both have your father's blood. I've always been afraid of this thing. I've debated over the years whether or not to show it to you . . . or when I would *have* to." That last comment was shot at me. I sort of understood her logic.

Christina stared at the *Mortem Mobo*, transfixed. She reached for it and picked it up, straining slightly under the weight. "So, how does it work? Who wrote it and gave it to Daddy?"

Poor Mom looked at a loss for words. "Gosh, I wish your father was here." She looked into our eyes as if we could provide her with some kind of idea of what to say. "It's magic bound. Your dad said it writes itself. I think a witch may have given it to the family. You two might have to take more of the research into your own hands. I could never get it to work for me."

I watched Christina gracefully turn pages and saw her energy change. "Mom," I said, my throat parched. "What was Daddy's power?"

"Whenever he did something bad . . . or wrong . . . and trust me, I know there's a thin line between what exactly constitutes each . . ." Her eyes averted. "Death followed."

—

Two days later I woke to the smell of French toast. Curious and confused, I exited my room and found my mother making breakfast.

"What the—"

"Merry Christmas, hon!" Mom said, turning around briefly to look at me.

"It's Christmas already? Why are you cooking?"

"Y'know we always have French toast on Christmas morning." She looked at me like I was crazy.

I turned to my twin with a raised brow. She was intensely focused on her breakfast and wouldn't meet my eyes. I rubbed my eyes hard and then blinked several times to try and figure out if all of this was real. In the past few days I had been killed, brought back to life by my magical twin, interrogated by cops, and given a magical book. My brain throbbed at the normalcy as I mechanically grabbed a plate from my mother.

I sat beside Christina and took a bite. It was delicious, as it always was, but my stomach turned uneasily. My mom turned off the eye and turned around to face us. She looked well rested and seemed genuinely happy. When I turned my attention towards Christina, I found her smiling as well. I pushed back from the table making the chair scrape loudly against the floor.

"I'm not that hungry."

My mom frowned and twisted her apron in her hands. "Casey, it's Christmas."

"But yesterday so many things happened. I mean, you were furious, and that makes sense, so why are you so calm right now?"

Mom sighed and made her plate. She walked over and sat down before deciding to answer. "Look, I know a lot has happened in the past few weeks and honestly I'm not too happy about what both of y'all have gotten yourself into. Christina, you helped your sister flee the county and Casey you stole evidence which made it 'necessary' to flee." She took a big bite as I glanced between both of them. "But it is

Christmas and we are going to act like it's Christmas. Today, all is for-given, and we can open presents and eat good food. Tomorrow, you'll be grounded again."

"Christina, are you okay with this?" I asked trying to make some sense out of this nonsense. She shrugged and went back to eating.

"Casey," my mother said with a deadly tone, "just drop it and eat your breakfast."

—

The day passed relatively nicely considering I was freaking out the entire time. My mother had gotten me a few books and a new set of paints and Christina had gotten me a movie we had both loved. I man-aged to find the unwrapped canvas I made for my mother but admitted to Christina that I didn't have hers yet. She seemed okay with it but hadn't said a word all day.

In fact, she hadn't said anything since we left the police station, and it was not only worrying but also annoying. I desperately wanted to talk to her about what had happened and why she didn't want me telling anyone that she saved me.

I looked down at my phone but there were no new messages. I was pretty sure Danny's mom wouldn't let him text me, or even have a phone, but I was slightly confused that I hadn't heard from Cameron.

I stared at the new paints and then my bedroom door. It may have been Christmas but that didn't mean I had to act like everything was fine. I walked out of my door and knocked on Christina's door. She opened it with wide eyes and let me enter.

I plopped down on Christina's bed. Her comforter, which was covered in a flowery design, was silky against my skin. I splayed out my hand on it and rubbed back and forth. I was enjoying the way it caressed me. Christina sat in her desk chair. She had been spinning around in it but was now leaning back with her feet propped up on the bed.

My mind was racing, and I couldn't figure out how to stop it and make it make sense. "So, um, can I talk to you?"

After about a minute of waiting for an answer, I forced myself into a sitting position and stared at her. She had her eyes closed and a faint smile played across her lips. "Come on, Chris, please? I need to talk to you about everything that has happened. I know it's only been a few days but so much happened and I need to talk to you. I tried the day we left the police station and then the day after that and I know it's Christmas, but ..." I tried to figure out what to say. I squeezed my eyes tightly and clasped my hands together. "Can we *please* talk?"

There was another pause. "It's Christmas, Casey." Her voice was so soft I almost missed it.

"Yeah, I know, and all day I've let it be, but it's been three days since I *died*." I swung my legs against her bed a few times. We stared at each other for a minute before quickly averting our eyes.

She pushed off her bed and spun around towards the blue leather book sitting on her desk. I hadn't really looked at it yet. Picking it up, she spun around back towards me and played with its edges. "I know. I'm sorry I haven't been talking. I've ... uh, I've learned a lot about my power already. This book is fascinating."

"That's . . . that's great, Chris." She had been immersed in the book ever since Mom had given it to us. I gripped at the silky comforter. The rose nearest my finger contorted into a bumpy ball. I couldn't believe it was something she could talk about, but I was glad she said something. "Speaking of which, we never got to talk about why I wasn't supposed to tell anyone that you saved me."

She looked down quickly and began playing with her hair. The book balanced precariously on her knee and I watched it wobble unsteadily. "Yeah, I know that was probably weird for you."

"It's not exactly that it was weird, but I just . . . didn't understand it? Still don't."

Letting out a deep breath, she locked eyes with me. "You're the first person I've ever saved."

"Okay." I stretched out the "ay."

"I didn't know what it would do to you, if anything, but when we came up to Cameron and he was dying . . ." My heart jumped against my chest and I looked at the ground. I could still feel his freezing skin and see his lifeless lips. "I knew I had to save him too. It's the same feeling I had during the wreck. I know, I know, you probably don't understand, but . . ." The hair in her fingers was wrapped tightly against her skin.

"I really do appreciate all that you did for me. I mean, saving me, and then Cameron. It was amazing of you, but I still don't understand why you don't want to tell anyone about me. I guess it's not really that important now, but . . ."

She stood up, careful not to drop the *Mortem Mobo*, and placed it back on her desk. Pacing the room, I watched as different emotions flitted across her face. Her eyes kept flashing to me but it took her a few minutes to say something. "I don't really understand my powers. I . . . I mean, I understand them more than you seem to understand yours, I think, and the book, the book helps but . . ." Standing still, I watched her shaking hands drag through her hair and grip it near her skull. I looked past her at the book and then back to her.

"I'm glad the book helps," I said, trying to think of something more to say. I wanted to help her. She looked so frightened. I stared at the book. It had only been in our lives for a few days but I had a bad feeling about it.

"The truth is . . . I didn't know what was going to happen to you. I've had animals not wake up and then I've seen some other stuff but I had to save you. But something felt different. Different than any other lifesaving experience. It . . . I don't know how it made me feel. Then, when I saw Cameron . . ." She turned her palms up toward the ceiling.

"Wait, what do you mean you've seen other stuff? Like what? And what do you mean it felt different?" As she looked at the ground, her mouth quirked down on one side.

"It is kind of hard to explain? I don't want you to hate me or any-thing, but . . ." She twirled around again so that she was facing her desk. "I felt like I could feel extra energy flowing through me and into you. Is that weird?"

I stared at the ground. Of course it was weird; all of it was weird. Looking up at her doe-like eyes I knew I couldn't say that. "What do you mean?"

She spun around. "I don't really know what I mean?" She shook her head. "I'm sorry, Casey, but I just don't know. For now, can you promise me you won't talk to anyone about what I did?"

"I- I guess I won't."

"Thanks." She put her hand on my knee. "So do you want to watch a movie?"

I shook my head. "I'm gonna go paint, but maybe later?"

She nodded and reached for the book again. I frowned but left her to it. It was definitely the weirdest Christmas I ever experienced.

CHAPTER SIX

when you find out the true strength of a word

Despite the oddities of everything that happened before Christmas, the next few days were nice. Christina and I hadn't talked anymore about what happened, but we did do our best to enjoy our grounding. True to form, my mother had indeed grounded us immediately after Christmas. My friends all seemed to be in a similar boat. Danny was on full lock-down and 'forbidden from ever seeing us again' (something he assured us he could fix). Cameron and Tiffany were MIA as well, but I assumed Cameron was grounded and Tiffany was on vacation or something.

Regardless, Christina and I were watching our favorite movie together when the world started to darken around me. As I tried to listen to the dialogue, the world around me changed. In an abandoned building, a few blocks away . . . a man was being yelled at. Strong hands wrapped around his collar, suspending and shaking him in midair. My heart twisted as I avoided looking at his killer. The man had on a suit that hadn't been washed in days. His brown eyes looked like murky seawater and his hair was greasy, dyed blond.

As his first memory tried to poke through his head, I started turning to look at his killer when I heard the thing that made everything click. "I wish you would just *DIE*," a familiar voice growled with great force.

Suddenly, the man's memories bombarded me, tearing hard into my mind. There was his first bike, his last kiss, his death, his drug addiction, all of it. I gasped out loud without meaning too. Since the man was dead, I knew I only had a moment before I would break out of my vision. Before I broke, I found myself face to face with the Golden Boy.

—

"HOW COULD YOU DO THAT!?" Christina screeched. In front of her, the body of the dead man lay on a broken mirror. My heart beating fast, I looked around the decaying building. Christina momentarily focused her energy on the man. "Breathe," she whispered over him. The man breathed in deeply but remained relatively still. Shakily standing up, Christina returned her attention to Cameron. Meanwhile, he seemed unable to look away from the now breathing body. "YOU JUST KILLED THAT MAN!"

"Christina, calm down!" I tried to wrap my head around what had happened. Part of me was happy that he was breathing, but the other part stayed with Cameron. Watching him gave me no clues as to what he was feeling. "We don't know the whole st—"

"I DO NOT CARE, CASEY! He died. And it's all *his* fault." She gestured to Cameron's now stiffened form. His eyes had moistened, and he looked down at the ground. "If it wasn't for me, he'd still be dead."

"Stop it, Christina," I replied sharply. "Cameron?" I stooped beside him. "Are you okay?"

His only response was to look up at me with pleading eyes. "HE DOESN'T EVEN CARE, DOES HE?!" Christina roared.

Cameron's head snapped to her. "I do care," he managed in a broken whisper.

"Oh, whatever." Christina seethed in anger. "You know, maybe *you're* the killer." The world around us froze. That accusation was harsh.

"Chris—"

"Don't you *Chris* me, Casey," she said angrily. "Where has he been during all of the killings? Huh?" She pushed me. "Think about it."

"Christina, the killer tried to kill *him*," I said, having begun to worry about her logic. I faced her and took a deep breath. "Remember?"

"Sure . . . or he could have just found a way to fake it so that we didn't suspect him," Christina said, building conviction.

"So, he ran his car off the road and killed himself to trick us? His eyes aren't blue, Christina."

"Maybe now. But there are contacts, *hello?* We have powers. Why can't he have one that changes his appearance? If he can kill someone right now, why not before?"

My twin was completely irrational. "That's not fair. Our powers come from a curse, Chris. I never noticed Cameron trying to kill anyone until *you* saved him."

"Stop. Calling. Me. Chris." Her voice was a tundra, embracing me in icy shards. "He just killed a man and you expect me to be okay with that? Really?"

"Christina—" I started but found myself cut off again.

"No! I know you're expecting me to shy away. To go into my mute stage, but I'm not. Not for this."

"It's your decision to be mute."

"It is a *disorder*." She shook her hair out of her face. Glaring at me she jabbed a finger toward Cameron. "I will not stand for this."

"Then sit down," I demanded, exasperated.

"Fine, Casey, be that way, but I will *not* share a room with a *murderer*." With that, she had begun to walk out of the room.

"DON'T CALL ME THAT!" Cameron bellowed, stopping her escape. "I was tracking the killer too. I've been doing it for a while." My brows furrowed together as I searched the ground in front of me. "That man right there was a shot-out drug dealer. He probably has as much blood as the killer does on his hands." Cameron's body shook violently. "I didn't mean to kill him . . . I just wanted more information. I've seen and dealt with his kind before. All it takes is a little fear and they'll talk a mile a minute. I didn't know I could kill him. Not with just a word." A sob wracked through him.

"What do you mean, a word?" I said. I walked over to the body and sure enough, I couldn't find any wounds. The man groaned lightly and rolled over. I jumped and went back to Cameron.

"I said, 'I wish you would just DIE.' When I said that word, he choked and . . ." Cameron clinched his eyes shut. "He just died. I didn't even touch him, I promise. He died when I said that word. Like it was some kind of spell or something. I don't know what's going on." Cameron opened his eyes and stared at me. "I was just trying to help."

"Killing isn't help," Christina said venomously. Cameron ran out of the building.

What does he mean by "I've dealt with his kind before." I took a step toward him before turning to my sister. "Stay here. I'll be back." Her snort made me pretty sure she wouldn't stay, but I didn't have a choice.

"Stop it right now, Cameron!" I shouted as I followed him outside. "We need to get out of here. There are cops just down the street."

"Why should I?" He didn't turn around. "Why do you care right

now? I just killed someone. And you saw it in your head, didn't you?!"
He slumped against his new car; something shiny reflected in his hand.

"Cameron?" I stepped closer to him. "What is that?" His hand readjusted the thing and I saw what it was: a small piece of the shattered mirror. By the time I was in front of him, he had gripped it firmly. "Put that down. You promised me."

"Why?" His breathing was shaky and heavy. I made a grab for it, but he held it high above him.

"Put that down." I jumped high, trying to get it. At that moment, he sidestepped me and put the mirror on his skin. Quicker than I would have expected, I covered his hand with mine. He stared down at my hand in helpless frustration. "Please stop," I whispered. Everything had gone downhill out of nowhere, but he simply couldn't hurt himself. There was a soft click as the mirror clattered on the ground. "Thank you."

I leaned my head against him and enveloped him into a hug. It was the first time I had really seen him cry hard. "I didn't mean to kill him. Please know I never meant to kill him. I'm not the killer." His voice broke on the last word.

"Shhh . . . I know you aren't. This doesn't make you a killer," I mumbled into his warm skin. Our contact had made me blush, but I tried to stay focused. It was windy outside, chilly and dreary, but with him it felt like summer. "I don't want you to worry about this, Cameron. We *will* figure out what happened."

He stepped back, his shoe crushing the mirror. "Maybe it's better if we're not friends . . . anymore."

My heart hit a wall. "What?"

He began furiously twisting his bracelet back and forth. "Your sister is really upset, and you need to be with her. I'm not a good influence." He turned his shoulder on me. "Maybe it's best if we don't talk for a while."

There was a moment of silence. "Friendship means sticking with people even when everything feels wrong." I circled him and grabbed his arm. Forcing his chin up, our eyes met. "What you did was wrong, but it's okay now and we can talk about it *together*. I have been a bad person in my life. For Pete's sake, I hid evidence from detectives!" I released him and took a step backwards. My eyes pled with him. "I've seen a lot of people die and have done nothing, *nothing*, to stop it."

"But that's not your fault—"

"And this isn't yours. You said you killed him by just saying a word. I don't understand it, but I believe you." My hands ached to comfort him, but I didn't know what to do. He stared right past me, unblinkingly. His hands continued to toy with his bracelet. "I am *here* for you, Cameron. And I can help you with this. We just need to talk and figure everything out. I want to help you."

He continued to stare unfocused past my shoulder. "Well, you shouldn't want to. And I don't blame you."

He walked to the front of his new red Beetle and got in the driver's seat. I pounded on his car windows, but he continued to avoid my gaze. He began slowly backing up and when I didn't move he put more force on the pedal. Knowing I couldn't do anything right then, I jumped back and allowed him to leave. Christina emerged from the warehouse. "Is he okay?" I asked through clenched teeth.

She blinked at me several times. "Yeah, he's fine. His breathing seems normal and I don't really sense that he needs more healing. We were lucky we showed up—"

"What the actual hell, Chris?" I turned quickly toward her, crunching the gravel beneath my feet.

She narrowed her eyes and put her hands on her hips. "You have that tone with me, because?"

"Because he's our *friend*. Yes, whatever happened is messed up and we are *going* to talk about it, but you were able to save him and—"

"And what if I hadn't been able to?" She threw her hands up in the air and let out a crazy chuckle. "That guy would have died, and we would have never known! How can you be okay with that?"

I copied her hand motion. "I'm not saying I'm okay with it, but we don't know everything. He said that the guy died by a word and there's no wounds, so I'm inclined to believe him." I rubbed my hands together. "He probably didn't mean to kill him and I need to talk to him before I can make any judgments!"

She rolled her eyes and stomped over to our car. "C'mon, let's continue this stupid conversation in the car." I glanced back at the warehouse and then quickly followed her. "I'm sure I'll get an earful, but I'm going to adopt my mute state and remain silent."

"Your choice. Not mine."

"It is not a choice." Each word had a slight pause before it. "Screw you and your thoughts anyway. That boy killed a man, *killed* him, and you expect me to be fine with it? Unless you can prove he isn't the killer, I'm not going to change my mind. But let's go home and *try* to forget this ever happened. I know that's what you want."

I didn't bother to talk her out of her state of mind. She was stubborn. I hated everything that happened, but it wasn't my call. Sighing, I reached for my keys and got in the driver's seat.

Christina practically destroyed the door as she got in the car. Sighing, I turned over the engine. I knew I was asking too much of the universe to have an easy night. "What is your problem?"

"What's my *problem*?" she howled. She was creating enough

noise to make me miss her quieter state. It was a wonder we got out of there without attracting every cop in town. "Well." She was suddenly calm. "First, I was finally getting to talk to you about truly important stuff when, second, you left me inside with the latest victim of the Bartow Slasher."

"Well, Christina, we will be able to talk about these things whenever. And Cameron is *not* the killer."

"There is no proof of that," she retaliated.

I gave her my best *are you kidding me* face. "What about Ryan? You seemed to be fine with that theory before."

I put on my seatbelt while I drove us home; her big blue-green eyes gazed at me sadly. "I still don't trust Cameron. I never have."

"Because he *accidentally* killed someone?"

"Yes. Because he accidentally *killed* someone, Casey. Do you not see how awful that is?" She mirrored my tone.

"Of course, I do. But Cameron didn't *mean* to kill anyone. We still don't know how he got this . . . 'power.' To kill someone with a word. A *word*." Christina froze at the mention of Cameron's "power." "Chris, please tell me what you know. You know something."

She took a giant breath. "Your visions are changing, aren't they? You're getting stronger in them; more in control?" I didn't nod, because she didn't give me time to. "Well, to just get straight to the point, sometimes when I breathe life into someone . . . I feel like I enhance them." I'm sure my jaw dropped like cartoon characters' do. "I don't know how it works and I don't know what all it can do, but I've seen animals that can move incredibly fast, and hamsters that can eat through a steel cage. After I've saved them. It doesn't happen every single time, but . . . when what I do . . . affects some of them, it's crazy. I felt it when I healed both of you."

"You enhance them?" I repeated, slowly digesting this thought as I maneuvered the car.

"It's like they now have so much energy thanks to me. Borrowed energy that they're not used to. And some of the bodies . . . react to it. Grow . . . stronger."

"Like with my visions?"

"And possibly with Cameron."

My head jerked toward her. "And you've been shunning *him*, knowing what you know, knowing it might be partially *your* fault. Saying *he's* the one killing everybody in town."

She reacted as if I slapped her. "That was *his* wrong, Casey, not mine."

"But *you* changed him."

"But he didn't control it. I had no way of knowing. And if he had truly been thoughtful of his actions . . . I probably never would have known. Before the giant car accident, I had only saved two humans. How was I to know that it would affect both of you that way?"

I nodded my head once. "So . . . that's why he has powers?" In some bizarre way, it actually made sense. He wasn't some freaky half cousin three times removed. I pulled into a gas station somewhat close to our home.

"Wait, what are you doing?"

I turned off the car and threw the keys at her. "Go home, Chris." She looked at me incredulously.

"Where are you going?"

"Where do you *think* I'm going?" I shot daggers at my sister before slamming the door. The night wasn't over.

—

"Cameron." I pounded on his front door. After five minutes of continual knocking, I figured out the door was unlocked and let myself in. "Cameron?" I called, walking in on him standing in front of a picture hidden behind the couch. I placed a hand on the small of his back.

"What are you doing here?" he asked stoically.

I shook off his coldness and began talking. "Christina told me that her power sometimes transfers extra energy into a person. Apparently enough to give them their own power."

His body rumbled with a short chuckle. "So, I'm saved by your sister and end up with the power to kill. Isn't that unbelievable."

"Cameron—"

"I killed someone. Why are you comforting me? I'm just like my dad. It's no wonder that I get the 'power' to kill."

"Stop. You didn't *know*. You would never have killed him if you knew that could happen, right?"

"Right . . ."

"So yes, you killed someone, but my sister doomed you when she saved you." I placed my palm on his cheek. My heart fluttered at the contact. "Right now, it's important for you to remember that he is actually alive and that we will find a way to get through this. You're a good friend, Cameron. Maybe . . . maybe even more than that. I promise you we're gonna figure this out." He looked into my eyes then closed his own tightly. "So, what is this picture of?"

"My father," Cameron whispered with quiet venom. Leaning around him, I focused in on the family picture that held his father. Cameron couldn't have been much older than seven, but his eyes held the secrets of a grown man. To his right, his mother stood tall and beautiful, clutching her son's hand, even as she looked like she might wither away. It was as if she was a walking contradiction. Finally, to his left, stood a man larger than Cameron was today, slightly distanced from the happy family. His hair was sandy blond and greasy, and his skin was a bit tanner than Cameron's, but there was no mistaking that it was Cameron's father. It wasn't the fact that he was Cameron's father that had me awestruck. Two perfectly cold, blue, snakelike eyes graced his features. They were the exact same eyes as the "Bartow Slasher."

CHAPTER SEVEN

a shattering of worlds

Those eyes had me hooked in every way possible. As impossible as it seemed, I was convinced that the man in the photograph was watching me. "Cameron . . ." I whispered, aware that my voice sounded off and strained. "Where did you say your father was?"

Even in his exhausted shape, his eyebrows shot up. "We never really talked about it, but he's basically in an insane asylum. Why? What's going on?"

"I think . . . I think your father is the killer, Cameron."

In an instant it looked like he had shut down. I put my hand on his shoulder. "Are you . . . how can you be so sure?"

"The eyes . . . Cameron, I can't forget those eyes."

He backed away from me and sat on the couch. The rest of the night passed by in a blur that felt like an eternity. I continued to stare at the photo, paralyzed, even as Cameron left me. When he finally sat beside me, he didn't acknowledge me at all. I didn't know what to do. At one moment, I had yawned which had made him jump. I looked down at my phone and wondered when Anne would be home. She needed to know. "I'll be right back," I whispered.

I walked away from him and went into the bathroom. Its sunny yellow paint made me squint when I turned on the light. Cozy and bright, the bathroom was relatively small but had a giant mirror and sink. I looked at my reflection. My silver-blue eyes reflected a bit of terror; for a second, I saw Cameron's father's eyes. I quickly shut mine and leaned my head against the cool mirror. Memories of the killer and what he did flitted across my mind, as did Cameron's target. Everything about me seemed to be burning, and it was definitely not in a good way.

The man that had tormented me for what felt like centuries was the father of someone I considered a friend and even a crush. *Who knew I'd have this kind of boy trouble?* I thought, half miserably, half hysterically.

I splashed some water on my face and felt slightly rejuvenated but the second I was face to face with the mirror that feeling disappeared. I rested my head on the cool glass. I knew I needed to go back out and check on Cameron, but I didn't know what to say.

Taking a deep breath, I reentered the living room and heard soft crying sounds. I picked up the pace and found tears falling lightly from Cameron's eyes. It didn't look like he had moved since I left. "Cameron," I said gently, kneeling in front of him. "Are you okay?" He dropped his chin to his chest and shook his head.

I got up and sat beside him. Moving slowly, I wrapped one arm around him. He leaned into me, his tears sprinkling my shirt. I must have fallen asleep, because the next thing I knew the front door was opening.

"I'm home," Anne announced, putting down her purse and shopping bags. "Well hey, Casey. How are you doing?" Cameron jumped

232

up and raced to her. "Cam, what's wrong?" I walked over and saw his mouth struggling to form a sentence.

She turned to me with a questioning stare.

I cleared my throat, surprised by how full it felt, and began talking. "When was the last time you were told about Cameron's dad?"

"Michael?" Her eyes narrowed ever so slightly, and I saw her glance at Cameron before starting again. "That man . . . was no son-in-law of mine, and I want no part of him. When I moved Cameron to Georgia, I changed back to my maiden name and made sure there was no forwarding address. We wanted to start over, and that's exactly what we've done." She threw the photo on the coffee table and sat down. "Why does it matter?"

I couldn't find it in me to look straight into her all-knowing eyes anymore. "You didn't think the hospital would ever need to contact someone? If nothing else, to let you know that he was dead? Or . . . escaped?"

Anne stood up in a no-nonsense way. "Casey, he killed my daughter. I don't want to hear anything else about him ever again."

"I know." I found the courage to look in her woeful eyes again. "I'm sorry."

"Why does this matter to you so much?" Even though Anne was trying to be calm, agitation rolled off of her.

"Because he's Cartersville's serial killer," I finally said.

The room dropped twenty degrees as Anne looked at Cameron. There was genuine fear in his eyes as he looked back at her. "It's not possible, right? Gran, please, tell me it's not possible." Behind his shoulder, I could see Anne. She stood erect, with almost tangible thought bubbles around her head. She looked at Cameron and panic erupted from her. She quickly walked over to the window and peered out. She did the same to all the windows in the room as I turned my attention back to Cameron.

"Cameron. I am so, *so* sorry, but it's him." I gestured backwards toward the photo. "That man is the man in my visions."

He spun away from me and searched for his grandmother who was still walking around the room irregularly. Every window was being double, and triple checked that it was locked. "Gran . . . how could he . . ."

Anne was by his side in an instant. She put both hands on his shoulders. "He was . . . well, is an intelligent man, Cameron. But you are safe, do you hear me?" He nodded but said nothing. The room's silence was deafening as they looked at each other. She seemed to come to a conclusion in her mind before leaving the room. "Excuse me. I need to go make a phone call."

Cameron started violently shaking the second she left. I reached for his arms to force him steady, but he shook me off and backed away. "Cameron, it's okay. I'm here, your grandmother's here. We're not gonna—"

"It doesn't matter, Casey!! There's no getting away from him. There's no getting away from him . . ." He rambled on and on until Anne came back into the room.

Her silence seemed to inch across every surface. She looked as if she had aged twenty years.

"What?" I asked, as Cameron mutely watched her.

"He escaped last August," Anne acknowledged. "They must have been desperate to reach me, because they told me straight off. I'm calling the police." At those words, I backed up hastily and almost fell over the coffee table. She looked at Cameron. They were both pleading with each other for some sort of answer that neither could provide.

"When the murders began." Cameron was broken. I wrung my hands together and held my breath. "He would have had plenty of time to find us."

Anne turned away and checked the doors. She had also picked up her phone and began to call the police. I looked at Cameron. "I . . . I can't be here."

He didn't say anything. I wasn't even sure if he could see me in that moment. I put my hand on his arm but he flinched and backed away again. "Don't. You need to go, right? So, go."

"Cameron . . . I'll stay if you want, but the cops . . ."

Anne was back in the room in a flash. She put her hand on my shoulder and gestured with her head that I should leave. I nodded and started to go. She had put down the phone and was talking to Cameron in a hushed voice. Something screamed at me to stay, but I walked out of the door and didn't look back. Right then and there, I felt our world shatter into a million pieces.

CHAPTER EIGHT

the final beginning

If a single pin dropped in Cartersville, we all could hear it. Who knew this little town would be ravaged by such devastating deaths? Agent Harling was the number one most contacted person in my phone since we found out Michael was responsible for the bloody chaos. In the remaining week before school knocked us into reality, Cameron began talking to me again. He had mostly been quiet since the discovery, but we finally talked about how to break the news to everyone. I hadn't told Christina, her view on death seemed to complicate everything, and besides that, she seemed quieter again. Plus, Danny was still grounded though he had managed to message me on social media a few times.

Still, when New Year's Eve rolled around, Cameron and I decided to talk to our group. Danny texted me earlier that day and said that he was able to meet us for once. Christina, though she had been mute for the past week, agreed to go with me so we could talk about everything. It wasn't going to be a good conversation. Especially since Cameron announced that he had more news to share.

The old covered bridge was a historical landmark. Cameron and I wanted to break the news in a special place. It rested in front of me, symbolically broken; both the end, and maybe the beginning. We watched the river flow beneath the creaky structure. The water reflected a pale sunset just as the air chilled everything to a standstill. Twilight was waning and the crescent moon was on the rise. Darkness crept from every direction. Danny and Christina chatted sweetly in the car; still no sign of Tiffany. I had asked her to come, but I couldn't blame her for not showing up. I'd basically been ignoring her. At first, she bought our story, but small towns have no privacy. It didn't take her long to figure out that she had been excluded from a lot more than we were letting on. Perhaps not my best decision. Losing a friend hurt.

Speaking of losing friends, Cameron appeared beside me with an ever-stoic face. It seemed to be his neutral expression nowadays and it worried me. "How are you?" we both said at the same time. Our soft chuckles mingled in the chilly wind. The life that arrived in his eyes again filled me with warmth.

"I'm okay, I think. The end is coming," I replied after a moment of consideration. Craning my head, I looked into his golden eyes. "It's you I'm worried about. What if this really is your dad we're talking about?"

A visible shudder shook his frame. "I'm not sure. But he won't continue." The force and venom in Cameron's voice worried me, but I let it go. I would have been pretty mad too, given the circumstances. "This town has suffered too much because of me."

"Don't say that. You know it isn't your fault." He replied with silence. My mind flashed to the body of the drug dealer, but I shook it off. Nothing had become of his almost death, at least there had been no cop involvement. Still, I hadn't known what to think of it. I wanted to find some words of comfort, but I came up short. "Are you ready?"

"No. Well, yes. I'm insanely nervous, but they deserve to know. And since Christina didn't drag Alex, I'll be fine."

"Okay." I tried to knead some warmth into my hands.

"Hey," Christina said, walking over to us. She peeked at Cameron before focusing her attention on me.

Danny bounced over. "Are we all here?"

"Yep." I tucked a stray piece of hair behind my ear. "Cause your boyfriend isn't coming, right, Christina?"

Her cheeks had probably never been that red before. It was actually kind of entertaining to see. "*Alex* had soccer tryouts. So, I told him I'd catch him up tomorrow. Besides, we've only been talking since Christmas." Cameron let out a small breath of relief.

Danny shrugged and reached into his backpack to retrieve four large candles. "That's okay. I only brought four candles anyway."

Cameron's eyebrow shot up. "Candles?"

I nodded once. "No fires are allowed here anymore." I gestured to the covered bridge. "Authorities aren't too keen on the idea of this going up in flames and I don't blame—"

"But . . ." Danny interrupted. "We need a place to talk and this is actually in Euharlee. It's kind of a brilliant plan to avoid curfew. The cops aren't giving people trouble who are coming back *into* town." He grew a huge grin. "We'll probably be out here a while, so when we go into the covered part of the bridge—"

"We're going inside?" Christina hugged the book tighter. "I've heard a lot of scary things about this place . . . . People say it's haunted."

Danny scoffed. "If I can do it, you can do it." She looked dubious as he led us into the tunnel and made a comfy pallet-type thing, because the bridge was "damp, dirty, and too dark to sit on without protection" in his opinion.

"Perfect setting for ghosts," Christina muttered, making her way to her spot.

Cameron had trudged himself to the edge of what looked like a growing pit of candlelight. I sat between him and Christina but situated a bit closer to his side. Danny finally sat, careful not to touch the left wall with one candle in front of him. A single candle sat in front of each of us. Christina sat with her back to the darkness, eerie shadows collecting on her face. The book sat on her right side, away from Danny, emitting its own creepy darkness. Our moment had the ambiance of a séance without a ghost ... currently.

"Well, I suppose I should start," Cameron began, he rotated his bracelet once. "Casey and I know who the killer is." Danny, who had been rhythmically patting his knees, stopped abruptly. Christina's shoulders straightened in the shadows.

"Who is it?" Christina's voice was a dull knife.

Cameron took a deep breath. "My father," he whispered. There was a moment of silence.

"Who?" Christina asked scooting forward. The shadows shifted her features into a sinister snarl. Or maybe that was just the look she was giving him.

He said it again a little stronger. "My father." I held my breath as another silence ensued.

"Your *father?*" Christina replied through gritted teeth.

"Christina ..." I warned. Danny's eyes were focused only on Cameron, gauging his reactions.

"No. Of course. It all makes sense now. You *would* kill that guy, because you're just like—"

"Don't you say another word, Christina," Cameron growled, jumping to his feet. The candles flickered from the sudden movement and one went out. "I. Am. NOT my father."

I reached for his hand and gently tugged him back down so that he was closer to me.

Cameron looked down at his hands in his lap. "My father killed my mother right before my eyes . . . Then he laughed and asked me to help. I've never been that afraid." His voice broke and he lifted his head so that he could look at everyone. "I tried to send him to prison because I hate him. Too bad he ended up in a psychiatric institution instead. Please, please never compare me to him. I never meant to kill that man. He *did*. He *enjoys* it. That makes all the difference, and I need you to back off."

Christina's blue eyes turned from steel to soft concern. As if she was afraid to anger him, she slowly reached over and rested a hand on his knee. A flame inched toward her now-close flesh. "I'm sorry, Cameron . . . I didn't know." She retracted her hand. "I guess I need to work on judging people before I understand . . . and on what I say."

He nodded graciously. Danny broke the quiet. "I'm sorry, can we hold the phone here? Did you just say you killed a guy?"

Cameron flinched. "Yeah, well I didn't do it on purpose." Danny pulled back, causing misery to form in Cameron's eyes. "Danny, I swear to you that it wasn't like that."

I jumped in for him. "Yeah, it turns out that Cameron has some sort of power because Christina saved him."

"Okay, okay, what is happening . . ." Danny said.

"Cameron got into a fight with a homeless person and said the word *die*. And the guy actually died. It was an accident, and the reason it happened is because when Christina saved Cameron, it gave him the ability to kill someone by saying the word *die*," I clarified.

Danny nodded his head. "I think I understand, but this is a lot."

"I know and I have some more information that I haven't even been able to tell Casey about," Cameron said. He took a deep breath and moved closer to his candle. It cast a flickering orange across his eyes. "The detectives told Gran how he escaped and it's terrifying."

"Why did they tell you that?" Christina asked with narrowed eyes.

"For our safety? Because they want us to be satisfied and not sue the mental asylum? I mean, they told Gran instantly that he escaped, because they knew they screwed up." He took a deep breath. "Anyway, Michael never showed up in his cell after breakfast on the same day that there was a shipment of supplies that arrived to the hospital. The detectives said a doctor wearing a dark, pinstriped suit and white lab coat was seen entering the back of the semi-trailer during the delivery. The guards must not have been interested in a doctor being on the shipping dock of a prison hospital, or were too distracted to notice that this doctor never exited the truck. The driver was given the go-ahead and the vehicle left with that devil inside it. He must have hidden somewhere inside and got out at a different place in San Francisco. From there, no one knows what happened. But here we are."

Wind whipped through the corridor and caused our candle flames to grow and then almost disappear. "My God," Christina said.

"Are you okay, Cameron?" I asked as I scooted even closer to him.

"I don't know. We ended up talking to Agent Harling a few days later, and he said that they weren't sure it was him but they would help us out with security. Still, if he's really here? I don't know what I feel."

"We're here for you," I said, giving him a half smile, which he returned.

Rubbing the sides of his face, Danny looked at me, then Cameron, and then back to me. "Yeah, we are, but I've got to ask: Casey, are you okay with all of this?"

I was thankful the darkness hid my warming cheeks. Peeking at Cameron, I found his eyes boring into me. "He's our friend. It's not right, but he didn't mean to. Plus, Christina managed to save the guy, so it's all good on that front. He's not actually dead and Cameron's not lying to us."

"It's true, Danny," Christina said with a short shrug.

"You're lucky you're a good and cute friend, Cam."

Cameron released yet another breath. "Thank you. Really. I promise we can talk about it later if you want."

He shook his head slightly. "We're gonna have to come back to the power part, but first the potential identity of K. Didn't you just say he was locked up?"

"Yeah . . . and this is where it gets complicated. When we moved here, Gran wanted nothing to do with him, nor did I. So, she changed our last name to her maiden one." I looked over to see Christina pursing her lips in thoughtful consideration. "We apparently were hidden a little too well, because when he escaped . . . they couldn't figure out where we were to let us know." He continued with an eye roll. "They're probably afraid Gran will sue them for not being able to stop him from escaping."

"Okay, you're saying that he's escaped?" Danny was still trying to make sure this wasn't the nightmare of reality it really was.

"Yes . . . somehow," Cameron confirmed.

"Okay, like, *when*?" Danny questioned, still in shock.

"Last August."

"Okay, so, this is, like, for real?"

"Yes. For real." Cameron looked tired at confirming everything but seemed to understand the need to.

"Like, for *real*, for real?"

This time I answered Danny. "Yes, Danny. This is for real, for real. Not a joke. This is a really upsetting situation and when people hear about this . . ." I looked at all of my friends. "It's going to get out at some point, and we'd like to prolong that as much as possible. It's not going to be easy for us to deal with, especially Cameron. So . . . can it not leave this bridge?"

"Oh my God . . . Cameron, I'm so sorry," Danny finally said.

"Don't be sorry. Just be my friend." Cameron looked at him with utmost sincerity.

"We love you, no matter what. At least we know who it is." He looked at me. "Wait, how do we know K is his father? Even if he escaped, could it be coincidence?"

"I know his eyes from my visions, and I found them in a photo at Cameron's. Plus, he got out in August, so the timelines match."

"Oh my God . . ."

I continued. "The police know. Agent Harling obviously knows." Cameron perched his chin on his knees, staring into the candlelight. "So, you won't tell anyone? Not even your parents?"

"Of course not." Danny put his hand on Cameron's shin. Christina mimed her lips being sealed.

Outside, a twig snapped. We glanced at each other. "Did you hear that?" Danny half-mouthed. We nodded.

"Just the wind," I offered, scooting closer to Cameron. "We weren't followed, guys. We can all agree. Absolutely no one in the world knows where we are right now. They couldn't possibly."

"Except I think I saw something," Christina said, her face paler than normal.

"It's probably a deer," I said attempting to ease everyone's mind. "Should . . . should we check?" Danny asked while craning his neck to look outside.

Cameron looked at me and shrugged. "Up to you guys."

I turned around and looked out into the wooded area but found mostly darkness. Trees crowded the clearing, making it appear more confined. Wind rattled the air and drew mysterious shapes near Cameron's car when my eyes adjusted to the night. "Let's wait," I decided, shifting uncomfortably under their gazes. "Okay, so we know a good bit about the killer. The key now is how to catch him." *I feel like a schoolteacher,* I marveled, annoyed at the thought.

"Right. Oh my God, we can be heroes." Danny was getting a little too excited. "And Beatrix will be dancing in heaven."

"I don't think people will look at *me* as a hero," Cameron's deadpan voice admitted. "But you're damn right we're going to catch the bastard."

Christina seemed to warm up to Cameron again as she shifted closer. "I can't believe he was able to escape," she said timidly.

Cameron's face darkened with the shadows. "My dad has his ways." A jolt of energy went down my spine as a loud *bang* shot through the night.

Cameron and Danny shot to their feet; Cameron from protective instinct and Danny from Scooby and Shaggy-like fear. "What was that?" Danny asked in a scared voice.

"Probably just the wind." But I felt uneasy. Danny slowly sunk back to the ground.

Looking around, he gave us a slightly sheepish smile. "Sorry, that was a bit nerve wracking."

"No worries, Danny," Cameron said as he stared down at his hands. He was twirling his bracelet around his wrist. I adverted my eyes and directed them toward Christina. At that moment, her fingers twitched over the cover of the book.

"Why did you bring it?" I asked, nodding my head in its direction.

Her hand lay protectively over it. "I thought tonight would be good for talking about the book. I feel like there is a lot we can learn from it." She shrugged and backed further into the dark abyss. "So, I brought it."

"I don't like that book. We can talk about it without it being here."

"Uh . . . not really," Christina said, as if my idea was ridiculous.

"You sure are—"

"Look, I'm just thinking that maybe the book can help us catch him." Christina's shoulders dropped and she rubbed her hand across the cover. "It's very *old, fragile,* and *powerful.*" With reluctance, she handed the book over to me. "Because of that, we *all* need to take a look at it . . . Well, I'm not sure about you, Danny; sorry."

He raised both hands in mock surrender. "Hey, I'm not complaining," he joked before his face fell to a more serious expression. "I'm here because of and for y'all."

I gave him an appreciative smile before focusing my attention back to the book. The cover seemed to hold nothing but secrets as I ran my fingers over it. I tilted my head slightly to the side and began to open it. "NO!" Christina yelled, almost causing me to fling the book out of the bridge. "Sorry," she continued sheepishly. "It's just that . . . you should read it when you're alone. It's really odd to read. Helpful, but odd. Besides, when you're done, you can pass it on to Cameron."

My eyes narrowed. "What do you mean it's odd to read?" At that very moment, Cameron's car alarm went off. I shot to my feet and took off toward the sound, everyone else in tow. No one or thing was around the car when we reached its high-pitched blaring. Cameron quickly hit the "quiet" button, fumbling with his keys.

"Let's go," Cameron said.

We all fervently nodded, and Danny and Christina ran back into the bridge to retrieve the candles and blanket. "Hurry!" I wrapped my arms around myself as I surveyed the car.

"Hey, Casey?" Cameron said in a shaken voice.

"What?" I stood up from the crouch I was in to look underneath the car.

"Look at this."

I moved to the hood where he was standing. A golden strand of hair was tied into a careful bow. Cameron picked it up. "This . . . I think this . . ."

Christina and Danny popped up beside us, out of breath. "What's that?" Danny gasped.

"Someone's *hair*. Some dead person's *hair*," I realized.

Everyone piled in the car immediately. "He knew we were here," Christina blurted in fear. "We were so careful. How did he know we were here?!"

Simmering for a minute, Danny spoke in a high-pitched voice. "I don't really think we need to try and 'capture' this guy." I bobbed my head in agreement.

"I think I need to talk to Harling about this."

"You *think*?" Danny snipped. "Watch out!" he said, as Cameron turned his Beetle around and sped away. "Let's not panic. Let's be smart. Let's not panic. Let's be smart—"

"Yeah. We're going to have to start being a *lot* more careful," I responded, watching Cameron's lips sag downward as he focused on the winding road. "This is not a good thing."

"This is *soooo* not a good thing," Danny agreed.

"This is *really* so not a good thing," Christina finished.

"Yes. I know. I promise to tell Agent Harling everything."

"*That* would be a good thing." Danny continued his hysterical encouragement. I couldn't argue with them. "Like, what does this hair mean?" Danny scoffed at me. "Wait a minute. I? You? Not *WE*," Danny suggested, realizing I just insinuated that I would be talking to Harling alone. "Cameron's dad is stalking all of us and you're going *alone?*"

I looked at him in the rearview mirror. "I would rather it be just the two of us, yes. I think he takes me more seriously when I'm alone."

"But we'll be coming with *dead people's hair*," he pleaded. "How less serious can he take us?"

"Sorry." I stood my ground but wondered if it really was smarter to go alone.

Danny could only breathe in and out like a woman in labor as we reached the main road, leaving Euharlee and heading toward Carters-ville's city limits.

killer problems

The next day I found myself at Cartersville's local chain coffee shop, which was overly crowded with people. Multiple voices loudly rang out, whether they were ordering or just talking to each other. After a few moments of searching, I managed to find Agent Harling. "Hello, Casey." One eyebrow rose up. "You said you needed to talk? Please sit down or order if you'd like. I'll pay." He gestured to the counter.

I declined his offer and slumped down in my chair. He had picked one of the places with comfy chairs and a large table. However, the sheer amount of paperwork spread out dwarfed the table. I briefly wondered if it was smart of him to have all of, what looked like important papers, out in the open. As he organized them into a singular stack, I figured he probably knew better than I did. Harling cleared his throat as he shoved the paperwork into a seemingly too small briefcase. Bright sunlight escaped a cloud outside and spread across our table.

For a moment, the room seemed to spin in an awkward web. I took time during the silence to really look at Harling. Since it was Saturday, he had on a simple white T-shirt and blue jeans. It was completely bizarre, but he didn't look bad. He took a quick sip of his coffee.

"So, I assume you're here about Cameron's father?" He crossed his arms. I was wondering what Anne had told the police and was dying to know what he thought. "CPD is conducting surveillance on Mrs. Lott's home. Not only are they concerned, the FBI is too." He paused. "Though I cannot really say much about our investigation, you shouldn't worry. Georgia is far enough from California. He should have made a scene elsewhere before he made it here. As we know, however, anything is possible."

Remembering Harling coming to my defense in front of Tal and Mary, I decided to help him out a bit before diving into my news. "Have you investigated any unsolved murders in California, where he lived before he killed Cameron's mom?"

A chuckle escaped him. "Like I said, I can't tell you much. But I admire your spunk." He took another sip of coffee before continuing. "So, what did you want to talk to me about?"

I shifted uncomfortably in the armchair. "Agent Harling, I want you to know that Cameron's father isn't just here but he's the killer. I can promise you that."

"Promise . . ." he said, running his finger around the lid. He pulled out a notepad from his briefcase. "How do you know this?"

"The eyes. When I saw that photo, I knew it was him, and the build matches perfectly as well. Besides, for the most part, doesn't he go for blond-haired boys and brown-haired girls that resemble Cameron and his mother?"

Harling digested the information and looked up from where he had been writing. "Okay, what else?"

"Do you have anything on him yet? How did he escape?"

Harling seemed amused by my sheer involvement in these matters and the absurdity of my presence in front of him. I watched as something shifted in his eyes. He took a deep breath and shook his head. "Casey, I think you're an important aspect in this investigation, but I really can't tell you much. I want you to know that we now know almost all the details of his escape." My eyes widened as he leaned closer. "But that is all I can say on the matter."

Exasperated, I threw my hands up in the air. "How can I help if I know nothing?" The chair made an awful squeaking sound as I scooted it backwards. "I'm going to get something to drink."

In front of the cashier I massaged my palms and contemplated what to drink and what Harling had said. Paying for my latte, I returned to my seat still unsure what to make of this FBI agent. In a way, I owed him my life. That didn't mean I had to be happy about his treatment of me as a kid. "I'm mature enough to handle this," I said plopping down.

He rubbed his forehead. "I don't doubt that. The things you must have seen." His eyes pierced through me. "But this has nothing to do with maturity and everything to do with my position with the FBI. If you were a part of the FBI or officially registered with a police force then it would be different, but you're still in high school."

"I thought you said it wasn't a maturity thing," I mumbled.

He made a *tsking* sound. "It's not. It's a job thing and you don't have one in my agency. Let me be straight with you. I trust you, Casey, and maybe one day you could be a part of the bureau and fight these kind of crimes, and I could actually give you information but for now you're not."

The barista called my name, so I went up and got my latte. Taking a sip, I contemplated what he said. *Maybe I could be a special agent one day.* The connotation of that sentence made me laugh out loud and almost choke on my coffee. Harling raised an eye at me. "Imagine if this information leaked out. Even if you didn't do it, look around. We're not in a private enough place to discuss this information and that's why I picked it."

"Why did you do that then?"

He gave me a half frown while shaking his head. "I need you to understand that I simply *cannot* share all of the information you want or really any of it. It's a hazard for my job and I take that very seriously." Looking into his eyes I finally nodded. My curiosity was killing me but after everything he did for me, I couldn't possibly ask him to do anything more. "Considering what we've learned, he seems more than capable to do some of the things you're suggesting. You are right to be nervous about Michael Townsend, but we are watching your houses."

I gave him a small smile of thanks for this bit of information. Even if it was miniscule.

"I have actually heard how he escaped, though." I dropped my voice lower and leaned forward. "Did he really sneak out of the facility as a doctor? How did he get the clothes?"

Exhaustedly, Harling rubbed his neck and took another sip of coffee. "I really can't discuss this, Casey." His eyes narrowed as he studied me. "I'm interested how you learned this information."

I grimaced. "It doesn't matter but I still have questions. Like, how is he getting around? Did you guys figure out how he got here from San Francisco? What do you think—"

I stopped talking when he raised his hands. "I think you and your friends should be careful. We will be watching you. You're playing with fire without any gloves and it worries me. I don't want you to be so alarmed and fixated on this possibility that you can't eat or sleep.

Cameron's a very nice young man. You should be happy. We will catch this killer. *Regardless* of who he is."

I blushed. "Cameron and I . . . we aren't . . . um, never mind." I quickly took another sip of my coffee. "Thank you."

Harling looked at his watch. "Is there anything else you have for me?"

"Yes." I pulled the plastic bag with the bow-tied hair out of my pocket. "Friday night . . . this was found on Cameron's Beetle by the covered bridge in Euharlee."

Harling raised his eyebrows. "When was this?"

I blushed slightly at the fact that we found a loophole in the curfew. "It was around nine-ish when we found it."

His mouth quirked upwards. "Ah, I see. Very smart to pick a location outside city limits if you want to break curfew. I like that bridge. A bit of southern nostalgia, isn't it?"

I shrugged at his strange sentiment. "I guess."

Frowning, he held out his hand for the bag, which I graciously dropped into his hands.

He looked at my frightened countenance and attempted a calming smile. "Whether or not this man is Cameron's father, or just another psycho, I'm glad you came to me with this new information. If he left this on Cameron's car, it means he was following you."

"So, it is from the killer?"

He studied me again and seemed to wrestle with the idea of what he could say to me. There was a bit of hesitation, but he finally continued. "For now, I need you and your friends to not go anywhere alone or after dark. We've had officers watching your house for months, but you need to still be careful when you're away from home." I nodded. He continued peering at the hair closely. "Any idea which victim it's from?"

"No," I said after a moment of thought.

"This is strange for you." He hid a smile. "Trying to be a detective."

I laughed lightly. "Yeah, that's quite an understatement. I just don't know what all I can do."

Harling leaned forward on the table. "I know you're not an official part of this investigation, but I respect any information you can provide." I nodded. "First, let me know ANY time there is a kill. Even if you just text me, right then, this is very important. Second, something like this . . ." he referred to the hair, "needs to be brought to me. Immediately. Because we can analyze DNA samples. It's evidence. We like evidence." I covered my face and released a shameful sigh. "Finally . . ." Agent Harling looked me dead in the eyes. "Be careful. Be extremely careful out there. And know that we are going to do everything we can to protect you, your friends, and everyone else in Cartersville."

I bobbled my head. "Okay, Agent."

"Do you trust me, Casey?"

"Yeah . . . I do," I admitted as we shared a small, equal smile.

—

I spun my chair around to focus on the *Mortem Mobo*. Without a crowd of people around, it didn't seem to have an ambiance of horror. It reminded me, more or less, of a really old, worn out book that you find in some ghost shop or flea market. I rolled over to the shelf and opened up the book. The first page it brought me to was my father's tale.

Curiosity bubbled in me as I started to skim the page.

I couldn't believe what had just happened. All I did was steal one piece of candy, no big deal . . . I looked back up at the television's screen.

"Five dead down by the Kangaroo station on 41," the reporter said. I glanced back down at the book my own father passed down to me. The section about me was completely empty, waiting to be filled with this sordid tale. If my dad was right, eventually it would hold everything I had ever done. He kept telling me that it would write itself; this book was a recorder for us. I knew I needed to research it.

I dragged my eyes from the page. I knew the book was magic. Mom had said our powers came from witches, but to actually experience my father's thoughts and see his story was something completely bizarre. Shutting the book, I allowed my shallow breathing to calm. I tilted my head slightly and was alerted to the dark blue leather that seemed to crackle with energy. *I need to research this,* I thought, mimicking my father. I scooted my chair closer. I tried to open the book to the beginning. However, the page refused to budge, and instead, opened up somewhere near the end.

"What's this?" a lanky black-haired boy asked in a British accent.

"Something crucial to your future generations, love," a brown-braided girl responded. The sky surrounding the two was a gloomy, London gray. There was no sign of life, but there were carriages on the street and the building reminded me of something you'd see in the 1800s.

"What does that mean? Why are you doing this, Abelyne?" Roderick said, stepping toward the pretty girl.

"Oh, you know why." She stepped closer and trailed a finger down his cheek. Roderick flinched. "Is seeing my death date so painful?"

"Only because it's so soon," he lamented bowing his head.

"We knew the cost and the reason."

He grabbed the Mortem Mobo from Abelyne. "What does it do?"

She laughed like soft rain. "So inquisitive. It records, it answers, it knows, it speaks . . ." Suddenly she quieted. "Your family is cursed. You know how and why, but that might be for-gotten. This book is one of my own." Her hand caressed the cover. "And it will guide anyone affected by your family's curse. It will decide what to tell you and how." Her eyes shut for a moment. "But just like your powers, it is a curse. Don't underestimate what it can do to you."

Roderick held the book tight against his chest and nodded. "Thank you." He leaned forward and kissed her on her lips.

"I only wish I could do more," she sighed. Taking a deep breath, she stared into Roderick's eyes.

Suddenly, the book jolted in my hands.

"How much longer?" she asked me, her blue eyes turning violet under a sudden burst of sun.

Numbers rolled through my mind and finally straightened themselves out: 0.0.0.0.0.5. I held her close, cringing at her final seconds.

"Now," I whispered as she burst into flames, burning me with her.

Yelping, I dropped the book. The smell of burning flesh filled my nostrils, but my actual flesh was unblemished.

"Scary, huh?" Christina asked casually, entering the room. "Did the same thing to me the first time," she recalled absentmindedly. She traveled over to my desk and played with the book's cover.

"Are they all . . ." I was at a loss for words.

Christina shrugged. "It's apparently a different experience for everyone, but they are all relatively vivid."

That's an understatement, I thought numbly. "I'll want to see it again." I watched my twin closely.

"Fine." Her voice clipped as her fingers tightened on the thick spine. An almost magnetic pull tried to convince me to keep looking, to drag it back from her. I sensed that this wouldn't be the last time I read from it. She pulled it up to her chest. "How was your talk with Harling?" Sighing, I recounted our conversation. "Hmm." Christina leaned against the desk, half sitting. "Have you told Cameron and Danny yet?"

"Danny, yes." I remembered his interest in every detail. "Because he called earlier, and he told me he would tell Cameron. So technically yes to him, too."

She nodded at what I said. I looked around my room and then back to my sister.

"I'm sorry." She breathed quickly, shocking me. "About blowing up on Cameron . . . and everything."

I stared at her. "You don't have to apologize. It's not exactly a normal situation. Also, I'm . . . sorry for all the crap I've said to you lately."

"Me, too." She hugged herself.

A thick silence covered us as Christina shrugged. "How much

have you read?" I asked, gesturing to the book she held in her hands like a child.

"It's not how much I've read as much as what I've learned." Her eyes sparkled disconcertingly. "Our powers date back to the 1000s. Everything we are came from the Dark Ages, which is poetic, isn't it?" Her voice was full of wonder. "And each ancestor had a unique power; almost none are the same." At this point, Christina was on my bed and bouncing. "Sure, they're similar, but not really. And what some of them have accomplished . . . Oh, Casey. These powers . . ." She trailed off, a smile in her eyes.

"Did you find out their effects on a person? Anything bad?" I watched as her face fell. "What problems are there? Why is it a curse?"

Her eyes darkened, and she stopped her bouncing. "I don't know what you mean," she said. "All the powers I saw had wonderful qualities and amazing benefits." Christina dropped the book back on my desk with a heavy *thump* and headed to the door. "You should consider that while you read." With that, she slammed the door, leaving the book alone with me.

CHAPTER TEN

the book and its plan

The rest of January went by with a rush of winter: Sleet, long nights, promises of snow with nothing to show. Though there were no more deaths, I held on tight to my friends as every day meant a potential victim. Fear ripped into my skin. Cartersville was in a panic, locking all doors. Roads became deserted at dusk as people realized it might be better to keep to the shadows of home. Though everyone was pissed about all the cancelled events. I had given Cameron the book, and he had been reading it for a few weeks. I shook off the familiar stares as I walked into Spanish class.

I cautiously took my seat as Alex gave me a sympathetic frown, sliding in the seat beside me. "You okay, Casey?" He normally sat across the room, so I vaguely wondered how the normal patron of that seat would react.

"I feel odd," I whispered, barely audible.

"¡Hola clase! Como es—" Señora Johnson continued, but I could no longer hear her, because a few blocks from the school, the killer had found a lonely Cameron's-mom-look-alike jogger.

Thanks to being resuscitated by Christina, my powers were becoming something I could control, but only slightly. The kill was quick, yet meaningful. My mind transferred into the woman. I felt his huge hand wrap around what was currently our neck. A sharp silver knife caressed the woman's skin and then quickly pierced through her heart.

"*Perhaps tonight should be a pizza night,*" the woman said, gripping her daughter's hand while looking lovingly into a man's eyes. "*We deserve a treat.*"

"*I think you're absolutely right.*" Just as he leaned down to kiss her, the vision shifted.

"*NO, you can't do that—*" she screeched. My mind whirled as I fought to escape back into the classroom.

"*Thanks again for the ri—*" the woman said, looking at a much older gentleman in front of an airport.

"*What do you mean she's dead?!*" Her face was twisted agony as she gripped a doctor. As the vision swirled more strongly out of control, I fought to return to my own mind.

If only I could have watched her grow up, the woman lamented finally, her biggest regret ending and pushing me back to my Spanish class.

About twenty pairs of eyes anxiously hovered over me, judging, searching, pitying. I froze and instantly assessed the fact that I was on my back, lying on the floor beside my desk.

"Casey?" Señora Johnson asked. Her brown eyes filled with worry. "Are you okay?"

He's still killing, I thought, blinking and trying to clear my head of the vision. "Yeah . . ." I muttered weakly.

"Please state your emergency." The voice over the intercom was

259

spitting static. I groaned quietly to myself. Of course, they would push the panic button.

"One of my students, Casey Darling, passed out," Mrs. Johnson said nervously.

"All right," the sweet southern voice said. "We'll send the nurse right away. Is she conscious?"

"Yes."

"Okay, just hang tight." The intercom clicked off.

A few minutes later, our school nurse, Miss Harden, came in. Considering I was surrounded by a ton of worried and skeptical people, she figured out who I was right away. "Okay, what happened?" she asked, all business.

"I've been feeling dizzy since this morning," I lied quickly. "So, I didn't eat anything and when I walked into the room it got really bad." Alex cocked his head slightly at my words. "And I just passed out."

The nurse nodded. Taking off her stethoscope, she listened to my heart rate. "Well, your heart rate is slightly elevated. Do you have any health issues?"

I peered over her shoulder at Alex. "No, ma'am."

"Okay . . . well, let's get you something to eat and call your mom to come get you."

"No," I said quickly, grabbing her hand. "I'm really fine." Everyone around the room stared at me for an uncomfortably long time. "I don't need to miss any school."

Miss Harden's lips tilted down. "I don't want you to get sick again."

"I won't . . . I just need some food." I mumbled the lie.

Seemingly not pleased with the fact, Miss Harden finally nodded. "Okay then. Everybody get back to work. Go get some food, and then do what you need to."

I sighed in relief as she shut the door. I pulled out my phone and quickly let Harling know what happened.

—

"Casey!" Cameron excitedly shouted from behind me in the parking lot. I blinked up at him as the sun shrank my pupils. School had been a rush of horribleness after my infamous episode, but that wasn't exactly uncommon at this point.

"Hey!" I was trying to muster up the same happiness.

He gave me a quick shoulder squeeze before dropping his arm. "Alex told me about what happened. Bad day?"

I bit my lip and closed my eyes. When I reopened them he was staring at me expectantly. "That's an understatement." I kicked the ground. "Anyway, you sounded like you had something to say?"

His eyes lingered on me for a second before he continued. "I found something in the book." His voice was filled with glee. "Something to help us with our . . ." He looked around to make sure we were definitely alone. "Powers."

He tilted his head towards his Beetle and together we walked over to it. He quickly opened my side to let me in before going to the driver's side and pulling the book out of his backpack. "Okay. So back in the old days, some of your family thought it would be helpful to practice their powers." He sat down in the driver's seat.

"Practice . . ." I said doubtfully.

"Yes, practice. It makes perfect." He ignored my sarcastic glare. "Now, some of them were lucky and their powers weren't dangerous, or not really, and they could just use it on a person. For instance, one of your ancestors, Ernesto, could explain in detail the way a death was going to happen, so he became a sort of fortuneteller for people. It worked, too." He continued his excitement, fading only for a moment. "Sadly, as he studied more and used his power to his advantage, the power intensified. The deaths started happening right after he predicted them . . . so people were literally dying after touching him."

A shudder rippled through me. "Did that happen to everyone's powers?"

He ran a hand through his hair forcefully. "Yes and no. It didn't change his powers or anyone else's. I personally think it just brought out . . . the 'curse.'" Slowly, he rested his head back on the seat. "The book made that clear to me."

We sat in silence for a moment. "Did it say anything about how *you* could have powers? Or *why* you have powers?"

A bark of a laugh escaped him. "No, not quite, but I'm a big anomaly. It kept bringing up these points on transferring powers, but it never lasted, and it was very dangerous. I don't even know what we would have done that could have even begun to transfer powers."

I frowned in thoughtful consideration. "I can try and do research on it," I said apprehensively, fully aware that the book could make my powers even more pronounced. *It's so strange,* I thought as I looked at the blue binding. *There is so much it must know and that I can learn.* As I thought of it, though, a shudder vibrated through me. This book had definitely become a new addition to our family.

"Don't be afraid, Casey. You aren't alone anymore." His fingers brushed mine as he handed the book back to me. "Now, about the practicing. Obviously, I'm not just going to start killing people."

"That's comforting."

"I was thinking animals."

My eyebrows knitted together. "Animals?"

262

"Yep. Actually, Danny thought about animals. I talked to him earlier and he's got some trapping equipment that we can use. I'll figure out *how* I can kill people while you're figuring out *why* I can kill people. Besides, maybe you can experience the deaths to try and control your powers more, since they are getting even more powerful."

"You want to kill animals?" I scoffed, my brain still fuzzy from school.

He let out a frustrated breath. "Of course not. But Casey, come on. If I don't understand whatever is going on with me . . . I could end up hurting a lot more than a bunny rabbit in the forest. I was angry when this happened." He slammed his hands against the steering wheel. "God, I was just like my dad."

"Hey," I said sharply, leaning against the door. "Shut up. You are *nothing* like your dad. You didn't do that intentionally."

Cameron stared at me for a long moment. "That night, when I killed that guy, you were on my side; why? I killed someone, and you saw it with your own eyes. Why didn't you freak out on me like your sister?"

The air was filled with reticence. "Because . . . you were so scared." I tried to capture his gaze, but he refused to look at me. "When your father . . . when Michael kills someone, it is full of hatred and contempt for the people he's killing, and that was the complete opposite of what happened with you. I could tell you were horrified, and then—" I took a deep breath. "And then, you tried to hurt yourself. I thought you were going to kill yourself right then and there and I couldn't bear it."

"But *why?*" His golden eyes were shining through their moisture.

I stared at him for a long time. My mouth parted to speak but no words came out. His own face was contorted in confusion. Moving slowly, I closed the space between us and kissed him.

He must have been shocked because he momentarily pulled away, but after a second he breathed in my air and leaned forward. Unlike the porch kiss, I felt in control, but that didn't mean it wasn't taking over me. I tangled my hand in his hair and pulled him closer once more before releasing him. Our breathing synced up in ravaged paces.

"I know I've only known you six months, but I feel this connection and . . . I trust you."

He used his thumb to trace his bottom lip. "That . . . was definitely not the response I was expecting."

I let out a breathy laugh as my cheeks warmed. "Yeah, um, sorry if that was weird?"

"No, no, no. That was the opposite, that was—" His phone chiming cut him off. He held up his index finger and read the text. "That's Danny." His eyes caught mine again and this time he blushed. "Do you mind if we meet up with him?"

"No problem, I'll text Christina." I fumbled in my pockets for my phone.

He placed a hand on my shoulder. "I also, um, I want to talk about this later, okay?"

I looked at his hand and placed my own on top of it. "Definitely." We shared a smile before Cameron began to drive. "Let's find Christina and Danny first. If you're going to start killing Bambi, we need Christina to bring him back to life," I said, texting my sister.

—

I couldn't stop admiring Danny's traps. I would always forget how into hunting his family was. He tightened the rope on one that he claimed would capture rabbits. "There we are." He took a step back to survey his work. "Y'all are lucky I'm here."

"I'm always lucky to have you as a friend, Danny," I said. He put his hand on his heart in mock flattery.

"So, you brought us all the way up here to do what, again?" Christina asked massaging the space between her eyebrows.

"The usual," Danny said, ushering us away from his hard work. He had mentioned earlier that we needed to give the traps time and space. "Murdering animals in the name of magic science."

I rolled my eyes. "I know we're not normal, but you could have phrased that better." I turned to my paler than normal sister. "The book mentioned practice was a good idea. Besides, you can heal anything we actually manage to kill. I don't really even know if my powers will work, but at least yours and probably Cameron's will."

Her face held a concerned expression. "Our powers aren't toys—" she started to interrupt, but I cut her off.

"And the book says this can help *strengthen* and help them." At the word "strengthen," she seemed to be satisfied.

Christina sat against a tree and began looking back through the book. Realizing he didn't have much to do, Cameron began playing on his phone. Danny gestured for me to walk over to a spot away from them. "What's up?" I asked him.

"Are you okay with doing this?"

I shrugged. "I'm really not sure, but it seems important to try?" I rubbed my neck.

He took a deep breath. "Fair enough." His eyes flashed to Cameron. "Have you talked to him about this new power of his?"

I pursed my lips together. "Not really."

"I was afraid of that."

265

"Why?" I searched his face.

"He seems really torn up about it. We talked it over and the boy doesn't have a clue what he's doing. I'm glad he's got you and the book, but I want to make sure you're safe and okay with everything." He grabbed my shoulder in a soft squeeze.

"Thanks, Danny. There's a lot I want to talk to him about. And, uh, actually we kissed earlier."

His face lit up just as a rustling sound appeared to our left. Cameron and Christina jumped up from their spots. "What was that?" Cameron asked from a couple feet away.

"I don't know." I looked around but didn't see anything. "Maybe it's an animal?" Danny and I considered each other. "Want to go check?"

He nodded, and we headed over to where he had put his closest trap. I thought about our encounter at the covered bridge and had to shake the impending fear out of me.

"He kissed you earlier??" Danny half whispered.

"Actually, I kissed him."

"O-m-g!" His eyes were bulging out of his head. Finding nothing at that trap we moved to the next one. At this point I couldn't see Cameron and Christina anymore.

"Yeah. I don't know what came over me, but he was asking why I was still with him after what happened and he looked so sad and I just, kissed him." I stooped down and picked a stick off the ground. Absentmindedly, I began to twirl it around. "That was stupid of me, huh?"

He crouched beside one of the traps that had a covering object. "I'm not sure if stupid is the right word." He eyed me from his shortened position. "But maybe y'all should talk about it. Heck, about everything."

"Agreed." Together we surveyed the rest of the traps but found no terrified animals. Just as we were about to head back to our group, we heard Christina scream. Fear propelling me, we raced through the woods to our friends.

CHAPTER ELEVEN

down the rabbit hole

It can't be him. I can't lose them, I thought as Danny and I jumped over roots and dodged pointy rocks. I don't think I've ever run as fast as I did that day. As we got closer, I was able to see a third figure beside our friends. Danny and I burst through the trees and found . . . *Tiffany?*

Christina stood in front of her best friend with her hands on her hips. Tiffany's face seemed conflicted as it danced between a sheepish smile and scrunched up lips. "Hey guys," she said as we caught our breaths. "Long time no see."

I turned my attention to Christina after staring at Tiffany for a while. "Why did you scream?"

"Don't worry," she said, shaking her head. "Tiffany practically jump scared us."

Tiffany rolled her eyes. "No. Y'all are just highly unobservant."

Cameron twisted his leather bracelet and addressed me. "What actually happened is that we heard more rustling after you guys left and decided to check it out. Christina looked behind a bush and screamed when she saw Tiffany."

Glaring at each other, Tiffany and Christina both let out a haughty huff. Tired of their behavior, I turned to Tiffany. "What are you doing here anyway?"

She dropped her arms and put her hands in her pockets. Staring at the ground, I watched as she moved the rocks around with her feet. "I may have been spying on you."

"What!? Why?"

Her eyes flashed angrily. "Because y'all have kept me in the dark for months. I haven't heard anything since *Christmas.* No one has said a word about what's happening and all I have to rely on is the rumors around school."

Danny *tsked.* "You know better than to listen to gossip, Tiff."

She kicked a rock hard enough to send it flying through the underbrush. "Well that's the only social interaction I've had, so . . ." She finally looked up at us and let out a large breath. "I saw Cameron leaving and decided to follow."

I rubbed my wrist in a similar fashion as Cameron does with his cuffs. "I'm sorry, Tiffany. A lot has happened and it's a long story—"

"But I'm your *friend!*" Her sudden outburst made us all jump. "At least, I thought I was."

Bright sunlight lit up her dark features. Her eyes were fierce, but I could see the pain they held as well. I had begun to walk to her when Christina moved in front of her. She wrapped her in a tight hug. Tiffany returned the gesture. "Tiffany, I'm so sorry! I should have put more effort into talking to you about everything."

"It's okay," she said with a small sniffle. She shook her head making the coils bounce crazily. "At least it will be if you tell me everything now?"

We all looked at each other.

Tiffany couldn't stand it any longer. "Will you please just talk to me? Are the rumors true? Is Cameron's dad *killing* people?!"

I looked at Cameron who had looked away. Then I gauged Christina's face the most carefully. This was her best friend, so I felt it was mostly up to her. We locked eyes and I shrugged at her. She turned her face back to Tiffany with a brazen expression in her eyes. The next hour was used for telling Tiffany everything.

—

"I think she handled that well," Cameron said as he drove me home. We were closing in on curfew, so the world was painted in dying golds and harsh indigos. "I mean, she seemed to fully embrace the powers part which was cool."

He was right. Despite my constant lookout for panic on her face, I never saw any. I was grateful now more than ever for her presence in our friend group. I leaned my head against the seatbelt and stared up at the sky. A glowing moon faintly shone out through some residual clouds. "I'm not sure how to feel about your power," I said without meaning to. In the darkened window I saw him face me. "I mean I'm sure I like you, and that you've been a really good friend, and even that you could be something more." My cheeks flushed. "But I don't know what to think about the killing."

As he turned left, I realized just how close we were to my house. I finally faced him to find his eyes fixated on the road. "That's fair," he said.

We drove in silence until we were at my house. The front porch light was on and our family's Escort sat silently to the side. He put the car in park and turned it off. After another few minutes of silence, we were plunged into darkness. I scooted around in my seat so that I was facing him a bit better. The seatbelt remained on.

"I honestly don't know how I feel about the killing . . . but I do know how I feel about you." He rubbed his bracelet.

"You do that a lot." I nodded to his hands.

"Yeah, nervous habit I guess." He turned to me. In the low light I could barely see his eyes. I felt the urge to get closer and look at him clearly. Since the nearest streetlight was at the edge of the street, I could only see fragments of skin, a patch of his iris, a smidgen of his cheek. "I don't blame you if you want to go away—"

"That's not it!" We recoiled at my loud voice. "I don't want to go away . . . or for you to go away."

"Okay."

"I just want to make sure that that isn't going to happen again and that you're okay."

"Okay."

"I think I want to be with you."

"Okay." We watched each other. I pinched the skin around my hands. Since the car had been off for a few minutes, whorls of cold had begun to interrupt our space. The coldness leeched into my hands, which caused me to rub them together a bit harder. Cameron stood remarkably still, but he was shivering periodically.

"What are you thinking?" I asked.

"That I want to kiss you." I blushed and looked down at my twiddling hands. "But I also am thinking that we should take things slow?"

I found a small smile curving across his face. "I'm . . . I'm okay with that."

"And if you think you know how you feel about the killing then you can tell me whenever you know."

I nodded. "Honestly, I prefer not to think about it."

"Okay." Slowly, he put his hand on mine and squeezed. "Thanks for being honest with me, Darling."

"Any time." We said our goodbyes and I disappeared into my house.

CHAPTER TWELVE

shop till you drop

"Settle down students," Principal Bullfrog said with a slight tremor to his voice. "This is an assembly, not a pep rally." I rolled my eyes as I sat down beside Cameron and Danny. "This is a very important meeting and we need all of you to understand what is going on." Hundreds of students chatted loudly as they poured into the sweaty, overcrowded gym.

Tal, Mary, and Police Chief Arnold stood patiently beside Bullfrog. They were an imposing trio that dwarfed the principal. Finally, Tal asked for the microphone. Waiting for the last of the student body to enter, he looked around the gym at all of us. I leaned against Cameron and sighed. "Today we are not talking about curfews, but about prom, and other events that were shut down earlier this school year."

As if a mute button had been pushed, everyone in the room shut up. Principal Benton gratefully took the microphone back. "As many of you know, prom was cancelled." Boos ruptured from the crowd. "Quiet!" he yelled sharply. "However," he continued, louder than he needed to be, "we realize that that is not only unfair but unrealistic. Everybody here who qualifies wants a prom, right?" The students answered back with cheers. Cameron squeezed my hand, and when I looked up at him I could see agreement on his face.

Mary grabbed the microphone, her red hair swishing, and looked out at everyone sternly until we quieted. "As a solution, we will be holding a delayed prom, in late April, rather than early March." Again, cheers exploded from everyone around us. Girls jumped up and down squealing, and the boys had their own form of enthusiasm. Danny practically radiated glee. "There will be only pre-approved after-parties and heavy police supervision, but we will still make it a night to remember." She grinned like a proud mom.

When the masses finally quieted enough, Police Chief Arnold took the microphone. "Also, since the Bartow County Fair was cancelled, we at the Cartersville Police Department and Mayor Santini have managed to get them to come back next month." There was another babble of excitement, although it was nothing compared to the prom uproar. The police chief, however, had a very happy, smug grin pasted on his face that looked just like his son's. Ryan sat in front of us beside Patricia. The two of them could have passed for royalty with all of their flair and posture. I turned toward Danny, the energy of all the news buzzing through me.

"We get our fair," I said excitedly.

Cameron laughed and put an arm on my shoulders. "You sound more excited for that than prom."

"Oh, she kinda is," Danny teased.

"It's her *favorite* thing," Christina added from behind us. The two of them shared a laugh as my cheeks began to turn red.

"I think it's cute," Cameron responded to my blushing.

My other friends exchanged looks.

"Despite these events, there will still be a curfew. This is still a dangerous and important time for each and every one of you." The police chief continued to drone on about safety and prom and what to do, but we blocked out the rest of the lecture.

"This is so exciting," Tiffany whisper-squealed, with a graceful smile splitting her features.

"Hey, Danny," Phoebe's sweet voice called out, breaking through the layers of our group.

"Hey," he responded, his earlier, happy emotion quickly becoming overwhelmed. "How are you, Phoebe?"

She mouthed her response. "I'm okay. You?"

"Good."

"Hey, let's make a plan to go dress shopping." Tiffany muffled her clapping.

"Sure," I agreed.

"Dress shopping?" It took me a second to realize what Cameron was asking.

"Oh, yeah, us girls have to have our shopping dates for big events."

"So . . . you're going to prom?" he asked.

"Yes, I've been planning on going for a while now."

"Oh, I see. Who with?" He shuffled his feet.

"Oh!" I was taken aback. "No one right now."

"Would you, would you want to maybe go with me?"

I clasped my hands in front of me and rocked forward. "I really would."

His eyes sparkled as I ran to Tiffany and Christina.

—

I plopped down on my bed. The colors of prom dresses still circled inside of my head. We had explored every formal shop within a forty-mile radius in the hopes of finding other wonderful dresses. In the end, the three we had tried on first had been put on layaway as we drove back to the madness of David's Bridal. It was overall a great day. Feeling inspired, I walked over to my easel and got my paints ready.

Just as I dipped the brush into a bright teal color, my phone rang. I walked over to my dresser and picked it up. "Hey," I answered.

"O-M-G, tell me allll about shopping and your new boyfriend." Danny buzzed in my ear. I shook my head and walked back over to my canvas. Cradling the phone between my ear and shoulder, I continued to paint.

I told him all about the exhausting world of dress shopping. "I did find a good one, though." He squealed so loudly in my ear, I almost dropped my paintbrush. The canvas now held a base layer of blues for what I was going to make an ocean. "Prom will be fun."

"You betcha! I cannot *wait!* I've been planning this thing since last year and I am so glad it's not cancelled." I smiled and worked on the sun portion of the canvas. "And you and Cameron?"

"We're taking it slow, but it's definitely something. Plus, I'm kind of disregarding the accidental almost killing because it was, you know, accidental."

"True, true." I wiped my forehead with the back of my paint-splattered hand. "Just be careful with him and keep yourself happy and safe."

I smiled. "Hey, speaking of being careful. I have sort of a weird question about Christina."

"Okay, shoot."

I put the paintbrush in my water and sat down on my bed. The painting was nowhere near finished but it had a good base. "What do you think about her and that book?"

There was a thoughtful pause. "It's troubling," he haltingly responded.

"More than troubling. You know she thinks that book is helping me. That these powers of mine are *good*," I said, desperately trying to keep quiet.

"Well—"

"Oh, not you too."

"It's not that, Casey. It's just . . . her powers are wonderful things to her. She *hates* death, just as much as you, if not more. And she has a way to stop it. Think about it. She has a way to *stop* it. I think maybe she wants you to see that."

I plopped backwards onto the bed. I was grateful for the soft sheets that cradled me. "Yes." I paused. "I understand that, but her obsession with that book is dangerous. It's always by her side when we don't have it, and she just looks so . . ."

"Tired?" he said.

I nodded but then shook my head. "It is almost worse than that. It's like the book or *something* is draining her. Like, she might become hollow."

"That's dark. I guess I see what you mean."

"If you lived with her, if you saw her at home, you'd have noticed it too. Besides, everything in that book says our powers are a *curse*. There will be no happy ending and she doesn't seem to get that."

There was a loud sigh through the phone. "Maybe I can talk to her? I definitely don't want anything bad to happen to her."

I returned his sigh. "No, no it's not your problem to deal with." I splayed out my fingers above me. "Thanks for letting me rant about it though."

"No problem! I'm always here for you, y'know."

I smiled. "I know, but I also know that it is late and I'm tired from all the shopping."

He chuckled in my ear. "I'm still jealous I didn't get to go. Alright, Casey, I'll talk to you tomorrow?"

"Tomorrow."

a whole new meaning to the word acrophobia

"I've always wanted to go on a fair date," I confessed as we pulled into the parking lot. A March sky meant the town was painted dark, but that just meant the fair was beautifully lit up.

"Well then, I'm glad you accepted my offer." Cameron got out of the car and walked over to my side to open the door. I smiled up at him as he offered me his hand. A few days ago, he had offered to take me as our first real date. It had all felt very magical. Feeling like a five-year old, I sprinted to the ticket booth.

Laughing behind me, Cameron wrapped his hand around mine and used the other one to get us all day passes. "This place looks slightly rickety."

I slapped his arm lightly. "It's wonderful, not rickety!" Though looking at the grounds, I saw what he meant. The park still filled me with the joy I had as a kid, but now I could see some of its flaws. Its ground was covered with trash, as the carnie custodians couldn't keep up with littering tots. Some of the rides looked in danger of toppling to the ground, and many adults had a look of *please let's go home, we've been here for hours.* I also noticed the volume of dark navy uniforms that belonged to the Cartersville Police Department walking about. I felt my lips squish into a grimace.

"Hey." Cameron tapped my scrunched-up mouth with his index finger. "No frowning allowed."

I beamed at him as we began our journey. The first ride we went on was the Tornado. I sat across from him and lowered my eyebrows suggestively. "Can you handle this ride if I control the spinners?"

He gave me a sizzling, smug look. "I'm sure I can, but you have to hand it over to let me have a shot too."

I agreed, and the ride began. Between the swirling of the ride and my own laughter, I couldn't remember a time I had so much fun. Cameron's laugh rung out clear as the ride continued to provide a true tornado of fun. After a few minutes of spinning us, he took the wheel and began turning us in the opposite direction. My earlier dizziness changed into a flop of elation and I felt my eyes crinkle happily against the wind.

We freely and somewhat drunkenly stumbled away onto another ride. After that, we went to another, and another, and another. "Let's get something to snack on," Cameron whined after we were released from the Scrambler. I nodded enthusiastically as we went to a stand and ordered a giant funnel cake and two water bottles. "I don't think I've ever seen you this happy. You haven't stopped smiling since we got here."

"What can I say? You picked the perfect date," I responded, tearing off a piece of the funnel cake and closing my eyes as I put it in my mouth. "Yuuum—I absolutely love funnel cake."

Cameron shook his head with a small smile on his face. "You're adorable." He tore off a piece of the delicious dough for himself.

I tilted my head to the left, thoughts plaguing the front of my mind. "You know, I've been thinking . . ." I started, swallowing my last bite loudly. "The woods by the highway really aren't all that far from Cartersville *proper*."

"Casey . . ." Cameron moaned.

"But this is serious, Cameron. Harling has probably extended his search radius to all the forests around Cartersville, but he still hasn't been found. I'm just wondering about how your dad would be able to move in and out—"

"Casey!" Cameron half-yelled, eyes somber. "This is a date. Our first ever date. The killer isn't here . . . I want *you* to be."

"I am."

"No, not right this moment." He put a hand over mine. "Earlier you were completely with me, but right now you're thinking about my dad and I wish you would stop. I want tonight to be perfect and fun and a *break*."

I looked at the Golden Boy and my heart stirred. If we were going to try and be together he was right. We needed to actually try the whole relationship thing. "Okay, I understand and agree." I gave him a fraction of the smile I had before. "Okie-doke. What's the plan now?"

He gave me a sly look. "I know just the thing."

—

The Ferris wheel seats tilted slightly back and forth as we rose above the ground. I normally didn't have a fear of heights, but that was a bit nerve-wracking. I was gripping the handle bar so tightly my knuckles turned the color of the moon.

"Afraid of heights?" Cameron teased, looking completely relaxed with his hands behind his head.

"No," I said, wincing at my rough voice. "Well, not normally." He chuckled and made the seat rock even more. Closing my eyes, I heard him attempt to hide his laughter.

"Yeah, definitely not scared." Slowly, making sure the seat stayed still, Cameron put his arm around my shoulder.

"Well, that might put a damper on things."

"What do you mean?"

"Open your eyes and see." Feeling silly about my fears, I opened my eyes. There we were at the very top of the Ferris wheel. My heart fluttered to a stop, but I wasn't sure if it was from the height or the beauty.

Because it was nighttime, the city looked like it was covered in glitter. All of the buildings shone beneath the trees; it was picture perfect. Taking care in my movements, I turned to look at Cameron. "Did you plan this?"

His sun-colored skin glowed red in the dark. "Yeah . . . I paid the guy down below. You know, this is always really romantic in movies. Of course, I should have checked whether or not you were afraid of heights."

I leaned my head on his shoulder. He jumped a bit before resting his head against mine. "I'm glad you paid him off." I giggled. As I snuggled into him, the inevitable happened.

Her brown hair was pulled into a tight ponytail, and she smiled down at a small boy with blond hair. My breathing hitched, and I felt Cameron look at me worriedly, but I was suddenly in that woman's brain, watching as she looked up at the tall Ferris wheel. The little boy pulled her toward the Twister, and just for a second, they were clouded by the shadow of a tree. That was all Michael Townsend needed.

Slipping through the shadows, Cameron's father stabbed the woman in the back. Our breath flew from our body and I saw her look into the young boy's terrified eyes. "*Run*," we whispered.

I yanked myself out of the vision. Hot tears fell down my face. "Casey, is it . . ." He trailed off, looking into my eyes. I guess they said it all, because he gave a short nod. Shouts erupted in the night air as Cameron eyed the crowds. "I know parents are supposed to interrupt you when you're with your girlfriend, but I didn't think it would be like this."

A half-sob half-laugh bubbled up from my lungs as loudspeakers echoed through the crowd. "Attention carnival guests: security asks that you remain where you are due to an incident near the south entrance. All rides will be shutting down and all guests are asked to remain where they are until authorities secure all areas of the fairgrounds. Do not panic. It is very important that no one exits the park. All operators are asked to stand by and keep guests in line." The announcer's voice attempted to stay positive but was unsuccessful.

Giving each other a nervous look, Cameron and I looked down from our high perch. Everybody glanced around at each other. It was as if you could read their doubting thoughts about people that they had probably come in contact with. The Ferris wheel operator looked very disgruntled as he got everyone off of the giant machine, one by one. He asked the riders to stand at the railing encircling the ride. It seemed like it took forever for the wheel to rotate, stopping every minute to let off each rider, until our seat reached the bottom. My feet on solid ground once more, I leaned heavily on Cameron. "What happened?" he asked quietly.

"A woman and her . . ." My mind flitted to the briefest flash of a memory from her. ". . . Child," I sadly noted. "I don't know about the child, but he managed to kill the mother."

His arm tightened around me. "Are you okay?"

I shook my head slightly as none other than Mary and Tal arrived in front of us. "Casey Darling." Mary drew out the first syllable of my last name. "This is an awfully big coincidence."

My cheeks flushed but I stood my ground. The Ferris wheel operator lingered; he looked curious as to why detectives had been zeroing in on us teenagers. Though theories about the killer had been thrown around, disdain for the police force grew, as they seemed incapable of catching him. The carnies were from out of town but certainly knew about everything.

Detective Tal cleared his throat. "You want to tell us where you have been for the last fifteen minutes?"

"Look, I don't know what happened tonight," the Ferris wheel operator butted in, "but they were at the very top of this here wheel when I heard that racket goin' on. So, they didn't do nothin', aright?" Cameron smiled at the man, glad his money went further than he expected. Mary's eyes cut to him.

"Exactly. And I'm on my first date right now." I pulled Cameron close to me. "Unless that's illegal now?"

Shaking her head, Mary crossed her arms. "There's no need to snark at me, young lady. You're still a suspect in my book." She tapped her foot several times and looked at her partner. "Lucky for you, this nice man is here to confirm that, while you're suspiciously at the fair, you didn't commit this crime."

"Half the town's here, lady. It ain't that weird that she is," the ride operator said.

Tal rested his hands by his sides. One hand fell close to his gun and made my eyes widen. He addressed Cameron. "I don't know if I buy the Michael Townsend story, son. But if it's true, better hope you don't end up like him."

At that moment, Mary's walky-talky went off, preventing us from reacting to such an affront. "Suspect has escaped over the north fence heading west on Martin Luther King. Repeat, suspect heading west on MLK." The device chirped. The two of them looked at each other and jetted off.

I looked at Cameron with wide eyes. He was pensively staring after Tal and Mary. "Cameron?" He looked down at me. Worry filled me to the core. "Don't listen to them."

"Casey . . . was he here because of *us*?" He pulled me further down the railing, gaining privacy from the operator and other carnival guests standing in place. "Was my dad here . . . because of *us*?"

I didn't answer for a long time, but right when I was about to, another voice came on to the speakers. "Citywide curfew is in effect. The fairgrounds are now closing. Citywide curfew is in effect. Please have a safe night, and if anyone has suspicious activity to report, please notify security personnel while exiting the gates."

I gripped Cameron's hand tightly as we left the park. We passed paramedics and a huddle of officers tending to the victim and her child, which had just been inside of my head. "We can't do anything until he's gone, can we?" I realized. "Or at least . . . not without consequences," I mumbled. He nodded solemnly. "We shouldn't go to prom."

He saw the hurt in my eyes. I saw a flash of anger pass through his. "It's not fair." I nodded lightly and pulled him into a walking hug. "Casey, it's our senior year."

"Prom isn't that important," I said, wondering about Christina's and Danny's reaction if they had to go without me.

"But it should be."

"We just have to find him. Put an end to this." I looked up into his golden brown eyes and saw my own determination reflected.

"And we will." His voice had an unnerving amount of steely resolve.

"I just hope it's sooner rather than later." I bobbed my head once and joined the squeezing herd moving through the gates.

"So much for a perfect night."

My frown slipped back onto my lips. "It was perfect, Cameron." He stared at the disappointed guests being forced to leave. "Thank you."

"I had a lot of fun."

"I'm glad. But prom, Casey?" He sounded exhausted as he cautiously maneuvered us through the parking lot. "What are you going to tell everyone? *Should* we go?"

I scratched my head and sighed. "Well . . . it depends. Do you really think he came here because of us?"

Cameron scowled. "Yes. Definitely."

"Okay . . . then maybe prom isn't the best place to go after all."

His eyes flickered toward me. "Have you picked out your dress?"

"It doesn't matter."

"Casey?" he inquired, his eyes terribly sad.

"Yes," I whispered as quietly as I could.

I could tell he wanted to say something, but he remained silent for about ten minutes as he drove me home. Obnoxious radio commercials filled the air as we neglected it. My house loomed in front of me, dark, and impossibly normal after tonight. "I'm sorry."

I wasn't sure how to respond, so I leaned over and kissed his cheek. "You don't have anything to be sorry about. I'll talk to my sister about prom sometime soon, okay? I really did enjoy the first part of our date." He nodded, stoic. "Hey," I said, poking his lip lightly. "No frowning allowed."

He blew at my finger and said, "Yeah, but I fear the rules might be changing."

CHAPTER FOURTEEN

the rabbit that lived

"Are you visualizing the death?" I said, softly placing a hand on Cameron's tense shoulders.

"Yes," he responded through a clenched jaw and eyes tightly shut. "Die," he breathed, opening his eyes and glaring at the frightened rabbit. After a few minutes, the rabbit attempted to bite through the metal cage again. "It's hopeless. Maybe my power has already faded?" Cameron bent down to the cage, hopeful.

"The *Mortem Mobo* states that you can't just lose a power bestowed unto you," Christina said, looking up from the blue leather.

"Thank you, Professor," Cameron replied sarcastically.

I sighed quietly. Ever since starting this in February, it had been two months of bickering, new strategies, new animals, Christina actually being able to do something with her powers on the near dying animals, Cameron frustratingly accomplishing nothing, and me giving lame encouragements since no animals had been killed yet. Considering the killing at the fair, we didn't spend much time in the woods but instead collected the traps and took them back to one of our houses. This time we ended up at mine, just the three of us. We thought we'd be more productive without the distraction of Danny and Tiffany. "What did you feel when you . . . killed that guy?" I asked cautiously.

One side of his mouth quirked down. "Anger, frustration, wanting knowledge . . . Maybe it doesn't work on animals?" he said.

"Mine does," Christina said perkily.

"Thank you, Captain Obvious," I said, half-jokingly and half sarcastically.

"So . . . yours should too, Cameron," she retorted.

"Yeah, yeah, yeah . . ." He stared at the rabbit. Despite the two animals in our backyard, the other one being a snake Christina had insisted we bring along, it was a depressing sight. Our grass was filled with dying patches and weeds in the healthy parts. A neglected garden sat to the side. Georgia's spring showers had yet to bring any April flowers.

"Think about the anger," I whispered in his ear, running my hand up and down his back. "Why were you so mad? Think about that again. Use it. It's literally your weapon."

"I can't think of anything but you right now," he whispered back, spinning me around to face him. His eyes were closed as he leaned his forehead against mine.

"You guys are wayyyy too close." Christina mimicked a puking motion.

"Be quiet, Chris," I said. Cameron winked at me. Christina continued to gripe about our "groping" as Cameron closed his eyes and took a deep breath. "Think *angry*. You are the Hulk," I said.

His body rumbled with laughter before going completely still. He drew in a sharp breath, and suddenly his body was shaking slightly. He opened his gorgeous golden eyes and glared at the poor bunny rabbit. The rabbit began twisting violently. "*Die.*" I watched in horror as the rabbit jerked around before dying. I waited to see if my power would take over, but it was silent. "I—I actually did it?" Cameron was baffled by his own powers.

"Yes. Yes, you did," I said carefully. I walked back over to him and enveloped him in a giant hug. He squeezed me tighter against him.

Behind me I heard dirt shuffling around. Confused, I broke away from Cameron to find Christina crouched over the rabbit. Having detached it from the trap, she held it in her hands and was stroking it distressingly. "*Breathe,*" she said softly, her throat clogged with sadness. The rabbit's chest kicked back into action frightfully. Small, wide brown eyes stared at us momentarily before it hopped off into the distance.

"You're getting really good at that," I said worriedly.

"You actually killed the rabbit," she said, ignoring me. Her stance was rigid as she glared up at Cameron.

"That's what this is all about, I thought." He took a step back. "Training our powers?"

"But you killed on command." She took a step forward, allowing a twig to snap underneath her.

"Yes, and you brought it back to life . . . *on command.*"

"Christina, didn't you want to practice this? The *Mortem Mobo* said this was important for us to do."

My sister turned her glare on me and suddenly it felt as if the temperature had dropped. A bird cast a shadow over my sister as we stood in an uncomfortable silence. "Yes," she said through clenched teeth. "But you can kill things . . . That isn't normal or good."

Cameron frowned. "What can I say? It's not like I want this curse."

Christina threw her hands up in the air. "What is it with you two and this being a curse?"

I exchanged a look with my boyfriend. *One second, Cameron's power is a curse. The next, it's not? What logic is this?* I thought as I knitted my brows together. "But you just said . . ."

"Cameron's powers aren't ours, Casey. He gained his powers through me . . . He's an abomination," she stated simply.

I gave her my best *"are you crazy"* look and felt my eyebrows pull together again. "He is *not* an abomination." She rolled her eyes at me but didn't try to intercede. "You're making no sense."

"Come on, we're wasting daylight arguing. Don't you want to be able to practice some more?" She walked to our next group of traps.

"Cameron . . . you can leave if you want," I told him once my twin was out of earshot.

He shook his head and stared after her. "No, the practice is good . . . but you might want to talk to her. Or have her committed."

"I've tried. It never works." I looked at the Golden Boy's trusting eyes. "Okay . . . one more shot." His hand pulsed in mine as we walked over to where a snake was ensnared in one of Danny's infallible traps.

"Think you can do it again?" Christina asked, stroking the snake's head. The snake's tail lashed violently. I was thankful it was just a garden snake.

"Yes, I can do it again if you promise not to freak out on me."

She gave us her best smile as her eyes darkened. "Pinky promise."

—

I paused outside of Christina's door and listened. There was no sound I could make out, but that wasn't going to stop me from having a serious talk with her. My phone let off a faint ringing sound. Looking down at it, I saw that it was Agent Harling.

Blowing out a breath of air, I turned around and went back into my room. "Hello?"

"Hello, Casey, it's Agent Harling." His normal wary voice was filled with a bit of spark. "I'm glad I caught you. You might have seen it on the news, but we know how the killer is getting around town." My eyebrows rose as I waited on him to continue. "He's been using dugouts to hide quickly and go undetected. I don't know if you know what that means, but basically he dug shallow holes scattered around town, covering them inconspicuously." My stomach dropped to my feet in a confusing swirl of dread and interest. "It doesn't help us find him, but it does help us determine how he's doing what he's doing. I'm only telling you this because it aired on the news. Didn't want you alarmed. We've checked; your yards are clear."

My throat felt parched and I tried to think of something to say. "Is there anything else you can tell me?"

He gave me a low chuckle. "No, not really. Like I said, I'm calling because the evidence was just released. Plus, I've appreciated your help. I also wanted to know if you've seen anything lately? Detectives Tal and Mary said they found you at the fair when he appeared."

I blushed. "Oh, yeah, I'm sorry I didn't tell you."

"No problem."

I kicked my bed before plopping down on it. "But I do want to help." Underneath my door, I saw the hall light turn on. My curiosity piqued as I tried to focus on our conversation.

"I know that." He sighed. "I wanted to let you know that we're making progress and that you are helping when you text me about your visions. That brings me to my next point. For now, I still need you and your friends to keep out of the woods." I fidgeted with my thumbs. "Casey?"

"It's just, maybe we can help . . . maybe we can figure something else out . . ."

There was a long pause. "My job is to keep you and the citizens of Cartersville safe. It's going to be much harder if you're running around the woods. Trust me. Stay out of the woods. Be as smart as I know you must be and keep diligent about your visions. It helps more than you know."

I bounced my legs against my bed. "Okay I will."

"Thanks, Casey. I hope you have a good night."

When we said our goodbyes, I texted Cameron and let him know everything, then went into my sister's room.

"Hey, sis." I perched on her silky comforter. She was lying on her stomach and reading the *Mortem Mobo*. "I know you hate talking about it, but I want to talk about the book."

Her relaxed body kept on reading. "What more do you possibly want to know?"

"Why are you so different now?"

She turned to me, clearly confused by the direction I was going. "What do you mean?"

"I know you must see it in the mirror," I continued lightly. "You look sick and tired *all* the time and you're always irrational."

Her mouth formed a tiny "Oh." "That's not the book, Casey . . . That's my soul." I raised one of my eyebrows. "Remember a while ago,

I told you that I enhance people? Well, the book revealed that when I heal . . . I lose bits of my soul, and that extra energy . . . . Well, it actually *does* enhance things in people and animals, apparently. The book tells me how much I'm giving up and when it's a bad thing . . . yadda, yadda."

I couldn't believe my sister's nonchalance. "Then you need to stop," I said obviously.

"I'm not just going to stop," she said flatly. "Besides, I can't reverse who I've saved, so there's no point."

I hopped off the bed and began to pace. Unlike my own room, hers seemed full of life. It was a stark contrast to the gaunt girl in front of me. "The point is that *you* are losing your mind. This needs to stop, Christina." She jumped off her bed and stopped me mid-pace, her eyes boring into mine; I could tell how horribly glassy her green-blue eyes were from even a distance.

"Make me," I wanted to respond, but she turned away from me and threw the book into my hands. "You want me to stop reading the book? Fine, I don't need it anymore. But I will *not* stop helping people just because you want me to." I looked around at the disaster area of a room. She had never been this careless before. "Without my powers, you wouldn't even be here."

"I'm so thankful you saved me, Chris, but I don't want anything bad to happen to you," I pleaded with her.

She frowned and began pushing me out the door. "It won't . . . I'm fine . . . Just get out."

I started to say something, but she shut the door in my face. I stared down at the book in my hands and went into my room with it. Carefully, and thinking as hard as I could, I opened the book to somewhere near the end.

"Help me," Christina cried despairingly flipping through the book. "What can I do?" The book flipped to a page about soul losing. "Yes, I know that." She flipped a few pages back. "Am I dying? Can I stop it?" Her eyes scanned the page and landed on a single word: irreversible. "Oh . . . I guess not."

My eyes watered with tears. My sister was losing her soul and there was absolutely nothing I could do about it. Closing my eyes tightly to keep from crying, I crawled into bed and tried to fall asleep.

CHAPTER FIFTEEN

a unique kind of prom

"Oh wow! Casey, Christina, y'all look beautiful," my mother crooned as we walked down the hall. I agreed that the maroon mermaid dress looked good on me, but it was uncomfortable when you factored in the leggings and tank top I was wearing underneath for hunting. I squirmed under her gaze. "When are the boys coming?"

I looked at my twin in her pale blue, short, and sparkly dress. Her hair was curled and stacked on her head in a way that rivaled Cinderella's bun. "Alex will be here in just a few minutes to pick me up." Her eyes shined bright beneath her makeup, but I couldn't help but notice the purple bags under them.

My mom frowned softly. "Cameron's not coming with him?"

"Oh no," I replied awkwardly. "He really wants to drive me since it's kinda our second date."

Mom nodded and inspected my sister and me once more. "Y'all are going to have an amazing time. I absolutely adored my prom. It was just your father and I, and it was marvelous." Her tone faded a bit near the end. At that moment, the doorbell rang. I excused myself to the bathroom as Alex came in.

The mirror and bright lights allowed me to see my own bags due to lack of sleep. I sighed and leaned heavily against the mirror, taking shallow breaths. "Casey? Are you okay in there?" my mom asked timidly.

"Yeah," I croaked quickly, shaking myself more awake. I unlocked the bathroom to find my mother standing by the door slightly nervous.

"Hi," she said delicately.

"Hi," I said, cocking an eyebrow up. "Are *you* okay, Momma?"

"I just—" she started, shuffling awkwardly. "About everything . . . over the past few years . . ."

"Mom—" I attempted to walk out of the bathroom. I felt bad for being so rude to her.

She stopped me. "You and Christina just look so *beautiful* tonight and I know y'all are going to have so, *so* much fun and I just realized y'all are all grown up. And I missed it."

"Mom, it's okay."

"No. It's not." She looked at me intently. "I'm glad you have your father's book. I wish I had given it to you before instead of forcing you and Christina to go through this alone. I know we'll never have a perfect family or relationship, but we can try again, right? More of an adult relationship?"

The doorbell rang at that moment, but I stayed where I was. "Yes." She gave me a hug that I uncomfortably returned. "I do love you, Momma."

Her grip tightened. "I love you, too." Together, we went to the door to get Cameron.

—

"So, is your sister all better?" Cameron asked as we drove toward the mountain trail. No cops were following us because it was prom night. Instead, they were generally crawling around the school and patrolling neighborhoods at random. Despite what Harling had said, we still intended on going to the woods and looking around. Part of me was screaming that it was a stupid idea, but at least I wasn't going alone.

"She isn't *all* better, but we've patched most everything up. Though I am still worried." The Golden Boy wiggled uncomfortably in his tuxedo. "Was the rental expensive?"

"Nah. Gran found this in the attic. It was my granddad's." His eyes gauged my appearance. "How about your dress?"

"I wasn't so lucky." I leaned my head against the headrest agitatedly. "You look amazing, by the way." He really did. His hair was rumpled slightly, courtesy of me. Calm hair on him didn't suit him and the tux fit him wonderfully. Even the red of the tie popped against his tan skin.

"As do you, my dear." He smiled, carefully picking my hand up and placing a swift kiss on it. "I'm almost glad the rest of the prom doesn't get to see you. They might be a little too jealous."

My cheeks colored as I blinked warmly at him. I looked out the window and realized that we were at his grandmother's house. "Are we here to change or something?" I looked down at my pretty dress.

"Well, not quite." His tone lilted upward.

"Cameron . . ." I said demurely. "What's going on?"

He turned sharply in the car so that he could really look at me. "Look, I know what we said about prom, but you look so beautiful and I already have the tux, so . . ." His eyes flashed in the dim light. "With

297

the help of Gran, I fixed up the living room for us. No killer. No hunting. You said it yourself. We aren't really supposed to anyway." Tracing warm patterns on my flesh, Cameron happily gripped my hand. "Just something a normal couple might do."

I was so shocked that I had nothing to say, so I let him lead me into the house. It was beautiful. Candles were carefully aligned everywhere above ground level, a giant white sheet was spread over the floor, along with a bunch of pillows, and the couch was nowhere to be seen. On the sheet there were two plates with actual silver coverings. "They even have silver coverings?" I managed to stumble out.

"That's all you can say?" He laughed gleefully. "Come on, let's eat." I leaned back on the pillows and Cameron sat next to me, his leg resting lightly against mine.

"Your grandmother is okay with us being alone here?" I inquired as he pulled one of the platters over to me.

"She trusts us," he said as he took off the lid coverings. Two delicious plates of chicken smothered in a cream sauce sat in front of us. "As she should, right? Besides, with the never-ending cycle of officers out front, she didn't have much reason to say no."

I bumped into him gently and picked up the plate. "Right." The two of us chatted comfortably as we ate on fine bone china with sterling silverware. I let my mind wander to the dance floor at the civic center where the prom was. "I'm glad we're both here," I said.

As we chomped away at the food, I smiled at the beautiful quiet of the place. It wasn't prom, but I'm not sure that was a bad thing. There were no loud, obnoxious, grinding students crowding us, or horrible music.

Finishing the last few bites of the meal, I stood up and stretched gingerly. "That was wonderful."

"Gran outdid herself again," he remarked, taking the plate from me and heading into the kitchen. I followed him as he sat the dishes in the sink, without turning on the lights, and ran hot water over them. When he was done, he turned around and took a step toward me. I looked up into his bright golden eyes, still ablaze despite the dark atmosphere. Standing on my tiptoes, I laid my forehead on his and closed my eyes. We shared a breath together for a minute, no kissing, no talking, just us together. Suddenly, Cameron leaned forward and pressed his lips against mine. I entangled my hands in his hair and pulled him to me once more.

I couldn't really believe we were doing this. After everything that's happened, it felt so normal. We stopped kissing and stared at each other. In the dim lighting his eyes had more of a brown tint to the normally golden irises.

He enveloped me in his arms and squeezed firmly. "You're a good boyfriend," I muttered into his neck. "No joking."

As my vision continued to adjust, I watched his expression shift to considerate confusion. "I know that." His head tilted downward as he took my hand. "I also know that I like you a lot more than I thought possible. I might love you. And you're the first, Casey Darling."

The butterflies in my stomach erupted into flames. "Yeah, that is a bit cheesy." I tried to sound nonchalant as pleasant feelings waged war inside me.

"No joking," he mimicked, tapping a finger lightly on my bottom lip.

"Yeah, yeah." I leaned my forehead against his chest, tightening my hand against our intertwining ones. "Silly boy."

"Silly girl." We headed back to his living room, grinning like idiots.

When we sat down, I was even more impressed as he produced a dainty dish of Godiva truffles. I felt guilty for wanting every single one of them but settled on the two that looked the most divine. We popped the candies in our mouths. I leaned against him. Fire enveloped me from the outside in. We melted together, heartbeats in sync, and rested by the candlelight for hours.

We must have fallen asleep, because we jerked awake at the *ding* of my phone. Cameron sighed softly on my face. "A text?" he asked dolefully.

"Sorry," I said with a small smile. "I'm glad we weren't actually after the killer, because that would have been bad." He snorted lightly as I read the text. "Oh, it's just from Danny. He wanted to know if we could spare some time in our '*hunt*' to come join them at the after-party at his lake cabin. Says prom went off without a hitch. No incidents."

"Guess Michael figured out we didn't go." Cameron furrowed his brows and continued on with his next train of thought. "Danny's having an after-party, in a cabin, in the middle of the woods, with a serial killer on the loose? I still can't believe they let him do that."

I tried to hide my smile. "Well, it was approved this week by his parents and the police. Mrs. Mardox usually gets what she wants, and I guess she wanted him to be happy." I kicked his leg casually. "And Danny is more popular than you would think. It's probably going to be a roaring spectacle." My tongue poked through my lips.

"I know." He stuck his tongue back at me. "It's hard not to like him, I guess. It just seems odd to me with everything that's happening but as far as parties go, it would be a pretty awesome end. Lake nearby. House all to themselves."

"I wish we could go. Danny really wants us to all be together, considering the occasion. Besides, he says we'll never find 'K' just by

randomly hunting. He's probably right. They'll have a blast, I'm sure."
I leaned back and closed my eyes. "Of course, they can't go *too* crazy."

"Why not? Because of the neighbors?"

A bubble of laughter left my lips. "Cameron, it's the beginning of spring. *No* one goes up to the cabins until Memorial Day." I reached over and grabbed his hand.

"Really?" His tone was full of astonishment.

"Yes, really. Danny's been up there a few times for a Christmas getaway, or just a parent getaway, and they all say it's like a ghost town. Their street is mostly vacation rentals."

"Well, okay then," he responded. "See, in California, the weather is perfect *all* year." I rolled my eyes at him sweetly. "Where is it anyway?"

"Just on the other side of Pine Mountain on Lake Allatoona. Well, not right on the other side . . ." I paused for a moment, my mind buzzing.

"Casey, what is it?"

I released his hand. Twisting my thumb, I looked around Cameron's house. The dimmed lights and candles suddenly cast eerie shadows instead of peaceful ones as I mulled over the empty cabins. "Cameron . . ." I looked back at my boyfriend. "Why did you think it was odd for them to be able to go?"

Cameron looked thoroughly confused, but said, "Just . . . because the woods are the only place anybody thinks Michael stays . . . and cabins are in the middle of woods, obviously . . ." He trailed off, his mind playing catch up with mine. "They're abandoned most of the year?"

"The ones by Danny's cabin. And those lake trails would be a perfect way to get to and from town without driving a car. He avoided the road blocks on Main Street . . ." I dropped his hand as terror shot through me.

"Right. The forest is vast and he's not exactly stupid. I mean, it's been about nine months and the cops are still clueless," he admitted.

"What if that's what we're missing? What everyone has been missing? There are empty houses and trails." My heart pounded loudly against my chest. "What if he knows we didn't go to prom, and is angry about it or something and wants to take it out on them? Or thinks we'll show up at the party?"

"But he'd have to know ahead of time about the party."

"He seems to know about everything. What if he went there and put a tracking device on one of their cars like he did yours?" I stood up and stared at the darkness of the house. "Danny and the others . . . any one of them."

"I know," he rushed, jumping to his feet. "We need to go. Now. Try calling him."

Together, we surged out the door, into the car, and toward Lake Allatoona.

CHAPTER SIXTEEN

it all comes crashing down

As carefully as I could, I forced the dress off of me. Despite Cameron's careful (if not fast) driving, it still took a good few minutes to get the maroon fabric to release me. "Couldn't you have just waited 'til we got to the cabin?" Cameron asked, frustrated, as I tossed the dress into the back seat.

"Probably, but now we're better prepared to just get out and go," I explained, grabbing the long-sleeved t-shirt I had stuck in the back seat a few days ago in preparation. I painstakingly put the shirt on over my tank top so that I wouldn't disturb Cameron.

"Casey." Cameron's hand rested on my shoulder briefly. I sensed our anxiety rolling off of us in a whirlwind. "Calm. It will be okay."

I nodded, even though I didn't really believe that. From the way his hand tightened on the steering wheel, I figured he felt the same way. We both discussed other possibilities to try and calm ourselves as we drove over there. The first few cabins whizzed by as we turned onto Danny's street. Each one of them dark and deserted, but with our understanding of how careful and reclusive Cameron's father was, I felt like every one of them harbored secrets that were unreachable in the moonlight. Even as the car sped past each one, too fast to reveal anything crucial, I couldn't stop studying them for the slightest clue.

Danny's cabin glowed like a firework in the dark Georgia woods. From the car, I could hear the bass of some dance song shaking the earth. I glanced at Cameron. He reached out his hand and I hustled over to grab it. On our way to the door, the patrol officer out front rolled down his window. It was none other than Officer Golding, who interviewed me at the Tay house the night Beatrix was murdered. He tilted his hat at me, but I ignored him and pressed on toward the pulsing music.

Since there was no sense in knocking, Cameron and I let ourselves in. The cabin was packed with elated teens screaming and dancing, even though by now they should have been exhausted. I was surprised to see that no one was overtly drunk or high, but realized that, since this party was already pushing limits, Danny had probably assured the cops out front that there would be no drugs or alcohol. Almost every light was on and the glaring lights blinded me. "Danny," I called out, dragging Cameron behind me.

Danny popped out of nowhere like a magician. "Casey! You made it!" His hug was crushing, but I couldn't find it in me to return the gesture. Always the observant one, he held me at arm's length and looked at me. "What's wrong?"

"Danny, 'K' is in one of the cabins around here." I was going for calm, but the words came out shaky.

All color drained from his face as he watched me, petrified by the news. "What. In. The. Hell? Why does K not let me have any fun?" Danny pouted his lips at Cameron as he whined. "Are you sure?"

"Not completely," Cameron answered. "But it's logical and likely. People at this party are prime targets if we're right."

Danny was obviously high on prom adrenaline and wasn't having any of this news. "Well if he is, I'm goin' have to let loose on K. Mkay? So we all can dance. K's now screwin' with my Gaga on top of screwin' with my friends! Don't nobody screw with my Gaga!"

"I'm sorry Michael's screwing with your Gaga," Cameron said in his signature deadpan baritone.

"Has anybody around here mentioned anything to your family?" I asked hopefully.

"About what? What do you mean?" Danny was growing more confused now than frustrated.

Christina showed up beside me, looking like she was on top of the moon. "Sis, you made it." I was confused by the sudden show of affection but attempted to give her a similar smile to the one she had given to me. "Prom was AH-mazing!" Alex showed up beside her, his arm casually entangling itself around my sister's tiny waist.

"I'm glad," I responded through clenched teeth.

"Nice outfit. Although I didn't know sweatpants were 'in' this season." Alex flashed his dazzling joker smile at my attire. I narrowed my eyes at him. Cameron gripped his leather bracelet tightly.

"Not now, guys. We might have to whoop some ass," Danny expressed curtly to them.

"Whoa, what's wrong?" Christina asked, her eyes darkening.

"K," I whispered as quietly as I could.

"I prefer Michael Townsend." Cameron's dripping sarcasm seemed to have come from embarrassment. We all stared at the floor momentarily.

Alex's grip tightened on Christina as he began to look afraid. Christina, however, looked . . . somewhat hungry. "Where?"

"Somewhere close by, maybe," Cameron answered.

Danny interjected before anyone could say anything else. "Oh my God! My mom said that the Lillians' alarm has gone off a couple of times. But when the police check it out, nobody's ever there. They assumed it was raccoons or something, because one of the screens in the basement was gnawed and the window was broken. But they sent someone to fix that."

"Didn't they look inside? Did they not find anything?" Cameron was now the investigator.

"Hell no, they live in Chicago. They only spend summers here." He turned to Alex. "And I *hate* the wife, because your mom told my mom that she—"

"Danny." I took back the wheel.

"Carry on," he said.

I looked at Cameron quizzically. He gave an almost imperceptible nod. "We'll start there; where is it?"

"Down the street. I'm coming with," Danny said, taking off his blue bowtie.

"No you're not—" I began.

"Yes he is, and so am I," Christina interrupted. "You need us." She turned in Alex's arms so that she could better look at him. "You need to stay here and actually watch over the cabin. You'll need to call the police as well. They're out front anyway." He agreed.

"The police won't really do anything because they're completely incompetent and can we *please* not get them involved? Call Harling," I huffed.

"Sorry," Christina said.

I reached into my pocket and pulled up Harling's number on my cell phone. "Call this guy, Agent Harling. He's with the FBI. Give him the address, everything we just discussed. Tell him to meet me there.

Let him know that you are friends with me." Alex took the phone with a bit of excitement.

"I need to tell everybody, so they don't run off." Danny disappeared to deal with the music and his social minions.

Tiffany had erupted from the mass and gave a small smile to our ragtag group. We quickly explained what was happening. "I'm gonna help Alex with the crowd, okay?" I thanked her and gave her a short hug.

"Lock all the doors, man. Windows, check the closets, basement. Under the beds. Check *everywhere*. He could be in the house already," Cameron said.

Alex and Cameron patted each other's backs. "I got this."

"Christina," I said crisply. "This is way too dangerous. *We* shouldn't even be doing it."

"But you are . . . So, so am I."

"Excuse me, ladies and gentlemen!" Danny said loudly as the music cut off abruptly. "I know we are all having the time of our lives, but it has been momentarily ruined by one man." He paused dramatically. "The notorious Bartow Slasher is rumored to be close to this here cabin." Screams, screeches, and gasps abounded. "But *I*, along with some of my dearest friends, are going to handle it, because we are not about to let him get away with destroying our party." Despite the general panic, the crowd cheered. "Do not leave for any reason! More officers are on their way and Mr. Greene is in charge. The drinks are to the left of the stairs, and by 'drinks' I mean non-alcoholic." He gave the crowd a pointed look. "Help yourself to the food, and *please* keep the music tasteful. If there is going to be any hero up in this joint, it'll be *me* . . ." he continued to a laughing, happy crowd.

"Be careful," Alex said fiercely into Christina's hair as he tugged her into a full-fledged hug. "Stay close to Danny and Cameron." I gestured for Christina and Cameron to follow me outside as Danny finished his speech. Alex Greene was christened the man in charge. The four of us left the cabin as he put my phone up to his ear and made his way to the first closet in sight.

—

The Lillian cabin was a tad smaller than Danny's, but just as nice. However, with no lights shining from within, it looked exactly like every horror movie you could possibly imagine.

"This looks fun," Danny said sarcastically. We stared up at the deserted cabin. "What do we do now?"

I shrugged, now angry for not really having a plan. I gazed at the knives everyone had in their hands. *We only have knives,* I thought dejectedly. "Just look around and see if you find anything that looks . . . weird." My group gazed at me, forlorn. "Don't split up; let's go in pairs."

Cameron and I headed to the back of the house. "We aren't exactly armed detectives," he agreed.

I carefully studied the back porch. "This may be silly, but it's the only thing we have." I gripped my knife tighter.

"I didn't say it was silly." He captured my hand, and together we walked up to the porch only to find there was nothing disturbed. "I just said we weren't detectives."

"That's for sure. But Harling will be here soon." We walked back around to the front, where Danny and Christina were looking intently at something in Christina's hand. "What's that?" I let go of Cameron's hand and moved closer. Danny held Christina's and his knife haphazardly in one hand.

Christina held up the thing so that we could see it better. It was some indistinguishable dark lock of hair that was tied into a knot. We exchanged looks. "He's been here, then?" Danny asked, a shiver rippling over him.

"I think so," I said, just as Christina said, "Hey, what's that?"

Off to the side, a figure in complete black emerged from the forest. The light from the waxing moon allowed me to see that the killer's mask was off, exposing his blond hair and stark blue eyes. He was ripped, just like Ryan. I could see how I had been confused before. It was astonishing for us to be staring at him as he stared back calmly, unmoving. We were frozen. His mouth opened, and "Cameron!" erupted from the bowels of his being.

Anger fueling him, Cameron launched himself at his father, but I managed to grab his shirtsleeve in the last minute. "Run!" I yelled to my friends.

Fear jolted the rest of us into action. Michael took out the infamous knife I had seen him use to kill so many people. Finding Cameron's hand again, I dragged him in the opposite way of his father. My knife remained awkwardly at my side as I attempted not to cut myself as I ran. Christina and Danny ran diagonally from us and, eventually, I lost sight of them. "Casey!" Cameron yelled at me, trying to release my hand so he could face his mother's killer. "We have weapons. I have a weapon. I can take him."

I shook my head, even though I knew he couldn't see me in the dark. "Cameron, we were stupid. Harling is on his way. We may have him outnumbered, but like you said, we aren't the police." I started to make us circle around the cabin and hopefully to my sister and best friend. "We need to call the police and make sure they know we're out here." I couldn't believe what I had just said, but knew it was true.

Back at the cabin, I froze and listened to our surroundings. Cameron seemed angry, but I saw that he too was making sure we were okay. "Christina? Danny?" I said in a semi-loud voice.

I heard footsteps running toward us, but no response. Cameron ducked into a crouch and I did the same. I saw a glint of silver as he brought out his own knife. I felt fear erupt inside me as I did the same. "Casey!" Danny screamed as his lanky form slammed into mine. Cameron stood up slowly and let out a sigh of relief.

"Where's Christina?" I asked. "And your knife?"

"Dropped it . . . She wasn't with you?" he responded, worry deep in his tone.

"No. We lost my sister!" I heard a low, deep chuckle behind me. I pushed the two boys toward a tree and hoped they would hide like I did. I scrambled upwards to a low branch that supported my weight. Seemingly safe from this height, I tried to shake the shock of my agility, but figured it was just because of how much adrenaline I had. Danny looked up at me with surprise but simply pressed himself tighter into the bushes.

"Here, little children. You came to find me, and you did." Michael's voice was the stuff of nightmares. It had all the cadence of a snake's, infused with a deep rumble. "I was always good at hide and seek. Remember, Cameron?" It took me a moment before I could find him in his spot behind a cluster of trees. Dread filled me as I couldn't reach him or really see his reaction. I shook my head and sent pleading thoughts to him. My attention turned to the rest of the forest. *Christina, where are you?* I asked myself.

Suddenly, Michael appeared under me. Pale moonlight lit his hair in a way that reminded me of Cameron's hair. "But I know you're here. I can almost smell your fear," he said with a mad laugh. "You don't want to keep me waiting. When I wait, I become more creative." My blood chilled to an unnatural cold. "Come out, come out, little children."

"Casey!" Christina yelled from somewhere to my left. The killer's head swiveled toward her voice and I realized I could only do one thing. Without another thought, I dropped off of the branch and landed on top of Michael. His breath left in a whoosh as I hit his shoulder. I groaned at the pain and attempted to get in a better position, one that would keep him from escaping, but would prevent me from acquiring a large bruise. Christina's pale form came into my view just as Michael lifted my body off of his and threw me. Flying through the air, I lost my knife to the dark forest's tendrils. *Great, there went another quarter of our arsenal. There really needs to be a gripper on those things.* Cameron pulled his knife out and began to lunge at his father, who was just about to get up. Danny ran out from the bushes to try and help me up. Despite his size and obvious pain from being the landing area for an eighteen-year-old girl, Michael was still fast enough to sidestep his son's wild swing.

Feeling useless without any weapon of my own, but wanting to help my boyfriend, I pushed away from Danny and Christina and swung at the killer. Without a thought, he grabbed my fist and hurled me to where Cameron had gone after he missed his swing at Michael. We both examined each other before stepping toward the killer once more. Christina stood off to the side, bewildered and looking completely out of place. Danny, however, headed toward the killer like a football player. I locked eyes with Cameron. As if we were reading each other's minds, we gave a slight nod and began after the killer, just like Danny, in the hopes of trapping him between the three of us. In front of us, the killer sliced his knife across Danny's throat.

I stopped dead in my tracks; horror wrapped around me tightly as I watched Danny fall limply to the ground. His dirty-blond hair flopped around him carelessly and I was forced into his memories. I watched all of the times we hung out, him with Phoebe, hanging out with friends, and just the overly happy person he always was. Then came the bad memories of his life. "Noooo!" I wailed, wrenching myself from the experience.

Hearing my distress, Christina shook herself out of her stupor and focused her attention on our dying friend. The killer was not as easily distracted and ran toward her. Fury boiling in my veins, I flew into him at the same time that Cameron did so. This created a mass jumble of bodies between the three of us; it also knocked my knife in the same direction as Christina and Danny. I screamed and attempted to rip out Michael's hair from his head.

Cameron rolled out of the pile and glared at his father. As I wrapped my small arms around the killer's contorted form, Cameron opened his mouth to kill the man responsible for so much carnage. At that moment, Christina launched at Cameron, forcing him to the floor. "No more death," she snarled.

The killer stood up and flung me from his body. Saving Danny appeared to have finally broken Christina. Looking into her wild eyes as she fought to control Cameron's mouth, I realized, like the book said, that her power had finally become her greatest curse: she would save everyone, even if it let the one responsible for so much death go free.

After I was shaken off by the killer, I came face-to-face with him. Suddenly, I was looking with my own eyes at the man that had raised Cameron. His eyes were still crystal blue, but they had sunken deep into his skin, which had a horrible sheen. The proof of evil was in his eyes.

I looked around me in a panic, hopeful that a knife was dropped somewhere close by. Unfortunately, all I had was a giant branch. The killer looked down at his knife with a small smile. "Are you ready to go to bed?" he whispered. His voice was slime and rust on an old car, which sent shivers down my back.

Helplessly, I looked back to Christina, whose focus was far from the present, and Cameron, whose panic over the situation was palpable, but we both knew he couldn't help.

Danny was nowhere in my sight. With a single glance at his son, Michael then turned to me. I raised the branch to defend myself, and just as I swung at the killer, I was sucked into yet another vision. The branch dropped out of my hand as the vision ripped me from the present moment.

Emptiness filled my soul as I looked at myself through Michael's eyes. Slowly and in awe, the killer looked down to find a knife sticking out from his shoulder. He glanced behind him to find Danny panting and pale, yet alive and victorious.

His gaze then oscillated toward his intentional prey: Cameron. Through his mind, I could see Christina's face twisted in a wrath worse than I'd ever seen, my boyfriend's arms restraining her. "I wanted you to stay," his father mumbled, disoriented.

"*DIE*," Cameron commanded with no remorse.

As Michael shut his eyes, I was transported back into my own mind. I waited for the memories to bombard me, but his death was blank. My head tilted to the side as I examined him in his death. He had been so evil, so twisted, that he had no good moments and no regrets. I could almost sigh in relief that I wouldn't have to understand his feelings, but his blankness unnerved me. Finally, a regret filtered through to me. By far, his biggest and only regret: The fact that Cameron still lived.

I dashed to my best friend and hooked my hands tightly around his waist. The blood from his neck wound was still slick, but the slash was perfectly healed. "Are you okay?" I choked out.

His head bobbed up and down as he returned the hug.

"What is your problem?" Christina's voice ripped through the air, startling everyone. I released Danny and looked at where Christina was standing, away from Cameron. "Someone is dead!"

She started to make her way to the killer's corpse, but Cameron stopped her. "Christina, you can't save *everyone*. You aren't God!" Cameron said authoritatively.

"But you can't just kill anyone you want!" She took another step forward.

"What is wrong with you? You're crazy! This is what we came here to do," I attempted wildly. We were all treating her like she was a wounded animal, about to bolt.

"But—"

"Look at what he did to me," Danny interrupted, gesturing at his blood-soaked tuxedo.

Her face momentarily lapsed into compassion, but she shook it away. "No, you listen to me!" she screamed. Her hands clawed at her barren eyes. "You have never cared for me or my powers. You've never understood me. But I understand that life is precious."

I walked over to her and put my hands on her shoulders. "You're my sister, Chris. Of course, I care about you. I may not fully under-stand you or this, but . . ." I glanced over my shoulder at Danny and Cameron. Danny was shaking and clutching himself. Cameron seemed drained but hovered beside me in a guarded stance. "You can't save him. Please don't."

Her head dropped against her chest and she sobbed. I wrapped her in my arms. Her black bun had fallen, and locks of hair were matted against her skin. Tentatively, I brushed a big chunk behind her ear.

"You will save more lives if he is dead," I whispered. She pressed her hands to her ears, despising her own insanity.

A few minutes later, I pulled myself off of the ground and pulled Cameron's phone from his pants to call Harling. He answered after the second ring. "Hello?"

"It's me," I answered with a frog in my throat.

"I'm on my way. What's going on?"

"We found the killer. We're at the Lillians' cabin—"

"I know. I just spoke to your friend, Alex. Is Michael detained?" Harling asked, obviously navigating roads that would lead to us.

"He's dead."

"Alright," he said after a pause. "Are you okay?"

I looked around my group. Danny was comforting Christina and Cameron stood beside me, unmoving, staring down at his father's body. "I'm not hurt," I said cautiously.

I could almost see Harling nod as he said, "Okay, good. I'm sending more units and paramedics out. I'll be there as soon as I can. Squad cars are arriving at the Mardox cabin, where the after-party is being held. Alex said they were panicked, so I sent more officers." I nodded despite the fact that he couldn't see me. "'Y'all did good,' as they say down here in Georgia."

I laughed out loud. "Thanks, Agent Harling." He hung up his phone.

I wrapped an arm around Cameron's waist and we leaned against each other. "Cops are on their way," I announced before looking back up at him. "Are you okay?" I asked, so only he could hear me.

"My father is dead," he said blankly. Turning to face me, he pulled me into a tight hug. "I'm so relieved."

I closed my eyes against his chest and listened to the sirens.

CHAPTER SEVENTEEN

graduating with honors and improvements

I looked around the field at my fellow graduating seniors. Danny buzzed up to the "D" section, where I stood with Christina, and gave me a huge hug. "Can you *believe* it?" he asked for the millionth time. "Today is our absolutely last day of high school! Never again will we be students at life's torture device."

"It is certainly a miracle," I admitted, fixing his bowtie for the millionth time that night.

Bouncing like a bunny, he scanned the crowd. "I think I may need to go, my Darling. BUT I will see you after." With a peck on the cheek, he sauntered to his spot.

Through the crowd, I spotted Alex, who gave me a thumbs-up and then spent the rest of the night staring wonderstruck at Christina. It was nice to see that it had worked out for the two of them. They were perfectly weird for each other, as he now seemed intrigued by her "gift" (both mine and hers had been explained in detail to those in our little group). Besides, every time he and

Christina locked eyes, I could see her becoming healthy again. *I wonder what that means?*

My eyes continued down the rows of people to Cameron, whose eyes crinkled when they met mine. There was no hint of pain left in those eyes. With his father's death, he was truly free. Danny chatted with some of his fellow "M" people. Finding my gaze, however, he winked at me. He was with me through thick and thin, and now, we had come to the end of a cycle.

As the principal began his speech, my eyes finally settled at the beginning of the crowd, where Tiffany stood tall amid the "A" section.

"This year has definitely been one of the hardest years Cartersville, Georgia, has ever faced. But we have persevered." Principal Benton's lower jaw quivered from talking to the entire student body. "This class has been one of our strongest classes, and we are very proud of its accomplishments. Despite a killer on the loose, these kids have managed to maintain their GPAs and their school spirit. Now, let's give our mayor some respect, as he has an important announcement."

The mayor of our town was a broad, slightly balding man named Mr. Santini. The general rumbling of the crowd quieted to hear his booming voice. "Thank you, Principal Benton. As he was saying, this school year has been no easy feat. This town has been subject to great loss. Today is a special day for our seniors as they leave, and our soon-to-be seniors as they take the stage. We have also decided to do something else on this day." He nodded to Chief Arnold, who walked off the stage and stood next to a giant rectangle covered in cloth. "We want to honor those whose lives have been taken." Chief Arnold removed the piece of cloth, revealing a giant collage of pictures and memorabilia.

The crowd let out a collective breath as if we had all been holding it. I shuddered as tears escaped my eyes. Beatrix's bright red hair drew me to her picture. Christina's arm wrapped around my shoulder, and when I looked at her, I found that she was crying, too. "It is tragic to have lost so many people, especially a senior who should be graduating today: Beatrix Tay. But we shall remember." Cheers erupted from the crowd. "There is one last thing I would like to do before we get this graduation back on schedule," Mayor Santini continued when the crowd quieted down. "Would Casey Darling please join us on the stage?"

As I walked near him, Danny gave me a thumbs up and winked. Trying not to step on anyone, I squeezed through the aisle and walked up the stairs. I looked back to see Christina's wide eyes mirroring mine. Cameron raised his eyebrows but offered a small smile as I joined the principal in front of the massive crowd. "All of the teenagers in Cartersville have done their best to keep moving forward and push past the horrid tragedies this town has faced, but Casey has managed to do some wonderful deeds. With the help of Casey's information, our town is safe again." Shock clouded my thoughts. "I would like to thank her on behalf of the Cartersville Police Department, the Georgia Bureau of Investigation, and the Federal Bureau of Investigation . . . with a medal." The crowd was absolutely devoid of sound.

Chief Arnold walked back onto the stage and smiled. He gestured to none other than Detectives Tal and Mary, who stepped onto the very same stage. I couldn't quite read their expressions. It wasn't exactly guilt but there was an apology hidden in Mary's smile. As Chief Arnold walked stiffly to the mic I couldn't help but feel bad for him. The wind almost knocked his cue cards out of his hand and for a split second a scowl plagued his lips. Detectives Tal and Mary stepped forward. "For aiding the police in their research, we would like to provide Casey Darling with this medal." Mary's face twisted into a small smile as Tal placed a gold medal with light purple ribbon around my neck. I hadn't talked to them since the killer had been caught. *Do you still hate me?* I asked myself. "We at the Cartersville Police Department thank you for what you helped us to achieve with your efforts. We are a free and safe community at last." I felt my cheeks grow hot when the crowd expelled a few timid claps. It then turned into confident appreciation, reaching a full thunder.

Despite the hundreds of people, I still managed to find my beaming mom and even Agent Harling, who bowed his head to me. It was nice to know that he traveled all the way from Washington strictly for me. He wore a smirk, making me wonder what he was thinking. When the crowd calmed down again, the principal walked up to the mic. "You can sit down now," he said politely before addressing the crowd once more. "Now let's get this show back on the road."

The high school staff vigorously handed out the diplomas and my heart swelled as I heard Tiffany's name called. Then Christina and I were called, and it was as if nothing like this could be possible. Beginning our senior year felt like an exciting dream that I had had as a child. Now I had a diploma in hand and a million possibilities in front of me. Names whizzed by, but happiness filled my every cell as I heard first Cameron and then Danny's name called. This moment couldn't feel more perfect.

After the varsity chorus finished their last song, all seniors raced to the center of the football field. Purple and white caps were flung into the air as we screamed in elation. The cap toss had successfully separated me from where my friends were, and now that families had joined us on the field it was absolute chaos. The end of high school was one of the happiest days . . . and the saddest. I felt the tear on my cheek long before I realized I was actually crying. Some of these people I would never see again—a blessing, sure, but I had been with most of them ever since I was five years old. Graduation suddenly turned into a bittersweet event.

Cameron waved from across the crowd and ran to me, lifting me into a hugging twirl. He had somehow managed to lose his footing. Together we fell straight down, him on his back and me on top of him. "Oops," he said in breathless laughter, and, just like that, all of my sadness was erased. "Maybe we should try that again?" He stared up at me like I was the only other person in the world.

"Are we having a pileup or whatever it's called?" Danny asked from somewhere behind me. "Because, though I'd never do something so stupid normally, I can make an exception for graduation."

"No, we were just—" I tried to say before I felt a body land on top of me.

"Okay, this is fun!" Danny yelled.

"Don't leave us out," Tiffany's small voice chimed from the crowd. Suddenly, she, my sister, and I'm pretty sure even Alex had added to our heap. It was bizarre, odd, weird, strange . . . and something that probably never would have happened before this year and I absolutely loved it.

The lovely Anne Lott had found us in the crowd and grabbed her camera. "Gran, can you take a picture? Quickly." Cameron's voice was muffled from all the bodies. I couldn't resist kissing him. Just as our lips touched, a bright flash erupted in front of us. We broke apart and the Golden Boy whispered, "Now that's a memory I want to keep forever."

I smiled as he placed another soft kiss on my cheek. "Okay guys, now *please* get off. Y'all are killing us!" I yelled at my small group, which seemed not-so-small anymore, which finally stood up, one by one. "What are y'all doing after graduation?" There was a collective shrug.

"My mom wants to see me at some point . . ." Danny began looking at the semicircle we had formed. "But after that, I say we meet up in Maximum's?"

"Yeah, that sounds great." Alex was finally an official member and no longer afraid to chime in. "My family is dying to hang out with me too, but we can meet there around ten-ish? No more curfews," he excitedly added, and all of us delivered a "Hell yeah." Christina leaned against him and let out a small breath as he kissed her right on the lips.

The rest of us agreed, and for a few hours, we separated and let the tidal wave of graduation descend upon us.

—

"We aren't late, Casey. Please calm down," Cameron pleaded as I dragged him from the inside of his car, where we had been for the past hour.

"I know we have all summer, but what if this is the last time we'll all be together? I don't want to miss a moment of it." I opened the door to Maximum's brightly lit décor from the 1950s.

Inside, I found the most picture-perfect moment. Danny was laughing at something a cute redheaded waiter said, his head back and teeth shining brightly. Tiffany was gesturing wildly as she revealed something that she clearly thought was monumental to Christina, who had her feet propped in Alex's lap. She was listening intently to her. Alex's face was completely relaxed as he traced patterns on Christina's bare leg. He waved at us, the earlier hostility to Cameron completely erased.

Danny was the next one to see us, and all he did was give us a small wink before continuing on with his new potential beau. Phoebe was a bit off to the side with Christina and Tiffany. During all of the chaos Danny had broken it off with her, because of all the stress. She seemed sad, but I was confident she would find someone. Tiffany stopped her story and gestured us over. Christina gave me another one of her hollow smiles, but when Alex's hand tightened over her leg it turned up a notch.

"Hey guys, have y'all already ordered?" I asked, sliding into a chair beside Phoebe. Cameron fell gracefully into the chair beside me.

"Oh, yeah, well, *we* have," Tiffany replied, answering for everyone. "Danny's still '*ordering,*'" she informed us with air quotes.

"Great—we may never get anything to eat," I said just loud enough for Danny to hear me. Phoebe let out a loud "ha" at his expense.

"Oh, all right." His voice was exasperated. "You should probably take their order or do some other cute waiter thing," Danny said to the waiter with a glow. When Phoebe's face fell a bit, Tiffany leaned on her.

Cameron and I ordered our food, and underneath the table, I intertwined my fingers with his. It was very hard to suppress the miraculous notion that I had finally fallen in love with life.

I looked at my herd of friends and marveled over what next year would bring. I was going to KSU, since a full scholarship and lack of other applications was hard to turn down, and Christina was settling for some college near Savannah, which just so happened to keep her snug with Alex. Cameron was accepted to Georgia Highlands, which happily only put us about thirty minutes from each other. Danny would be a fabulous University of Georgia freshman, and though that was a bit further away, I was confident we'd find some friend time. Phoebe and Tiffany were still considering their options, but it was only a matter of time. "Let's be sure to meet up during the holidays this year, okay?" I asked my friends, already feeling nervous about the distance.

"Of course!" Danny exclaimed, wrapping an arm around me. "You aren't getting rid of us that quickly, Miss Darling. Besides, next year we better not have a killer cramping our style." At the upset frowns on our faces, Danny backpedaled a bit. "I mean, like, I know we have family, but we at least have to see each other once."

"Maybe y'all can come to my annual New Year's Eve party," Alex chimed in. With affirmations from the rest of the group, I felt that maybe college wouldn't end my adventures with my friends.

I reached for my float and gasped as I saw an old woman reach out her hand to a small child with pitch-black hair. "There, there, dear. The monsters are gone now."

Maximum's flew back into perspective. I got a small flash of my friends' concerned faces before being yanked back into the vision. The little girl's black hair had faded to silver as she lay on a hospital bed, staring out the window. She knew death was coming soon.

"Casey? Casey, are you okay?" Danny's voice broke through the surface, and I was able to focus on the present scene at Maximum's again. "What's going on, is it another—?"

I fell back into the vision. "Mom, are you sure there's nothing more I can do?" a woman asked, fidgeting nervously next to the old woman's bedside.

She chuckled weakly. "Yes, dear, I'm sure. Now please go home and have a good night." When the daughter left, the old woman closed her eyes and the memories began to blur before me.

"Casey, just tell us—are you okay?"

"Yes, I'm—" My voice dropped as I watched her get married, have a child, see her off to college, and then witness her granddaughter's first day of school. Bad memories started to come, but I quickly flashed through them, only skimming over her divorce and something that looked like a fire. Finally, the deep regret of not getting to talk to her granddaughter one last time surfaced before she drifted into oblivion.

I opened my eyes. "Yes, I'm fine," I whispered, giving them a soothing smile. "No, it wasn't a killing, Danny. An old woman in the nursing home by the high school just died." Everyone stared at me silently and sadly. "This is my curse, guys . . . I'm okay. Really," I promised. Phoebe, Alex, and Tiffany still acted a bit perplexed about Christina's and my powers, but they were trying to take it in stride. I was just glad that we finally talked to them about it before graduation.

Christina gave me a tiny smile and a nod. Alex looked concerned but offered a full-fledged grin to show his understanding. Tiffany took her arms from around Phoebe and Danny and rested her hand on my arm. Cameron squeezed my hand back. It wasn't going to be the last vision I would ever have, but I had my friends. And, not to sound cheesy, I figured with them by my side and a killer long gone, life was going to be a lot better. Now, I just needed to survive college.

ABOUT THE AUTHOR

Jessica Branton has performed at Camp Broadway in Las Vegas and the Grande Theatre and Act One Theatre in Cartersville, Georgia. Her play *The Prince's Doctor* was produced by Act One. She performed and wrote for "On the Spot", a professional improv troupe in Athens, Georgia. Her play *Building 3200* was produced by The Oak Theatre in Atlanta.

Jessica obtained her bachelor's degree in English from the University of Georgia where she studied abroad at Oxford. She was awarded a teaching assistantship at Georgia Southern University where she is a graduate student. Jessica has several novels in development.

CPSIA information can be obtained
at www.ICGtesting.com
Printed in the USA
LVHW041112040219
606286LV00003BA/208/P